To Moira
Love and Be~~
Pamela Gaull.
7 · 9 · 2010 .

The Darkness
of
Dreams

By

Pamela Gaull

i

Published by

Cauliay Publishing & Distribution
PO Box 12076
Aberdeen
AB16 9AL
www.cauliaybooks.com

First Edition
ISBN 978-0-9564624-5-9
Copyright © Pamela Gaull 2010
Cover design by Fiona Swapp www.silversea-design.co.uk.

A CIP catalogue record for this book is available from the British Library.

For
My mother Janet
who has encouraged me from the beginning.

Acknowledgements

I have to thank the following who have taken the trouble to read this book in its various stages of editing and given their comments and advice:
Bryan Baird, Liz Campbell, Betty Clark, Angela Cotus, Cathy Cowie, Pete Davies, Vera Edwards, Sue Fehlinger, Paddy Fussell, Avril McQuiggan, James Scott, Jim Stott, Jackie Shaves and Fiona Swapp.

I am grateful also to my daughter, Paula, and my sister, Susan, for her patience and support.

My thanks also go to Pamela and Bill Kelly of Better Read Bookshop, Ellon for their helpful advice. www.better-read.co.uk

A special mention must be made of Charlie the Jack Russell for his loving companionship during the many long hours of editing.

Chapter I

As everywhere else blighted by World War II, 1944 was pretty bleak in Aberdeen, and the drawing in of the October nights as winter approached threw a dismal pall over the town. The countless tragedies that years of war bring to a nation might have been expected to bring the population to their knees, and for some individuals who were pushed beyond human endurance this was unfortunately the case. However, it was astonishingly true that although years of enemy bombardment had flattened streets of buildings in every major city, the fighting spirit of the British people not only remained uncrushed, but grew remarkably stronger in defiance. In Aberdeen it was no different. Its inhabitants endeavoured to withstand the sorrow of separation and lost lives with a stoicism as impenetrable as the grey granite of their town.

It must also be said that living with the ever present thought that there may not be a tomorrow produced a devil may care attitude to pleasure, and every last person made the most of any opportunity to have a good time. So it was that the Clark family were enjoying a lively evening in their top floor tenement flat to celebrate their only son Kenny being home on leave. Joe Clark and his wife Daisy had broken into their Christmas fund to pay for the party. Ration coupons that had been saved for special occasions were used at the butcher, the grocer and the baker by Daisy who was joyfully shopping in a way she had almost forgotten was possible after years of frugal living. 'In a war you learn to live for the moment,' the normally prudent Joe had explained to Maggie and Jane, his twin daughters, who were shocked yet delighted by their father's unexpected burst of extravagance. It was his weekend off from driving tramcars and he was in a particularly ecstatic mood at having two long lies to look forward to. 'And see

5

to it that you two come straight home from work this afternoon and give your mother a hand to set out the food. No hanging around with these soldiers that drop in past your bake house for cheap second day's buns and cakes.' But they needed no reminding. Even more than usual they couldn't wait for Friday night to come and had squabbled and laughed like schoolgirls, falling over each other in their rush upstairs to help their mother prepare the rare delicacies such as sandwiches with egg and ham and the luxury of a couple of tins of salmon. Joe even managed to rustle up some bottles of beer and stout. And why not? Kenny would be gone from them in only a matter of days for God knows how long, so hang the expense.

All the neighbours turned up and the bustling tenement kitchen echoed with such laughter and singing that it might have been Hogmanay come early. Kenny played his violin with great gusto, and Joe had everyone in fits with his hilarious bothy ballads, while blind Mr. Sharpe from across the landing gave it laldy on the spoons.

It was late and the last of the neighbours had gone, leaving the family to enjoy a few precious minutes together. 'This has been the happiest night of my life!' shouted Maggie, a lively redhead, as she kicked off her high heels and danced, feet flashing, round the cramped kitchen in time to Kenny's brisk fiddling. His shirtsleeves were rolled up to reveal a physical strength that belied the sensitivity of his musician's hands. The bow flew over the strings, scarcely taking time to touch, and the music sprang forth, jaunty, familiar, tugging at toes. Maggie's twin sister, Jane, sat close by Kenny, her face glowing with happiness.

Huddled together in a billowing floral armchair, cosy conspirators in the flickering firelight, their parents, Daisy and Joe Clark clapped their hands and tapped their feet, Daisy in her good pink slippers with the fur round the ankles, and Joe in his thick-knitted socks that had worked their way down his legs and now flapped a good two inches beyond the end of each foot. He obviously thought this was great fun and began flapping them against each other as if they were puppets dancing. Daisy gave him a playful slap before turning her attention back to Kenny, gazing at him with adoring eyes and swaying with her husband in time to the music.

Suddenly she stopped clapping and held out her hands in front of her, but instead of singing, she cried out in a voice that shook with suffering, 'Why can't you be here with us every night of the week where you belong?' The music stopped and everyone turned to look at her. Daisy began wringing her hands, fingers clasped so tightly that the nails were banded with white. Then, placing them together as if in prayer, fingertips gently brushing the tremor of her lips, she raised her brimming eyes heavenwards and called out in protest, 'God save us, a young laddie like him shouldn't be fighting in wars. War's not natural. Never has been. Never will be.' Slowly she shook her grey head that had been made wise by the hardships of time. Over the past five years, her hair had become thin in places allowing a pink scalp to shine through, and new lines of worry had etched themselves on her face among the laughter lines of happier times.

Kenny and his sisters froze in horror to hear their long-suffering mother finally give voice to her pain. The muscles along her husband's jaw line noticeably tightened and he closed his eyes and took a long slow breath before answering. 'They're all mothers' sons, the young soldier laddies,' he said, taking Daisy's hands in his. 'How else do we stop Hitler and his evil Nazis from marching through every land?' he argued. 'It's the sacrifice we parents have to make, and I'm proud of our Kenny.'

Joe began clapping even louder than before and stamped his stocking feet to drown out the lingering implication of his words. He turned to his son and shouted gruffly, 'Go on lad, keep playing, and you girls, I want to see you up dancing again. There's no point in us all being miserable.' Daisy reached for her glass of whisky that sat on the cabinet between the chair and the bed in the recess. She took a long sip and then another. Joe rubbed his forehead with the flat of his hand, and taking his own drink from off the kitchen table, he knocked it back in one, and closing his eyes, allowed the amber liquid to soothe him. He patted his wife's hands that lay still in her lap now and said gently, trying to reassure her, 'It might not be for much longer. Don't let worry cloud our pleasure, if only for tonight.' After squeezing her knee to make her ticklish, to make her smile again, he began slapping his thigh with the other hand, which he cupped for more resonance, so providing his own personal percussion to the lively tune. Behind round-rimmed spectacles his lively eyes sparkled with joy. 'Certainly haven't lost your magic touch, Kenny lad,' he called out. 'It's a treat to have you home beside us. We've had a night to remember and no mistake, and all our friends had a great time.'

Death, however, needed no invitation to the party and, comfortably seated, feet under the table, the gatecrasher waited unseen for his unsuspecting victims. The music flowed faster, bewitching the feet and, unaware of the silent watcher in their midst, Maggie pulled Jane from the comfort of her chair, and in the space between sink and table, they crossed hands and swung each other round, toes twinkling like the northern lights, those heavenly dancers that dart across black night skies in winter. The girls' long hair fanned behind them, Maggie's a rich red tangle of curls, and Jane's blonde and straight. 'Just look at the pair of them,' sighed their mother, 'chalk and cheese, Maggie wild as the wind and Jane soft as the snow.' The sisters continued their reel, spinning and shrieking till the floorboards bounced below them and dizziness had them staggering for chairs, where they sat gasping for breath and rocking with laughter.

Joe had moved to the arm of the chair where he bounced himself up and down so vigorously that he tumbled backwards on to Daisy's lap. She screamed in false protest, kicking her legs in the air as they rolled together, the fullness of her thick pleated skirt wrapping itself round his trousers, entwining them in a giggling,

8

struggling tangle. Daisy managed to fight herself free and bent over Joe to give him a kiss on the cheek. Joe drew her to him and gave her a kiss on the lips before straightening his spectacles that were perched askew on the point of his nose. His nose was by now tinged with purple from having consumed the lion's share of the whisky he'd bought in especially for the occasion.

Kenny let out a low whistle and Maggie chided the two lovebirds playfully as she tucked in her blouse that had worked its way loose during the dancing. 'Behave yourselves at your age. You're tiddly, both of you.'

'We've a right to be,' answered Daisy, holding out her glass to Jane who came over to refill it with the now near empty bottle. 'And go easy with the water this time, Jane; I like to taste my drink.'

'No water in mine,' added Joe. 'I'm allergic to it.'

'Only a wee smidgeon of the hard stuff for me,' said Kenny as he mopped his brow and placed the fiddle lovingly back in its case. 'We've a busy day tomorrow.' He cleared his throat to draw everyone's attention and then standing up straight with his back to the fire, he raised his glass. 'To victory!' he shouted. Everyone got to their feet. 'To victory!' they echoed in unison.

'We'll soon have Hitler and his Nazis running scared,' said Joe, 'and then we can have evenings like this any time we want.' After taking a long slug, he held his glass up towards a framed photograph on the mantelpiece of a young man in uniform. 'And not forgetting Eddie. Here's to my kid brother wherever he is. May the good Lord bring him safely home.'

'To Eddie!' they shouted in response, and followed Joe's example by draining their glasses and banging them down hard on the table.

Joe took a piece of neatly folded paper from under the photo frame, glanced at it quickly and replaced it. Everyone knew by heart the harsh telegram message and that no matter how many times Joe read it, it would always say the same – Missing Presumed

Dead Stop.

Maggie watched her father slump back into the chair with her mother. He took off his spectacles and brushed away tears. Maggie went over to the photograph. 'I love my Uncle Eddie. I pray for him every night,' she said quietly. 'I know he's still alive.'

'I believe that too,' said Jane who stopped clearing away the remains of their party in order to kiss her father gently on his balding head.

'Right, you bairns, time for bed,' said Joe huskily. 'We've our day out tomorrow and I'm taking you somewhere posh for tea.'

'You're the best father in the world,' said Maggie affectionately, rushing over to throw her arms round his neck, squashing her mother in the process. But Daisy scarcely noticed. She was staring straight ahead lost in her own thoughts. 'My own dear Celtic princess,' said Joe fondly, stroking Maggie's wild mane. He looked over at Jane and Kenny who had taken down the photograph and were gazing at it wistfully. 'No matter how old any of you three are, you will always be my bairns.' Daisy prised herself from Joe's side and, one-by-one, kissed her brood goodnight.

In bed, Maggie cuddled into Jane's back as they whispered and giggled together like children, the years slipping away like vague dreams. 'Just listen to Kenny snoring in his room,' sniggered Maggie. 'He's making more noise than the Luftwaffe.'

'Sh! We'll be keeping everyone awake,' answered Jane, but she needn't have bothered, Maggie was already asleep.

Chapter 2

No bombers flew that night. High in the frosty heavens, the pale, waning moon peeped cheekily out from behind slow moving clouds and tiptoed over a patch of midnight blue sky before hiding again. No wind came to whistle down chimneys or through cracks in doors and windows. No sirens sounded to summon the family from their cosy beds. After exhausting nights of relentless air raids when the moon had been shining full and bright, the family slipped easily into lead-heavy sleep, and were soon in the drowsy depths of oblivion unaware of any menace that might lurk in their own quiet haven.

And, as they slept, Fate sneaked in without warning to play one of her twisted tricks of cruelty. In the lobby of their flat, exposed live electric wires near the fuse box happened to touch and fired angry sparks across at each other. The crackling heat spread rapidly along the partly chewed cables. In a trap in a dusty corner, broken-necked and blood-bespattered, lay the little grey mouse that had gnawed so vigorously at the frayed cloth covering of the old flex and laid bare the copper strands that carried the current. But the sharp toothed rodent's execution had come too late; his deadly damage was done.

Quivering fingers of smoke reached into the darkness of the night. Smouldering wires burst into flames and the hungry fire that stretched longingly for sustenance found it readily in bed sheets drying on the pulley. From there, it went on to consume the thick wool-fibred coats behind the door. Fiercely, the flames tried to devour a roll of linoleum that had been stored against the wall waiting until Joe and Kenny found the time to lay it in the kitchen. Foul stinking smoke belched from the top of it in the same way that it billows from the great chimneys of the factories and mills that pollute and blacken the townships and countryside around them.

Maggie's nose twitched like an animal's, involuntarily, giving

11

warning. The smoke wafted up her nostrils, interrupting dreams of beach walks and happy laughter, and carried her back to awareness. She realised the danger and was wide awake in an instant. She sat up and looked round the room. Her eyes fell on the outline of the bedroom door illuminated by the blaze behind it. 'Fire! Fire!' she screamed and frantically shook Jane till she too was awake. She reached down for the torch they always kept close at hand and leapt out of bed. Kenny was already banging on the walls and stamping on the floor to raise the alarm. Then she heard him shouting from his window down to the street below. In no time at all the tenement stairs echoed to the sound of neighbours vacating their flats. The white stick of their immediate neighbour, Mr. Sharpe, struck with an eerie regularity against their door and then rattled the stair railings as he made good his escape.

'Don't open the bedroom door,' Maggie screamed at Jane who, still groggy with sleep, was heading in that direction, 'we'll have to go out the window!' Maggie had already hauled back the heavy curtains, rolled up the blackout blinds and was wrenching open the window. Kenny's earlier cries had alarmed the patrolling air raid wardens and sent them scurrying for help. A distant clang of bells drew closer and grew louder. Two fire engines swerved round the corner of the street careering together like chariots in a race. Firemen jumped from them even before they'd stopped outside the door. Maggie leaned out of the top window waving her arms and shouting. Excitedly, she pulled herself back inside the room. 'The Fire Brigade, Jane. We're saved!' She ran over and dragged her sister towards the window.

'I can't jump,' Jane protested. 'We're two floors up. What about Mum and Dad?' She was shrieking, tearing her hair out, hysterical.

'We've no choice. They'll be rescued too.'

Maggie let go of Jane and struggled out of the attic window feet first. The pale half-moon offered a gentle white light and, silhouetted below her, a circle of men held open a fire blanket and urged her to jump. She turned to hurry Jane on, only to see her

12

swallowed into the jaws of the flames that had come tearing round the bedroom door when she'd opened it in blind desperation. Jane's cries were stifled in the asphyxiating black clouds that attacked the back of her throat. In a final farewell, her outstretched hands pawed the air, her arms flailing through the flames and smoke. Maggie heard a loud scream tearing through the night air but failed to recognise it as her own.

She clung like a limpet to the window frame, immobile. 'Jump, lass, jump!' shouted the gathering crowd below. Rising above the deep voices of the men, the shrill cries of the women carried eerily through the night air. Surely this must be a dream, a nightmare brought on by fear. But why couldn't she waken? Maggie looked at the band of rescuers and froze. They seemed so far away. What if she fell? She felt dizzy and the ground below her started to spin. 'Jump, lass, jump! It's your only chance!' Maggie closed her eyes and swallowed back the bile that filled the back of her throat. 'It's all right. We'll catch you!' The firemen's voices were hoarse from shouting. They shook the fire blanket up and down and she allowed herself to be seduced with the promise of life. She lowered her body and slithered it down the slope of the roof. The cold damp of the slates penetrated the seat of her pyjamas and the ridge of the guttering dug into the soles of her bare feet. Her whole body shivered. 'Jump, lass, jump!' A nerve twitching in her right hip made her leg tremble, causing her foot to slip from its hold. In order to steady herself, Maggie's grip intensified so much so that her nails pierced the soft weatherworn wood. Having regained her foothold, she bent up both her knees and placed her feet flat on the slates. If she wanted to live, she had to jump now. Maggie heard the fire raging behind her and felt its hot breath on the back of her neck. She released her grip on the window frame and rocked herself backwards and forwards at the edge of the roof in order to increase momentum. With every last ounce of her bodily strength, Maggie propelled herself forwards and downwards and landed with a bump in safe hands.

13

Kenny had meanwhile thrown a blanket over his head and shoulders to protect himself from the flames as he rushed through the lobby, heading for the kitchen to rescue his parents. As if timed to happen, with the precision that is peculiar to accidents, the blazing pillar of linoleum fell across his back at the exact moment that two firemen burst through the door. Crushed under the burning weight, Kenny was attacked by flames from every side. His pyjamas, his hair, his body caught fire. With a desperate heave, Kenny threw the scorching cylinder off him and rushed headlong past the men. Fragments of linoleum and cloth adhered to his body and he tumbled, a human fireball, down the stairs and lay burning like a log on the landing below. His body could be heard sizzling like a pig roasting on a spit and a Sunday morning smell of burning bacon filled the building.

Poisonous black smoke had long since seeped in through the always open kitchen door and penetrated every single nook and cranny. It was followed soon after by rip-roaring fire. The firemen who stormed in from the stairs were too late to rescue the couple. Joe, in his long johns and vest, lay sprawled on his back across an armchair where he'd been overcome as he stumbled through the intoxication of sleep and drink in a last ditch attempt at escape. Daisy lay near the door like a bundle of burned out rags in her charred nightdress. Finger-wide smears were etched through the black smoke residue on the wall nearby where she had blindly tried to claw her way out before collapsing. All the fire fighters were able to do now was drag out the bodies. Another two had entered from a ladder at the window and were subduing the flames with powerful jets of water.

Wrapped in a thick, warm blanket, Maggie lay on the ground, her head nestled in the arm of an air raid warden. From somewhere among the gathered crowd a woman's voice, sobbing, fell on her ears, softly spoken but harsh to hear: 'Poor little mite. All alone in the world. What will happen to her now?'

Maggie raised her head weakly and whispered, 'I had to leave them. I had to jump. I wanted to live!' A lit cigarette was placed between her lips. She inhaled it deeply and coughed. She took a second puff and the dizziness brought a welcome sense of calm.

'I'll take her!' It was Ina Scott, a neighbour from two doors down. 'Better with us than sharing some church hall with the rest of the homeless.'

Chapter 3

The day of the funeral arrived. In the Scotts' house, people had been coming and going all morning, opening doors, shutting doors, talking, whispering and crying. From the street outside came the sound of car engines revving. Maggie lay under the covers in the little bedroom. The blinds were down and heavy curtains at the window created a daytime darkness that Maggie was glad to escape into. She tossed and turned and then lay on her right side facing the wall. She covered her head with her arms to block out the noise and rocked herself, but in spite of her efforts to hide away, she couldn't help but overhear the concerned voices of women outside her bedroom. They stopped and she knew they were listening for some sign of movement from her. There was a gentle tap and the door squeaked open. 'Are you coming?'

'Nyrahh!' She yelled without even turning round. The door was closed again with as much speed as someone would close the cage of a frightened animal before it could bite. 'I told you she wouldn't come.' It was Ina's voice clearly now and unmistakable in its matter of fact tone. 'The doctor said to leave her. She needs time.'

At last, after more to-ing and fro-ing, the house grew still. Outside, the street too had fallen silent. Maggie lay taught as a wire. An occasional tremor ran through her like ticker tape. For five days she'd not washed, and paid no heed to the basin of lukewarm water and soap that Ina put daily on the dressing table. Only once a day did she rise and put on a coat from the pile of clothes on the chair at the foot of her bed, clothes that neighbours had gathered for her, digging deep into their own almost empty wardrobes and drawers. Leaning into the wall like a shadow, she would slip unnoticed down the stairs to the outside toilet with her pee pail and out into the chill November nights, where chimney smoke hung heavy in the moisture of the air, making it nearly too thick to breathe. Werewolf nights, her dad used to call them. Maggie remembered him reading a tale about vampires to Jane and

16

her round the fire one evening when they were only twelve, scaring them so much they had to spend the night in the safety of their mother's big bed while their father was banished along with his book through to their room.

Maggie caught a whiff of cold porridge reminding her of Ina's offering on the table by her bed. Sometimes there was soup or mashed potatoes and turnips. Maggie didn't want food. She wanted to die. But every time she wished that she too had lost her life, she heard her own voice again, calling loudly over the rooftops: 'I want to live!' And the part of her that wanted to live reached out to the food and ate just enough. Today, however, there was no room in her throat for food; it was too choked full of sorrow.

Still Maggie rocked. She remembered how as a child she'd been shunted on a trolley into a side-room near the hospital theatre, pain slicing her throat where her tonsils had been. No Mummy or Daddy came to give comfort, only bad-tempered nurses telling her to sleep.

Maggie felt the same panic now. 'Mummy!' she shouted, 'Mummy!' but she knew there would be no answer. 'No one will ever come again,' she sobbed. Behind closed eyelids the faces of her family shimmered in a perpetual re-enactment of their last night of life. Maggie lay in a mirage of flames, willing herself to burn, but staying alive.

For four more weeks Maggie dug herself deep into the foxhole, only sometimes washing or eating, until the day dawned that was different from other days. Even misery must come to an end. Maggie rubbed sleep from her eyes and sat up. She had wakened without tears. On every previous morning, tears had burst from her eyes like springs of clear water that force their way through the cracks and crevices of great boulders on the sides of mountains. Now, today, her eyes were desert dry, scorched with the pain of lamentation that had seared its way out of her, carrying in its

17

deluge the grief of her soul. Emptied of emotion, she felt ready at last to face the life she had bravely decided was her right. But was it always to be a life so heavily burdened with sorrow? Would she ever find anyone to love again?

Chapter 4

Maggie heard Ina and Sandy Scott quarrelling. Sandy's voice, full of rage, jarred against the walls of her hideaway. 'What kind of stupid fool act was that of yours to take that derelict girl into our house?' he yelled at his wife.

'But it's not as if anyone's using that bed,' Ina came back at him sounding just as angry, 'Robbie's away and I could be doing with help in the house and some company, not to mention some rent.' She banged a plate of watery porridge down in front of her husband so hard that it lapped over the side and spilled glutinously on to the table. 'A bit of board money and we might be able to afford an occasional egg and a drop more milk,' she argued, wiping up the gooey mess with a corner of her apron.

'But she's lain in that bed refusing to budge for weeks now. She never even dressed for her family's funeral. She just lies there day after day eating us out of house and home. And her wailing through the night would send a chill through the bravest of hearts. Either she starts paying her way or she's out. We're not a charity.'

'I'll have a word with her, but it won't be easy. We've known that family for five years ever since we moved into the street,' answered Ina.

'There's a war on and there's no time for sentimental slush,' declared Sandy, swinging over his shoulder the haversack that contained his meagre lunch of bread and syrup and a flask of black tea. 'I want things different when I come home tonight.' He slammed his way out of the house and off to work as a labourer gathering the rubble from bombsites, the only work he could find since the war started.

Maggie rose and, after rummaging among the cast-offs, managed to find a skirt and jumper that didn't have any stains and was near enough the right size. Yesterday she had felt able to wash her hair and now she brushed and combed the unruly waves till they shone, before pinning them into a neat tight roll along the nape of her neck. She could hear Ina cleaning the fireside in the kitchen, a homely sound, reassuring that a new day had dawned, that life would continue, that there was work to be done. Maggie shoved her feet into a pair of down-at-heel court shoes and, straightening her shoulders, walked through to the kitchen with the poise of a stylish mannequin modelling garments of haute couture.

Ina turned from her duties and, masking her surprise, smiled more with relief than in welcome. Maggie returned the smile. Why cause more hostility? 'Fancy a cup of tea?' she offered brashly and thought to herself, 'I must hold my own. I won't crumble under their criticism.' Without waiting for Ina's answer she started filling the kettle at the sink.

'There's some porridge in the pan if you want it,' offered Ina from the recess where she was making the bed, crawling over the top of it and tucking the blankets securely into the side against the wall.

'I can't thank you enough, Ina, for putting me up like this,' Maggie said between mouthfuls of porridge, which she guzzled like a hungry calf, milk trickling from the sides of her mouth. Her lips were anaemia pale and her cheeks were hollow, a shadow of the lively young woman she'd so recently been. However, a hint of vibrancy had returned to her eyes and her shoulders were no longer hunched in defeat. Determination was suggested in the way she held her head high like the proud princess she'd always been for her father. She cleared her plate and washed it at the sink along with the other breakfast dishes lying there. Without hesitation, Maggie dried every one and stacked them back into the cupboard with the same confidence she would have had in her own home. Ina stood at last beside the neat, smooth bed and looked grimly at the milk bottle, empty now. She placed her hands on her hips and asked outright, 'When are you going back to work?'

'I can't go back to the bakery. Their sympathy would finish me off. I need a fresh start and I must earn money for clothes.' As she spoke, she pulled at the waistband of the loose fitting hand-me-down skirt whose lining showed a good quarter inch below the hemline.

'You'll be fine back at work. Good for you to be among people you know,' said Ina, deliberately ignoring what Maggie had just said. Going to the cupboard, she took out a partly filled pillowcase. 'I think you're ready for this now,' she said placing it on the table in front of her. 'You have a look through it while I get on with lighting this blessed fire.'

Maggie sat at the table and stared at the bundle. She closed her eyes and braced herself. 'Is this all that's left?' she asked, steadying a quiver in her voice.

'I'm sorry, lass, but it is,' said Ina, concentrating on the fire. She screwed sheets of newspaper into balls and laid them in the clean grate. 'Mind the table though. Use these to lay your things on,' she said as she handed over a couple of papers from her pile.

The pillowcase showed one unmistakable bulge, Kenny's violin. Maggie drew it out slowly, as if frightened to encounter this reminder of happier times that could never be any more than memory. Thick greasy soot covered its case which was burnt through in parts round the edges and she caught a whiff of the acrid smell of burnt linoleum. Maggie set her jaw and continued the grisly task. Picking up a sheet of newspaper and using it as a towel, she wiped her hands thoroughly before releasing the two tarnished metal catches on the side. To her amazement and joy, the instrument was intact. Reverently she passed her hand over the curved outline of its shape and lifted it out. Holding it up by the neck in her left hand, the bottom resting against her waist, she plucked the four strings one-by-one with the long thumbnail of her right hand, starting with the thick G-string and ending with the fine gut A. 'It sounds fine,' she said. 'Kenny's violin is perfect!'

'I hope you're not going to start crying again.' Ina rose from the fireplace and went over to the sink to wash her hands. She sounded more impatient than concerned.

Maggie shuddered. 'No, Ina, don't worry. I have been to the pits of Hell and back. I've experienced the horrors that lie in wait for us there, and now I've had enough. I've no more tears and it's time to move on, find a job and somewhere to live.'

'You don't have to leave,' said Ina, bending down to open the little door under the sink. She took out a large pan containing a butcher's bone. 'Look what I have for us today.' She lifted out the bone and held it up temptingly to show off the slivers of meat that still stuck to it. 'I'll simmer it slowly over the fire all day to draw out the marrow. It will make us a right healthy pot of soup.'

'We'll see,' was all that Maggie said as she rummaged among the relics of her home. At last a cry of triumph broke through her lips which she'd been chewing anxiously as she searched. 'Thank God I still have these!' She pulled out a metal box and wiped it clean. It was a beige and brown tin with Milky Favourites written on the lid. Pictures of chocolates that had once decorated it so temptingly were now faded in some places and blackened in others. Maggie removed the lid and reached inside for the treasure. One-by-one she set out in front of her the handful of family photographs. After scrutinising the valuable bundle closely, she gathered them back into the tin, hugged it and placed it on the sideboard behind her.

Maggie resumed her search, carefully emptying the contents piece by piece. She dug deep into the pillowcase and ran her fingers along the seam at the bottom. 'At last, here it is.' Joy shone in her face as she held up the prize and shouted, 'Uncle Eddie's photo!' The back of the frame was scorched and it crumbled as soon as she touched it. The glass was cracked and part of it fell into her hands as she touched it. With great care, as if the whole thing might disintegrate and be lost in the irretrievable dust of time, she removed the photograph from its frame and, laying it on the newspapers, smoothed it flat with her hand.

'You can't see who it is. It's covered in smoke,' said Ina over Maggie's shoulder.

'Have you a cloth?'

'Let's see what I can find, but I've more to do with my day than polish old photos.' However, in spite of herself she was intrigued. Might be a bit of gossip to brighten up her life. She scurried over to her cleaning basket at the foot of the cupboard and produced a piece of soft white cloth. 'Here, try this,' she said with a hint of excitement.

Maggie took the cloth and unfolded it. An unfamiliar sound hit her eardrums, a sound she hadn't heard for a long time. She stopped and listened. Sure enough, she was laughing, and amusement ran through her voice as she spoke, 'I hope these belong to your Sandy,' she said, holding up a pair of men's underpants, the material worn thin, almost transparent in places.

'Of course they do,' answered Ina turning a deep shade of pink. 'Who else?' She hurried back to the bone on the sink and began preparing the soup.

'It's ideal, Ina,' said Maggie, still smiling. 'I've used many an old vest of Dad's for polishing.' Her laughter stopped but she managed to hold her mouth firmly in its smile. She must not let herself down by crying whenever she mentioned one of her family by name. Gently she wiped the photograph, painstakingly, as if restoring a grand master from one of the world's finest art galleries, rubbing just hard enough to remove the cloying soot, but not so hard that the surface would be damaged. Eventually she held the picture up to Ina. 'There he is, my Uncle Eddie.'

'Fine looking man,' Ina said, coming over from the hob where the soup was heating at the flames of the fire on the range. 'I think I've seen him visiting. Your dad's brother, isn't he? I see the likeness, except for the lovely head of hair.'

'It's auburn, something like mine but darker,' said Maggie wistfully. 'You don't see it in the black and white. He's a lot younger than Dad though, only twenty-seven, five years older than me.' Maggie touched his face. 'He was with his regiment in Italy. He wrote as often as he could. I'll never forget the day the telegram boy stopped at our door. Those three words - missing presumed dead - brought my father to his knees. It's the only time I've seen him cry. We all howled that day, but we prayed as well, and I live in hope, especially now, that one day he'll come back. He's all I have.'

Ina's voice dropped to a whisper and was unusually gentle. 'I live for the day the war will end and our Robbie will be back safely home with us.' She handed the picture back to Maggie. 'Never give up hope,' she said in a gruff whisper. Her eyes were moist and she gave Maggie's hand a squeeze.

'That's what Eddie always said, "Nihil desperandum". He and Dad used that phrase as if it were a family motto.' Maggie tenderly placed the photograph with the others. 'But now I'm off out. There are things I have to do.'

Ina's eyes had softened but now her expression darkened again and she drew her brow into a deep frown. 'I wouldn't have minded a hand with the baking later on, but you please yourself.' She turned away sharply and, snatching the papers from the table, threw them into the fire where, matching her own anger, they flared up the chimney.

It was early evening before Maggie returned. Slowly she turned the door handle and crept in. She stood silently with her back against the sideboard, chewing her lips and swallowing, as she waited for the interrogation she knew would ensue. Ina was knitting by the sparse fire. Sandy was bent over a cobbler's last at the table, hammer in hand and a supply of nails secreted in the front of his mouth. To eke out the few pounds a week he made gathering rubble, Sandy took in neighbours' shoes to mend. He was a proud though sullen provider. Grey hair and a grey, weather-toughened face gave him the appearance of having himself been hewn from granite. His temperament too was harsh and unyielding. Bending to his every whim, Ina's own personality had been chipped away over the years till she no longer remembered who or what she was.

24

She merely replicated her husband, but this she considered to be the epitome of success for any decent woman.

On seeing Maggie, Ina shoved the knitting behind her into the corner of the chair, eager to find out whether or not she would have free help in the house as well as possible income. Sandy continued to file the rough edges of the sole of the shoe he was working on. His only acknowledgement of Maggie was the barely discernable upturning of his eyes as he listened closely, desperate to hear that there was financial benefit in the offing. There was no friendly greeting from Ina either and she lost no time in launching the attack. 'Where the hell have you been? We were worried sick during the air raid at lunchtime?' Maggie remained stock still at the door of the kitchen. She put her hand into her coat pocket and produced a purse. Ina's eyes narrowed. 'Where on God's earth did you get that?' she demanded, hands on hips accusingly. Maggie gave her a defiant look and kept her lips sealed. She opened out the wallet part of the purse and, with meticulous care, flicked through the notes inside with her fingertips. She drew out four singles and folded them into her palm before closing up the purse again and stuffing it deep into her pocket. Ina's eyes had followed each and every movement, as had Sandy's, and the scrape of his file on leather had ceased.

Maggie smoothed the creases from the notes and held them out to Ina who nearly knocked her husband off his seat in the rush past him to grab the money. Only after she had tucked it down her front did she take a closer look at Maggie who had sat herself wearily at the table opposite Sandy without even taking off her coat. Ina drew in her breath in a gasp of astonishment before speaking, and her voice took on a more kindly tone as she uttered: 'Your bonnie hair, Maggie! You look like a boy.' Indeed, Maggie's small white face peeped out from a frame of tight red curls that wound themselves closely to her scalp.

'Pride is worth more to me than vanity,' she answered icily, not taken in by Ina's sudden kindness. 'My hair will soon grow.' She placed her hands flat down on the table as if symbolic of business now finished. 'I only hope that was enough to repay you for taking me in.' She stared at Sandy as she spoke, willing some response. His stubborn refusal to show her anything other than callous disregard all the time she had lived under his roof had made her feel worthless. Her voice trembled as she continued with her explanation, and she clutched nervously at the skin of her throat. 'I sold Kenny's fiddle as well. It nearly broke my heart, but I knew he'd understand.'

Sandy was scrutinising his handiwork. 'Nothing for nothing in this life,' he muttered before feeding some tackets into his mouth and gripping them between his lips. Although he had at last spoken, he still never looked her way; instead he started hammering with steady strokes of satisfaction and flicked the segs out of his mouth with his tongue as he needed them.

'Come, Maggie, take your coat off,' Ina said, mellowed by the money. 'You must be worn out.' As she helped Maggie off with her coat she noticed the label that denoted a garment of quality. 'That's some coat you're wearing, and a new skirt and shoes. Where did the likes of you get them?'

'The Salvation Army. How could I expect to find work looking the way I did? And that's where I was during the air raid, searching through dead people's clothing for something suitable to wear.' Maggie swayed slightly and sat down again at the table opposite Sandy. 'When we heard the sirens, the Salvation Army officers took us to their shelter and prayed for us. They led us in singing hymns so I wasn't frightened. It made me feel better and, as I sang, I prayed to God, and I knew my family were up in Heaven safe with Him.'

'Maybe it's time to forget about all that now,' Ina said offhandedly. 'We must get on with life whether we like it or not.' She went over to the fire and ladled some hot soup into a deep plate before sliding it across the table. Maggie wolfed it down with chunks of bread, packing it into her mouth until her cheeks

26

bulged. She wiped her face with the back of her hand and braced herself to tell them her news. 'I found myself a job so I'll soon be out from under your feet.' She said this pointedly to Sandy who was tidying away his tools so that he too could have some soup. 'I start work tomorrow morning washing dishes in the Regent Hotel, so I'll away now and get ready. I've an early start.'

'But you can't leave us now after all we've done for you!' Ina ran and blocked Maggie's path to the door. Maggie dodged to the side of her and pushed past and disappeared into Robbie's room to pack the best of the cast offs and the precious tin of photographs into a scuffed old suitcase that she had to tie round with the belt of an old dress to keep it from falling open.

'Well, whatever happens to you now,' said Ina, brushing herself down, 'you've only yourself to blame.'

Chapter 5

At the Regent Hotel, Sadie Dewar, the manageress came round from behind the reception desk and shook Maggie's hand in warm welcome. She exuded efficiency along with the subtle aroma of expensive perfume. Her black hair was scraped back with tortoiseshell combs into a tight bun so smooth it looked as if it had been painted on by those Japanese artists who decorate cups and plates with delicate brush strokes.

'We're so pleased to have you, Maggie,' Sadie said, ushering her through to the back and along a dark lobby. 'I'll show you to your room now and leave you to it.' Tucked away at the end of a long dark corridor at the top of the building was a white door with the number seventy-three on it in polished brass figures. Sadie opened the door with a flourish. She knew Maggie would be pleased. Although it was a tiny room, Maggie gasped with delight. Nestled cosily under the slope of the roof was a single bed already made up with a pale blue satin cover and floral quilt. A wardrobe with a mirror set into the door stood against the far wall. In the corner was a wash hand basin with a cane chair beside it. On it, beautifully folded, were towels, nighties and work overalls.

'The bathroom's back there on the landing,' said Sadie in her rich contralto voice, 'but you'll have to share it with the other girls who live in. They like it kept clean and tidy and no cigarette ends down the sink.'

'Of course,' said Maggie. A vague recollection caused her to hesitate before adding, 'I don't usually smoke.' She turned to Sadie. 'I'll rest now if you don't mind. I'll be down in the morning at seven o'clock sharp.'

'By the way,' said Sadie, 'feel free to use any of the soaps and perfumes. They've been left behind by various residents over the years and they're just lying there going to waste. Hardly had Sadie turned the corner of the stairs than Maggie had deposited the old battered suitcase in front of the wardrobe and made a beeline for the bathroom with the towels and a nightie. In her twenty-two years Maggie had never been in a real bath. She'd washed in the spluttering sprays before and after swimming at the municipal pool but she'd never experienced anything like this. At home they'd just had to take the big basin through from the kitchen to the bedroom for their private ablutions.

This was luxury. In the centre of the spacious bathroom, a vast Victorian bath stood proudly on carved brass feet shaped like those of a lion. Maggie turned on the nearest of the gold taps and allowed the water to run through her fingers. In no time at all it was running hot. On the shelf above the sink were two bottles with glass stoppers. One was half-full of pale rose water and the other held rich oil with the faraway fragrance of blossom and countryside. It had *Jasmine* written in elaborate yellow letters on the green label. On the sparkling white china bath, in the space between the taps, was a new cake of lavender soap lying in a mother of pearl dish shaped like an oyster shell.

Maggie stripped off and folded her clothes on to a pale pink basket chair. She looked at herself in the mirror and drew in her breath with shock. Was that really her, the emaciated creature with bones sticking out all over the place? Where was the figure she'd so proudly displayed when dancing at the Plaza, drawing the soldiers who kept her up on the floor waltzing all night? Her shorn hair received little more than a cursory glance. Her long red locks had served her well and more would soon grow back.

Maggie held the soap under the hot tap. The water rose perfumed and frothing to fill the tub, enticing her in like the protective arms of a lover. She dipped a toe into the cloud-soft cushions of foam. It felt heavenly. Slowly, she slipped into the water and soaped herself all over. She breathed in the calming lavender smell of the soap and felt the pain of recent weeks being washed away. The tub was so big she could float in the water and woozy sleep nearly overcame her as she relaxed into its soothing warmth.

Refreshed and brand new, Maggie climbed out of the tub and wrapped herself in the fluffy towel that held the smell of fresh air. She took the bottle of jasmine and oiled her body with the lingering scent and allowed it to soak into her undernourished skin. Last of all she slipped on the crisp white cotton nightie with pink smocking and little puff sleeves. Looking herself straight in the eye in the mirror, she made a solemn vow: 'One day, no matter how hard I have to work and whatever I have to sacrifice, I swear to God that I'll have this kind of luxury all to myself in a home of my own.'

Chapter 6

As the days melted one into another at the Regent Hotel, Maggie fell into a comfortable routine. Long hours left her little time or energy for pining, and instead of crying over her dead family, she used the fond memory of them all to drive her on to make something of her life. Every night she spoke to them in her mind, telling them how successful she was going to be one day, and every night she prayed to God that He would bring Uncle Eddie safely back home to her. Good food, the sound sleep that comes from satisfied exhaustion and regular walks during her time off soon brought the colour back to her cheeks and the strength to her body.

Occasionally, Maggie was asked to help in the cocktail lounge when old Charlie Grant, the resident barman, had nights off. She would wear her new navy dress with padded shoulders and gold buttons down the front. Conversation lifted her spirits and the customers were charmed by her polite manner. Christmas was in the air. Tessa Mearns, a large middle-aged woman, tickled the ivories of the grand piano in the corner, playing a medley of jazzed up carols. Her frizzy hair, dyed blue-black, had an orange tinge at the roots and her face was heavy with makeup. Her more than generous hips swelled copiously over the sides of the piano stool as she played, giving her the appearance of riding a horse, rocking backwards and forwards, her playing fingers pulling the reins, galloping with Rudolph in ragtime rhythm. The crowds loved her and flocked to the Regent every weekend to join with Tessa in raucous, fun-filled evenings.

Three young soldiers were seated round one of the marble topped tables of the lounge. They laughed and joked in fine humour, happy at being home amongst friends. Two of the soldiers went up to the piano and spoke to Tessa. She squealed with pleasure as they kissed her on the cheek. With great gusto she played their request while they sang. The third soldier approached

Maggie at the bar. He was tall, and although he had the regulation short back and sides, his tight brown waves prevented him from having that institutional look. 'Hi there,' he said in a voice that warmed her like sunshine, 'I'd like to order.' Maggie looked up from the glass she was drying and her eyes were caught in his. Neither looked away. They gazed as if they already knew each other well and wanted to find out more. Maggie's face grew hot. 'What can I get you?' she asked and started to wipe the top of the bar with a cloth in order to hide how flustered she was.

'Three pints of beer,' he said, 'and something for yourself.'

'I'll have a small port, thanks, but I'll take it later if it's all right with you.' She put the price of the drink into a jar beside the till, a jar that was nearly full of shillings, sixpences and thruppeny bits. Her savings were growing and that cheered her more than any alcohol could.

'You must be new here,' he said. 'I'm Frank, Frank Rae.'

'My name's Maggie, Maggie Clark,' she answered, and pulled the three pints without talking, her cheeks pink, unusually stuck for words.

Frank watched her closely. Maggie fiddled with the buttons of her dress with her left hand while she lifted the pints with the other, slowly and carefully, one by one, on to the counter. 'Why am I trembling so much?' she thought. 'I must have served hundreds of men before.'

'Must say you're a great improvement on Cheerful Charlie,' said Frank taking a sip from one of the glasses. Maggie felt a tingle just below her ribs. Maybe there was life in her after all.

'Charlie's decided to cut his hours,' Maggie replied casually, but looked straight at Frank as she continued, 'He's only here during the week.'

'So you're on at weekends,' Frank replied with a nod as he paid for the drinks. 'It's been terrific meeting you, Maggie. However, must get back to my pals before their singing drives your customers away. None of them is a great singer, I'm afraid.' For the rest of the evening it was Frank who came to the bar to order and they enjoyed a few more snatched snippets of conversation. When he left with his friends at the end of the night he smiled over in a way that made her heart give a lurch.

The following Friday Maggie's pulse started to race when she saw Frank striding into the lounge. Her smile froze and the hand she had been about to raise in a welcoming wave fell back to her side. There was a woman with him, petite with short blonde hair cut into a bob. She wore a light blue suit and her soft, feminine appearance made Maggie think of fluffy toys, ribbons and bows. Frank led her over to a table in the far corner. Slowly, almost reluctantly, he approached Maggie. Despite his manliness, he looked somewhat sheepish and embarrassed. Maggie kept her cool. 'Hi,' he said, 'pint of beer, sweet sherry for Sarah and whatever you want for yourself.' He didn't look directly at Maggie but fumbled with his wallet. 'Sarah's my fiancée. We're getting married when the war's over - whenever that might be.'

'Could be sooner than you think; says so in all the papers,' Maggie replied as she wiped a pool of spilt drink from the bar counter with businesslike nonchalance. Throughout the evening, whenever Frank came to the bar to order, he stopped for a chat. He turned up on the Saturday night too and on the next two weekends. Sometimes he was with Sarah and sometimes with friends. Maggie determined to stay friendly but aloof. When he finally said 'Goodbye' to Maggie at the end of his leave, he squeezed her hand. 'I'll miss you, Maggie; you've brightened up my time here.' His face grew serious, almost sad and his eyes burned into her as he spoke. 'Why weren't you here this time last year?' Maggie knew exactly what he meant. 'Look after yourself,' she replied with a forced smile. 'You've been a good customer. I hope you and Sarah will be happy.' She looked over towards Sarah and gave her a wave. After all, what was one more soldier in uniform when the town was full of them? So why did she feel a sinking heaviness in her heart when he disappeared into the revolving doors and out into the dark street?

'Cheer up! He's not worth it,' said a voice beside her. It was Andy, an elderly friend of Charlie's who spent more time in the bar as a customer than anyone who worked there. 'Here, have one of these;' he said, offering her a cigarette, 'it's one of these new fangled ones, tipped so you don't cough so much.' Maggie thanked him and drew one from the packet, slowly and deliberately, and put it between her lips. She inhaled the warm petrol smell of Andy's lighter and drew in the cool menthol flavour of the cigarette. Giddy now, and comforted, it didn't seem to bother her so much that she wouldn't see Frank again.

Chapter 7

On her day off, Maggie walked through the town where regiments of grim grey tenements stood guard, street after dreary street, over the wartime city of Aberdeen. Hard granite walls, which adequately protected the inhabitants from a harsh northern climate, had succumbed in places to direct hits from the Luftwaffe, tumbling into depressing piles of rock and dust, leaving swathes of nothingness in the sombre rows of colourless buildings.

However, it did not take long before Maggie's naturally ebullient nature thirsted after stimulation, and, in order to escape the monotony, she took to strolling round the harbour where she could watch the ships berth in order to load and unload cargo. From there she would wander along the coast right down to where the sand changed to rocks, and the rocks changed to cliffs. Windswept and exhilarated, she watched the climate reveal its mercurial moods over the sea. The raw vibrancy of nature was far and away preferable to the encroachment of death among the buildings.

Maggie sat on a bench one frosty Sunday in March. She was enjoying the long uninterrupted stretch of vision across the turbulent sea, which for once had a turquoise glow in the sunshine as opposed to the usual slate grey viewed through wet wintry fog. Scarves of white foam unfurled themselves over the surface, tossing their fringes carelessly, and losing them in the swell. Hypnotised by the soothing repetition, Maggie's mind emptied itself of all worries for the first time in months. She inhaled the refreshing salt air and felt the remnants of her old energy take root inside her and start to grow. Relishing the sense of renewal, Maggie lingered on the seat aware of nothing except the sea and the ceaseless crying of the gulls. Through the haze of her reverie she heard distant footsteps on the sandy path drawing closer. She opened her eyes and turned. A muscular young man, head thrown back in the wind, strolled towards her. She caught his eye and he smiled. She smiled back. He bowed his head and put his hand up to the black cloth cap he wore over dark curly hair. Quite the gentleman thought Maggie to herself and it seemed only natural that he should stop and sit down beside her.

'I hope I'm not disturbing you. You looked so peaceful.'

Maggie laughed. 'Of course it's all right. It would be nice to have some company.'

'I've never seen you walking here before.'

'I like to get away from the town on my day off.' A feeling of camaraderie quickly grew between them as they looked out towards the horizon.

'Can't say I blame you, and the sea has a way of making you forget your troubles.' He was an amiable fellow and chatted about the weather before asking her all about herself. Finally he stood up. 'I'm sorry; I'll have to go now. I was just having a walk before I join my boat. I'm first mate on the Brave Harvest.' He nodded towards the harbour and headed off in that direction. Left alone, Maggie gazed after him but smiled again when, after a few steps, he turned back. 'Hope you don't think I'm being cheeky, but I would like to see you again, or are you already spoken for?'

Maggie noticed that he glanced at her left hand as he spoke. She shrugged. 'Nobody to speak of,' she answered casually. What had she to lose? 'I'm here on Wednesdays or you can find me at work.'

His eyes sparkled. 'Look forward to it, and, by the way, my name's Sam, Sam Taylor.' Maggie introduced herself and they agreed to meet again.

Over the next few months Sam's open nature and genuine affection removed stone by stone the fortress wall that Maggie had built around herself. She began to look forward to seeing him when he returned from fishing trips, and would hurry to see those sharp blue eyes and soft black hair that hung in ringlets over his forehead. There was no regulation haircut for this free spirit and, as they walked out together, arm in arm, Sam wooed Maggie with romantic tales of the sea, of midsummer nights in the Arctic Ocean, when the sun shines all night and sparkles on diamante ice flows creating a fairy tale landscape at the ends of the earth. Sam seemed to be the one who would bring into her life a sense of adventure, a means of escape.

'It was my father who first introduced me to the sea,' he told her. 'Dad took me for frequent walks round the harbour and told me all he knew about shipping and trading. His favourite yarn was about his docker friend who'd had the questionable delight of sampling some opium on board a Chinese vessel and who always said with a twinkle in his eye, "It sure beat a full strength. By the end of the day, I was speaking Chinese with the best of them!"'

Maggie always laughed out loud at that story. She enjoyed the nonconformist edge to Sam's personality. Thankfully, he was also the steady hard working type that she knew she must have if her life were to be a success. 'Quite a character, your father,' commented Maggie. 'I wish I'd met him.' Sam's smile always broadened when he heard Maggie laugh and he would squeeze her tighter to him. On cold days, he held her hand deep inside his jacket pocket and wound a long, thick scarf, which he'd knitted for her during one of his trips, round and round her neck until it covered her mouth and cherry red nose.

'After the First World War Dad worked on a trawler. When he fell heir to some money from an uncle who'd owned a farm, he put it past and never touched a penny. He always said it was for me to use for a share in a fishing boat, and when he died and left it to me last year, I made up my mind that once this war's over that's exactly what I'll do.'

'You'll be well off then, Sam. A man of means,' said Maggie, tightening her grip on his hand.

Chapter 8

(Aberdeen, October 1945)

It was a year after the fateful fire and the war had been over for five months. A tall young man with auburn hair, dressed in standard demob suit, carrying a small suitcase and a gabardine raincoat over his arm, stood outside the tall tenement building, looking up at the attic windows where the Clark family had lived. A net curtain twitched but no face could be seen. 'I'll hang on for you,' said the taxi driver, 'but not too long mind.'

'Don't worry; I'll be back in a tick. It's just that I've had no reply to my letters. Maybe they've moved and I'll need you to take me to their new address.' He checked the nameplates. None of them said Clark. He rushed up the flights of stairs taking them two at a time until the top floor. He stopped momentarily to catch his breath before banging desperately at the door. It was opened by a young man he'd never seen before. He barely had a chance to ask if he knew where the Clarks had moved to when a girl flung the door wide open and chipped in, 'If it's the Clarks you're after, they all died in the fire.' Their white-faced caller swayed against the banisters and wiped his brow with the flat of his hand. 'O, I'm so sorry,' she added, and put her hand over her mouth. Her husband shook his head and glared at her before holding out his hands to the stranger. 'Come inside and look if you don't believe us. You can see how it's all been done up.'

'No thanks. I'll take your word for it.'

The girl stepped forward, trying to redeem herself. She sounded concerned. 'Try the Scotts two doors up. I did hear a story that one of the Clark girls went to live with them, but we're new round here and the Scotts keep themselves to themselves.' The man just nodded a 'Thank you', picked up his case and coat from where he'd dropped them, took a last lingering look at the new nameplate and headed off down the stairs.

Two doors up, Sandy Scott sat at the kitchen table, listening to the sports news, waiting to check his football coupon. Ina broke a couple of eggs into the frying pan. They spat hot fat at her. She blinked away the smarting pain that stung her cheeks and forehead and shook the basket of browning chips in the other pan.

There was a loud, urgent knock at the door. 'God almighty, who the hell's that?' groaned Sandy, 'Robbie's not due home from the Army hospital until next week at least.'

Ina flinched at the mention of her wounded son's name. 'Well, I can't answer it, not unless you want the house to go up in flames,' she replied, turning the eggs. The whites were flecked with black and starting to curl up crisp at the edges.

The announcer started to read the results.

'You know this is the highlight of my week. We could be worth a fortune.' Sandy put a cross opposite one of his draws.

'You'll get the results tomorrow in the Sunday papers. If I answer the door now there's no tea for us. That's the last of the eggs.'

A second knock brought more venom from Sandy. 'Sod this!' he exclaimed, shoving the pencil behind his ear and turning up the wireless so he could follow the results from outside. 'Keep your hair on, I'm coming!' He creaked to his feet and, gritting his teeth against the pain in his joints, shambled to the door. Throwing it open, he glared at the intruder.

'Does a Maggie or Jane Clark live here? Do you know where any of them could be?' The questions were fired anxiously like gunfire, drowning out a result that Sandy strained his ears to listen to as he was sure it was one of his draws. But he stiffened when he heard the name Clark and his jaw tightened when he caught sight of the suitcase. He'd no intention of playing host to any more waifs and strays.

His face curled into a sneer as he told the stranger, 'Maggie, the only one left from the fire was here but she's gone long ago and never been in touch. Probably down south somewhere chasing the big money.' He slammed the door and headed back to his coupon.

'Who was it?' asked Ina, dishing up the chips, making sure they covered the blackened egg. She didn't feel she could face another night of his moaning.

'Some bloke sniffing after Maggie Clark. He'd a suitcase, probably on the lookout for somewhere to doss down. I soon sent him packing.'

'What did he look like?' asked Ina, her curious mind switching on to the possibility of who he might be.

'He was tall, with reddish hair. Looked the sort who would fancy himself.'

Ina banged her husband's supper down in front of him, on top of his beloved coupon, and shuffled down the stairs as fast as her worn carpet slippers would allow.

She stood at the front door, scanning the street in both directions. There was neither hide nor hair of anyone, only a taxi turning the corner.

'Thanks for waiting, driver,' said Eddie, 'boot her up and head for the station. I'll catch the overnight train to King's Cross in an hour. There's nothing to keep me here now.'

Chapter 9

(Aberdeen, March 1946)

It was the anniversary of Maggie and Sam's first meeting and they were strolling towards 'their bench'. The war had been over since last May and people's lives were returning to normal. Maggie had begun to seriously consider the possibility of a future with Sam, but she must wait to be asked. She didn't want a husband who was weak and always looking to her for direction.

They sat in silence watching a ship sail into the distance. Sam closed his eyes and swallowed repeatedly. All the time he was playing nervously with his hands, twisting the fingers round each other. Suddenly he cleared his throat and spoke without drawing breath: 'It's all very well having plans but they're meaningless if they're not shared, know what I mean? What about you and me, Maggie? D'you think we could make a go of it?'

For a few moments Maggie said nothing. Sam took out his handkerchief to mop his brow. In spite of the cold weather, beads of sweat stood out on his forehead. Maggie heaved a long sigh before turning to Sam with a wry smile. 'Is this a proposal, Sam Taylor?' she asked, managing to hold her voice steady. Maggie's recent dreams had turned to beautifully whitewashed cottages owned by well-off skippers in the picturesque villages that nestled in little havens all along the coast. Sam turned, took her hands firmly in his and declared, 'Yes, it is.' Keeping hold of her hands, he went down on one knee on the wet ground. 'Maggie Clark, will you do me the honour of becoming my wife?'

Maggie laughed and pulled him up beside her. 'Of course I'll marry you, Sam Taylor. I thought you'd never ask. I love you as much as I can ever love again.' She pulled her scarf down from where it covered her mouth and kissed him till they were both left breathless. 'Let's go for a drink to celebrate.'

'There's only the Bosun's Locker round here. It's a bit of a rough house and I haven't been there for years, not since my father took me when I was a boy.'

'The perfect place!' declared Maggie. 'You can tell me all about it while we're in there.' Maggie wanted to know everything about her future husband. Since they'd no friends or acquaintances in common, listening to Sam's tales and visiting his haunts were ideal for finding out about his past.

'After our harbour walks,' Sam began, 'Dad would take me in here so he could have a yarn with his mates. Mum would have killed him if she'd known. Poor Mum; she didn't live to see forty.' He pushed the swing door open for her. The warm air that smelled of beer, smoke and stale fish wafted over them like a cosy blanket after the brisk salt air of their walk. It was a small intimate pub of the kind where everyone joins in everyone else's conversation. Although the bar was small, the gantry was extremely well furnished with row upon row of bright shining bottles of every kind of spirit. 'Let's sit here,' said Sam, guiding Maggie to a corner table. 'Dad and I used to sit here when I was a child so I wouldn't be spotted through the window. I used to practise my reading on the names of these bottles. I was mesmerised by them. They reminded me of the sweetie jars in the local shop and they seemed to be as alluring to the drinkers as the lucky tatties and sherbet lemons were to us children. Dad always had the dark rum – for his chest – with a dash of ginger to make it even more warming. I had raspberry cordial.'

'You're excited just talking about it,' commented Maggie, unwinding the long cosy scarf, which in the warmth of the pub was beginning to stifle her. The barman came over to wipe the table and take their order. 'Port and lemon, please,' Maggie said. Her cheeks glowed red now with the heat of the coal fire beside them. Sam's face glowed with love.

'You can have anything you want, Maggie,' replied Sam, bending over and kissing her lips again. 'You've made me the happiest man in Aberdeen.'

The barman rolled his eyes to the ceiling. 'So a port for Juliet and what for you, Romeo?'

'Lager and a whisky to celebrate,' smiled Sam, clearing the gruffness of emotion from his throat.

Maggie's eyes darted round the bar. She felt exhilarated, excited by its 'away from it all' atmosphere and heady masculine smell, so different from the lounge at the Regent where young men courted their sweethearts with sweet cherry brandy or eggnog.

They clinked glasses in a toast to the future. Maggie snuggled close into Sam's side while he continued his tale. 'The barman would bring me a little stool and I'd sit there making patterns in the sawdust with my feet, piling it up between my shoes. Everyone made a fuss of me, especially the women who, as my father would say, "Came in looking for men to go and play games with." They gave me pennies and sweets. The men were usually just there for a drink and to play dominoes or darts and there was such a lot of laughter, the loud, hearty laughter that you only hear when a crowd of men gather together, rough and ready and relaxed, with no wives to restrain them, to refine them.'

Maggie nudged him hard in the ribs. 'Watch it. I hope you don't mean me. I would hate to end up as some dragon whose husband had to go to pubs in order to escape. Promise me, Sam, we won't end up like that.'

'Of course not, Maggie. We're different. We're best friends.' He wound his fingers through her red, spiralling curls and kissed her again.

Maggie smiled. 'I know Sam. I was just being silly. Go on with your story.'

Sam took a long drink of his pint. 'Sometimes the men played cards for money and even though I was just a child I found it thrilling. When the stakes were high, I sat there absorbing the tension, drawing on their raw energy till I felt I was big and strong like them. I feel that buzz in my innards even yet.'

'Did your father gamble? Do you gamble?' Maggie asked this

question seriously. Sam wasn't a hard drinking man like many were these days, especially since the war, singing and roaring through the streets at weekends. She was so relieved at his indifference to alcohol that she'd never until now even contemplated any of the other demons that can ruin a man.

'My father never gambled. He called it a mug's game.' Maggie opened her mouth to repeat the last part of her question, but the words remained unformed on her lips. A short man, who made up for his lack of height in width, came rolling over to their table as if the floor were the deck of a ship heaving up and down.

'Game of cards, Sam?'

'Not today, Victor, but thanks all the same,' replied Sam, stumbling over his words nervously.

'You don't gamble do you?' Maggie was quick to repeat her question. She had to know.

Sam glared at his fat little friend and stood up. 'Come on, Maggie, this is no place for a lady.' He took her hand. 'Let's get out of here.'

Victor laughed a coarse, unwholesome laugh. He'd overheard the tail end of their conversation. 'Does Sam gamble? Is the Pope a Catholic? I bet you'll find a pack of cards in his back pocket right now.'

Maggie didn't take time to ask. She slid her hand behind Sam and deftly pick pocketed the evidence.

'So, you do!' She tipped the cards out of their box and waved them in front of Sam's face till they blurred with the fierceness of the movement. Victor stood close by. His wide grin exposed a row of yellow, widely spaced teeth sitting like neglected gravestones in dark red gums that were heavy with saliva.

'I, I did gamble, Maggie,' Sam stuttered lamely, 'but that's all in the past. Since I've met you I'm different. I have you to make me happy.'

'That's rich,' guffawed the fat informer, 'you were playing pontoon in the Ship Aground last Saturday night with Bobby

Black.'

'Is that true, Sam? Don't lie to me.' Maggie's face had turned from crimson to white and her hands were shaking with emotion.

'It is true; I can't lie to you, Maggie, but I promise you faithfully that from now on I'm all through with cards.' Sam's voice faltered and failed to settle the fluttering uncertainty in her stomach, but she chose to ignore the warning. All she could think of was the little house that marriage to Sam would bring her.

'You'd bloody better be!' she shouted and, swinging her hand back in the action of a shot putter adding strength to their throw, she flung the cards so high in the air that they struck the nicotine stained ceiling before fluttering down on Sam and Victor's heads like giant pieces of confetti.

Chapter 10

Although Maggie had accepted Sam's proposal and the engagement was short, wedding bells had to compete with the warning bells that rang in her confused mind. She couldn't forget the cards hidden in his pocket, but neither could she face a life alone. Falling for Sam had made her lose her single minded strength of purpose and she'd become dependent on his strong manly presence. Whether it was love or just habit, Maggie had been robbed of her ability to stand on her own two feet. The determination to seek her own salvation that had first guided Maggie in her desperate quest for hotel work had dispersed in the comforting sense of safety she had grown accustomed to in her relationship with Sam, and it was only too easy to mistake familiarity for happiness and security.

So, in line with the many who are weakened by life, Maggie decided to take a mere mortal as her saviour and, on a warm sunny day with tree blossom showering down upon them in a gentle breeze, the happy couple posed for photographs outside St. Matthew's Church where they had just taken their vows. Surely God's blessing would ensure a change in Sam and guarantee a fairy tale ending.

Sadie Dewar, her boss, and Charlie Grant, the old barman, were delighted to act as matron of honour and best man. They had grown as fond of Sam as they were of Maggie. After all, didn't he make her smile? Didn't they look good together? However, Maggie never revealed to them Sam's weakness for gambling. Why should she? Hadn't he said he was done with all that?

Colleagues at the Regent had taken the place of family for Maggie and, although she had sworn that no one would matter to her any more, she wept like a child when she packed her few possessions into boxes in order to set up home with Sam, although she did work part-time during the week while Sam was at sea. Every penny counted and every penny was a prisoner once Maggie had her hands on it, each one a contribution towards her beautiful cottage.

Until the fulfilment of that dream, she and Sam rented an attic room and kitchen in one of the streets of tenements that Maggie had vowed she would never return to. In fact it was an even older building than that of her parents and the rooms were tiny. Cramped living conditions and trips to the outside toilet in all weathers contrasted unfavourably with evenings of pampered luxury in the huge Victorian bath in the Regent Hotel, and so it didn't take long before Maggie's endeavours to be happy were tainted with bitterness as she struggled to come to terms with this retrograde step. 'We're only living where we do until Sam buys a share in a boat and then we're moving to a little fishing village,' she would say. She told this story often in an effort to convince herself of its truth.

The matter of buying a fishing vessel was a constant bone of contention between Maggie and Sam. 'When are you going to invest in a boat?' Maggie wheedled in his ear at every opportunity.

'When the right one comes along,' was always Sam's curt reply.

Summer was nearing its height and Maggie had wanted her life to be seeing some improvement by then. 'I'm tired of that old song,' Maggie said with a whine in her voice. 'Find out more about the Sunset Glory that you said was up for sale.' She harped on about this particular one for weeks and Sam was running out of excuses when tragedy struck the Sunset Glory. It went down in a freak storm, taking a lump of water that sent it plummeting to the bottom of the sea with all hands. Bearing in mind that fishermen were superstitious and Sam had said this accident made him feel like a Jonah, Maggie managed to keep quiet for a few weeks.

However, things came to a head one Sunday while she and Sam sauntered along the seashore in the sunshine. Maggie's dream had resurfaced with a vengeance now that there was an urgent reason to improve their circumstances. Only that week she'd been to the doctor and he'd confirmed that she was pregnant. She must have fallen almost immediately they were married although they had planned to wait a while. Maggie had no desire to start a family in the poky attic rooms she had already grown to hate. She needed a proper home for her child. It was time Sam made a move to get his own boat underway.

Maggie clung on to her husband's arm, comforted by his large presence. 'I wish we could do this every day,' she said, making pleasant overtures in order to win him over. 'It's so relaxing to get out from those four walls. That flat of ours hems us in. There's hardly room to breathe, not like out here in the open by the sea where the air is fresh.' Sam nodded but said nothing. He knew exactly where comments like these were heading. Maggie put her hand on to her belly that was already swelling below her coat and she burst with impatience to tell Sam her secret.

She had been watching the surf play on the golden sand, tickling it and then rolling back out again. She couldn't help but allow her eyes to wander lazily along the coast to where she knew a little white house was waiting for her, snuggled in a sandy bay with private little rock pools. 'Look out there, Sam, that's where we'll live one day. We'll have a pretty little living room and on cold winter evenings we'll draw the curtains against the dark storms. I really think it's high time you invested your money in a boat. We'll never be well off as long as you keep working for somebody else.' Still Sam made no reply and noticeably quickened his step.

Maggie was used to him avoiding the issue and continued to give voice to her dream. 'At nights, you know, I can see these villages from the kitchen window, their lights twinkling, mingling with the stars.' In playful mood she swung Sam's hand in hers and then she turned and was giving little steps backwards, facing him, high with excitement, waiting for the precise moment when she would tell him her news. She wanted to see his eyes, his expression. Suddenly Maggie stopped walking. It was now or never. She stood directly in front of her husband and looked straight into his azure blue eyes that stood out vividly against the velvet black of his eyebrows and the outdoor ruddiness of his cheeks. 'Sam,' she said, 'you know I've been putting past my wages every week. Why don't I add my savings to yours? Then you can bid for a better and newer vessel.'

Her suggestion met with stony silence. 'Sam, speak to me. What's wrong?' The silence rose like a barricade between them. Sam's eyes clouded into steely grey and narrowed. Roughly he pushed Maggie off him and walked on alone. He had never spurned her before. Maggie ran after him, thinking he was playing a game. She forced her hand between his arm and his side but he shrugged her off. 'Leave me alone, can't you?' he snapped. 'Nag, nag, nag! Never a moment's peace!' He marched off in high dudgeon but Maggie chased alongside him like a child who is struggling to keep up with a hurrying parent.

Sam's long strides and Maggie's quick steps soon brought them to the estuary of the river. Sam squatted down on the shingle, his head in his hands. Maggie crouched beside him. He turned towards her with a look so dark it seemed to come from a demon of possession rather than from her loving husband. 'I'm no damned use to you, Maggie. If you've any sense at all you'll leave me,' he said.

Maggie's knew now that this was no game. 'You can't treat me like this,' she said. His words had driven her from his side and she had risen in shock to her feet and now stood several feet away, looking down on him as he cowered like a frightened schoolboy caught in the middle of some mischief and frightened of the outcome.

'I've been trying to pluck up the courage to tell you,' Sam said. He had looked up at her just long enough to mutter these words and then cast his eyes downwards again.

'Tell me what?' shouted Maggie. She was pacing backwards and forwards and clutched her arms round herself in an effort to soothe her agitation.

Sam was still curled forward as if protecting himself from imminent attack, and he burrowed his hand down behind the lapel of his jacket towards the inside pocket. Maggie stamped her feet impatiently, making her high heels sink deep into the softness of the beach. 'Hurry up! What do you want to show me?' She lifted first one foot and then the other in order to remove her shoes, showering Sam with sand as she did so. He offered no word of protest or sign of annoyance, but sat cowed, all dignity gone. Without a word he offered her a slim red book, his Savings Bank book, a book he always kept private. 'Go on, open it,' he urged. 'Find out exactly what kind of a worthless waster you've married.'

Maggie leaned forward and took it from him gently. Intuition told her what to expect, and when she opened it and read the columns of withdrawals over several pages, she knew she was right. In small amounts, ever since the day it had been deposited, the original sum of money had been steadily depleted until only a few pounds remained. Maggie remained remarkably calm. She closed the book and handed it back to Sam who, all the while she had been scrutinising it, had been drawing patterns in the sand with his fingers. 'What did you do with the money?' she asked, but from the tightness of her mouth and the disappointment in her eyes, it was obvious she knew the answer already.

'I've gambled it, Maggie,' he whispered. 'In dribs and drabs round dockside pubs and out at sea, in every kind of card game it's been my misfortune to play, I've squandered the lot, every single penny my father assigned to me for the future.' He paused, waiting for Maggie's red-haired temper to strike him the hail of blows that he felt he deserved.

There were no punches and not one angry word. There was no punishment possible for a sin of such magnitude. Instead, Maggie gathered up her discarded shoes and put them back on her feet, all the while heaving one long sigh after another. She looked out at the waves of the sea and was tempted by them. It would be so quick. No more struggle. If it weren't for the new life inside her, she would have surely abandoned the future that stretched ahead of her like a dark, endless tunnel. She gave one last look out across the horizon before reaching a hand down to help her husband to his feet. 'Come on, I want to go home,' was all she said. Sam brushed the sand from his clothes and fell into step beside her, a docile, obedient shadow. Maggie's heart weighed heavy as lead inside her. If only she had faced reality on the day he'd proposed, instead of pushing the truth to the back of her mind. Then she wouldn't have made such an incredible mess of the life she'd been spared when everyone else in the world who mattered had lost theirs. She turned to look at Sam who had stopped walking. She noticed his hands were shaking as he tried to light a cigarette. Maggie took the matches from him and lit it for him. She watched and breathed with him as he took his first draw. 'Don't put them away,' she said. 'I'll have one as well.' Maggie inhaled deeply, the nicotine helping to fill her with resignation, and so, arm-in-arm, the unhappy couple walked home without another word, but this final hurt had compounded Maggie's regrets, and every last vestige of passion drained from her wounded heart.

Maggie had no choice now but to make the most of her marriage. There was a new life to consider. At least her awful mistake would bring her someone to love. Maggie enjoyed a healthy pregnancy although she couldn't help having a cigarette now and then. 'Well, tea makes me feel sick now and I need something to make me relax,' she would tell her neighbour, Rosie Simpson, who lived in the flat below. Rosie had also become her best friend and confidante. 'I'll stop when the baby comes. I'll be happy then.'

Sure enough, baby Catherine's birth in March, 1947, almost two years to the day since she had met Sam, brought renewal to Maggie. It was love at first sight and Maggie regained her womanly warmth in the adoration of this beautiful child. Sam was besotted. During weekends at home he rocked the tiny bundle in his huge arms giving Maggie time to tend to other chores.

'Why shouldn't he help?' Maggie said to Rosie. 'Catherine's his baby too. It's right that he should help to look after her.' Sam loved Maggie with all his heart and took her cold indifference in his stride. Without her and his precious lamb, Catherine, there was no life at all. But just how long could Maggie endure?

Chapter 11

(Aberdeen 3 years later in 1950)

Another three years passed. Maggie knew that if it were not for Catherine she would have left Sam and so she felt trapped in a cage of boredom and drudgery. She sat dejectedly on the back steps with a basket of washing on the ground in front of her. Rosie was shovelling coal from the cellar into a scuttle. 'All these years of struggle, Rosie, and I'm no further on or better off than my parents were.'

'You're too ambitious,' Rosie replied. 'Why can't you be content with your lot? You're ruining your own happiness.'

Maggie tutted and shook her head in irritation. 'Ambition's not a dirty word, Rosie. All I want is a little house. And you know something? One of these days that's exactly what I'll have.'

'You're a dreamer, Maggie. Life's not that bad.'

'It's the poverty of our lives, Rosie; it gnaws away at human self-respect. I should have done better, made something of myself. You know something, Rosie, I'm ashamed of how we live - everybody scraping by, putting on a brave face. Sam's one of those people who live a life of acceptance and look where that's got us.' Rosie clapped her hands together to clean off the coal dust before sitting down beside her friend. She knew snippets about the lost money and how devastating it had been, but Maggie had withheld the whole truth out of loyalty to Sam even though she did complain about his lack of drive. 'He has no real concern for the future. He missed the boat - literally - and it doesn't bother him.'

'What you've never had, you can live without, that's my philosophy,' said Rosie, putting an arm round Maggie. 'Don't be so scornful of him. He works hard and dotes on you.'

'I've no choice but to suffer him. There's Catherine to think of,' Maggie said with a sigh and stood up. 'Better take this lot upstairs and get it ironed before Catherine wakes from her nap.'

'Your head's too full of pipe dreams, Maggie. Why don't you take Catherine for a walk; come back down to earth,' answered Rosie and she heaved the coal bucket past Maggie on her way upstairs to light the fire. 'Come in past later for a cup of tea. I've something to show you.'

Maggie had never lost the practice of taking long walks to clear her mind, and as a result she never lost her trim figure or optimistic drive, but today her resentment knew no bounds. She was trapped in the life she'd wanted so desperately to escape. Perhaps a chat with Rosie would help.

Rosie Simpson, her best friend and confidante, was tall, blonde and fair-skinned, an obvious descendant of some Viking raider from the Norse lands of yore and yet she was a placid woman whose easygoing nature had deposited many pounds of unwelcome flesh on her sturdy frame. She picked up a currant bun that was thickly spread with margarine and looked down at her generous curves. 'I'd be happy with a flat stomach.' So hard did Rosie pull in the muscles of her stomach as she spoke, that the pink cheeks of her plump face were sucked in too. She took a bite of the bun, and as she munched it, she reached over to a catalogue and pulled it towards her. She opened it at a page of corsets. 'What do you think of these here? If I wear something like this maybe I'll look slim like you.'

Maggie laughed at the pictures of women whose bodies were encased in an assortment of shapely elasticated garments. 'Oh, Rosie, you do cheer me up. I wish I could see life as simply as you. I wish that all I had to worry about was what I looked like in the mirror. I'm going to try, really I am, to be more contented with my life.'

Maggie did try. She strove as hard as any other woman to maintain a clean, respectable home, but it was never enough. Her mind frequently turned to the dream cottage that might have been hers had Sam not been a gambler. Sam, meanwhile, sailed on from crisis to crisis, continuing to lose money on cards and occasionally on horses. Gambling was his fix and promises to Maggie and to himself came to nothing. Maggie did sometimes believe she should take a share of the blame for driving him on to fill the emptiness that her lack of affection had hollowed out in him, but what could she do when she didn't yearn for him any more and was aware of her body stiffening whenever he came near her?

Chapter 12

Sam made great efforts to dedicate his life to Maggie and Catherine, swallowing down the guilt that haunted him daily. But no matter how he tried he couldn't resist gambling. Weeks and even months would pass and he would hold firm to his promises, and then, out of the blue, the thrill of gambling would lure him in. He thought his punishment had come at last one Saturday when he hurried home as usual from a trip to find an empty house. At first he panicked that Maggie had finally left him, as she often swore she would, and he feared the worst as he picked up the note lying on the kitchen table. Maggie hadn't gone but it was just as serious.

Desperately he banged at Rosie's door. 'What's happened to Catherine?' he shouted, waving a piece of paper. 'I've just come home to find this scribbled note on the kitchen table from Maggie. Says she's taken Catherine to hospital.'

'That's right, Sam, Catherine's got whooping cough real bad.' Sam bounded down the stairs. At the Sick Children's Hospital he followed the nurse to where Catherine lay in an isolation ward. Maggie was crouched over the low bed. 'Come on little one, breathe,' Maggie whispered. Sam looked on in shock. The usually podgy three year old was thin and drawn. Her eyes blazed with fever, and when she coughed, it was as if she would never catch her breath again. 'Take a rest, Maggie, I'll sit with her,' said Sam quietly. He put a comforting hand on Maggie's shoulder.

Maggie turned on Sam. 'Leave her? How can I leave her? She might die.' Sam pulled up a chair to be near her. 'There's no point in living without my baby,' she raged on. 'I need someone to love.' Sam stood up. His eyes were glistening. 'I'll get you some tea,' was all he said. He returned to find Maggie on her knees by the bed, calling out audibly and without inhibition for God's mercy. Catherine's long shuddering in-breaths, the whoops that gave the illness its name, sounded like ghosts calling from the graveyard.

But Maggie would not relinquish her child. Day and night she kept her watch, praying to God and breathing along with her daughter. She willed the frail body to draw in every single drop of life-giving air to her lungs and not give in to the call of advancing death. Sam brought flasks of soup and thick sandwiches made by Rosie. Maggie refused to give up her vigil and it was not until after nearly three days that Maggie finally heard Catherine's breathing grow steady and the coughing subsided. She had won this round against the grim reaper. Catherine was her miracle, a true gift from God, and Maggie felt that Catherine was fully hers now, a child for her to mould and develop as she saw fit.

Her love for Catherine that verged on obsession only intensified Maggie's refusal to accept their lot in life. Catherine must have more. Catherine must escape the deprivation. Maggie was determined that her child must have the education that she herself had been denied because her own father had considered it wasted on a girl. Catherine must never be tied to a loveless marriage by dependency on a man she could not respect. Dissatisfaction fuelled her ambition like petrol on a blazing fire.

Chapter 13

(Five years later, February 1955)

The years passed uneventfully and Maggie felt that life was at a standstill. Catherine, however, continued to thrive and remained the focus of her mother's life. One stormy February night, Maggie sat in front of the fire in her cramped attic kitchen. She was darning Sam's working socks and listening to the wireless. Catherine, who had grown strong and healthy, was crushed in beside her mother in the armchair. Sam was at sea and so cosy they were, just the two of them, mother and daughter, tucked together, listening to the gentle music of the Light Programme. Catherine snoozed off and on between moments of watching pictures in the fire. The tall flames danced round the coals and then pranced high into the chimney like wild horses pawing in protest against the intrusion of the cold night air.

Maggie stopped sewing, her darning needle poised over the wooden mushroom which held the heel of a sock in place. Catherine squeezed out from beside her and drew a dining chair so close to the fire that her feet were in the fireplace. Her woollen socks had slipped down round her ankles leaving her legs bare and exposed. 'Don't sit so near the fire, Catherine, you'll get tinkers' tartan,' Maggie said gently, hitching up her own skirt to show the evidence on her own bare legs, which were patterned from the knees right down to the ankles with dark red lines reminiscent of a complicated road map. 'It's a mess and it doesn't fade. You won't find a rich husband with legs like mine.' Catherine looked at the ugly marks and then looked away quite undeterred by the warning and pulled her chair even closer to the fire in defiance. 'I don't care. I like to feel the heat. It's freezing tonight.'

'Please yourself.' Maggie masked a smile as she recognised her own wilfulness in her daughter.

She bit the strand of wool that connected the needle to the

sock. 'You don't want to spend your time knitting and mending thick working socks like these of your father's. You want a better life.' She looked with a critical eye round the kitchen that was furnished in the same way as most of her neighbours'. The table was the centre round which all social activities took place: meals, board games, discussions, cosy chats, baking and even yet, in some homes, the laying out of bodies. The sink had only one cold-water tap, and even that had frozen the week before when the temperature had dropped below freezing and the windows had been patterned with ornate ferns and flowers made of ice.

'O, Mum, I've told you before; I don't want to get married. I'm going to stay here with you and Dad forever.' Catherine jumped back up and gave her mother a quick hug.

Maggie looked fondly down at her daughter and said nothing. 'Let her be happy, she's a child yet,' she thought inwardly. The strains of violin music filled the room and a golden silence fell between Maggie and Catherine once more. Catherine examined her knees closely, looking for the tell tale marks. 'Mum, can I sleep with you tonight; I couldn't get warm in my bed last night?' The cold February wind howled its agreement, rattling the ill-fitting window frames as it battered the rain against the glass like a bombardment of rifle shot.

Maggie crept over to the window, too cold to straighten up, huddling the heat from the fire into herself and drawing her cardigan tight around her. She looked out but could see nothing but silvery pellets of sleet trickling down the windowpane against the black backdrop of the night. She withdrew quickly and pulled the heavy brocade curtains close together, overlapping them where they met to secure the house from draughts. She hurried back to the fire, hunching her shoulders and rubbing her hands together. Catherine was curled into the armchair now and moved over to make room for her mother. She repeated her plea in a most pitiful little voice. 'Can I, Mum, can I sleep with you tonight?'

'Of course you can.' Maggie stretched her palms out to the

flames. She hadn't the heart to refuse. 'It's bitter tonight so we'd best snuggle up close and keep each other warm.' Catherine turned and hugged her mother. 'We can play Fairies in the Wood,' she said excitedly. Maggie laughed, delighted that her daughter's imagination equalled her own. 'That bed has seen the dramatisation of more stories than the stage of His Majesty's Theatre,' she said, putting her darning safely in a drawer. 'That's enough of that for one night,' she said. 'Let's have some cocoa to warm us up. There's plenty milk.' Just as she made her way to the cooker, heavy steps sounded on the stairs.

'It's Dad!' shouted Catherine and she jumped up to welcome him.

'It can't be; he's not due home till tomorrow,' answered Maggie, a worried expression flashing across her face. 'I hope nothing's wrong.'

'See, it is Dad!' shouted a jubilant Catherine as her father appeared in the doorway, filling it with his robust frame. Sam's black curly hair fell wet with rain in loose ringlets over his forehead. Scarcely had he lowered his heavy kit bag from his shoulder on to the floor, than Catherine ran over to him and climbed up his front like a monkey and clung tightly to him. Sam rocked her up and down and jokingly threatened to throw her into the air. Catherine screamed with mock terror. What could be safer than her daddy's arms?

Maggie flounced her tangled hair with her hands before welcoming him with a quick hug. 'Engine trouble with the storm,' Sam explained as he swung Catherine back down to the floor again and embraced his wife. 'My two girls!' he exclaimed, grinning from ear to ear, unable to hide his joy at being home. But Maggie could read him. She knew that in spite of the weather he'd been to the Jolly Fisherman and had won a couple of pounds at cards. She knew this from the deep red of his face and the broad smile of the gambler on a winning streak. 'You're too open to be a successful gambler,' Maggie would sneer. 'A gullible fool that people see coming a mile off.'

He dug into his donkey jacket pocket and gave her two ten shilling notes in addition to her usual housekeeping. 'And here's half a crown for your piggybank,' he declared, handing a delighted Catherine a large, silver coin. Maggie opened the door of the large cupboard just along from the fireplace and put the money in an old tea caddy at the back of the shelf. Catherine chinked the half crown into a pink and white china pig on the sideboard.

'What a night; let me into the heat!' Sam exclaimed, striding across the room which was really too small to accommodate such a man. He always had to crouch and bend when he went anywhere near the window where the lie-ins sloped steeply following the shape of the roof. His gaze fixed on Maggie who was acutely aware of the gleam in his eye that revealed he had plans for her later.

'I take it you'll need feeding,' Maggie said in the hope that food might occupy his mind instead. She hurried to fill the kettle and started to prepare the cheese on toast he always had for supper.

'Do you want me to leave again?' he laughed, sitting down to pull off his wet boots before depositing them in the fireplace to dry out. An all-pervading fishy smell spread round the room. He padded over towards Maggie. 'There was some kind of trouble with the bilge pumps. I wouldn't care but we'd found a right good shoal of fish and were doing well.' He came up behind her and, pulling her into his arms, burrowed his unshaven face into the nape of her neck. Maggie tensed and a cold shudder ran down her back. She pulled away. 'Stop messing about, Catherine's watching.'

'Okay, I can wait,' he replied, loosening his grip. He lumbered back to his chair like a great soft dog sent lolloping back to its basket. Maggie started to set the table. 'Never mind that,' he said, leaning back into the comfort of the easy chair. 'I'll have it on my knee. No point standing on ceremony.' Maggie placed some cutlery on the arm of the chair beside him but he waved these away too. 'God gave me hands to eat with. If I needed knives and forks, I'd have them growing out of my wrists.' He looked at Catherine and laughed.

Catherine laughed back at him. 'O, Daddy, you're such fun,' she squealed.

Maggie cleared away the cutlery and scowled over at them from where she was now toasting the bread and cheese at the grill. 'You'll have her as rough and ready as yourself, Sam Taylor. I sometimes wonder why I bother.' She put his supper on a plate and handed it over to him. He devoured it quickly and wiped his mouth with the back of his hand.

'You're too good for me,' he said quietly when she went over to him for the empty plate. As he spoke he patted her just above the knee, allowing his hand to linger long enough to feel the warmth of her thigh. He pulled her gently on to his lap. Catherine ran over and climbed on too, throwing her arms round the two of them. She liked to see them happy and laughing. It wasn't always like this though. Sometimes, especially on Saturday nights, there would be shouting, usually about money, and she would hear her mum crying. Catherine squashed herself against the warmth of their bodies. Sam started to kiss Maggie. 'Come on then, Catherine,' he said, 'it's bedtime for you.'

'Let me stay for my cocoa, and can I not get changed in front of the fire? It's freezing in my bedroom.'

'Oh, all right then,' he laughed. 'It's as cold as a witch's tit out there.' Maggie scowled at him. 'It's freezing in her room so she was going to sleep with me tonight. You'll have to carry some fire through to her room.'

''Course I will. I know what will happen if I don't, she'll be wandering in beside us. After two weeks on a trawler, I need, ahem, my sleep.' He squeezed Maggie's waist meaningfully as he spoke and stood up to deal with the fire. He took the small hand shovel that was lying in the fireplace beside his boots and, digging it right into the back of the blaze, gathered up some burning coals. 'Stand back. Open the doors.' Holding the flaming shovelful high in front of him like the Olympic torch, he carried it through to Catherine's room and deposited it in the grate. 'I'll put some coal on top and that should keep you warm through the night.' White vapour clouds puffed in front of him as his breath met the icy cold air. 'You can get changed in the kitchen, Catherine; give this room time to heat up.'

A millionaire couldn't have bought the happiness shared by the little family as they cuddled close drinking hot chocolate. It was one of those simple pleasures that become a lasting memory.

Maggie would have liked the evening to last forever but the night was closing fast around them. Compared to many families they were happy and they did get by. An old saying of her mother's sprang to mind: A contented heart is an eternal feast. 'How true that is,' thought Maggie to herself as she remembered the life her mother had endured with little complaint. 'Perhaps we're not doing so badly after all,' she mused. Sam held his hand protectively over hers and she turned her own hand round until it faced his and she squeezed it. He bent down and kissed her. Maggie's lips softened as she returned his kiss. He kissed her some more and she felt his hot breath brushing against her ear.

Maggie stood up suddenly, shaking Sam's clinging hand away. She had remembered something. She must go and check. 'Aw, Mum, why did you have to move?' whimpered Catherine.

'It's getting late,' Maggie answered, avoiding Sam's quizzical eyes. She went to the cupboard and, stretching up to the top shelf, brought down a little glass tube. At the sink, she furtively turned her back to take the top off it. She felt embarrassed about this little tube even in front of Sam. Good, she had one left of the spermicidal pessaries she had to use as protection because Sam refused to use condoms.

Maggie, secreted behind the curtains, tipped this last tablet into her hand. She would keep it safe in her cardigan pocket and insert it later when they went downstairs to the toilet. Nervousness caused her fingertips to twitch and the tablet seemed to leap from them and all she could do was watch it fall and land in the sink. Maggie was devastated. It had happened in a flash and the horrific realisation that once done it couldn't be undone struck her immediately. 'Damn it!' she cursed. 'That was the last one. If only I was back sitting by the fire!' She struggled to turn back time with the power of desperate regret, but knew she willed in vain as she watched the dropped pessary effervesce in the dregs of water that lay in the bottom of the black iron sink. Panic stabbed Maggie hard as if a knife had been plunged into her solar plexus right up to the hilt as she stared transfixed and helpless at the fizzling foam that would have saved her.

'Come on then, Maggie,' urged Sam, peeling Catherine off him, 'let's get downstairs and back again. I'll fetch the torch.' He gave Maggie a smile. His sparkling eyes twinkled with expectation. Maggie forced a smile. What would she do? If she refused Sam, his mood would change like quicksilver and then he'd be out gambling all weekend. Maybe, if she could persuade him to be careful, it would be all right. However, that was wishful thinking because he never was. How did wives with husbands at home every night cope with the worry? Hers was only at home every two weeks and that was more than enough.

'Maggie, you're dreaming again,' said Sam, joining her behind the curtains at the sink and, hidden from young eyes, started squeezing her breasts. Maggie wondered why he had to be so rough. All this twiddling and tweaking of his did nothing for her. She had once asked him if he wasn't trying to tune in to the Home Service on the wireless and he had squeezed her nipple so hard with indignation it was bruised for a week. Maggie wriggled free. 'What are you doing over here anyway?' he asked, obviously puzzled. 'You can do the dishes in the morning.'

'Just looking out at the weather,' she lied. Maggie stiffened and drew back from him. 'Behave yourself, Sam; we're not youngsters any more.' She turned away from his hard stubbly face, which felt like sandpaper against her own smooth skin. 'You need a shave and you're hurting me.'

'I remember those days, Maggie, when we were courting,' he answered. 'I can hear your laugh now. You were always laughing. And you liked my rough face. You said it was manly and reassuring.'

'I'm older now and my tastes have changed,' she said under her breath, but Sam had gone to put his jacket on and didn't hear.

'Women,' he said with a shake of his head, 'I'll never understand them.'

Maggie had set her mind on having one of the new council houses. It was just a matter of waiting and when she moved into a nice new house, she wanted everything of the best. A child might bring them more points, but would bring endless years of doing without if she was no longer able to work. It would mean years of poverty and always being dependant on Sam. Now that Catherine was becoming more independent there was at least a chance of freedom some day if she were able to work full time. With another child she'd never be able to leave Sam if life with him became too much to bear.

As she helped Catherine prepare for bed, her mind went to a conversation she'd had with the neighbours in the wash house a few months earlier. Babs Green, who lived through from Rosie Simpson had amused everyone with her ideas for contraception. She swore that she'd kept her family down to only two by tying a penny to her belly button with tape. 'If you tie it tight you can't get pregnant.' She had spoken with the authority of a medical practitioner.

'It's not your belly button you have to cover, you daft woman,' Rosie had replied. 'We've moved on from the dark ages you know.' They'd had such a laugh that day, doubled up and laughing until they were sore. At thirty-three, Maggie was young enough to consider more modern methods of birth control instead of listening to old wives' tales. However, Maggie couldn't help wondering if she had any broad tape, but quickly shook her head in utter disbelief at her own stupidity. 'I'm thinking like an ignorant old woman,' she scolded herself inwardly. 'Sam will just have to do without.'

Once Catherine was in bed, Sam became unstoppably amorous. Maggie tried to explain about the lost pessary but Sam was totally unconcerned. 'We both like children, so what's the problem? A few more like Catherine would be a godsend. Maggie, don't you realise how much I need you?' he murmured, kissing her hard on the mouth regardless of her struggling. 'Don't I work hard and risk my life for you? I'm entitled to have this. I'll be careful, I promise.' Aroused and demanding, he half carried Maggie towards the bed. 'Seriously, the chances of you getting pregnant the only time you're not protected are pretty slim. Surely the odds are stacked against it.'

Tiredness caused Maggie's firm resolve to weaken as her immediate need for rest began to overwhelm her. She wanted to be left alone to sink into the soft, welcoming bed. 'All right then,' she said, trusting her future to fate, 'but pull out before you finish.'

'Trust me,' he said breathlessly. In less than a moment Sam was on top of her and started his lovemaking. There never was much foreplay. In fact, Maggie often felt there was more of a thrill from the spermicide sizzling inside her than from her husband. He wanted instant gratification and wouldn't take time to explore the intricacies of a woman's body. His hips moved up and down like the pistons of a well-oiled engine and it mattered nothing to him that Maggie lay wooden and detached beneath him. His grunting, heavy thrusts were more numbing than exhilarating. Rigid, Maggie blanked her mind to everything but the immediacy of an opportunity to sleep. At last he pulled back and pretended to use his hand for a couple of seconds to complete the business. 'I told you I'd be careful.' He turned over and pulled the bed covers over his broad back, not only to sleep, but also to hide from having lied to his wife. He'd lost control. He'd cheated her.

Relieved it was over, Maggie tried hard to convince herself that

66

she was safe. She couldn't be pregnant. She turned over too but couldn't relax. Behind her, Sam was already sleeping and snoring. The storm outside raged furiously in accompaniment to his steady drone. Lightning flashed and thunder roared as if twin giants were calling a warning to her from the heavens. Somewhere outside, a dustbin lid clattered and crashed as the wind whipped it up and threw it down like a top. Worry made her grow hot. She slunk out of bed and went to the sink for a glass of water. The white froth of earlier had subsided into a pool of pale liquid. Choking anxiety rose in her throat, fluttering up her windpipe like a bird caught in a chimney. She clutched the edge of the sink to steady herself and wiped sweat from her brow with the fingers of her other hand. She gulped in the cold air and reached over to turn the tap full on to flush the sink clean. Warning phrases from talks the health visitor had given at women's meetings competed with the storm outside to blast against her inner ear: 'It only takes the once.'

'How could I have been so stupid? What's a row compared to what I could be facing now?' she moaned, her face in her hands.

Chapter 14

Maggie was in Rosie's kitchen chatting over a cup of tea and she drew the conversation round to the laugh they'd had in the washhouse with Babs. 'Imagine believing that old story about taping your belly button,' she said as she spread homemade rhubarb jam thickly over her scone. 'She needs her head examined.'

Rosie wasn't listening; she had issues of her own. 'Remember those corsets in the catalogue? Well, I sent away for them and they're no damned good. Just look at the size of me, like a barrage balloon. I used to be so slim before I had young Jimmy.' She pressed her hands into her stomach to flatten it. 'Jim used to say I was his Hollywood star.' And true enough, there could still be seen buried in the plumpness of Rosie's face the high cheekbones and shapely nose of the stunner that she'd been in her younger days. She pulled up her blouse and pinched a flange of flesh that protruded between the two pieces of corset.

'Hey,' said Maggie, toying with the plate in front of her, 'You're putting me off my tea.'

Rosie carried on hauling at her body. 'These ones are no good. They separate at the waist. I'm buying an all-in-one next time so I don't have a gap that lets the fat spill out like a great blancmange.'

'Rosie, you look fine.' Irritation made her voice unusually harsh. 'After all, you are thirty-six. If you're not turning your hair into steel wool with the latest home perm, you're pouring yourself into these steel reinforced suits of armour. You're Rosie Simpson, remember, not a pin-up.'

Releasing her grip on the surplus fat of her midriff, Rosie pulled her clothes together, sniffed loudly and tossed her blonde frizzy head in the air.

'Sorry,' said Maggie, realising she'd struck a raw nerve. 'I've a headache. I'm not feeling myself.'

Rosie turned her back. 'All right, Maggie, forget it,' she said, but her eyes glistened with tears of hurt.

'I was just wondering what you thought of Babs Green's ideas on birth control,' persisted Maggie. She pointed to the chair opposite to make her friend sit down and listen.

'There's only one thing that works and that's to keep your knees together,' answered Rosie drily, obviously still smarting. 'Jim gets nothing from me if he doesn't wear a rubber Johnnie. He gets them from the barber's. No raincoat no fun.' She straightened her back and stood up, proud to be in control of her man.

Maggie squirmed at the thought of Rosie's Jim all set for action. 'Not a pretty picture,' she said but she was pleased that the way was now clear for an open discussion on the subject. She continued, 'I use pessaries from the chemist to stop me getting pregnant. Dr. Menzies says he uses them too.' She spoke with contrived confidence, with the air of a woman who would never take the chance of falling pregnant by accident.

Rosie was at the mirror again combing her hair, teasing out the latest perm till it resembled candy floss on a stick. She stopped immediately, alert at last to what Maggie was saying, her eyes wide and inquiring. 'Pastries, did you say pastries?' She laid the comb on the mantelpiece and hurried over to the table and sat down again. She stared at Maggie. 'What's the connection between home baking and sex?' Her puzzled eyes darted back and forth as she contemplated that perhaps she was about to hear something she did not already know.

'No, no, not pastries, Rosie. Clean your ears out!' scoffed Maggie glad that the conversation was taking a comical turn. Maggie always enjoyed a laugh. It helped her to cope with whatever was on her mind at the time. 'Now, just listen carefully, pess - a - ries, pessaries.'

'And what are pessaries when they're at home? Why have I never heard of them?' Rosie wasn't too happy that Maggie knew something she didn't.

'Well,' Maggie said, not exactly sure how she was going to

explain them, 'they're like fizzy tablets except you don't put them in your mouth.' She cleared her throat wondering what she would say next.

'Well, if you don't swallow them, what the hell do you do with them?' Rosie was beginning to think that Maggie was making fun of her.

Maggie took a deep breath and continued, 'You don't put them in your mouth, you put them in there, down there,' she finished, pointing down to her lap.

'You don't mean ... down there! Surely not! And what happens then? What do they do?' Rosie's face was a mixture of confusion, interest and disbelief.

Maggie cleared her throat. 'You put them inside yourself and they dissolve. They kill the sperm.'

'Well, I'll be blowed!' answered Rosie. She looked over at Maggie and the two of them suddenly burst into gales of laughter. Rosie slapped the table, making the cups rattle in their saucers. 'I've heard it all now;' she squealed, 'and your doctor's wife does that. My God, not much wonder he always looks so cheery. It must tickle him a lot. I'm never going to be able to look him or your Sam in the face again. Oh dear, I must try them with my Jim.' Rosie went to the sink for the cold cloth to wipe her face that was moist with perspiration and tears.

Maggie stopped laughing too. Although the laugh had done her good, her voice was barely a whisper when she asked anxiously, 'Do you think it works if they take their thing out before they're finished? You know what I mean, withdraw before the end.'

There were a few moments of silence before Rosie spoke. 'Well,' she replied, giving Maggie a penetrating look, 'if you've tried that trick then God help you. That's what Mrs. Riley round the corner does and she's got five. But she's a Roman Catholic and got no choice. She can't go using condoms or these pessaries. And she's only twenty-six so God knows how many she'll end up with.' Rosie looked closely at the unusually quiet Maggie who seemed to have suddenly lost her sense of humour. 'You're in a weird mood today. There's nothing bothering you is there?' Seeds of suspicion were sprouting in her mind as pieces of Maggie's conversations drifted back and slotted together to make a disturbing picture. She didn't voice her suspicions outright. She'd wait until she was more certain.

'No, Rosie. It just occurred to me out of the blue. I don't know why.' She fumbled in her overall pocket and brought out a packet of cigarettes and matches. She lit one, closed her eyes and inhaled deeply. 'You want one, Rosie?' she asked through the side of her mouth. Rosie's jaw dropped and she had to wipe away the crumbs that trickled from her mouth. 'No thanks, I stopped that caper long ago and so did you. You said they cost too much money and even started poor Sam on roll-ups.'

'I was feeling fed up, that's all. It'll be different when I move to my new house,' she said as she watched the smoke swirling up to the ceiling.

'You and your new house,' exclaimed Rosie. 'You can't live in a dream. Anyway, Jim and I have decided to stay put here with a cheap rent. As sitting tenants we're quids in. Council rents are extortionate.'

'Well, I believe in dreams. How else are we supposed to make anything of our lives?' She snibbed her cigarette and tucked it carefully into her apron pocket before flouncing out and slamming the door.

Chapter 15

A distraught Maggie sat in the outside toilet crying into her apron. She used her long red coils of hair to wipe away tears. Her face was blotched with smeared make-up and her even features were swollen beyond recognition. Desperation turned her to prayer as she tried to strike a deal with the Almighty. 'This can't be happening to me. Please, God, please, I'll do anything if only you let me off this once. I'll go to church more often and not just at Communion.' Maggie was not a particularly religious woman, but she did in her own way believe that divine intervention was possible at times of trouble. Hadn't He answered her prayers to save Catherine when she was ill? Her skirt hitched high round her hips, Maggie sat on the wooden toilet seat and mulled over the last six weeks of anxious suspense. A split in the wood nipped the soft flesh of her thigh, but she hardly noticed the pain. Her second period was now a day late.

After one last check Maggie decided to leave the sanctuary of the toilet. The church clock had just struck three. It had been striking two when she first sat down. She reached for the packet of cigarettes on the damp floor at her feet. It was empty. She'd smoked all five. Her legs had gone numb and she struggled to stand up. The crack in the seat had raised a long weal in her bare flesh but Maggie didn't care. She pulled down her skirt and straightened herself up. Clenching both fists tightly so that the box of matches and cigarette packet cut into her hand, she marched out into the rain. 'I won't go through with it. I won't. I'll shift this if it kills me!'

Catherine wouldn't be home from school for another hour. There was enough time. She'd make sure there would be no baby. She wasn't going to be the latest subject of gossip that would excite her neighbours out of their drudgery.

Maggie ran upstairs and put on the pinafore apron she wore in the mornings. She tied her hair back with a head square made into a turban and put on a pair of ankle socks and her old working shoes. Starting at the top of the building she swept all the way down. She swept out the front lobby, the back stairs and the front path right out to the street and deposited a large pile of dust and grime into the gutter. She swept the concrete outside the back door, reaching into every tiny crevice with the corner of her brush. The regular cleaning of the tenements played an important part in these women's lives. They liked to see the shining evidence that they cared, that their lives meant something.

As she clattered and banged with the brush, her neighbours looked out to see what all the noise was about. 'Hi there, Maggie,' they shouted, 'go easy on the stairs or you'll have the building down!' but they knew that fervent cleaning of this sort meant trouble. It was a tried and trusted method of letting off steam, of getting anger, worry or even grief out of the system. The neighbours knew there was no need to hang around waiting to find out the reason. They would know soon enough through the network of stair landings, shop doorways and street corners.

Maggie worked on. Although it was a cold day in early spring, Maggie worked herself up to a frenzy of heat. Drops of perspiration rolled down her face and ran down her neck before their wetness penetrated under and around the collar of her dress. The warm rivulets trickled between her breasts. Down from the nape of her neck the sticky sweat flowed between her shoulder blades and into the small of her back. From her armpits it poured in torrents converging with the other streams like the tributaries of a great river to flow down her sides, round her groins, down between her buttocks and down her thighs. Maggie was awash. Her face had lost all form and expression. Only the fixed ice-blue eyes were a reminder that this demoniac creature was in fact a human being.

The sound of the repetitive sweeping echoed round the walls of the tenement and its outhouses filling the frosty air, as Maggie, a desperate dancing dervish, contrived to rid her body of the clot

73

of gristle growing within. She had no sense of wonder or joy. There was no mother love, just a monstrous urge to destroy.

Half way through Maggie's gruelling endeavours, Catherine came home from school. She stood aghast at the sight of her mother whose clothes were dishevelled and her face flushed red. 'What are you doing, Mum? Why are you doing everybody's stairs?'

Quite out of character, and frightening the child still further, she hissed at her through clenched teeth, 'Get into Rosie's. Do you hear? Stop standing there gawping at me. Get into Rosie's!'

Rosie, who had been listening from behind her door, came out and, keeping her head down, slunk past Maggie and took Catherine's hand. 'Come with me, lass,' she said kindly. There was no doubt in her mind now as to what was wrong with Maggie. She led the child gently inside and, shoving the ghastly problem to the back of her mind, put on a great show of kindness to comfort the children by giving Catherine and her son, Jimmy, some bread and jam and lemonade. 'What's this for?' Jimmy asked. 'Why are we having lemonade on a Wednesday?'

'Because we are, that's all,' replied his mother. 'Just drink it up before I change my mind.' He did not need telling twice. Catherine sat silently, looking down at her feet, studying the buckles on her shoes. 'I'm not thirsty, Auntie Rosie,' she murmured and pushed the tumbler away.

'Your Mum's just had a busy day cleaning that's all,' Rosie replied, softly stroking the little girl's hair as she spoke. She turned away to hide the tears that had welled up in her eyes. 'Right then, kids, let's put on the wireless for "Children's Hour",' she said, tuning in the wireless to the correct station. She put out the jam dish usually reserved for visitors. In it was the special silver spoon with an enamel shield on the handle bearing the word Blackpool in red lettering. No one knew where it had come from. No one they knew had ever been to Blackpool.

'I don't want jam!' shouted Catherine and she dragged her chair to the sink and stood on it to climb on to the wooden draining board. She leaned precariously forwards, with outstretched hands against the glass, to catch a glimpse of her frantic mother. Rosie had tried to stop her but the child was near to tears, so eventually she let her be while keeping a protective arm around her in case she should fall.

'Your mum's going off her head,' said Jimmy. He was a constant irritation to Catherine. His appearance was more like that of his father than his mother. He had thick black hair that stood up in greasy spikes and one of his ears stuck out. His eyebrows were heavy over staring eyes. Always staring at her he was, like a googly-eyed goldfish peering out from the confines of his limited life and even more limited mind. And his mouth was too big, large rubbery lips, opening and shutting, spouting rubbish that she didn't want to hear. Normally, Catherine would have chased him and hit him, but today she was too distraught for retaliation. 'I'm frightened,' she cried, 'Mummy's making me feel creepy.' Rosie lifted the child down from the window and cradled her in her cosy bosom.

At last the noise of scrubbing stopped, and Maggie dragged herself up to Rosie's flat. She stood just inside the door. Her eyes were sunken and dark in a face that was no longer flushed but had turned translucently pale with a light bluish tinge around her mouth. Her clothes were crumpled and sticking to her. She looked so ghastly that no-one, not even Jimmy, passed comment. 'I'll take Catherine home now,' she gasped, 'we'll be having an early night.' Her emphasis on the word 'early' made it clear that she did not want Rosie to come up later, as she sometimes did, for a warm heart-to-heart over a glass of sweet stout.

Chapter 16

Maggie woke early with the April sun softly stroking her eyes like a kindly nurse bringing a patient gently into the day. Her first waking thought was a happy one. A lovely day, just ideal for washing. It was a long time since the sun had shone so brightly. Maggie always responded joyfully to sunshine, whatever her circumstances. She was glad to see the end of the long dark winter that was a breeding ground for the brooding dark thoughts that wormed their way into the underworld of a mind deprived of sunshine and light, eating it away with depression and regret. Spring was her customary guide back to reason and optimism.

She stretched and yawned, taking the full benefit of having the bed to herself. She arched her back in a full luxurious stretch, but sore muscles reminded her sharply of her troubles, striking her a stunning blow dead centre in her forehead between the eyes. The memory of yesterday ached through her whole body. The pain of her situation made her close her eyes tightly again and she curled up into a ball and buried her face in the pillows like a hedgehog hiding from danger. No amount of sunshine could cure this.

For a few minutes she lay, allowing panic to build up into sweat. This was a problem that wouldn't fade with time. This was a problem that needed action. Maggie drew a deep breath and reaffirmed her vow, bracing herself for the next step of her plan. She rose, had a wash in cold water at the sink and dressed in her working clothes.

As soon as Catherine left for school, Maggie stood at the back door breathing in the freshness of the morning. She looked over at the washhouse and prepared herself mentally for the operation. The washhouse served as a meeting place as well as a work place. Washing day could be arduous and the women often helped each other. Sunny days were best. Neighbours would sit on the back steps chatting, while others folded sheets and blankets together or laid out the whites on the green grass to bleach in the sun. But

Maggie wanted no such help today. She wanted to work herself into having a miscarriage. It was her only hope.

Maggie entered the small cool washhouse. Firstly she prepared the newspapers and sticks for the fire under the boiler, which snuggled in the corner, looking like a giant wasps' nest but made of bricks and concrete. A small grate for holding a fire was built into the front. The boiler was a favourite place for children playing hide and seek. There was just enough room to curl up inside unnoticed, especially if they skilfully pulled the cover over the top. Along the opposite wall were two wooden sinks with a wringer fixed between them. A huge iron mangle stood behind the door on the clear wall.

Maggie set to filling the boiler. Like a workhorse under the whiplash of a cruel master, she filled bucket after bucket with icy water at the sink and carried it over to the boiler where, each time she lifted the bucket high for pouring, a quantity spilled chillingly up her sleeve and down her front. At last it was full and she immersed the sheets to soak.

Now for the fire. Many a time she would be close to tears trying to light it, especially on a damp windless day when the cold moisture seeped into her very bones. Today was dry and warm, but Maggie still allowed herself the luxury of firelighters. She held one now to her nostrils to inhale the warm smell of petrol that triggered thoughts of oil wells in distant Arabia and transported her to the exotic East, sheikhs and magic carpets. She loved the coconut texture as she crumbled it amongst the newspapers and sticks. Taking a match she set the papers alight. She watched the little flames grow larger and longer as they licked their way round the sticks, melting them like children's lollies and turning them into fire. Now the coal could be added lump by lump till it too started to burn freely. Maggie gazed into the rich, orange-red blaze allowing herself a minute or two of blessed oblivion from the questionable purpose of this awful washing day.

Thoughts of the Orient turned her mind to the Persian poetry her Uncle Eddie had loved and often quoted. Whenever he came to visit he'd say, 'Always live your own life, just the way you want it to be.'

'I miss you, Eddie,' she said into the fire. 'Did you really die? I feel as if you're still around somewhere. Oh, Eddie, if you could see me now in this mess!' She started to cry and then stopped herself. 'I will sort it out, just you see.' Acceptance was alien to Maggie and she rebelled against her present situation. There was no going back to the weak moment she agreed to let Sam make love to her, but she was going to do her best to rid herself of the consequences.

A figure behind her made her start suddenly. It was no eastern sheikh or poet. It was the robust figure of Rosie, brawny arms folded over her chest, staring down at the crouched and much slighter figure of Maggie. The only resemblance she bore to anyone exotic was in her pink chiffon turban complete with four metal curlers lined up on her forehead. Her face shone with face cream. It may well have only been margarine if money was tight. She always wore a moisturiser on washing days convinced that the steam would help to soak it deep into her pores. Her hands were slippery and shiny too. Rosie's endless attempts to regain the lost glamour of youth never failed to amaze Maggie.

'Right, Madam,' Rosie boomed down at Maggie who ignored her and remained squatting at the fire, stabbing at it with the bent little poker, avoiding unwanted confrontation with her neighbour. Rosie formidably folded her arms tighter over her bulging breasts. She was determined. 'Out with it,' she said in a deep drum major voice. 'There's something you have to tell me and I have a good idea what it is. I'm not going to stand by and let you kill yourself. Yesterday was bad enough.'

'I don't know what you mean,' replied Maggie, rising to her feet and squeezing herself out through the gap between Rosie and the boiler so that she no longer felt trapped. She lifted the boiler lid and started stirring the water with the wooden tongs. She longed to make a start on scrubbing the blankets in the sink. Normally, she would wash them on a hot summer's day by trampling them with her feet in the zinc bath and hanging them out in the sun to dry. But that was too easy. Today she would wash them by hand on the scrubbing board.

'I know what's up, Maggie,' Rosie said following her around.

Maggie ignored her and made to go upstairs to put on a large kettle for hot water to augment what she had in the boiler. Looking neither left nor right she brushed past Rosie and out of the washhouse, but reached no further than the back stairs when a rushing sound rose coldly past her ears and suddenly everything went black. Maggie crumpled to the ground, her pregnant body weakened from overwork and lack of food. Rosie rushed to her and helped her to sit on the step with her head between her knees. 'Look, Maggie dear, it's obvious what's wrong with you. I'll finish off your sheets and towels and the blankets can wait for another day.'

Maggie tried to protest but her voice turned into a cry and she wept into Rosie's bosom just as her daughter, Catherine, had done the day before. 'What can I do? Please, Rosie, just leave me to it.' She wailed like a little child wanting her own way.

'Believe me, Maggie, once a baby's taken a hold it'll hang on in there for dear life. If nothing happened after yesterday then nothing will shift it,' she said, speaking with the authority of someone who knows what's what from many years of stair head conversations. 'The best you can do now is look after your health. Just get yourself to the doctor, and this time next year you'll be glad you did. There'd be no one left on the planet if everyone waited till they could afford children. It's nature, that's what it is. You're a churchgoer. Talk to Reverend McKimmie; he seems a reasonable chap, not like some of them fire and brimstone lads that would put the fear of God into you.'

'How can I ask a minister for help?' retorted Maggie. 'He'll lecture me about souls and Heaven. I don't want a baby. I won't

79

have it. And that's that.'

Suddenly Maggie pushed herself roughly from Rosie's comforting arms and ran to the toilet. The deep retching sounds that emanated from the closet where she had sat sobbing the day before were all the confirmation Rosie needed that she was correct in her diagnosis. Without a second thought she marched into the washhouse and stirred the now boiling water, foaming and white. The submerged sheets were heavy and resisting against her muscular strength. She added a lump or two of coal to the fire and, after bailing a couple of bucketsful of boiling water into a deep wooden sink, started to wash and scrub the pile of clothes that lay ready on the draining board.

Chapter 17

On the Brave Harvest Sam lay on his bunk mulling over his life. He shared a tiny cabin with a friendly young lad, Billy, who slept on the bunk below. 'I hate having nothing to do,' he said. 'It leaves too much time to think.'

'Never mind, Sam, we arrive at the fishing grounds tomorrow and that'll be a different story. I'm only too glad to rest now and conserve my energy. Here, have one of my fags, a full strength. Relax. Enjoy yourself.'

'Thanks, Bill,' Sam replied, hanging his head and shoulders over the edge of his bed in order to reach the proffered cigarette. 'The trouble with me is that I need to be busy.' Still suspended, like a trapeze artist, he took a packet of matches from his pocket and lit first his own cigarette and then Billy's. 'I've worries on my mind and Skipper doesn't take too kindly to us blotting it out with alcohol.' He lay back, inhaled deeply and blew the large smoke rings of a man deep in thought.

'Too true,' answered Billy. 'We can't have you falling overboard into the nets, or screaming mad with the horrors when the effects have worn off. Remember Old Gus that we had to tie down because he thought his cabin was full of snakes. Nearly lost him over the side we did.'

'Good God, Billy, you know I never drink anywhere near that amount. I just wanted something to take the edge off.' Sam sat up and swung his legs over the side in front of his cabin mate, blocking his vision.

'What's up, Sam? Nothing usually bothers you,' said Billy swiping Sam's legs away with the flat of his hand. 'And get your stinking feet out of my face.'

'I miss Maggie. A man needs a woman out here with nothing but grey waves for miles.' Sam sighed and lay back, chewing on the end of the used matchstick. 'Maggie's got me worried. She's been bad tempered and even more distant recently. She won't have anything to do with me.'

'Another man!' came the tetchy reply from below. 'The problem's always other men for blokes in our position away from home most of the time. Women get lonely for attention too you know.'

'Don't think so, Maggie's straight as a die.'

Billy rolled his eyes and smiled. Young as he was, he'd seen a bit of life. 'Where have I heard that before?'

Sam drew hard on his cigarette. 'Watch your mouth, son. You've never met my wife. I wish I could tell her how I feel about her but the words won't come.' Sam hoisted himself on to the floor. 'Fancy a game of cards?'

'Better that than listening to you getting all maudlin,' said Billy with a sigh. 'It's obvious you're not going to settle, like a monkey with fleas. But no money mind, just a game to pass the time.'

'Okay, don't start your preaching. I know all about you Bible thumpers from up North. So just matches. I gamble too much anyway. I'll find Fred and Davy and ask them to join us. Add to the crack.' Sam wandered off. No need to hurry. Eke out the time. Do anything rather than think. As he tossed the butt of yet another cigarette into the foaming sea, a dreadful thought occurred to him, something that reminded him of the early months of Maggie's pregnancy with Catherine. Only last week Maggie had asked him for one of his cigarettes. She'd taken up smoking again. 'Bugger it!' he shouted into the wind, his voice rising loud above the drone of the engines.

Chapter 18

At home Maggie sat alone by the fire. She took a cigarette from the second pack she'd bought in a day. She put on the wireless for company. The words of a favourite song about love everlasting on a paradise isle made her acutely aware that her life was not unfolding the way she intended. She hadn't amounted to anything. She was a failure. She stormed over to the wireless and switched it off.

She knew exactly what she had to do, but it was a risky business. She knew about such things from years of gossip in the washhouse. But surely the wall of the womb was thick. If it could stretch to carry a child, it would be impossible to burst. Just scrape away the surface a little. That's all she had to do. Maggie fetched her knitting bag and searched inside until she found what she was looking for - a crochet hook, a thin size ten. She also had a size eight but that seemed too thick. There were plenty towels in the chest of drawers. Carefully she laid them out on the bed. It was only a matter of bringing on a late period. But do it quick. Get it over with.

Maggie put on the kettle and fetched a glass bowl from the cupboard. The hook would need sterilising. Climbing on a chair so she could reach far into the depths of the top shelf where all the medications were kept out of Catherine's reach, she searched among the liver salts, the bottle of crumbling aspirin, the liniment and the myriad of mysterious concoctions for curing all ills. At last she found what she wanted, the dark brown ridged bottle of iodine.

She boiled the implement in the pan and then placed it in a glass bowl and smeared it with the brown antiseptic. In a trance, she carried out the procedure with business like precision. She had to scrub up thoroughly to avoid infection. First of all she washed herself, standing in the big basin soaping herself before rinsing herself thoroughly with the sponge. She wiped on the iodine and recognised the stinging as reassurance that all the germs were killed. Maggie forced herself on. This time tomorrow everything would be back to normal.

Now for it! She took several deep breaths, squatted down and placed a towel below her on the linoleum. The towels were sterile from being boiled and ironed. The bowl with the crochet hook was beside her on the floor. She held it carefully and inserted it. With a struggle she managed to locate her cervix and with pounding heart and shaky hands, she managed to manoeuvre the head of the hook into its centre. Repeating aloud, 'I must do this. I must do this,' she pushed it in. It wasn't as easy as she thought it would be. She pushed hard again. Perspiration prickled her forehead. Ever so slowly the crochet hook started to slide in. 'I must do this. I must do this.' She pushed again. Surely it must be inside her now. She twisted it, not stopping until a pain stabbed through her, right deep inside. It spread across her belly and round her back. Switching off to the mounting pain, she held the instrument steady for a good minute. Nearly over. When the agony became unbearable she stopped and withdrew it. It was covered in brown red gunge, a mixture of blood and iodine. She threw it quickly out of sight into the sink.

Doubled in pain, she struggled to a chair, the towel from the floor held under her. She rested for a while and the pain subsided. 'Well, if this fails then it's meant to be,' she said. 'What will be, will be. I've done my best and can do no more.' Maggie lay back in the chair, absolutely still, until her racing heart had slowed and she had stopped sweating. Robotically, she cleared away the evidence and made herself a cup of strong, sweet, milky tea and lit another cigarette. She felt she could do with a drink to calm her but the alcohol in whisky would make any bleeding worse. Suddenly with horror she remembered something that had slipped her mind. Red haired people bleed more. At the start of the war, a beautiful redhead in the next street, Josephine Lamond, had died giving birth to twins. Maggie felt faint. She prepared herself with two large sanitary towels and lay down on the bath towels she had placed on the bed earlier.

Surprisingly, Maggie fell straight off to sleep, but in the early hours of the morning a searing pain tore through her innards. Gingerly, she stretched out her arm to put on the bedside light. It was two o'clock. She felt down between her legs. The towels were sodden and her thighs were soaking. At first Maggie thought it was sweat, but on withdrawing her hand she saw it was covered in blood up past the wrist. Had this really been her intention? She called to Catherine. She had no choice now but to involve the child. She had to save her own life. Catherine would suffer if she died.

'Catherine, wake up!' she screamed. 'Get Rosie!' Catherine's sleepy face appeared at the door. 'What's the matter, Mummy?' She stood at the door, frozen to the spot, staring at her mother who could barely lift her head. Maggie screamed for Rosie at the top of her voice. A hammering at the door soon heralded Rosie's arrival. She took Catherine by the shoulders and swung her round so that her face was buried in the soft fat of her stomach. 'Send Catherine out!' Maggie gasped.

'What's happening?' shouted Rosie. 'I couldn't sleep for worry about you. It's not like us to fall out, and then I heard you screaming.'

She gave Catherine a shove towards the door. Her mind worked fast and she knew that what lay in the bed recess was not for a child's eyes. 'Go downstairs quickly. Tell my Jim he's needed. Tell him he must come!'

Rosie was over by the bed looking down at Maggie. She was afraid to draw back the blankets. 'You fool. You damned stupid fool!' she shouted. 'Now lie still. You mustn't move. I'll get Jim to phone an ambulance. He can run round the corner to the phone box in a flash.' Maggie didn't dare move, knowing that if she did so she might be endangering her life even more. She could feel herself fading, growing steadily weaker. When Rosie made a move

85

to lift the blankets Maggie grabbed her wrist with a blood soaked hand. 'My God, where is that man? What the hell is he doing?' gasped Rosie, leaning over the back of the fireside chair, her hand over her mouth in an effort to stop the retching.

Footsteps and a slow creak of the door brought Jim wandering in, still doing up his trouser buttons. 'There's no time to talk, Jim. Just throw on your coat and get round to the phone box. Dial 999 and get an ambulance here as fast as you can. Tell them someone's losing blood fast. Go on, man, MOVE!' The volume of Rosie's voice and the pallor of Maggie's face spurred him into action. Women's problems were bad enough at the best of times but this was a matter of life or death. He rushed out the door and clattered hell for leather down the stairs. Rosie turned her attention back to Maggie whose vivid red hair was splayed around the stark white of her face, which now matched the colour of the bleached pillowcase. She mopped her friend's forehead with a damp flannel while they waited for help to arrive.

It wasn't long before two ambulance men burst in through the door. There was predictably no sign of Jim who had scuttled back in to the refuge of his own flat. With one look at Maggie, the ambulance driver shook his head and turned to his companion. 'She's haemorrhaging badly. We'll need a stretcher.'

'Another silly woman too desperate to see sense,' replied his mate coldly. Years of dealing with human suffering had desensitised him.

Rosie's face blanched when Maggie was lifted off the bed. A large pool of blood was gradually seeping into the sheet, pillows and mattress. Near to fainting, she had to sit with her head between her knees for a minute before making it through to Catherine's room for a blanket to throw over the mess.

From downstairs could be heard Catherine's anxious cry: 'Is my mummy dead?'

Chapter 19

Sam continued to worry. After some serious thinking he had convinced himself that Maggie had been pregnant. All the signs were there and he knew he'd taken a chance the night of the storm. Anxious and guilt ridden, no amount of work could prevent his preoccupation with Maggie's plight. His tortured mind churned with the fish that tumbled in the nets that he and his fellow crewmen dragged from the turbulent waves. Since Peter Merchant, the skipper, had told him the gist of the message wired from the shipping agents, he had known no rest. Whatever stupid thing she'd done, it was his fault. What if she died! Why hadn't he put two and two together when he was ashore? All the signs had been there.

Suddenly, the voice of the skipper carried across the cold night air, shouting at him to stop shirking. There was a lot of money for everyone at stake if he didn't get his finger out. Glad of the heavy catch to use up his strength, Sam turned his attention to work. Frustration added power to the steel hard muscles of his neck and shoulders as he strained to haul in the bulging net, gripping the rope firmly with his bare, broad hands. He knew that to let it slip would disrupt the unified pulling of his mates. Grateful for the weight on which to vent his rage, Sam used every last ounce of his energy to drag the fish aboard and roared fiercely at his seemingly weaker comrades, 'Get in there, you bloody slackers, pull them in! Heave them up and over they go!'

The fishing ground was yielding a prize harvest and they'd worked by the light of the moon to rake it all in. Now, it was almost daybreak and they would be heading off soon to follow the shoal of haddock that was their daily bread. But worry stopped Sam from sharing the joy of his shipmates. 'If anything happens to Maggie I may as well have killed her myself with my bare hands,' he muttered to himself as he wiped the sweat from his face. The voice of conscience, merciless as the sea, disturbed his every waking hour. 'It's all my fault! I tricked her and took a chance. I'm no better than a murderer.' Sam tilted back his head and roared his confession to the four winds, and they alone heard it, so busy were the fishermen sorting the catch, and they carried the words away and howled them round the globe mingled with the screams of seabirds. Tears of repentance burned his eyes as he watched the first shafts of sunlight break through the morning clouds and give sparkle to the silvery scales of the wriggling fish as they poured, like a massive spill of liquid mercury, through the hatch and into the hold.

Old Peter had done his best for him, taking him into his cabin for privacy to break the news. He had listened patiently and impartially to everything Sam had to say, and although he himself was teetotal, had given Sam a shot of whisky from the bottle of single malt that he kept for emergencies. There was practically nothing this seasoned trawlerman hadn't heard before, after years of having men in his care far from their families miles out at sea. From what it said in the wire from the ship's agents, it appeared that Maggie had been rushed to hospital and given a couple of pints of blood. Now there was nothing for it but the long wait and the wondering.

'I was right about the smoking. Why didn't I guess sooner and speak to her about it?' Sam cursed himself, but it was always the same, however deep his feelings, the words always stuck in his throat like barbs, reinforcing the barrier between him and Maggie over the years.

The work finished, Sam looked out across the bubbling sea. The seagulls that wisely followed the boats, allowing men to do their fishing for them, squabbled around his head, ducking and diving like the thieves that they were. Sam continued to gaze trancelike at the seemingly endless ocean and allowed its magnitude to calm him. In the distance, on the curve of the horizon, he saw the blow of a mighty sperm whale shooting up like a fountain, and the vast grey brow rising clearly as it coursed the cruel waves.

However, as Sam soon noticed, this one was not solitary as many of these old gentlemen of the sea commonly were. Close behind came a family group of six mature females with their calves, serenely unaware that they were soon to be hunted down by the whaling ship that he knew was only a few miles away. Sam took time to savour the vision. With the ice flows glistening behind them, the whales created a show that no human artist could ever bring to canvas. In no time at all these beautiful beasts would be killed and chopped to pieces, the spermaceti wax cut from their huge heads to be used as the finest of lubricating oil, and rich ladies would delight in the perfumes made from the lumps of ambergris gouged from deep within these creatures' intestines.

The rest of the crew had gathered to watch the spectacle. 'You know, I love the sea,' said Sam. 'I love the sense of remoteness from all that is unsavoury in the world. So, when I see Man's destruction out here on the waves, I feel a pain deep in my heart. Men have always tarnished the oceans with piracy and pillaging, but that's man against man. It's the killing of its gentle inhabitants that I find most abhorrent. Sometimes I ask myself why I continue to be part of it all.' The rest of the crew continued to watch the whales without comment. Peter the skipper moved closer to Sam. 'You think too much,' he said gently, sensitive to Sam's present state of mind. 'You're here to earn a living. Surely our families matter more than a few fish.'

'That's right,' added Billy in an effort to console him further. 'Jesus himself went out with the fishermen and helped them with their catch.'

'I know that,' snapped Sam, quite out of character, 'but you won't ever catch me killing a magnificent creature such as these beautiful giants. No one has the right to take life. It's obscene!'

Chapter 20

By the time Sam came home, the offensive mattress had been taken away by the council to fester on the tip, its gruesome story exposed to the elements, and, as it rotted, it became a home to the rats that scurried amongst the piles of human waste.

Maggie fought to keep gossip at bay. 'It's hard, Rosie,' she said. 'They all know. Going to the shops gives me the jitters.'

'You hold your head high, pet,' answered Rosie. 'People's memories are short. Another nine-day wonder will soon remove you from centre stage.'

'You're right,' said Maggie, power returning to her voice. 'Now, where's the embroidery you were going to show me?'

'This is my passion,' said Rosie. 'When I sew I forget all my troubles.' She held up a beautiful tray cloth. 'It's easy; you just do some satin stitch here with one colour and change it there for another. A few lazy daisies and Bob's your uncle. It'll do you good to create something beautiful that you can admire.' Rosie opened a drawer and produced some samples of needlework that made Maggie gasp with amazement. She unwrapped a tablecloth from tissue paper and spread it on the table so she could examine it more closely. 'Rosie, this is incredible work. You've made these pansies stand proud of the material,' she said, lightly touching the purple and yellow flowers at the corner of the masterpiece. 'How on earth do you do that?'

'My grandmother taught me. Anytime I feel down I embroider. Your mind can be a terrible enemy, you know. The concentration of sewing keeps mine from running on to things I'd rather not think about.' Lovingly, Rosie folded up the display of cloths and stored them away again in the dark recesses of the mahogany chest of drawers.

'I've heard of hiding your light under a bushel, Rosie Simpson,' exclaimed Maggie, 'but this takes the biscuit. It's criminal not to show these off. They're wonderful.'

'Lot's of people embroider, Maggie, not just me. I'll give you a couple of pieces for your church sale of work. Now, on to important matters. How are you and Sam getting along?'

'You know Sam, he never talks about personal matters, but he has been much more attentive. No, not in that way, Rosie; you have a one-track mind. I can go to bed and sleep undisturbed. He has started making me breakfast in bed and asks if I'm all right. It's a weird experience.'

'Make the most of it, Maggie, while it lasts. Jim has never so much as made a cup of tea for me,' complained Rosie.

Disturbing changes had taken place in Catherine, however. She had nightmares and was frightened to leave her mother. In the mornings she would cry and refuse to go to school. If it wasn't stomach ache it was a sore throat. One morning, she stood holding on to a chair, unable to walk. Maggie took her to Dr. Menzies who said she would forget in time and in the meantime, to smother her with love and attention. He called for the receptionist to take Catherine into the waiting room to read comics and turned to Maggie. 'You see, she has the fear of death in her,' he explained, 'fear that you might die and leave her alone. Spend as much time on her as possible and do what you can to keep her mind occupied.'

Dr. Menzies wasn't finished though, and continued to look straight at her, making sure his words would penetrate deep. 'You took a terrible risk that nearly cost a little girl her mother, but I can understand your desperation. I can't possibly condone your actions,' he continued, playing with the top of his fountain pen, 'because I've witnessed the grim aftermath of a number of messed-up abortions. However, I have also seen the dire consequences of unwanted pregnancies - women dragged to an early grave by the strain of carrying baby after baby without adequate nutrition. You, Maggie, are most fortunate to be alive, so let's just leave it at that.' Maggie felt her cheeks redden with the

91

shame of the reprimand. 'Abortion is illegal, but who knows what another ten years might bring,' said Dr. Menzies thoughtfully as he pressed the top firmly back on the pen before placing it centrally on the prescription pad.

He walked round to the front of his desk where Maggie sat shamefaced and silent. 'You don't look too well even yet,' he murmured as he leaned over and gently pulled down the lower lid of her left eye. 'You're anaemic,' he said, straightening up as far as his arthritic spine would allow. He returned to his swivel chair and pulled the prescription pad towards him. He hesitated and thought for a moment before spinning himself round to the cupboard behind him where he opened a drawer and took out a bottle of round red pills. 'Here, Maggie, some iron tablets. These are free samples from the traveller. No point wasting a shilling on a prescription. Take one a day. You'll feel stronger. They'll improve your appetite too. And try to eat liver, raw, if you can stomach it.' Maggie muttered a quiet thank you, put the bottle in her bag and made to leave. Dr. Menzies laid his hand on her back, on the part between the shoulder blades that seems to bring healing. 'Go easy on yourself, lass,' he said and opened the door for her.

Maggie dutifully swallowed the tablets and found that they really did increase her appetite. She was even gaining weight, which, after a few more weeks began to cause her concern. Maggie was not unduly vain and had no aspirations to look like a film star, as Rosie did, but neither did she want to be fat and unable to wear what few clothes she had. She had been accustomed to remaining trim whatever she ate.

Sam had noticed but said nothing. The best route for him for the time being was a silent one. It was the outspoken but caring Rosie who first brought what everyone else was thinking out into the open. 'You're fairly blossoming, Maggie love,' she commented blithely as they bumped into each other at the front door one afternoon, each returning home from the opposite direction. 'I was watching you just now walking up the road. You're beginning to waddle. I never thought I'd see the day that you'd grow to anywhere near my size and just look at the bust on you.'

Maggie looked down at her bulging summer dress. She'd removed the belt from it and let out the side seams. 'It's these iron tablets. I'm eating like a horse.' She held on to the fence as she spoke. 'I don't feel comfortable carrying all this weight. And I'm so hot all the time. Why don't you come in for a chat, Rosie, I could murder a cup of tea.'

Rosie needed no further invitation. Her favourite topics - weight and dieting - were going to be thrashed out. 'I hear that Americans are losing weight by living on nothing but bananas and milk. Wouldn't it be fun if we both tried it together?' She hurried in the door instead of plodding as she usually did, and managed to skip lightly up the stairs in joyful anticipation of a new food fad. 'This one's going to work. I'm certain of it.'

Maggie had the tea ready when Rosie arrived. She had set out the cups, sugar and milk and also a plate with two sugary buns. 'I just had to buy these;' she announced, 'something sweet makes me feel better. I don't enjoy my tea the same though, it tastes funny.'

Rosie gave her an old-fashioned look. 'I notice you're still smoking. I thought you'd stopped. Something worrying you?' she asked as she reached over for a bun and took a large bite from it. Cheeks bulging like a hamster's, she continued, 'We're not on a diet yet, so may as well enjoy this while we can.'

Maggie left her bun untouched. She drew on the cigarette and blew the smoke out slowly. 'As a matter of fact, I am worried,' she answered. 'I've never had a period yet. After Catherine, I'd started back to normal by this time. I don't understand it.' She twisted the cigarette end into a pile of others in a brown cut-glass ashtray and continued, 'If I weren't so sure that I've never been with Sam since all the trouble, I'd swear I was pregnant.' She paused and waited for Rosie's reaction, but Rosie remained silent. 'You don't think I could still be pregnant, do you?' Maggie asked outright and waited again for an answer.

Rosie took a breath and then pursed her lips together thoughtfully furrowing her brows like a high court judge deciding on a sentence. 'I really don't know,' was all she could say. She thought back to the mattress. Surely nothing could have been left behind after that. 'If I'm honest, though, you are getting fat. You must go to the doctor, Maggie. Go up there this evening. I'll look after Catherine, the poor little mite.'

'I'm going to be sensible this time, Rosie. I'll see Dr. Menzies tonight. In fact, I'll get ready now so I'm first in the queue.'

Dr. Menzies sat behind his desk, grim faced. He had carried out an examination and struggled to explain the result to her carefully and gently. 'You are indeed pregnant, Maggie,' he said, looking down at his hands, which he clasped in front of him, the fingers intertwined as he prepared himself to give out the news. 'It can happen that a baby is left behind even after such a heavy blood loss and I see here in your notes that you never had a dilation and curettage to clear away anything left behind in your womb. Also, it might even have been a tear in one of the blood vessels at the neck of the womb that caused the haemorrhage and not a miscarriage. We'll never know.' He stopped for a minute to let his words sink in. 'The other reason could be that there were in fact two babies. After all, you yourself are a twin. It's not totally unheard of for one baby to be miscarried and the other remain.'

'Thank you, Dr Menzies,' was all that Maggie said.

'You do understand, don't you, Maggie, that there's nothing can be done. I'll make an appointment for you at the ante-natal. Keep on with the iron tablets and the clinic will give you vitamins, cod liver oil and orange juice.'

Maggie nodded like an obedient child. 'Don't worry, Doctor, I'll do everything now to make sure the baby's healthy. I just hope it's not too late.'

Chapter 21

Maggie accepted her fate without question or opposition. This would be a much wanted and much loved baby. Sam worried at first and even offered to stay at home for a couple of trips rather than leave her alone, but she insisted she was happy, glad to have the opportunity to put right the terrible deed. Catherine was delighted. At last a little brother or sister. Maggie bloomed. Her world started and finished with the unborn infant. She would have two miracle children now. Who could ask for more?

Sam was at sea when Maggie's time came a month early, and when she felt the contractions strong and certain, she handed Catherine to the safekeeping of Rosie and took a taxi to the nursing home. Just after midnight, into Sunday morning, Lucy Louise emerged. The tiny baby hung limp and apparently lifeless from the midwife's hands. The poor woman was scared to be too drastic in her efforts to make the fragile infant breathe, to make her live. 'Eight months is tricky for a baby,' said one of the nurses. 'Seven months or nine is what we like.'

'Are you trying to say my baby won't survive?' said Maggie angrily. 'Let me have her,' she demanded. The midwife handed the slippery little bundle to the anxious mother. Maggie cradled her dripping infant in the hollow of her hands and, animal like, blew gently into the nostrils and mouth, caressing her with her breath. Lucy Louise drew in her mother's offer of life, shuddered and then uttered a piteous mew, which, although no louder than that of a newborn kitten, broke the silent tension of the labour ward where those who were gathered round had also held their breath. Maggie looked down at her daughter and fell in love with her instantly. She snuggled Lucy to her left breast, beside the heart, and the little girl right away attached herself to the moist nipple and suckled with an enthusiasm for life that stunned the onlookers back into silence.

Lucy lay in Maggie's arms wrapped in cotton wool, Sunday's child, bonnie and blithe and good and gay. The tiny baby girl weighed only two pounds, the same as a bag of sugar. Her face, no bigger than the top of a bone china cup, looked like that of a doll. The features were perfectly formed, but in miniature. Anyone looking at her without knowing she was a real live baby might have said she was made of wax. There were none of the wrinkles and redness that lying in the womb for too long can cause, so having arrived early, her skin was satin smooth and unblemished. She soon became known by the nurses as the beautiful alabaster baby. Round her face, a shock of blonde hair burst out like the rays of the sun, silky soft but too stubborn to lie flat. Her fingers and toes were like the prongs of a dessert fork and the nails were not yet formed on them. Sometimes she would curl herself up tightly in a little ball and then she would stretch out her limbs and demand to be fed.

Maggie adored her. All the clothes she had knitted were far too large. Everything that was done for Lucy was special. The nurses bathed her, not with water, but by wiping her with nourishing olive oil. She was wrapped in pieces of cotton wool instead of baby gowns and was allowed to sleep in the tiny cot beside Maggie instead of being taken away to the nursery. However, Maggie was only allowed to hold her at feeding times and she accepted this without question. Whatever was best for Lucy, that's what she would do. Neither was it a problem waiting a few weeks till they were allowed home. Maggie stuck by the rules. She couldn't do enough in her efforts at recompense.

Chapter 22

Maggie continued to indulge her sickly little baby and, as the years passed by, Catherine felt the despair of neglect at being ousted from prime position in her mother's life. It was Lucy now who received all her love and attention and Maggie seemed oblivious to the hurt that was burrowing its way through her first born.

Catherine was the picture of misery as she dragged herself aimlessly round the playground, head bowed, shoulders hunched, ignoring the melee of children around her. 'Come on, Catherine, play ropes with us,' they called, but the only voice that Catherine heard or cared about was her mother's, repeating itself in her head since morning, impatient and rejecting, 'I haven't time. Lucy's crying. Do it yourself.'

'That sickly toddler Lucy takes all my mother's energy,' she grumbled to herself. Lucy had usurped Catherine's position in the Taylor household and it was she who now held sway over all proceedings. 'Lucy! Lucy! Lucy! I'm sick of it!' Catherine, the deposed prima donna smarted from the stinging injustice. 'Ringlets in my hair was all I asked for. Only ten minutes it would've taken Mum to tong my hair. I even got them ready myself, heating them in the embers of the fire to save her the bother.' Catherine pushed her hands even deeper into her pockets and scowled at her friends. She sucked in the cold air through her teeth but exhaled her words hotly with temper. 'I have to do everything for myself these days.' In a deep sulk she stalked the playground, gathering resentment instead of friends, plotting instead of playing.

Later, in the classroom, the teacher's voice rose and fell in the distance, failing to penetrate Catherine's thoughts. Miss Walker was notoriously strict to the point of tyranny. Her word was law even among the parents. The children sat bolt upright, listening carefully in case she should pounce with a question and they'd face punishment if they couldn't answer. 'Farmers plant their crops in rotation,' declared the teacher waving the long wooden pointer at a plan of four differently planted fields that she'd drawn on the blackboard. Distractedly, Catherine looked out of the window and watched clouds drift slowly past. In their shapes she could make out faces, creatures and characters weaving intricate dramas against the pale blue of the sky. Isobel Robertson had bragged that she could see her dead granny amongst them. 'Don't be such an idiot,' Catherine had replied, deliberately denying her grieving friend a sense of importance. 'Your granny's dead. She's not anywhere any more.' However, in the privacy of her own mind, Catherine allowed her curiosity full rein and was scouring the heavens for Isobel's granny when a thick black belt swung down in front of her eyes only inches from her face. 'Why doesn't the farmer plant oats in the same field two years in succession?' demanded Miss Walker. She had removed her horn-rimmed spectacles and laid them on her desk as a sign she meant business.

'I don't know,' Catherine answered lamely. 'I've never been on a farm. Why don't you ask a farmer?' She moved her head backwards away from the belt.

'Smell the leather.' Miss Walker's voice struck fear in every watching heart. No one dared laugh. The teacher stood there in a fury, towering over Catherine. The teacher's anger drew the flesh so tightly back from the bones of her face that her eyes seemed to bulge from the sockets of an elongated skull. 'Why do farmers rotate their crops?' she insisted.

'If I knew the answer I would tell you,' Catherine said with a scowl. Frightened now by her own audacity, she darted her eyes from classmate to classmate seeking support, but their blatant lack of courage set them in silent collusion with the teacher's cruelty. 'Somebody, please say something,' her eyes implored, but the teacher misread her fearful search for support as an arrogant attempt to instigate trouble and her face flushed scarlet. 'Come out to the floor, you impertinent girl!' She enunciated each syllable slowly as she spoke and she fingered the belt lovingly. She turned and strode, mannish in her tweed suit, towards the clear space beside the heavy oak desk at the front of the room. Catherine, knowing it was folly to protest, followed behind, head hanging, ready to accept her fate. With uncharacteristic meekness she faced her executioner.

Miss Walker steadied her body on sturdy lisle-stockinged legs, her brogue shoes set apart like those of a golfer preparing to swing. 'Hold out your hand!' she bellowed at the ten year old beneath her. 'Swing it up. Bring it down,' she chanted. The belt hit home, right in the centre of Catherine's flat hand. 'And the other one!' she roared. 'Swing it up. Bring it down,' she chanted again. Her second shot was stronger than the first and the girl buckled beneath it.

Fear of involvement meant that, although there was condemnation in the eyes of the silent onlookers, there were no words of opposition or acts of compassion. The child's eyes widened with silent suffering, but it was triumph that shone in the eyes of the sadist whose face, no longer skeletal, was suffused with blood.

Bent double with hot red hands between her legs, Catherine hobbled to her seat. Slowly, very slowly, she moved her hands from the folds of her skirt and placed them on the desk, palms upwards to the cooling air. Carefully, in case even a single strand of hair might brush the swollen hands and sting them, she laid her head on her upper arms and sobbed. The submissiveness of moments before evaporated and was replaced by a deep seething anger at the injustice. Deep tendrils of revenge twisted their roots into the rich young soil of Catherine's mind and fixed themselves there.

Without a word, Emily Walker replaced the belt in the desk drawer. She stood straight-backed staring ahead at the class, but her dull eyes didn't see them. Neither was she aware of the rising protests of the children who grew brave in her indifference. Her eyes saw only the horrific spectacle of a war, the image of which, even after thirty-nine years, was not yet erased from her battle-scarred memory. She heard only the howl of death as a bayonet plunged deep and tearing into a young man's heart and spilled his blood on foreign soil. Life's energy drained from a vibrant young girl at that same moment and mingled with her lover's on the bloody battlefield, leaving her empty and brittle to function alone on a pointless path through life.

Nor were there any men who might have resurrected this withered flower of womanhood; they too lay dead on Flanders' fields among the poppies and they too left shadows of women who scuttled through life in black widows' weeds, lonely and bitterly barren. This particular harridan, Miss Walker, had since wrought vengeance on many a naughty child for simply having the insolence to be born - but born to another and not to her.

Chapter 23

Sam was no happier than Catherine during those days of Maggie's obsession with Lucy. It was a crisp autumn Saturday lunchtime as Sam walked slowly from the Brave Harvest with a mate, young Davy, in tow. They'd had a good trip and carried a good wage in their pocket. 'Fancy a pint?' asked Sam.

'Are you not hurrying home to your wife and the girls?' answered Davy. 'You've spent the whole trip moaning about how much you miss them.'

'I do, but my being there makes no difference to Maggie,' replied Sam bitterly. She hardly speaks to me and hands me my food with the detachment of an overworked waitress whose only concern is sore feet. Lucy's her focus now. Even Catherine's needs are glossed over these days.' He turned up the side road that led to the Jolly Fisherman. 'Any time I lift Lucy, Maggie snatches her away and holds her tight with the ferocity of a she wolf with her cub.' He pushed his way into the smoke filled sanctuary of the pub to join the ranks of men who choose the cheerful banter of the bar over the quiet of the fireside with their wives at home. 'To hell with it all, I need a drink. I've enough time too for a quick card game.'

'You sound as if you resent your daughter,' said Davy.

'Of course I don't. I want a share of her. I want to belong in that family of mine.' He threw his duffle bag on the floor and called to the barman who was polishing glasses and laughing with a huddle of fish market porters who had finished work for the day. 'Two pints of lager, Tom, when you've a minute.'

'Coming right up, Sam. Good trip?' Tom pulled the pints for Sam into the tall thin glasses he and Davy preferred over thick chunky mugs.

'This lager's pretty good, nice and cool, slakes the thirst. Put a dash of lime in that, would you?' he asked, holding out his glass to Tom. A peroxide blonde next to them flashed her eyes round the bar touting for trade.

'Clear off, Millie,' said Tom, 'I run a respectable place.'

'Easy, Tom,' said Sam. 'It is a woman you're talking to.'

'You're too soft. They're a hard lot her type. Roll you for your money as soon as look at you.'

'D'you think I don't know that? I wouldn't touch one of them with a ten foot barge pole.' Sam closed his eyes and drew in a sharp breath through his teeth. 'I've heard grown men scream in pain trying to pass water when they've caught a dose of the clap from one of those.'

'Off you go, back to the Bosun's Locker where you belong.' Tom stood at the door ushering Millie out with a drunken customer. She staggered and fell heavily on the floor, but her companion quickly hauled her to her feet again, and with an arm round her waist dragged her out. With a glint in his eye he turned and gave the thumbs up. He was looking forward to a good time that he might not even have to pay for.

Sam switched his glance to a gloomy corner and there, in the dim light of the recess, he saw what he'd come for – a card game. 'Any chance of a game, lads?' he called, ambling over to them.

'Count me out, Sam,' said Davy, leaving him in order to join a group of younger men who were talking football at a table by the door.

'See you next trip, Davy lad,' replied Sam who was already introducing himself to the card players.

'Aye, sure you can join us,' replied a round fat man called Ronnie who bore an uncanny resemblance to Humpty Dumpty due to the skinny little legs beneath his round fat body. He stretched out the toe of his winkle picker shoe and with it slid an empty chair towards Sam. 'I've watched you playing cards in here before. You're just the man we need to liven things up. Three card brag okay?' Ronnie shuffled the cards deftly. He finished off by cutting the pack, riffling the two halves between his fingers and thumbs and letting them spring back quickly into one pile again.

'Brag's fine by me, pal,' answered Sam as he settled himself at the table, his jacket over the back of the chair. A wad of notes in his pocket pressed against his thigh in reassurance. He had twenty-three pounds, a princely sum for a fortnight's work. 'Right then, lads,' he said, pushing up the sleeves of his thick woollen jersey with his broad, calloused hands, 'let's get down to business.' Sam could afford to gamble eight pounds. That would be his limit.

A few games later saw Sam three pounds down. 'You all right, Sam?' asked Ronnie. 'Not wanting to pull out yet are you?' He rubbed his thumb and first finger backwards and forwards along his heavy jowls. Then, as his thinking intensified, he moved his hand up to his open mouth and rubbed the sides of his protruding wet tongue before continuing to shuffle the cards which he covered with sticky saliva.

'No problem. Plenty time yet,' replied Sam confidently. Sam could hold his drink but wasn't a hardened boozer. This third pint was enough to make the game go with a buzz. He had reached that happy stage where problems start to fade and life becomes hopeful. Optimism high and his wits not yet clouded, he played astutely. The next two games were his. He was even again.

It was Ronnie's turn to deal. 'This game's too tame,' said the fat man, 'let's go for big ones this time, fivers to start.' His voice rang loudly round the pub, drawing the rest of the customers' attention to their table.

'Steady on, you lot,' shouted Tom, a slight edge to his voice. 'I don't want to lose my licence.' Tom expertly manoeuvred his way through several tables of drinkers to reach the card players, his usually fair complexion had turned a deep shade of pink and dew drops of sweat sparkled on his forehead. 'Hurry it up. I want this game over and done with before the cops come calling on their lunchtime round.' He heaved a worried sigh and looked at the clock before clearing away their empty glasses and full ashtrays.

'You worry too much Tom, but never fear, Ronnie's here.' Ronnie shuffled the cards, cut them and shuffled them again. He smiled at his companions. Sam smiled back, a wide confident grin. Then he remembered what Maggie always said about being too open. In cards, the eyes were the giveaway. He chewed the inside of his mouth. Whatever his feelings, whatever his hand, no-one must know.

Sam felt the adrenalin coursing his veins, making his fingertips tingle and his heart pound. He could afford 'big ones' for one game. He was on a winning streak. 'Why are we waiting? Deal them out, Ronnie,' he said with authority, shoulders back and chest thrust out. Show confidence and unnerve the opponents. He finished his drink in one and wiped his mouth clean with the palm of his hand. It felt clammy against his face, but no one must know he was nervous. 'Tom, over here, mate. Get the boys a drink – and one for yourself.'

Slowly, he fanned open the cards. He gripped his hands close into his chest to stop them trembling. Three aces. In all his gambling days Sam had never had such a hand. It was a dream come true. Calmly, and even managing to feign disappointment, he put his hand face down on the table. The others had done the same. For blank expressions, this table took the prize. Four fivers were thrown in the middle. No one touched their cards. They didn't have to look; each remembered clearly what they were. Jake, the quiet old man to Ronnie's left raised them another five. So did Sam and so did Ronnie. Colin packed. The next time round Ronnie raised five and this time Jake packed too. This game of bluff could be expensive. And who could tell if bluff it really was? Sam played his hand with certainty. He too raised five. He would have to see Ronnie the next time. This was all he could afford. With this winning hand he wished he had more money. If he saw Ronnie now, he would be thirty pounds up, but if the money in the middle increased then his prize would be more worthwhile. Ronnie saw his consternation. 'Want to pack?' he asked with a smug smile.

Sam pretended to waver. If Ronnie suspected Sam was bluffing he might be tempted to keep upping the stakes that would eventually land in Sam's pocket. 'I'd like to chance another go,' Sam answered and chewed his lower lip.

'I can lend you some, if you like,' offered Ronnie, temptingly peeling fivers from a tight roll.

Sam hesitated. 'Right you are then,' he agreed. 'Give me twenty. I'll raise you the twenty and see you for five. If you're willing to match my twenty quid, that is. And that's my final word. That's as far as I'll go.'

Ronnie hesitated. 'I don't know. I don't want to see you skint.'

Sam took the hesitation as proof that Ronnie was indeed bluffing and really wanted to pull out. Already in his mind he was at home handing Maggie a hundred quid. 'Hand them over then,' he said and held out his hand. He felt a slight tremor, a sign of nerves to the opposition, but Ronnie gave no inkling he'd seen it. He counted out the notes and placed them in front of Sam.

Ninety pounds lay in the middle of the table. The other drinkers in the bar filtered over, poking their beaks in, like vultures wanting to be in at the kill. This was no casual card game. Tom looked worried and kept glancing at his watch. Two sets of three cards still lay on the table. Inwardly Sam smiled. Outwardly he kept serious. 'Okay, Ronnie, over to you,' he said. Ronnie deferred. 'No, you go first. I can wait.' He rested back in his chair. Sam turned over his cards one by one but quickly. He wasn't one for dramatics. He just wanted the money now and then head for home. 'Good God!' the crowd gasped together. 'Well done, Sam!' shouted Davy who'd made his way over, slapping him on the back and laughing. Sam looked over at Ronnie, all set to make a clean sweep.

Ronnie waved him back. 'Hold on there,' he said, leaning forwards over the table, 'The game's not over till the fat lady sings, or in this case, the fat man.'

105

'Well, get a move on, Ronnie, start singing. Get it over with. Be a sport!' shouted Jake who thought Ronnie was delaying the proceedings out of bad sportsmanship.

'Okay. Give's a chance,' Ronnie replied, draining his pint slowly. 'Are you sure you're ready for this?'

'Get a move on will you!' urged the watchers, beginning to weary. Ronnie was renowned for being a lad who liked the limelight, but surely this was carrying it a bit too far.

Ronnie, one by one, slowly turned over his cards, shouting aloud their value as he did so. 'Three!' he declared and looked around him like a performer seeking applause. Sam felt his body stiffen and the hairs stood up on the back of his neck.' Surely it wasn't possible. The chances of Ronnie having that hand, in the same deal as his own three aces, must be many millions to one. It must be a bluff. 'Three!' Ronnie called for a second time and waved the card in the air for added emphasis. Silence fell over the bar and everyone held their breath. Sam went visibly pale. With a flourish and a shout of triumph Ronnie bellowed as he turned over the final card 'Three! A prile of threes!' There was uproar as Ronnie swiped the notes off the table and stuffed them willy-nilly into his trouser pockets.

Cymbals of doom crashed in Sam's ears and the bar started spinning. Even seated, he had to hold on to the table to stop himself from keeling over. Ronnie jeered at him. 'Sorry, mate! So verrry sorrry, but I've won!' Ronnie was already heading for the door. 'You can pay me back my twenty in instalments. See you!'

Sam felt in his pockets for the last of his money. Davy come over and put a comforting arm on his shoulder. Sam shrugged it off. 'I'm finished,' he croaked huskily. 'All washed up.' All he had now to his name was three pounds and a handful of silver and copper. He'd rather face fifteen rounds with a heavy weight champion right now than face Maggie's wrath. The worries of a few hours earlier were paltry by comparison now. He could see no future. Maggie would throw him out this time for sure.

'What will you do now?' asked Davy, who stood next to him, his arms dangling helplessly by his sides.

'Head home,' Sam replied. 'What else can I do? I've nowhere else to go.'

Sam walked heart-heavy along the back streets leading to his house. A green shooting brake drew up alongside him. It was Gordon Black, the bookie. He parked there to ply his illegal trade. Housewives and old folk would queue in all weathers to place their sixpence each-way bets in an effort to spice up their humdrum lives with some hope mingled with suspense, and maybe make an extra bob or two if they were lucky. Among them there were always the two or three who were out of their depth, trying week after week, day after day even, to regain their losses and pay back the ever-increasing fortune they owed. They provided the bookie with willing lookouts who were always ready to keep qui vive on street corners for a buckshee sixpence, and on first signal that a copper was near, the car would take off and the crowd disperse back to their houses. Even if caught, what was a fine compared to the overall takings?

'You all right, Sam?' Gordon asked, winding down the window and sticking his well-fed face out into the wind. The dyed black strands of his thickly greased comb-over fluttered straight up like a flag flapping in the wind, revealing the loose pink skin of his scalp, which was as soft and smooth as a newly born piglet.

'Fine, just fine,' lied Sam. 'And how are you? How's business?'

'Brisk,' answered Gordon, flattening the flyaway locks on his bald head with his heavily ringed hand. 'Don't fancy a flutter yourself, do you? I've got a hot tip. Wouldn't tell just anybody, but then you've always been a special customer of mine.' He gave a sleazy laugh, and his eyes twinkled as he licked the corners of his wide mouth with a long wet tongue, like a slimy frog watching and waiting on his lily pad to catch a passing fly.

'I'm not in the mood for gambling today,' replied Sam, but

Gordon knew that the fact he had stopped for a chat told a different story, and he was right. Despite the disastrous card game, Sam was nonetheless drawn by the tempting words. 'I'm not a horsy man as you know, Gordon. I prefer the involvement of the cards, the touch, the skill, the interaction. Anyway, what's this gee gee's name?' The fact he was asking a question indicated to Gordon that he'd lured Sam and snared him. A gambler was a gambler was a gambler. Sam took a pack of cigarettes from his pocket, put one in his mouth and offered one to Gordon. Gordon took one gladly and, quick as a flash, took a lighter from his pocket and lit first Sam's and then his own. Calculations were taking place in Sam's head and Gordon recognised the signs, the moving of eyes from side to side as the sums went on internally.

'Eastern Rocket it's called,' said Gordon. 'A dead cert if ever there was one. Five to one, a good price. However, I've got a Sporting News in the back of the car if you want to look for something else.' He spoke amiably, stalking his victim, offering a choice, seemingly giving control. Sam said nothing. He had some figuring out to do first. In order to win and regain forty pounds from the three in his pocket he would need odds of fifteen to one.

'Let me see that paper,' he said, holding out his hand. 'What's the time of the next race?' People were gathering round the car, shoving pieces of paper and money through the window. Sam stood aside and flicked through the pages of the racing section.

'It's ten past two now. See what you fancy for the two-thirty,' shouted Gordon over the heads of the punters, his voice changing from friendly to businesslike. 'Time's money, so hurry up.' Sam scanned the list. Ignoring the names, ignoring the jockeys, ignoring the trainers, he moved his finger quickly down, searching for the numbers 20/1 in case a 15/1 might be reduced by the time the race was run. Here we go; this was more like it; an omen. Pretty Baby, 30/1 outsider. When he handed over the slip of paper Gordon guffawed. 'Do yourself a favour, Sam, and take my tip. This one's a loser.' He handed the betting slip back to Sam.

Sam shoved it back through the car window again into Gordon's face and it fluttered on to the floor. 'It's what I want,' he said, standing his ground. 'Put it on for me. I'll be back here at three for the money.' Gordon retrieved the piece of paper and stashed it with the rest in a leather pouch under the driver's seat and drove off.

Sam went into the Dog and Duck to wait. Some Scottish music was blaring from the wireless on a shelf beside the gantry. He pushed a shilling across the polished bar. 'Half-pint shandy,' he said to the gangly young barman, 'and any chance of listening to the horses instead of that heedrum hodrum rubbish?'

'Please yourself,' the new lad shrugged. Sam went behind the counter and tuned in the wireless to the racing before returning to a bar stool to listen, leaning forward on the counter and straining his ears so he wouldn't miss any of the commentary. His fists closed round imaginary reins and he pulled the heels of his boots tight against the rungs of the stool as if digging his feet into the stirrups. His knees pressed hard together as if against the warm sides of the galloping horse. 'Go girl!' he urged.

The barman gawped at him. 'You all right, mate?' he asked, but Sam was hurtling headlong on Pretty Baby down the last furlong and didn't hear him. For once in his life, and without any effort, his face remained expressionless. The final seconds of the race came and went. Sam sat motionless, staring straight ahead for a good minute. Ever so slowly he drained the glass and smacked his lips. No need for hurry. Rising from the saddle, he tossed a half-crown to the youngster who was struggling to shine tumblers, which he'd managed to cover in tiny pieces of white lint. 'Here's a tip for you,' Sam said nodding in the direction of the coin, 'and here's another one,' he added with a smile, 'use hot water and a dry cloth.'

Head high and whistling cheerfully, Sam swaggered across the road to where Gordon sat counting notes in the front seat. 'You've the luck of the devil, you bastard. You've cleaned me out!'

he snarled as he passed the winnings into Sam's eager grasp.

'It would take more than me to clean you out; you're rolling in it,' answered Sam pertly, eyeing the heavy gold rings on the bookie's podgy fingers. He tried to keep the transaction serious but, with a new hold on life, was unable to stop the broad grin spreading across his face. 'This should please the missus,' he added, thumbing through the notes, before putting seventy-three pounds into his jacket and stuffing the twenty he owed Ronnie deep into his kit bag. For the first time in ages he was looking forward to going home.

'Take more than that to keep a woman happy,' came Gordon's bitter reply as he started to rev the engine. 'They just keep on wanting more. It's in their bloody nature.' Gordon crashed through the gears as he drove off in a furious rage. Sam sang a happy song to himself as he strolled pleased as Punch home to his wife. He'd almost hit rock bottom and the jolt it gave him had finally hit home. From that day onward, Sam never gambled again.

Chapter 24

'And how are my three favourite girls?' Sam shouted as he burst in through the kitchen door throwing his bag down in front of the fire and filling the room with his joyful masculine presence.

Maggie turned on him from the sink where she was pounding at a scrubbing board with a bar of green soap. 'Where the hell have you been?' she screamed in shrewish welcome. 'Catherine's been sick all day, all over our bed, and you should have been here to help – not out getting drunk. You're away again on Monday morning and I'll be left to manage everything on my own as per usual. Just don't expect me to start cooking.' Maggie poured out her torrent of complaint with barely a pause for breath.

'It should be easier with these new fangled bri-nylon sheets,' Sam ventured but his clumsy efforts at appeasement met with more fury. Maggie slapped the soiled bedding on the washboard and pummelled it till the sweat on her brow soaked through the matted hair on her forehead. She plunged the washing into the soapsuds again and kneaded it murderously till her wrath was vented. Exhausted, she leaned against the sink, her front drenched with soapy water and her face running with tears.

Sam watched in quiet apprehension. Now that Maggie had stopped for a breather, he dared to offer a suggestion. 'Tell me what to do and I'll do it.' He spoke with the meekness of a timorous mouse, his voice barely a squeak. Maggie made no answer, but quietly wiped her red face on her damp apron and began rinsing the sheets. Sam took off his jacket and threw it over a chair before turning to the cot to pick up Lucy. 'Lucy Locket lost her pocket, Kitty Fisher found it,' he sang as he walked round the kitchen with the baby, bouncing her in time to the nursery rhyme. Maggie flew over from the sink and grabbed the child from him with her dripping wet hands that were red raw from the icy water she'd been working in. 'Leave that child alone! I don't want her breathing in your beery breath!' she shouted. She dropped a now

111

crying Lucy into the cot before heading back to the sink to wring out the washing.

'If you ask me, you're the one that's upsetting everyone,' Sam retorted, his voice steadier now. He stood with his back to the fire warming himself, not daring to take a seat. 'Why don't you sit down and I'll make you a cup of tea?' He raised his eyes to the ceiling and bit his lip impatiently. There was still no answer from his wife. 'I'll just take a quick look through to see if Catherine's settled.' He was determined to get a welcome from someone. 'Have you called a doctor?' he asked lightly, trying to bring normal conversation into their exchange.

'You know damned well that you can't get a doctor to come in on a Saturday unless it's a matter of life and death, and by the time it comes to Monday you'll be gone again,' she snapped, her face and body rigid with the effort of twisting the washing into tight cords as she wrung every drop of water from it. 'And keep away from that door!' She rushed over and grabbed him back by the arm. She slammed the door and positioned her body flat against it blocking his way. 'You're not going through there disturbing Catherine with your drunken carry on.'

Sam finally lost patience and rage overwhelmed him. 'There's not much point in me being here at all if that's how you feel!' he roared and dug into his trouser pocket for the fivers, which he flung on to the floor over by the sink where they fluttered down in a scatter around Maggie's feet. 'Here's your housekeeping. That's all I am to you, someone to bring in money. I thought you'd be pleased to have something extra for the new house.'

Maggie's jaw dropped and, oblivious even to Lucy's screaming, she was immediately on her knees scrambling on the sodden rug to pick the banknotes up. Sam watched her and for the first time in their married life it was he who felt disgust.

'We had a good trip this time and you can guess the rest, you that knows everything,' he sneered and, without waiting for a response, he continued in a wearied voice that conveyed his exasperation with the misery they caused each other, 'I've had enough. I'm away out. There's still time to catch the second half of the match.' Snatching up his jacket, he turned on his heel and was gone, crashing the door hard behind him before banging his way down the stairs and out, glad he'd had the foresight to keep back a couple of fivers for himself.

Maggie ran to the door and shouted after the disappearing figure, 'Fine help you are! Take your stink of fish and go; and don't come back!' The door was slammed for a second time but a smile tickled the corners of her mouth as she counted the notes slowly. From under the bed she took a metal cash box and added nine of the notes to the bundle already in there. 'Mummy!' It was Catherine coming through, wakened by the noise. Hurriedly, Maggie put the box on the floor and kicked it under the bed with her foot. 'It's all right, love, Mummy's here.' She tucked Catherine into the freshly made bed and gathered Lucy into her arms, rocking her and crooning. 'One day, my darlings,' she said. 'One day!'

Chapter 25

Catherine was sick into the bowl again, but being ill had its compensations. Illness meant she could stay off school and spend the day in her mother's bed. In the cot on the wall near the bed, Lucy bounced up and down like a jack-in-the-box. Maggie quietened her. 'Hush, my little sweetheart, Catherine's not well. Here's dolly to play with.' Catherine loved hearing her rival admonished in favour of herself and smiled smugly. 'Mum,' she whined, making the most of a situation that was actually running in her favour for once, 'Catherine's giving me a sore head. Could she not go and stay with someone till I'm better?'

'I know it's hard for you with Lucy dancing about,' replied her mother, wiping clean her mouth with a hot soapy cloth, 'but you were once little like that. If I take her out of the cot, she'll want to climb in beside you.' Maggie gently rubbed some eau de cologne on Catherine's hot brow. 'Remember, Catherine, Lucy's not too strong. She'll soon tire.' Maggie lifted Lucy from the cot and carried her round the room, rocking her and singing. 'Try to rest, Catherine. Can't you see I've got my hands full?' Catherine put her hand to her mouth as if about to vomit. Maggie had no choice. 'All right, Catherine, you win. I'll put Lucy down to Auntie Rosie's.'

'Thanks, Mum,' Catherine replied, trying not to smirk as Maggie carried her little sister downstairs. She lay back and gave herself over to dark thoughts. 'Now we can enjoy being together just the two of us, Mum and me. Why was I ever so stupid as to wish for a little sister? I wish there was only me again.'

Doctor Menzies was speedy in his diagnosis and speedy in his actions. 'Scarlet fever,' he announced. 'It's the fever hospital I'm afraid. In no time at all the ambulance bell sounded in the street outside their door. This disease could kill.

In hospital, Catherine lay between starched white sheets. It was two weeks since her admission and she was almost ready to go home. The doctor had said so this morning. She felt no excitement though. Instead she lay still and listened, straining her ears for any sound from the next room.

In the isolation ward next door a frail child was rasping her last feeble breaths through an ever tightly closing throat. Unable to speak or even cry, her eyes, bright with fever in a tiny flushed face, would occasionally open and do the talking for her. 'Why is it so sore, Mummy? What's happening to me?' they seemed to say. Her limp little body was covered in angry red skin that was burned dry and flaking in patches. Maggie and Sam sat beside their daughter at opposite sides of the bed, watching, waiting and praying for another miracle.

'God, where are you now? Surely you can't allow this to happen to a poor defenceless child,' Sam shouted, his eyes turned skywards as he wrung his hands and wept openly. Maggie gazed silently at her baby girl as if willing her to rise up, but there was to be no miracle this time. The rattle in the child's throat grew louder and more laboured. Maggie and Sam reached across the bed to clutch each other's hands for comfort. Their free hands grasped Lucy's gently, refusing to let her leave them. The child's neck arched and her body went into spasm. Her tiny face contorted as the fit took over. Maggie and Sam leaned further forward, their heads almost touching above that of their dying daughter. Neither dared to breathe. Little Lucy's fragile body relaxed and the life in it was finally extinguished. Serene beauty returned to her face. 'I'm sorry,' said the registrar softly, 'there's nothing more we can do. She's gone.'

Chapter 26

Flowers and wreaths surrounded the tiny white coffin, which lay open on the kitchen table specially laid out so that neighbours and friends could come and view the body. The roller blinds in every house in the street were down. Death had come calling. Everyone felt the chill of it. The miracle baby had died. The little face that was waxen at birth was waxen once more. The blonde wisps of a toddler had replaced the shock of new baby hair and the features were shaped into a pretty pert nose and cheeky cherub lips that were no longer moist and red, but pallid and dry. Neighbours wept to see the lifeless doll dressed in a long silk shroud laid to rest among the white satin cushioning that lined the box. It was painful to look at Maggie, and most mourners only glanced and then looked quickly away again. None could remember such grief as they saw now in her anguished face and bowed frame.

When Maggie first saw Lucy resting in the coffin, she almost passed out and Sam had to hold her steady. 'Jane,' she whispered. 'She looks just like my twin sister, Jane.' Maggie couldn't stand the strain and, after only a day of visitors, took to her bed. Waves of tears flooded her eyes and she lay washed out and laid waste. Sam fetched and carried for her and made all the funeral arrangements. Rosie took Catherine into her home. Maggie's life came to a standstill.

'Buy yourself something new for the funeral, Maggie. That'll help you to cope with the day,' Sam said as he tried to encourage her back to life from where she was hiding under the bedclothes day after day.

'I can't go. I can't face it,' she wailed. 'I don't care what I look like.' On the day of the funeral, Sam hauled the blankets off her and lifted her bodily from the bed to the chair. She was too limp with depression to resist. 'Come on, lass, you've got to go.' Sam knew the seriousness of what would happen if she were allowed to give in and avoid reality. 'I'll carry you if I have to. You must say

"Goodbye" to the wee one or else you'll never get over her, never really believe that she's gone.'

'All right, I'll go,' Maggie whispered huskily. She knew that Sam was right. She put on her black skirt and long black cardigan, her 'old faithful' that had kept her warm through the last two winters. There was no fine funeral outfit. Downstairs, at Rosie's, Catherine dressed and readied herself, oblivious to her mother's pain. Inside her head was a thick cloudy sensation that she couldn't shake off. Her limbs were made of jelly. Life around her was a bad dream, but there was no waking up.

From somewhere deep inside Sam drew strength. He surprised even himself, but then Sam's solution to worry was to keep busy. He shirked nothing as he worked off his aching heart, dulling the pain with action. Today was the test. They must survive it. Sam half carried, half dragged Maggie from the taxi into the crematorium while Catherine's fingers gripped tightly to the edge of his jacket. Pity was etched on all the neighbours' faces as they watched the bereaved family arrive and walk down the aisle to take their seats at the front. Many sat heads bowed, weeping sympathetically, yet relieved it had happened to someone else and not to them, as they were faced with the grim reminder that they lived every day in the shadow of death.

Reverend Stephen McKimmie took the service. Maggie absorbed only fragments of what he said through the grief. 'The Lord giveth and the Lord taketh away. . .' The tiny white container, buried beneath masses of mourning floral tributes lay on display at the front. The sun streamed in through the stained glass windows and gently fell on the coffin. Through stinging tears, Maggie watched the dust motes dancing in the sunbeam and marvelled to see rainbow colours spread in a canopy above Lucy. It seemed that the angels really were waiting to welcome her child.

The service drew to its conclusion and the organ's dirge filled the air as the coffin sank slowly down and the final curtain drew round it. Maggie stood up, opened her mouth wide and howled, her haunting cry reaching into every corner of the chapel and wrapping itself round every heart. 'I didn't deserve her,' shouted Maggie. 'She's far better off with Jesus in Heaven.'

'We must pull together as a family,' Sam said to Maggie a few weeks after the funeral. He'd just come back from paying the bill at the undertaker's and sat on the edge of the bed, his face haggard and unusually sombre. Recent responsibilities had cultivated in him a maturity that made him seem like a stranger to Maggie who had taken sanctuary again in her bed. However, as Sam spoke to her, even sternly at times, his words began to register like a conscience. 'I can't find the right words to say to you,' he started, 'I never could, but I want us to be able to help each other. We have to come out of the shadows and live again, if not for ourselves, then for Catherine. You know how much I love you, and I'm willing to accept you don't feel the same for me. That's always been the way of it, but I'll do anything for you, Maggie, if only we can stay together.'

Maggie was astounded by this little speech from Sam, her usually reticent husband. She longed to be allowed to wallow endlessly in self-hatred but his words gave her no rest. If Sam was man enough to say such words, then she must equal his drive for survival by facing life's daily grind. 'You're right,' she said, suitably chastened, 'I'm going to try.' And true to her word she emerged next day from where she'd lain brooding. 'There has to be a future for us all,' she said quietly. 'We're still young and Catherine hasn't even started to live yet. We owe it to her, but we must never forget Lucy.' With these words she dressed, brushed her hair and vowed to live everyday life as before.

Chapter 27

Grief drew Maggie and Sam together in a comforting closeness. The wounds of the past began to heal in their newfound friendship, and friendship was all it could be now. Since Lucy's conception they had shared a bed in icy separation, each turned from the other, Maggie flinching if Sam's leg inadvertently brushed hers, repellence more electric than attraction. Only occasional lust brought them together, and afterwards they would pull apart in cold satisfaction. Sam had endured contempt as his punishment and kept hope as his companion. Maggie's own guilt made forgiving Sam easier, but forgiveness for herself was another matter.

The Reverend Stephen McKimmie sat with Maggie at her fireside trying to console her. 'Come to the service on Sunday, Mrs. Taylor,' he said encouragingly. 'Jesus forgives us all. You can't continue with such guilt.'

'I'll try, if only for Catherine's sake,' she answered, wringing her hands and staring at the floor. 'Without her I'm not sure I even want to be alive.'

In church, the minister looked down from the high pulpit at the Sunday faces gathered before him. They looked up expectantly, all seeking answers to their various dilemmas. He spotted Maggie's grey face in a pew near the front. She stared him straight in the eye as if willing some power to manifest itself through him and he looked startled, fearful almost. Did he have it in him? With a little cough, he pushed strands of grey hair back from his forehead and placed his hands on the pulpit to begin the sermon. 'When the human mind has plumbed the depths of despair and self-loathing, and the unbearable future offers nothing but the deep pit of darkness, that is the time when a person will reach out for God's helping hand to lead them.' He paused, stood back and held his own hands heavenwards. 'Fortunate indeed are those who never know the sorrow that brings people to their knees to call out in the wilderness for a cradling love.' He leaned forward and lowered his voice, creating an atmosphere of intimacy.

'Perhaps he really does care after all,' thought Maggie.

'So, I urge you now, take your troubles to Jesus on the cross and lay them at his feet.' The minister's voice trembled with heartfelt emotion.

Maggie knew he was preaching directly to her and felt herself drawn to the words, recognising in them her own desperate quest for comfort and love. In her mind she saw Jesus, bleeding on the cross, and heard His dying words so full of compassion, 'Father, forgive them for they know not what they do.'

Maggie heard the familiar phrase and railed against it. 'But I did know. I knew exactly what I was doing.' She felt like screaming and running out, but the church was no place for her to cause a disturbance. Composing herself, she stood with the others to sing: 'Lay yourself in the Lord's arms, and find safe refuge there . . . '

Scarcely were the first few words out of her mouth than she grew even more pale and swayed as if about to faint. She sat down again on the narrow pew, put her head in her hands and prayed. 'Jesus, Jesus,' she mouthed in a silent whisper, 'what have I done? I tried to kill my little Lucy before she was even born. Surely, even you must despise me. You gave me a wonderful girl and I killed her. O, Jesus, can you ever forgive me this crime? Please help me. I loathe myself.'

Through in the Sunday school class Catherine coloured a picture of Moses crossing the Red Sea. Miss Walker, her primary teacher, also taught Sunday school. Today, they'd had to bring something from home relating to the story of the Exodus. Catherine had brought a small metal toy cow as a reminder of the calves in Joseph's dream. Tommy Paterson had made a whip out of a bamboo cane and a piece of twine to represent the cruelty of the Egyptian overseers.

Little Freddie Tulloch, however, had brought a small grimy bandage complete with safety pin stuck in it. Expecting praise for his participation, Freddie looked hopefully up at Emily Walker who had stationed herself at his side. Her stern face wore a puzzled look. 'What does this represent, Freddie? Where is this mentioned in the story of Moses?' Mockingly, she held up the grubby offering between her thumb and first finger as if it carried some dreadful contagion she would rather do without.

The children avoided each other's eyes. Freddie always had to be different. They longed to laugh, but any tittering could set Miss Walker off in the wrong mood. 'It's a bandage, Miss Walker,' he said in a halting, strangled voice, twisting his sweaty, dirt engrained hands together. All eyes were upon him. Freddie's parents were desperately poor due to the fact that both of them drank. He was turned out to Sunday school unkempt and unfed so that his father could have a lie-in. Everyone knew the situation and felt sorry for him, but the children were also glad to have someone to bear the brunt of their fun on a Sunday.

'Come on, Freddie, speak up,' urged Miss Walker, but her impatient words only added to his nervousness and he opened and closed his mouth like a stranded fish. At last he whimpered in a voice high and apologetic, 'It's a bandage, Miss Walker, from the story. You told us that Moses led his people out of the land of bandage.' He let go the words in a rush to bring his ordeal quickly to an end.

Miss Walker's face was a picture. She breathed deeply through flaring nostrils. Her eyes widened. 'What?' she stammered. 'Bondage, you fool, not bandage. Out of the land of bondage.' She pressed her lips even more tightly together. Her face became increasingly redder. And then – the explosion! Emily Walker erupted in laughter the likes of which the children had never seen or heard before. She trembled and shook. Her loud roars rent the silence of the austere little side room. Her horn-rimmed glasses fell off. Tears flowed down her cheeks streaking the caked on powder and rouge. The children were too overawed to join in. Freddie's jaw hung loosely open in disbelief. Catherine gasped to see the formidable features of the stern teacher contort into a caricature face, the likes of which one might only expect to see on a comic seaside postcard.

Fear controlled the children. They were uncannily quiet. Uncertain smiles played on their lips but came to nothing. Eventually, the laughter subsided and Miss Walker gathered herself. She took a lace handkerchief from the pocket of her suit jacket and patted her face, which was now covered in a pink soup. Red greasy lipstick was smeared round her mouth. No trace of makeup remained round her bleary pink eyes, which peered from deep sockets that were surrounded by heavy wrinkles. Spectacles on again, she surveyed the startled faces. 'I think that's all for today, children,' she declared, regaining some of her former composure. 'Off you go.'

It had been frightening for the children to witness such an unpredictable performance, and, pushing their chairs from them, they escaped with Freddie in the lead, whooping and cheering out through the front door of the church, down the steps and away home for their Sunday roast, Freddie to a plate of spam and chips, if he was lucky. Only one remained behind – Catherine. Laughter had released the cork on her bottled-up emotions, which burst forth now with as much vehemence as her teacher's hysteria. Her body shook as she cried into her arms in much the same way as it had done after the belting in class a few months before. Miss Walker looked on, but offered no comforting touch. 'Don't cry, Catherine?' she said. This was as near to showing compassion as her personality would allow. She stood awkwardly at the side of the large table where Catherine offloaded her grief.

'My sister!' wailed Catherine, her mouth wide open, drooling liquid from the corners of her mouth as she called out through tears and snot and spittle. 'My sister! I miss my little sister!' She put her hands over her eyes. Would life be any better in the dark? 'I didn't mean it, God. I didn't mean for You to take her away.' Her voice grew louder, calling from the depths of her being, from the inner part that knows the real truth of what we want and not the superficial part that reacts to the day-to-day irritations of people around us. 'God, please send her back. I loved my sister. I want my baby sister. I want Lucy now. I've changed my mind.'

Such was the scene that greeted Maggie when she came to fetch her daughter. Maggie narrowed her eyes at Emily Walker. 'What in heaven's name is happening here? Where are the other children? What has *she* been saying to you now? She hasn't hurt you again I hope.' Maggie moved threateningly towards the teacher, fists clenching and eyes blazing, a mother protecting her young. 'And why is your face in such a mess, Miss Walker?'

'No, Mum, no,' Catherine managed to utter between shuddering breaths. 'She hasn't done anything.'

Maggie crouched beside Catherine to soothe her. Miss Walker slipped out without a word, still looking awkward and uncomfortable with her hands up to her face, trying to hide it from view.

'It wasn't her this time,' Catherine reassured her mother. 'Honest. I was only upset because of Lucy.' Maggie asked no more questions but cast a distasteful glance after the departing teacher. 'I don't trust that one,' she said. 'I don't understand why the likes of her is allowed near children. If she ever touches you again, she'll have me to answer to.'

Maggie, after the belting, had complained bitterly to the head teacher, Mr. Bruce, but all her protests had gone unheeded. The head teacher had explained the situation clearly to her. 'It's the law, Mrs. Taylor. Teachers may belt the children but not smack them with their bare hands. Surely you agree we must have discipline in our schools. Miss Walker is a first rate teacher. She's done nothing wrong.' He had stood by the door holding it open. 'Good day, Mrs. Taylor, I have a school to run.' And so it was that Maggie's complaint was dismissed, but she would never forget the purple bruises running from the palms and along the wrists of her young child.

Reverend McKimmie had likewise defended the teacher when Maggie sought his advice. 'She sacrifices her Sundays to teach the children,' he'd said while pouring her a cup of tea in a bone china cup. 'We are privileged to have such dedicated service.' He had continued with his appeasement by offering her a custard cream from a plate of the same pattern as the cup and saucer. 'Emily Walker's severe exterior hides a truly kind heart, believe me.' He'd finished off the proceedings by biting hard into a biscuit, scattering crumbs all over his black robes.

Maggie remembered these excuses, which had done nothing to quell the anger she'd felt. 'I'll be keeping an eye on her,' she muttered, wiping away Catherine's tears and helping her on with her coat. When they'd left home that morning, each still yearned in their grief for God's help. Each had hoped for a sign of Lucy's forgiveness, but instead, each had come face to face with their own self-recrimination, which, for many people, is the true meaning of Hell on this earth.

Chapter 28

Meanwhile, Emily Walker marched, head up, face washed, along the Sunday-still streets to her house in the west end of the city. She closed the heavy front door behind her and headed straight for the bedroom. It was a room like her, dowdy and old fashioned. Brown velvet curtains hung at the north-facing window. The furniture was dark and overbearing. On each piece of furniture lay yellowing lace doilies to protect the polished mahogany from an array of dusty ornaments. A single bed cowered in the corner. From the table beside it rose the tall straight leaves of an aspidistra growing in a large earthenware pot. The clinging smell of lavender polish provided the only perfume in this barren boudoir. On the walls were various faded pictures of dead relatives, some in family groups and others alone, large as life. Their prying eyes followed her every move as if in defiance that even the grave could not make them relinquish control.

Hurriedly Emily drew the curtains. No one must see. This was her secret, her treat. She grinned, baring her teeth up to the gums. There was a spring in her step as she walked over to the portraits and one-by-one turned their prying eyes to the wall. She switched on the bedside lamp which cast only vague shadows round the room. Carefully, she positioned the dressing table mirrors so she could catch sight of herself from every angle.

And then, slowly and deliberately, Emily Walker started to strip, beginning with the mauve and pink heather mixture jacket of her tweed suit and finishing with the pale pink flesh coloured bloomers. Although Emily's vital statistics had barely changed in forty years, the once firm body now sagged with sinewy loose skin covering stick-like bones. As each article of clothing was removed, Emily's yellow-toothed grin grew wider like a turnip lantern grinning through the darkness of a Hallowe'en mist. White saliva crusts cracked at the corners of her mouth.

Coarse textured skin replaced what had once been a flawless

peach cheek and the chic beauty spot had thickened and spread until now, wart like, it sprouted black, wiry hairs. Long grey spirals dangled down from her chin.

Stretching her arm up and round the back of her neck, she released her hair from the bun and let it straggle to her shoulders like teased out string. She posed in the mirror, turning this way and that, swivelling her head to watch her every movement. Her deceptive mind's eye registered a past picture of a youthful girl with burnished-brown tresses that flowed like a shawl round milk-smooth shoulders.

Emily kicked the clothes into a corner and walked over to the wardrobe. She reached into the mothballed recesses and withdrew some dusty boxes, which she placed lovingly on the bed. From the first one she withdrew flimsy undergarments and set them out in front of her on the bed, stroking their softness with her shrivelled fingertips before lifting each one in turn and putting it on. The broderie anglaise brassiere, matching French knickers and suspender belt were incongruous adornments to her withered frame. The pure silk stockings brushed the knots in the veins of her muscular legs. Over her head she slipped a soft satin petticoat which hugged her waist and clung to her hips as she ran her hands up and down her thighs in a meaningful massage.

From the largest box, Emily drew out the once white dress, which was now dingy grey and smelt of mothballs. She held it up against herself and then, with the nervousness of a teenage bride, she stepped delicately into the brocade, which was beautifully patterned with lovebirds and vine leaves. She drew the soft, clinging fabric up over her body whose substance had changed from dewy ripeness to quickening decay. From among flimsy tissue paper came the head dress and veil. Emily pinned them to her hair and, as the soft netting dropped down to the floor, the years fell away. She blushed. From out of a drawer in the dressing table she took a gilt edged portrait, which she gazed at with longing and love. Her groom, a handsome young boy in soldier's

126

uniform, smiled back. She propped him up on the mantelpiece and pulled the veil over her face.

Along from the window, in the corner opposite her bed, lay a gramophone on a small table. Miss Walker ran her hand along and around the curved horn. Holding the contraption steady, she wound its handle till it felt tight and resisting as she grasped it in the palm of her hand. She placed on the turntable the first of two records that she took from a drawer. Emily released the handle and carefully positioned the tone arm on the outer grooves of the revolving disc. The crackling strains of an old bridal march eerily filled the room. In time to the music, Emily glided as gracefully towards the portrait as her stiffened joints would allow. In front of her groom now, she swept back the veil with both hands and with passionate mouth kissed the cold glass lips of the soldier while hot tears pricked her eyes.

With trembling fingers, Emily removed the headdress and walked back to the gramophone and changed the record. Placing the picture of her young man on the pillow of her bed, she lay down on her back among the boxes and rustling papers. Slowly, in time to an increasingly stirring piece of marching music, she pulled up her dress. Cool fingertips stroked her thigh. Up and down they played her, tantalising and tingling. Gently they moved to the soft inner parts of her thigh and her responses grew stronger. Fully aroused now, she touched her paradise part and was lifted and lilted to the ecstasy that only her own gnarled hand could bring her, an act of delight never shared with her one true love. Louder and louder grew the music in rhythmic crescendo till it reached its earth trembling climax. Emily stiffened. 'Quentin! Quentin!' she gasped and then lay breathless and still as the music faltered to its end.

Chapter 29

Maggie and Catherine continued to seek solace each Sunday, until, over the passing years, the fragile threads of self-forgiveness stitched up their wounds, bringing comfort and calm to their souls; and, as self-acceptance eventually triumphed, their original reason for going to church was replaced by habit.

As she no longer had to suffer the tedium of colouring books in Miss Walker's Sunday school class, Catherine now enjoyed the thrust and parry of Bible class discussions. 'You can be proud of Catherine, Maggie,' gushed Sybil Patterson, the Bible class teacher, at the weekly after-service get together. 'She has such original ideas for a girl of fifteen. I can see she'll go far, perhaps into missionary service.'

'Why, thank you, Sybil. That's kind of you to say such a thing,' replied Maggie, offering round the plate of biscuits to the other women who were sharing their table. 'Catherine is making a great success of school; she's in the top class and should qualify for a place at university. No one in either of our families has ever had the chance of an education, although my Uncle Eddie, I must say, was a brilliant man, a great reader, especially the great poets and philosophers. Entirely self-taught he was. And he lived by his principles. When he was only a lad of nineteen, he joined the International Brigade to fight against Franco in the Spanish Civil War, and he was among the first to sign up for the people's war against fascism. In fact, he was fighting in Anzio in Italy when he went missing. If he really did die there, it was a shameful waste of a good life. Now we're banking on Catherine to compensate for all that.'

Maggie's heart burst with pride on these occasions. What she lacked in social status was more than rewarded by the potential success of Catherine, who had already outstripped their cosseted yet academically inferior offspring. Catherine's education would enable her to hold her own in any society. Maggie held the eyes of the women round the table, as if daring them to vent their superiority over her because they had pen-pushing husbands and hers went to sea to catch fish. And as she spoke, they listened, munching on their lemon puffs.

'Hasn't Miss Walker been giving Catherine some coaching?' asked Mary Ogilvie, a sharp faced, yet still pretty, old maid who always shared a table with Maggie. She dusted the crumbs from her skirt into her hand and deposited them onto her floral side plate. 'Just look at the two of them talking together over there by the hatch. And too engrossed in each other to even drink their tea. They are very close.' She put great emphasis on her last two words and repeated them with relish: 'Very close.' She licked biscuit crumbs from her lips, which were heavily lipsticked well beyond the shape of her natural mouth. When she began sipping her tea, with her little finger held daintily out to the side, her eyes smiled wickedly over the top of her cup.

All heads turned, held at a slight angle for hearing better, to watch Catherine and Emily. 'I'm so delighted to be able to help you with that essay,' said Emily to a similarly animated Catherine. Right enough, the charge between them was electric. The teacher clasped her hands together in front of her chest as if in triumph. 'It was from the Ancient Greeks, you know, that we inherited the ideas of democracy. I believe they imported them from North India during the time of Alexander the Great's wide explorations.' She paused and clapped her hands together. 'O dear, just listen to me rambling on. It's so seldom I have the opportunity to share the delights of my studies, that this chat with you has been a rare treat.' The old spinster leaned even closer in towards her companion with an air of intimacy that had never been witnessed before. 'Young people such as yourself are scattered thinly on the ground. You, Catherine, are a rare orchid amongst weeds.'

Miss Ogilvie screwed up her sharp little nose. In spite of

sharing Emily's fate of having lost a promised husband in the nineteen-fourteen to eighteen war, she had retained a birdlike femininity. 'I've always thought Emily strangely masculine, you know what I mean.' She sniffed and tossed her head instead of using the incriminating words that were clearly insinuated. Then she looked Maggie knowingly in the eye and took another sip of tea.

Maggie watched Catherine and Emily together for a moment or two before replying firmly, 'Miss Walker is only helping Catherine with her work. She may be a strange sort of woman, but she is an excellent tutor, and she has many sets of encyclopaediae in her home. She's an inspiration to Catherine and has opened her mind to many experiences.' Maggie hoped she was convincing the others more successfully than she was convincing herself.

Sybil coughed. 'There are some experiences best done without.'

Catherine and Emily were standing over at the hatch now, waiting for the tea they had been too busy to fetch earlier. Doris Goodman, a rather matronly woman, who guarded her position as tea maker more jealously than if she'd been an office bearer of the Scottish Assembly, hurriedly poured them a cup each, pretending she had heard nothing of the gossip about them. Emily and Catherine didn't care anyway; they were too engrossed in matters of ancient history and unaware that everyone was watching. Emily cupped the girl's face in her wrinkled hands. 'You are special, Catherine. You remind me of myself, how I once was many years ago, so eager for life. And your hair, it's beautiful too.' Emily's mind had flashed back to the lustrous haired student she herself had been forty years previously, and she started to caress Catherine's hazel locks fondly.

'Please don't do that,' said Catherine trying to toss her hair out of Emily's searching fingers that were weaving their way through the strands like a spider preparing its web. Catherine was drawn by the teachings but certainly not to the teacher. An instinctive revulsion made her recoil and shudder with disgust. Her loathing

130

of Miss Walker first kindled by the belting of five years ago resurfaced like a firebrand of hatred. It had never really gone out despite the teacher's recent attempts at kindness. Maggie and her table of friends watched Catherine's increasing discomfiture. Emily, however, was lost, entranced in a distant memory. Present loneliness and despair since her retirement had caused memories of past joy to register as if being experienced in the present. Catherine stepped backwards. 'Don't do that!' Her shrill voice vibrated clearly across the thin air of the sparsely furnished hall to the ears of the tea drinkers that were thirsty for scandal. She shook her hair free and reached into her shoulder bag for a brush, which she pulled through her hair fiercely to remove all trace of Emily's touch.

Maggie was beside them in an instant. 'What do you think you're doing, Miss Walker? Leave my daughter alone!' She shoved her away from Catherine. 'Can't you see she doesn't like you touching her?'

Emily managed to catch her balance and took a step forward, this time into the present. 'I'm sorry,' she said, 'I forgot myself.' Her voice was soft, even womanly.

'It's all right, Mum,' said Catherine sharply in embarrassment, aware that she was caught in the middle of a scene. 'Why does everyone have to stare as if I were a freak show? Why do you have to draw attention to me all the time?' She marched over to an empty table, which was neither Emily's nor her mother's, and sat clear away by herself, arms folded.

All eyes were on her; eyes that longed to see trouble. Maggie walked gingerly, almost on tiptoe, over to her daughter. 'Was she annoying you?' Maggie spoke in a cautious whisper, sensing Catherine's need to hide away. Catherine said nothing, so Maggie dared to sit down beside her, all the time keeping a watchful eye on Emily. Catherine looked round the onlookers and the memory of that past occasion when she and Miss Walker had similarly captivated an audience sprang vividly to mind. She felt pain in her hands and fear in her guts. She looked up at Maggie who drew her close, like a mother hen protecting her chick with its wing. 'Yes, Mum,' she said in a quiet voice, 'she is annoying me. I don't like her touching me. I asked her to stop but she wouldn't.' The long awaited moment of retribution had arrived and Catherine was ready to make a meal of it.

'Well, what have you to say for yourself?' Maggie demanded. 'Why were you touching my daughter in such a personal way? She's only a child. You ought to know better.'

'I don't know why you're making such a fuss,' Emily replied innocently, not quite grasping the grave implications of the accusation. 'I was only admiring her hair and telling her how beautiful she is.' She looked fondly at Catherine, naively unaware that she was making her situation worse. The watching women pursed their lips and exchanged glances. Maggie marched Catherine towards the minister who had been standing by the hall door talking to a group of male elders, quite oblivious to the unfolding drama. Maggie made no effort to keep her voice down. 'Come with me, Catherine. Reverend McKimmie must hear about this. He can sort it out.' Taken completely by surprise, the confused minister blurted an excuse to his fellow churchmen and led Catherine and her mother into the vestry.

'I don't understand what's happening,' he whined.

'Miss Walker's been making unwanted advances to my daughter,' explained Maggie, and she recounted the events as she'd seen them. Catherine stood by and said nothing, incriminating Emily with her silence. 'This isn't the first time I've had cause to complain about that, ahem, woman,' Maggie argued. 'I want something done.' The others who were only too willing to act for the prosecution were called in one-by-one.

Once all the testimonies had been heard, Miss Walker was sent for. 'I don't know what I've done wrong,' she protested. She turned her eyes continually towards her protégée, pleading with her to utter some words in her defence, some proof of her innocence. The only response was a fixed glare of utter contempt. The minister watched their exchange closely. 'Have you anything to add, Miss Walker?'

'It's my opinion that jealousy is at the root of the problem,' declared Emily, her voice growing stronger. 'Mrs. Taylor is angry simply because I can do something for her daughter that she can't do herself.'

Maggie's hackles rose. The minister held up his hand like a traffic policeman. He was trembling. This was a far more serious argument than the regular rows over whose turn it was to put flowers in the church. 'Ladies, please,' he squeaked, 'you mustn't fight.' He rubbed his chin thoughtfully. 'I really must sit down.' He lowered himself into a high-backed, brown leather chair, a reluctant judge. He closed his eyes, the loose puckered skin of his eyelids twitched. The three women were silent, though their eyes collided in unrestrained battle as they waited for the verdict. At length he looked at them. Had contemplation led to enlightenment? What wise words were they about to hear? He squashed his lips together, turning them inwards to make a straight line of his mouth before unrolling them again and licking them as he prepared to give his verdict. 'Miss Walker,' he said, his voice quavering, 'it is with the deepest regret that I must ask you to forfeit your duties as Sunday school teacher. We are all truly grateful for your faithful service over the years, but perhaps now it might be better for all concerned if you have a well-deserved rest and leave. I hope you will continue to attend church, and, in your day-to-day activities, reap the benefits of a religious life.'

He wasn't guided by insight. His main concern was for his own survival, and that was best achieved by his congregation viewing him as someone who would always try to please them. Nerves made the sinews in his neck stand out in thick cords, causing his dog collar to rise and fall as he spoke. He pulled at it desperately, trying to loosen its tightening grip, but his neck bulged increasingly redder and fatter above it. Never before had he made such a

133

speech. He wiped his sweating hands furiously with his handkerchief and struggled to his feet. He placed a damp hand on Emily's back, just above the waist, and ushered her out. She walked quickly away, head hanging in defeat, out of the hall and out of the church. Catherine's head was held high, her eyes shining victoriously as she watched the beaten old teacher's wretched retreat.

'That's the last we'll be seeing of her,' said Mary Ogilvie with a detectable note of glee in her voice as she and her friends rushed to gather Maggie and Catherine to the bosom of the group. Although once beautiful, Mary had always been jealous of Emily's brains, which she knew would continue to shine long after her own assets had faded. 'Who does Emily think she is?' and 'How dare she hold court with the young folk!' had been frequent thoughts of hers over the years, but instead of revealing her dark side, she turned to Catherine and asked with treacly sweetness, 'And how are you my dear? I hope you're none the worse for your dreadful ordeal. Always remember you have us to support you at any time.' However, she couldn't stop a gleeful smile from playing on her lips as she looked towards the door and murmured more to herself than to her companions, 'I wonder what Emily will do now.'

'Thank you all so much. I really appreciate how you've all helped me today,' said Catherine halfheartedly. She wasn't looking at them however. Her eyes too were fixed on the door that Emily's slumped figure had disappeared through. In only a few minutes her expression had changed from someone flushed with the glory of just revenge to someone nauseated by their own behaviour. She looked pale as if it had been herself that had been shamed. 'Let's go home now, Mum, I want to rest,' she said quietly.

Chapter 30

Emily Walker never showed her face in church again, and many were the rumours that flew thick and fast among her curious erstwhile friends. However, one warm Sunday morning, after an absence of several weeks, her true fate was announced to all and sundry as the church bells rang out to summon good Christian folk to worship. It was Miss Ogilvie, at the top of the church steps, who addressed the congregation as they arrived for the morning service. Standing with regal poise before the gathered crowd, her head tilted to one side, she began: 'Well, I thought I'd better pay Emily a visit.' She held out her hands like a gospel preacher reaching for new converts as her shrill voice continued to cut sharply through the crisp Sunday morning air. She spoke with great gusto, revelling in the rapt attention of a crowd gathered to listen intently to what she, Mary Ogilvie, had to say. 'I was concerned for her, you see; after all she was, ahem, my friend. I went to her house, but when I knocked I got no answer. The curtains were drawn and the place was in darkness. I rang the bell but there was no answer. I was so worried that I tried the door handle. It wasn't locked, so I went in and called to Emily, but still no reply. I crept slowly in, afraid of what I might find.' Miss Ogilvie paused and looked round her eager audience. Slowly, in the same way that she sucked pandrops, letting them dissolve gradually to release a steady flow of peppermint succulence, so she tantalised the crowd with snippets that titillated their taste for gossip and whetted their appetite for more.

'Go on, Miss Ogilvie, tell us what happened. How was poor Emily?' called Mr. Petrie, the choirmaster, licking his lips. 'We're all waiting.'

The speech giver continued in a voice that was tremulous with excitement. 'Emily wasn't in the living room so I carried on through to the kitchen. Well, you'll never guess what I saw there . . .' She paused for effect. As every skilled orator knows, it is the

135

silence between words that lends emphasis to a speech. Mary Ogilvie was a past master at turning any tale into an epic.

'Yes, hurry up, get on with it,' urged Sybil Patterson who knew what was coming, but was nonetheless impatient to see the reaction on the faces of the listeners.

'Well,' said Miss Ogilvie in a hushed voice that let it be known they were about to be shocked, 'you won't believe it, but this is what I saw.' She cleared her throat and like a once-upon-a-time storyteller promising magic, began her story: 'Are you listening carefully, then, I'll tell you. I went through to the kitchen, and there she was, sitting at the table with the light out. And she was wearing ... she was wearing a ... wedding dress, yes, a wedding dress...' A hush fell over the crowd. Nobody spoke. Nobody asked any questions. They didn't want any interruption to spoil the story. Satisfied she had them enthralled, Mary continued. 'And the dress, it was filthy, all spilled on with tea stains, jam and green juice from the peas she was eating – straight from the tin with a spoon! It was a terrible sight. Really it was. The tea in the teapot was stone cold and that's what she was drinking. There was green mould growing on bits of stale bread that lay scattered on the table, and slices of cold ham had turned black, all curled at the edges. I don't know how long she'd been like that. It might have been weeks. I phoned Reverend McKimmie right away and he sent for the doctor. Poor, poor Emily!'

'Poor, poor Emily,' the audience repeated.

Mary took up the tale again, wringing her hands and shaking her head. 'I said to her, "Just sit there quietly, my dear. I'm here to help you."' There was a catch in Mary Ogilvie's voice and she wiped a tear from her eye. 'Poor, dear Emily looked up and said to me, "I'm so glad to see the face of a friend."' Her voice quivered, and she allowed herself to dissolve into tears. The choirmaster rushed to her aid and put his long, snakelike arm round her waist to steady her, and gave her a comforting squeeze with his dry, bony fingers. Mary leaned into him for support and closed her eyes, giving a gentle sigh as if the whole procedure had been too much for her mild disposition.

The gasps from the crowd sounded just as shocked as Sybil Patterson had imagined they would. Silence had turned to clamour. Everyone was asking Mary questions at once. Through the cacophony of voices filtered a repetition of certain words: 'white coats, asylum, taken away'. On the steps of the Sunday morning church was a scene more akin to a rabble in riot than worshippers in reverence.

Enraged, Stephen McKimmie swooped out of the door in his black robes, appearing more like the Angel of Death than a good shepherd. Frantically, he waved his arms like a windmill and bellowed above the turmoil, struggling to gain the attention of his flock as he called them to prayer. Red in the face with embarrassment, he kept looking from side to side along the street to check just how many passersby had witnessed this shameful display. 'Quiet please, the service is about to start!' he proclaimed, holding his hands to his mouth like a megaphone to make his voice carry better, as if advertising a fairground sideshow. 'Come in! Come in! There's a welcome here for everyone!'

Amid the sea of heads in the unusually packed church, there were two spaces in the pew where Catherine and Maggie always sat. One by one, the congregation glanced over and then quickly averted their gaze before starting to rummage in pockets and handbags for lozenges and mint sweets, although today, this latest snippet of tasty gossip would be sufficient to stop them from dropping off to sleep in their rows.

Reverend McKimmie took his place in the high pulpit. He cleared his throat and began: 'The theme of today's sermon is the Good Samaritan.' The wavering voice of the minister struggled to achieve its usual resonance that normally rose like a brisk wind into the high hollows of the church. As he spoke, his eyes scoured the many heads which were now bowed in temporary repentance. 'A man went down from Jerusalem to Jericho. It was a robber's road. And, just as our lives are, it too was fraught with many dangers. Indeed, on the path we all travel, our chances of meeting kindness on the way are rather slim.'

The congregation sucked hard on their sweets and some even had the good grace to fidget uncomfortably in their hard, narrow pews. The minister continued to scan the faces with penetrating eyes as he expounded on the kindness of the Samaritan and denounced the hypocrisy of the priest. Miss Ogilvie's face drew in on itself with guilt, like a crumpling soft leather glove, but she had to keep up the pretence of considering herself a good Samaritan? She sniffed, feigning grief, and daintily wiped the tears from her eyes with an embroidered lace handkerchief.

Chapter 31

Catherine sat on the landing steps. She needed space to think away from her parents' quarrelling voices. 'No, I'm not going to church to face that mob of judges!' shouted Maggie, her voice rising loudly through the closed door of the flat. Sam's voice echoed back, 'You have nothing to be ashamed of. That Walker woman was making advances on our Catherine for God's sake. You were right to complain.'

'But she was ill and now she's in the mental hospital. Just because she's an old maid doesn't mean she's after girls,' came Maggie's reply. 'All she did was stroke Catherine's hair, but in the light of what's happened, maybe we were too condemning. I wish now that I'd turned a blind eye.'

'I don't understand you. How do you know she was innocent? Surely Catherine's worth more to you than to risk chancing her safety with a bloody pervert.'

'But,' continued Maggie, 'if she did have on a wedding dress surely she must have been normal. Would she really be after young girls if she'd once been getting married? I never intended for her to end up like this.' Maggie was drawn to justice rather than judgement in the aftermath of Emily Walker's incarceration in an asylum.

'You've changed your tune. You were all for calling the Police only a few weeks ago and now you're feeling pangs of guilt. You can't carry the can for her state of mind. How were you to know?' shouted Sam. 'It's guilt that made you go there on a Sunday anyway! You never went to church all that regularly before you had Lucy. Now this has happened it's resurrected all your black thoughts. You went calling on God over your last mistake, and now it seems you can't face Him over this one.'

Sam's brutal words hit home and Maggie reacted with venom in her tongue. 'Look, Sam, you especially of all people know nothing about how I feel. I could go out into the street and find a

139

stranger who would understand me better. What's it to you anyway, you that's no better than a heathen? Apart from Catherine, God is all I have now.'

'Oh yes, turn it round against me as usual. You live so much in the past that God's the only one you can talk to any more. Come down to earth, Maggie, from your ivory tower of superiority. You're a human being like the rest of us and you get things wrong. So what! All that Bible bashing won't help. You're just as bitter and twisted as that Emily Walker!' Sam railed against his wife's rejection with the painful arrows of plain truth.

'You're a bastard, Sam. You always have been. A worthwhile husband would sympathise. You know fine I wouldn't have come through without God's help. It's certainly no thanks to you.'

'O yes, blame me since you seem incapable of carrying your own blame. Look, Maggie, you did nothing wrong. Forget Miss bloody Walker! Forget Lucy!' He picked up the Sunday paper that lay on the floor beside his chair and shook it out and began to read. 'There's less trouble in the rest of the bloody world than there is in here with you. Why can't we have any peace?'

'Peace!' roared Maggie. 'You're a fine one to speak about peace. You keep such a close eye on Catherine these days that you're always causing rows with her. You're on her top at every turn. What she says. What she wears. What she eats. Let the girl grow up. She's fifteen for God's sake.' Maggie rattled the pans under the sink and crashed them one after another on to the cooker ready for preparing Sunday dinner. Some baking trays clattered as they fell on top of each other crashing and scraping. Maggie made no effort to stop them.

The back of Sam's neck went rigid with annoyance. He put the paper down on his knee. 'For the love of God, what's happening? It sounds as if all Hell has been let loose.' He strode angrily to the cupboard and poured himself a bottle of beer.

'That's right,' shouted Maggie, 'turn to drink. That'll solve everything, and I don't think.' She hurled some potatoes at his

140

head. Sam ducked and held his newspaper up as a shield. She threw another potato, harder this time. He stopped it deftly with his right hand just before it struck the shepherdess figurine on the mantelpiece. 'Howzat!' he shouted and threw the potato back. Maggie caught it, and in spite of the argument, turned away to stifle a laugh. Sam glanced over at his wife. In spite of his frustration he did appreciate just how fragile she could become in such situations, and added in a much softer tone, 'Forget the funny looks and the wagging tongues, Maggie, you're a good woman, one of the best.'

His words made Maggie catch her breath. 'What is it about him that sometimes I just want to throw myself into his arms even though I can't stand him the rest of the time?' she thought. As she agonised over this inner conflict, she pared the remaining potatoes so fast that her hands blurred in her vision. Sam sat in silence, supping his beer and shaking his head at the latest news.

Catherine meantime leaned against the hard wrought iron banisters. Her eyes were shut and she had her hands over her ears. 'Why can't you two shut up once in a while!' she screamed up at the door, but nobody heard her through their own shouting. 'I've had enough. I'm going out and I don't know when I'll be back.' As she ran downstairs she bumped into Jimmy Simpson coming out of his flat. 'Steady on there, you'll have me over,' he laughed, enjoying the unexpected physical contact. 'Not at church today?'

'Don't you start. You know perfectly well what's happened,' retorted Catherine, brushing herself down to get rid of the contamination of their brief touch. 'You enjoy seeing me suffer and you're only fishing for more details. Why doesn't everybody just shut up?'

'You're looking attractive today. I like polka dots.' He cast an appreciative glance at her dress.

'Now you're patronising me. Leave me alone.'

'Fancy a walk in the park? Take your mind off things,' suggested Jimmy seizing a long sought after opportunity to have

Catherine spend some time with him.

'All right then. I could do with some fresh air,' she answered. She wiped away the salt tears from her face but the scowl remained.

'I was only going round to see my mate, Stan, but he can wait.'

They set off along the street in the direction of the park, side by side, but with a safe distance between them. 'See that Miss Walker? She deserves everything coming to her,' said Catherine, still sniffing but no longer crying. 'She's a cruel bitch. I don't care what happens to her.'

'If you ask me, I think you do care. That's what's eating you up. That's why you're so angry. You thought you'd get even but it's all gone too far.' Jimmy stopped walking and turned towards her with a smug smile.

'Well, Jimmy Simpson, I'm not asking you. And anyway, you've got me all wrong.' However, Catherine did look startled. She too had stopped walking, but she quickly hurried on as if to escape his words. Surely Jimmy didn't know her so well that could read her so accurately.

'I remember what you said to me years ago when she belted you,' Jimmy continued, adhering strongly to his theory. 'You swore revenge then, and now that you have it, you're not finding it quite as sweet as you anticipated.'

And even as they spoke, events were running their course in the mental hospital. An emaciated, terror-stricken woman was being dragged from where she cowered in a corner of her grey cell-like room by two muscular men in white coats. 'Just come along with us, Emily. It's for your own good,' snapped the nurse, a thick set woman with black bushy eyebrows. The attendants twisted her arms up her back and forced her struggling on to a trolley. Whimpers escaped her slavering mouth as they wheeled her in the direction of the theatre. 'Help me. I haven't done anything wrong. Please help me.'

Screams filled the air in the theatre of the asylum until they managed to force a gag into her mouth and a grey haired doctor attached electrodes to the shaved parts of Emily Walker's head. He pulled a small lever on a complicated machine that had wires coming out of it in every direction and stepped back quickly as the contraption whirred into action. The electricity jolted forth from it and along the wires to attack the tissues of Emily's brain with wave after wave of punishment. Convulsions shook her bony body and then she lay still, a twisted grimace on her face. The two attendants, one at her head and one at her feet, slung Emily back on to the hard metal trolley with no more concern than if she had been a sack of potatoes. 'Now then, my dear,' wheedled the nurse, 'that wasn't so bad after all, was it?' Emily stared back at her with eyes that were as blank now as her innermost soul. There was no utterance from her squint mouth.

In the warm, soothing sunshine, Catherine and Jimmy sat silently on an ornamental park bench among the perfumed roses. Courting couples wandered hand-in-hand, and families enjoyed a peaceful Sunday stroll. 'I wonder where she is now,' said Jimmy, desperate to break the silence. 'Maybe she wasn't that bad. After all, I thought you were glad she was helping you with your school work.'

'You're worse than my mother!' shouted Catherine, getting to her feet. 'Emily Walker will get all the help she needs in hospital. Anyway, it's too late to worry about her now.' She turned on her heel and ran off to the other side of the park to be by herself.

Jimmy shrugged. 'I give up,' he said with a shrug of his shoulders. 'I'm off round to Stan's.'

Chapter 32

(Aberdeen, June 1965)

Success for the Taylor family was measured in Catherine's test results at school. It was their raison d'être. Catherine studied, Maggie encouraged and Sam worked. Maggie's own missed opportunities would be more than compensated for in Catherine who had blossomed like a forced flower in a greenhouse and her destiny, a clearly mapped out journey, smooth and fruitful, apparently lay before her for the taking.

'Lord, please guide us on our way . . .' The voices of the sixth year rose joyfully into the ceremonial atmosphere of the assembly hall in Highfield Senior School for Girls. It was the final day for Catherine and her fellow students. The head teacher, Miss Groves, sent them into the future with an uplifting speech full of hope and aspiration. They were top drawer, privileged, prepared. The world was truly their oyster but would they harvest its pearls or merely be swine?

Many of the young hopefuls did not view the ceremony in quite the same serious vein as Miss Groves, their mentor for six years. They couldn't wait to escape the confines of school life. The hedonistic lures of adulthood, like fat juicy bait, attracted them and, once hooked, reeled them in like so many young fry, and lifted them out of the safety of a well cared for pond and placed them in the limitless sea of adventure and danger. Academic and spiritual practices held no great appeal in comparison.

An hour later and the farewell ceremony completed, some of the girls were chatting in the toilets. Joyce Baxter, her voice shaking with excitement, was doing her best to urge Catherine to join them for a night out on the town the following Saturday. 'You must come! It'll be such fun. You're not a school kid anymore and everyone's coming. It may be the last time we'll ever be together.' Joyce's pretty schoolgirl face now looked ghostly under the heavy coating of pan stick and pale, almost white lipstick and, as she spoke, she applied numerous coats of black mascara to her long eyelashes. She always said that eight were necessary to have the desired effect. Already she looked as if twin spiders had settled where her eyes had once been.

'Enjoy yourself for once, Catherine. Come with us,' she continued, rubbing her lips together and pouting into the mirror. Catherine continued to brush her hair, uninterested. Joyce glanced round at her friends who nodded her on to persevere with her persuasion. 'We're having a night out at the Bosun's Locker. A live band plays there so we can have a dance too.' Catherine found this group boring. They had no interest in anything but makeup and nail varnish. Envious eyes watched Catherine's long dark curls stretch and coil as she brushed them. 'It's not really my scene,' she answered, rolling a long length of soft, scented hair in her hand to make it smooth.

The girls wrinkled their noses in mock disappointment. 'Don't be like that,' they whinged. 'It won't be the same without you. You must come.'

'I'll think about it. Where exactly are you going?' Casually, Catherine flicked her hair out of her eyes and put the brush back in her bag.

'The Bosun's Locker. It's down by the harbour just along from the tattooist. It's the in-place to go; but we're meeting up first at the Duchess Café so we can all go down together. We're making a real night of it.' Joyce put a clingy arm round Catherine and smiled at her in the mirror. She genuinely thought this night out was the be-all and end-all of growing up.

'There's a late licence till eleven,' added June Dawson, a tall spindly girl who was fumbling under her blouse to adjust the cotton wool padding in her otherwise empty bra. 'They serve stovies too. You'll really enjoy yourself. Everybody goes there.'

'And it has a juke box! You can choose any pop song you want till the band comes on,' Shirley Sangster added jubilantly. 'It's going to be a fab night. Such a change from this boring place.' She jumped up and down with excitement just as a child might do before a party, her heavy bust bouncing out of control inside her school blouse like two excited puppies rolling around at play.

Although endless discussions about lipstick and pan stick left her cold, Catherine wanted to try something new. Her father didn't like her going anywhere. He was restricting her life. Why not give this place a try? What could she lose? 'All right, you've convinced me. See you all seven o'clock in the Duchess next Saturday,' she called, trying to sound happier than she really felt as she left her acquaintances to their giggling gossip. Catherine had no interests in common with these girls, but she would be meeting them again at university and it could be advantageous, or so she thought, to have their friendship, at least in the early days, until she made new friends of her own kind.

Going to university filled her with paralysing apprehension. Miss Walker's caustic comments of earlier years about her being working class were still etched deep into her psyche. She always had to prove herself worthy of her education. Among neighbours too she stood out as being different but for the opposite reason. Not one of them or anyone they knew had ever studied. She no longer felt she was accepted anywhere. The youngsters she had grown up with had already started work, even Jimmy, who was now an apprentice welder. She was desperate to fit in somewhere, somehow and make a way of life for herself.

Why did her parents, her mother especially, always want her to better herself? Everyone else was allowed to live contentedly where they were and seemed to have happy, carefree lives. 'Why can't I be the same?' she kept thinking. 'What is it about me that I don't feel entitled to have a good time? Will it be any different now I've left school?' Her stomach started doing cartwheels and bile rose in her throat as her mind raced, full of trepidation about the future. She walked slowly from the cosy sanctuary of the girls' toilets and through the dark building, savouring for the last time the stuffy familiarity of the senior secondary that had been central to her life for six years. The empty corridors seemed to echo with ghostly voices from the past, and when she reached the front entrance she hesitated; but she must be brave. She swung the heavy door open and took her first shaky steps into the waiting world – a schoolgirl no longer.

The coven had fallen about themselves laughing as soon as Catherine was safely out of earshot. 'I can't wait to see Miss Brain-box drunk,' shrieked Joyce maliciously. 'She's too full of herself by far.'

'I know, and her father's only a trawlerman,' sneered Shirley. 'I can't wait to see her brought down a peg or two.'

Chapter 33

Their progress on the housing list had slowed almost to a halt. The post-war baby boom had meant there were many more people wanting houses and they were being allocated to families with two or more children of different sexes. Even if Lucy had lived, their position would be no different. There were always people with bigger families adding to it, so they faced years of waiting. Maggie had long since given up her plans to leave Sam. She didn't want to leave him now she could trust him never to gamble and even more importantly, she respected him. There was no denying he had been a tower of strength even if at times they had had their differences. There was a genuine fondness between them that had strengthened over their years of struggle.

Maggie kept their names on the council housing list, but decided that it might be possible one day to buy a little house and had taken a part time job, hoping to make it full-time once Catherine left school. Even if it took years, paying up a mortgage on a little place of their own was a possibility worth considering, and it did at least provide her with the hope she needed to keep going.

She had allowed herself to spend some money on updating their flat, but these improvements were only intended as a stopgap until her dream of a lovely home was fulfilled. As she helped Catherine to prepare for her first ever night out, Maggie had feelings of optimism she hadn't experienced since the days before her marriage. Life was taking off again.

'You look just fine,' she said, admiring Catherine in the chiffon blouse and mohair skirt she'd chosen.

'It's far too short,' Sam interjected, interrupting the woman-to-woman exchange that was disturbing his sports programme on the new television set.

'You get back to the box, square eyes,' Maggie said dismissively. 'What do you know about modern fashion in your boots and big jerseys?'

'I know enough about life to know that Catherine's clothes could be longer,' he said, defending his stance while pulling his chair closer to the screen. 'Where are you going anyway?' he snapped, concern bringing sharpness to his voice.

'We're meeting at the Duchess Café and then going on to that new Chinese restaurant along from it,' replied Catherine who felt quite comfortable to be able to tell at least half the truth. 'You can get a meal there for four and six.' She added this last snippet for good measure in order to lend authenticity to her words.

'I wouldn't pay one and six for it. The Chinese eat dogs and cats you know. With all that curry, how can you taste the difference between seagull and chicken?'

Catherine glared at her father. 'Sarcasm doesn't suit you, Dad. Why can't you move with the times? You're so narrow-minded. The Chinese civilisation is one of the oldest in the world. They could teach us a thing or two. They lived in cities with beautiful architecture when we were still living in caves. Who knows, they might even be able to civilise you out of sitting around the house in that god awful string vest.'

'I would like to know why it's so important to be modern anyway,' he retorted. 'I'm all right as I am. I don't need to change. And as for string vests, they're a new invention and ultra scientific. The holes trap air and so they are more efficient at keeping you warm than even wool.' A smile crossed his previously angry face. He enjoyed a banter with his daughter.

'Leave her alone, Sam, and don't make excuses. Admit it, you're just old-fashioned.' Maggie was poring over the TV listings in search of a programme other than sport. 'You're happy in your old underwear in the same way a pig's happy in muck.'

'I'll tell you what's not new or modern,' he replied, 'and that's the fact that girls going out half-naked and covered in makeup will draw the same looks and put the same ideas in men's heads as they've always done since time began. You'll have to castrate the

149

whole male population before women can expect to tease them and escape untouched. I don't want a daughter of mine getting into trouble, that's all.'

'Are you trying to say that our Catherine isn't decent? Take back these filthy words, Sam Taylor! It's you that's got a dirty mind,' said Maggie, turning round to face Sam hands on hips, her face colouring.

'Will you two stop it? It's like living with children,' begged Catherine, squinting into the mirror above the fireplace to apply more eye shadow. 'Why can't you have a quiet conversation?' Catherine was really angry now, no longer arguing for fun. 'I can't wait to get away from here!' She picked up her new leather jacket and handbag and stormed out without a goodbye. Sam turned to the back page of the evening paper. Maggie marched over to the television set and changed channels to a pop show.

'Hey, I was watching the highlights,' shouted Sam.

'Get back to your paper and leave me in peace,' quipped Maggie as she flicked the centre of the wide spreading paper with her fingernail and made it fall out of his hands into a muddle on his knee. They looked at each other momentarily, and just managed to stop themselves from laughing as the tension between them eased with the letting off of some steam.

'Do you fancy some sweetheart stout?' asked Sam noticing the softening of his wife's eyes. 'I think I'll stay in tonight and just have a couple of bottles here by the fireside with you. I've been feeling tired lately, and I've got indigestion from that pie supper from the chip shop.'

'You're always getting indigestion these days,' answered Maggie. 'You should try chewing your food more thoroughly instead of gulping it down like a hungry bear.'

'Never mind me and my manners. Hurry up with the glasses.' Sam put away the paper and settled down for a night in with his wife.

'It'll be nice to relax just the two of us,' said Maggie. 'We'll have to get used to each other's company now that Catherine's growing up.'

Chapter 34

The three witches, Joyce, June and Shirley were waiting in the Duchess Café as arranged. Along with them were two other former classmates, Brenda and Shona. Brenda, because of her teeth braces, was a welcome member of the gathering as was Shona with her thick spectacles. Their unattractiveness enhanced the average looks of the main players in the group. It was not surprising, therefore, that their faces fell as a radiant Catherine arrived. 'I didn't know you had a leather coat,' said Joyce, the self-appointed leader of the pack. She scowled and added, 'I've never seen one in red before.' She had meant this last comment as a put down but her eyes held an unmistakably envious look.

'My parents bought it for me for passing my exams,' Catherine replied with a smile. 'My goodness, doesn't everyone look terrific,' she added cheerfully.

'What's that smell of fish?' Joyce asked. Her voice was serious but her eyes twinkled with malice. Everyone started laughing. Catherine said nothing but the muscles of her jaw tightened. Had she made a mistake in trusting them as friends?

They gulped down their espressos and headed for the harbour. Their stilettos clacked on the cobbles of the quayside and their squealing voices blended with the cries of greedy seagulls that circled the ships and trawlers berthed for the weekend. Wolf whistles followed them from the men that lurked among the ropes, nets and mysterious machinery that cluttered their decks.

At the door of the Bosun's Locker, the girls stopped to straighten their clothes and preen their hair. They giggled and pushed at each other. Since no-one wanted to be conspicuous by being first, they rolled through the swing door as one, a tangled mass of legs, high heels, mini-skirts and hair. 'In you come, girls,' the catcalls greeted them. The jukebox was playing a popular rock 'n' roll number. A grossly overweight man who would have benefited from an encounter with some soap and water and a razor blade danced solo in the middle of the floor among the tables. His long, lank hair was plastered with drips of sweat to his forehead, face and neck. All the while, as he gyrated his hips, he fondled the layers of fat that bulged under a tight blue woollen jumper in such a way, that from behind, it looked as if he had a partner caressing him.

'Come on, darling, give's a dance,' he said grabbing hold of Catherine and squeezing her to him, his hand planked firmly across her buttocks.

'Leave off, will you?' she cried, pushing him back so that he stumbled against the jukebox. Her friends looked on in relief that he hadn't picked on them. The old lothario struggled to regain his balance and smoothed his greasy hair back from his eyes that peered piggy-like from eyelids that were puffed up from drink. 'Oh, pardon me, Miss Hoity Toity,' he sneered. 'Better get the crystal out tonight, Harry,' he called to the barman, 'Royalty's arrived.'

'Leave the girls alone, Mike, and sit down,' said Harry. He turned to the girls. 'Sorry 'bout that, girls. Never mind Mike, he's harmless. Now, what would you lovely young ladies like to drink?'

They put in their orders for an assortment of cocktails and spirits. Catherine asked for a ginger beer. 'For God's sake, Catherine, loosen up will you,' exclaimed Joyce. 'Have a vodka and lemonade. You'll like it, I promise.'

Catherine, still shaking from her encounter with the dancing man, allowed herself to be persuaded. Tentatively, she took a sip of the clear liquid as she and her companions walked over to an empty table near to the Ladies. They pulled up two chairs so the six of them could sit together. A group of young men sat in the corner next to them. 'They're medical students,' said June. 'You can tell that from the colours on their scarves.'

Joyce stared at the young lads and spoke loudly to attract their attention. 'I see the Twotones are singing here tonight. They're brilliant. A local couple, Marian and Allan and they sing all the latest hits.' She looked around knowingly and grinned over to the next table as if expecting their admiration, but the young men carried on drinking with scarcely a glance her way.

'They're obviously school girls on a night out. We don't want to get involved with that sort,' whispered one, a red-haired stocky lad called Charlie.

'Isn't that exactly what we do want? Teach them a thing or two,' came the response from his curly haired friend, Norman, sitting directly opposite who was leering over at the girls.

'Schoolgirls spell trouble if you ask me,' opined a third, a fox-like character, called Steve, who, all the while he was drawing on his cigarette, looked past the girls at a dusky beauty of about thirty whose husband was at the Gents. The last of the group followed his friend's gaze and allowed his eyes to linger lazily on the married woman's shapely legs, which crossed and uncrossed impatiently, causing her short black skirt to ride up and reveal the tops of sheer black stockings. He was a tall, dark-eyed chap called Gregor whose straight black hair flopped over his brow, and, although he continually tried to brush it back with his hand, it kept falling down again. 'You should try hair cream like me,' suggested Charlie whose hair, which was thick with grease, had been shaped into a sharp quiff sticking out from his forehead like the peak of a cap.

Gregor laughed. 'No thank you,' he quipped, 'I like my hair to feel free, not clogged up and sticky. There's enough oil on your head to open a chip shop.' The students all laughed. They were enjoying themselves, light hearted and carefree. 'Real women enjoy running their hands through a man's hair, and that's what I call a real woman.' Gregor indicated with a quick nod of his head the seductive beauty whose hair swung over her face mysteriously. 'I want nothing to do with them,' he said, looking back in the direction of the giggling girls. 'The one in the mohair skirt is quite fanciable but she's still a kid. I'd rather tango with someone who's got a bit of experience behind them. Don't want some little girl

154

bursting into tears as soon as I try to kiss her.' They turned to watch the recent schoolgirls who were singing along with the music from the jukebox, swaying in their seats and snapping their fingers. Shirley stopped every four or five clicks in order to hitch up her huge bust which jiggled out of control under a clinging black sweater, a cardigan worn fashionably back to front.

'Things are beginning to liven up at last,' commented Norman with a smirk. He fingered his almost empty pint glass as he observed every movement of Shirley's unruly breasts with concentrated interest. Gregor had resumed his study of the beautiful woman's thighs until her muscular husband returned from the Gents and gave him a warning look and moved his head forwards and downwards as if demonstrating what to expect if he didn't back off. 'I'm heading up to the dance at the Students' Union shortly,' Gregor said loudly as if to appease the jealous husband. 'This joint isn't really my scene.' Lowering his voice, he informed his companions, 'There's a smell of fighting in the air. Don't want to end the night with a glass in my face.'

The heart stirring crescendo of electric guitars and drums that accompanied the falsetto voice of an American pop star were adding even more energy to the atmosphere when, all of a sudden they stopped in mid chorus and an empty silence hung in the air. Heads turned and voices rose in complaint. 'Hoi, Harry, I was listening to that!'

Harry stood up from the back of the juke box. 'Never mind that rubbish. We've got live music tonight. Let me introduce . . . The Twotones!'

'Yea, yea, yea. . .' came the high-pitched reply from Marian, the singer to the accompaniment of Allan's twanging guitar. Marian, in her blonde elfin haircut, heavy makeup and bright pink lipstick, looked not a day over sixteen and she only just passed the laws of decency in her psychedelic mini dress. As she sang she danced, precariously perched on white four-inch-high stilettos, and more than once nearly tripped over the cable of her huge microphone

155

that squealed with agonised feedback every time she hit a high note. Allan was a fresh-faced lad in his early twenties wearing black leather trousers and a red satin shirt open to the navel, exposing a smooth white chest. His long hair fell in blonde waves down his back like a girl's and, although he moved rhythmically to everything they played, his cheerful smile remained rigidly fixed on his soft-skinned face. They were like a pair of plastic dress-up dolls come to life. The couple had stationed themselves to the side of the bar just in front of the toilets near the girls' table, and as they sang, they had to regularly perform cleverly orchestrated side steps to allow the patrons past to pee.

Harry leaned on the bar for a break and drew hard on his roll-up. Mike, the ageing swinger, eyed him critically. 'You'd need a poultice on the back of your neck to keep those few strands of cheap tobacco lit,' he said, opening up a pack of his own cigarettes. 'And I don't think much of the band. What barrel did you scrape them out of?'

'Are you deaf? They're the Twotones, one of the most popular groups around,' Harry answered, accepting a 'real' cigarette from his disgruntled companion. 'They bring in the crowds; the students like them.'

'Aye,' replied Mike, 'and every weekend we've to tolerate our pub being filled with visiting voyeurs seeking the excitement of dockside life. I wish they would stay at their own end of the town where they belong and leave us in peace to enjoy a pint on a Saturday.'

'That's all very well but it's them that have the money. They've all got grants these days, and the brewery knows it.' Harry pressed his cigarette end into the ashtray, lifted the wooden flap of the bar and hurried through to go round collecting empty glasses in preparation for the rush during the singers' break.

'More money than sense,' muttered Mike cynically. He finished his pint and left. 'I'm off to a real pub,' he called over to Harry who just laughed as the till rang out its merry tune.

156

Catherine and her companions were singing along to some latest hits. Marian and Allan had the audience in the palms of their hands, singing a wide range of requests that suited everyone's taste. The girls were on their third drink. Joyce and Shirley were standing up now, singing and swaying. 'Get up and sing,' they called to their friends. They didn't have to wait long. Soon the six girls were swaying together in a line, their arms round each other's waists and shoulders. 'Something faster!' called Joyce.

'Will this do you?' shouted Allan as he played the introduction to a current hit. With squeals of delight, the girls broke free of their line and started twisting round the floor of the bar. Opportunistic unattached men, only too keen to be given the chance of a dance and a grope, quickly joined them. The rest of the clientele cleared out of the way. Up and down and round and round they went. More than one chair was knocked over and more than one girl slithered on to her bottom having slipped in a pool of spilt drink. Undeterred they clambered to their feet again, hair dishevelled, nylons ripped, shoes thrown off. Who was caring? Not they. They were having a ball.

Breathless and laughing, they staggered back to their table at the end of the number and threw themselves exhausted into the chairs, their legs splayed out in all directions. Spare men fussed round them offering drinks and more dances. Joyce and June went to another table with two of them. 'Slow one now if you don't mind,' begged Harry whose voice had been drowned out during the commotion.

Catherine asked her partner for a white rum and black currant. She had heard the dark-haired woman ordering one and thought it had a nice ring to it. 'Make it a double,' called the red-faced man who was buying it for her. Catherine thanked him and gulped her drink which was more palatable than the whisky. The face of her partner started to blur and the walls of the room seemed to be closing in around her. 'Thank you so awfully much,' she said to him slowly, concentrating carefully on each syllable and mimicking a posh accent. Holding the glass delicately with her little finger sticking out, she tipped the last of the contents down her throat in one. When she reached unsteadily over to put the glass down on a nearby table, it slipped past the polished wood that dripped with spilled lager and beer and crashed to the floor. Her laughter stopped and a tear rolled down her cheek followed by another and then another. 'I've dropped my glass!' she wailed before slumping drunkenly on to a chair, and there she sat in the middle of the crowded bar crying through drink. The words 'making a right exhibition of yourself' rang in her ears. It was a flashback to Miss Walker's voice, mocking her when she'd cried after the belting. 'Leave me alone!' she screamed aloud.

'See what I mean about school girls?' commented the sharp faced Steve to his companions as they turned to look at her. 'They're a liability.'

'Leave her alone,' interrupted Gregor, 'She's only a kid. Can't you see she's upset? We've all been where she is at some point in our drinking careers. She's obviously out of her depth here and not used to alcohol.'

Brenda and Shona tried to comfort Catherine. They wiped her eyes and kept asking what was wrong. The florid faced man who had bought her the drink had drawn his own chair next to hers and sat with his arm possessively round her. Catherine tried to stand up. 'I don't feel well,' she wailed. 'I think I'm going to be sick.' Shona helped her to the toilet and her 'partner' quickly got up and disappeared into the company.

There was only one toilet in the Ladies. The floor was awash and there was no paper or soap. Catherine knelt on the soaking wet floor and vomited her vodka, whisky and pink rum into the stinking, stained faucet where they swirled in a multi-coloured mixture among the cigarette butts and stale urine. She heaved till there was nothing left. On shaky legs, she slopped over to the sink where she splashed her face with cold water and ran her wrists under the tap till the water flowed out and on to the floor, the sink being blocked with fag ends and pieces of tissue. Sober enough now to be aware of her appearance, Catherine removed her sodden, ripped stockings and threw them into a corner below the cistern. She brushed her hair and re-applied makeup.

'I'm going home now,' was all Catherine said to Shona before pushing her way back to her table for her shoes and coat. Shona was no longer concerned. She was next in the queue to be sick. Catherine sat quietly for a few minutes. No one looked her way. The students at the next table sat drinking and talking. Spectators on the sidelines all evening, they were not about to involve themselves readily now that there was a problem. Catherine was on her own.

She donned her new red leather coat which, by some stroke of luck, was still over the back of the chair where she'd left it. Dishevelled clothing covered up, and with shoes on her feet, Catherine looked reasonably presentable as she slipped away by herself.

Outside, Catherine breathed in the cool, tangy salt air. It was almost ten o'clock and the midsummer sun was still shining brightly, creating silver spangles on the water in the harbour. The ship engines droned comfortingly. Some seagulls bobbed between vessels in evening contentment, like ducks, spreading rings of water round them as they paddled their feet. But this was no place for a decent young girl to loiter. She looked in her purse. There was enough for a taxi, but best keep walking till one came. 'Hey you!' a voice called after her. She quickened her step. How was anyone to know the difference between her and the other solitary women who paced these pavements touting their illicit trade? Heavy, fast-falling footsteps followed hers. A burly figure drew alongside her, stepping in time with her hurried pace. 'Haven't seen you round here before. You new at this game?'

Without looking, Catherine could feel his heavy presence and smell his sour breath. Head down, she walked faster. 'Right then, darling, up here will do just nicely,' he said as they reached a narrow lane between two shops, a ships chandler and a tattooist.

'Get lost will you! You've got me all wrong,' protested Catherine. She carried on walking, but he was determined. He grabbed her by the shoulders and swung her round, nearly spinning her off her feet, and pushed her up the foul smelling, rubbish filled alleyway. Roughly, he pinned her against the wall and tried to cover her lips with his own plump, slavering mouth. She turned her head away, and in the struggle, managed to scrape her nails down his face and twist his ear. 'Like it rough do you, little bitch? We'll soon see about that,' he said, spraying her face with saliva as he spoke. She felt the acid of it stinging the soft skin of her face and smelt its rancid tang as it dried on her. 'Think you're smart, do you, filthy little tart?' he growled, releasing yet another spray, which this time struck her on the eyes and lips as well. Footsteps sounded in the street beyond. They stopped and the shadowy figure of a man appeared at the entrance of the alley. He swayed slowly towards them. Catherine held her breath. She would be saved. Her attacker pushed her hard against the stone wall and leaned heavily on her so she couldn't move a muscle. He held a ringed knuckle threateningly against her face before jamming his hand firmly over her mouth so that she tasted the bitterness of his hot leathery palms.

'Sorry to interrupt and all that,' came the apologetic voice of the passerby who had nipped in to make his water. 'Soon be finished.' He unzipped himself and started to piss up against the wall opposite. Catherine prayed that he would linger; maybe even sense her danger. But she knew he was drunk and no doubt thought they were a courting couple or a streetwalker carrying on her business. Catherine tried to bite the fat-fingered hand that her assailant had wedged in her mouth, but her teeth met the heavy gold ring instead. She felt the beery smell of the urine enter her nostrils and settle in the back of her throat. A zipping sound was followed by the rapid thwack, thwack of footsteps retreating out to the street and away.

Alone with Catherine again, her attacker took his hand from her mouth and curled it into a fist. He scraped the jewel in the ring hard down the side of her face from just below her left ear, following the line of her jaw all the way to her chin. 'Go to hell, you whore,' he shouted as he flung her aside on to the grimy, litter-strewn ground before taking to his heels. Catherine felt a warm trickle of blood as it ran down the side of her face and neck and into her blouse.

She crawled to a dustbin nearby and, grabbing hold of the handles, pulled herself to her feet. Tiptoeing over the debris, she located her shoes and slipped them back on. She staggered her way out of the alley holding on to the walls for support till she reached the street. She took gulp after gulp of fresh sea air, trying in vain to cleanse the intrusive stench of garbage from her throat and nostrils. She glanced nervously from side to side as she lurched along the road, her eyes searching desperately through her tears for a taxi. After only a few yards she heard again a steady thwack, thwack behind her. This time she froze in her tracks. Her heart pounded its way up from her chest to her mouth and back again so hard that she nearly choked. 'By all that's holy, what's happened to you?' said a voice breathless in its surprise. Catherine teetered blindly towards it. She was sure she recognised it. Familiar features began to take shape through the haze of terror. Relief surged through her and she started to cry. It was Gregor, the young medic, as kindly a face as she was likely to see around these godforsaken streets.

'We'll have to get you to hospital,' he said, taking out his handkerchief and pressing it to the wound on her face. 'It's all right, it's clean,' he reassured her. She flinched with pain. 'We're in luck,' he said, wiping blood from her cheek. 'Here comes a taxi.'

The good Samaritan sat in front with the driver while Catherine sat in the back. 'Casualty if you please, driver,' Gregor urged. 'Found this young lass injured at the side of the road here.'

'Good of you to get involved, but rather foolhardy,' said the driver. 'The women along here take some chances you know. Always somebody coming a cropper. Just dropped a couple of young kids at the corner, no more than fourteen and working the streets. Full of drink too. Dutch courage I expect. It makes you wonder what sort of animal takes advantage of them.' The driver leaned out of the window and spat the tobacco he'd been chewing into the gutter.

'This isn't one of your street girls,' explained Gregor. 'She's one of those silly schoolgirls who come down here for a bit of fun in the pubs. Lucky for her it was me that found her.'

Catherine was too dazed to say anything. She held the blood soaked handkerchief against her face. Her new coat was ruined. What would her mother say? What would her father say?

Chapter 35

It was two o'clock in the morning before a taxi turned into Catherine's street carrying her home from the hospital, her wound stitched and dressed. Gregor sat in the front. He turned round to check she was all right. 'I'll just see you safely into your house and then I'll be off,' he said, stifling a yawn.

'I can't let you do that. You've done enough for me already,' Catherine replied anxiously.

'Losing all that blood, and with the shock of the attack, you run the risk of fainting,' said Gregor. 'I have to see you home to your parents.'

Catherine was too busy thinking of the angry reception from her father to argue. 'Just leave it running,' Gregor said to the driver when they arrived in front of Catherine's grey tenement building, 'I'll see her in and then come straight down.'

'Right you are, lad,' the driver replied, looking at his watch impatiently, 'but hurry up mind. I want home to bed as well you know.'

'Sorry, is your wife expecting you?' Gregor apologised.

'Not the wife exactly, but somebody is.' The driver's scowl changed to a smile.

Catherine tried to usher Gregor away, but once started on his mercy mission he seemed reluctant to leave until he had seen it right through to the end. It would be light again in an hour, but for the time being the stairs were dark and it was difficult to climb them noiselessly. 'Hush!' whispered Catherine. 'Everyone's sleeping.'

'How many people live here?' asked her companion. Catherine assumed it was because he had never been in a tenement before.

'There are six families,' she replied. 'We're at the top. Please do try to be quiet.'

'It's just like my Gran's was, except there were four floors and eight families.' Gregor was making everyday conversation in an attempt to reduce Catherine's anxiety at having to face her parents, but nothing could stop Catherine's mouth from going dry and her legs from shaking.

Through the dark silence came the sound of a door handle turning, the creak of a door opening and the concerned voice of her father calling, 'Is that you Catherine?' Satisfied it was his daughter, his anxiety turned quickly to anger. 'Get up these stairs this minute! Your mother's worried half to death,' he snarled.

At the turn of the stairs, facing Catherine's door, they saw Sam who was wearing nothing but his underpants and string vest, his hair tousled and heavy black stubble on his chin. They heard Maggie's voice from the house behind him, 'Is it Catherine? Where has she been?'

Gregor turned immediately away from the surreal vision, ready to make good his escape in the waiting taxi. 'Not so fast, my lad,' hissed Sam. 'I want a word with you.'

Catherine remembered the row they'd had before she went out and kept sensibly quiet. 'Get in here the pair of you,' he ordered. In the kitchen, Maggie lay in bed, obviously naked, the bedclothes pulled up to her chin. The nightie that she'd cast off while she and Sam had made love was strewn across the quilt. A line of empty beer bottles and two empty glasses decorated the mantelpiece. Sam hauled on a pair of trousers in an effort to make himself presentable, and immediately started the inquisition. 'Have you been drinking? Who the devil's this?'

'Your father was just about to go and phone the Police,' added Maggie.

Sam persisted with his cross examination but all his questions were met with a defiant silence from Catherine. It was Gregor who finally spoke up: 'It wasn't Catherine's fault.'

'So, where have you been till this hour? Where did you take her?' shouted Sam, advancing towards Gregor with his hands out as if ready to take him by the throat.

Catherine pushed in between them. 'Leave him alone, Dad!'

she shouted. 'Let me explain. It was Gregor here who saved me.'

At length the panic-stricken parents paused for breath and took a proper look at Catherine, noticing for the first time the dried in mud smeared down her coat and, even more significantly, the padding on the side of her neck, mostly hidden by hair. 'What's happened to you?' screamed Maggie, all modesty forgotten as she leapt from the bed trailing a sheet, toga fashion, behind her. She dragged Catherine in from the doorway and nearer to the main light. She pulled the hair back and put her hand out to touch the dressing as if proving to herself that what she was seeing was true. Sure enough, she felt the soft springiness of the cotton wool and saw the reddish brown crusts of dried blood on the collar of the new chiffon blouse. 'You've been stabbed. Sam, Catherine's been stabbed. My little girl, what's happened to you?' Maggie was on the verge of hysteria. Sam took her by the shoulders and led her back to bed.' He turned on Catherine. 'Don't you think your mother's been through enough?'

Catherine started to cry and sat on the edge of a fireside chair. Sam turned to Gregor. 'What happened? Who did this?'

'Catherine, speak!' shouted Maggie. 'For God's sake!'

Sam took hold of Gregor's shirt front again. His face was going a funny shade of puce and veins stood out on his forehead and neck like cords of flex surging electricity through him.

Gregor stepped backwards away from Sam and into the doorway again. His face was reddening too as Sam pulled at his collar almost choking him. 'I was only trying to help her. Honestly. Can't you people listen?'

Sam released him but his fists continued to clench ever tighter. His eyes were blazing red and his right foot pawed the floor as he poised himself ready to charge at Gregor like an enraged bull. Gregor took another step backwards, ready for flight. Beads of sweat sparkled on the young man's forehead and started to trickle slowly down his face that was now grey with fear. His mouth opened and closed wordlessly as he mentally prepared himself for speech should he ever be given an opportunity to clear himself.

'Let him be, Sam!' shouted Maggie who had gone back over beside Catherine and pulled on her dressing gown. 'We'll never arrive at the truth by these heavy handed methods. Listen to Catherine. Allow her to speak.' She drew Catherine close to her. She was far beyond worry now and couldn't think any more. Nothing else mattered but her daughter's safety. But who was this gangly young upstart? Why was he still hanging around, stirring Sam into a frenzy? 'It doesn't matter what you've done, Catherine,' she soothed. In fits and starts, Catherine gave her parents an edited version of the events leading up to the attack. It was when she said 'Bosun's Locker' that Sam lost control. 'That's nothing but a whore's den,' he shouted. 'What the hell were you doing in there?'

He remembered when his father used to take him there as a little boy and he could feel even yet the tingling sensation of having his palm tickled by the blonde lady who went out to play games with men. Why had that corner of stolen pleasure he'd visited as a child returned to haunt him? How could his daughter have ended up there? Was he being punished in some roundabout way? Memories of card games, sawdust and raspberry cordial flooded his mind, eerie phantoms floating in from the past. He saw too the gin soaked Millie tumbling out through the door of the Jolly Fisherman. Fatherly concern made him lose hold of all reason. Was this really the path Catherine had chosen after all their hopes and dreams?

Suddenly, crashing in his ears and through his brain, came a screeching sound like heavy metal machinery that had run out of oil. He struggled to speak but the words wouldn't take form in his mouth. Was this how it felt to go mad? Sam shook his head vigorously to clear the insanity and he managed to speak. 'Have you been drinking?' he demanded again, banging his fist on the table. Catherine had never seen her father like this. She said nothing. Sam glared at Gregor. 'I know for a fact that he has. I can

166

smell it on his breath.'

'That's enough now. Just leave her alone,' urged Maggie, her face a ghastly pale. She didn't recognise this Sam. 'Let's all calm down. Maybe we should be thanking this young man instead of attacking him.' She just wanted him to leave. She had squeezed herself in beside Catherine on the chair and the two of them held each other, not knowing which one needed the most comforting.

Sam was taking gulping breaths and had paled too. It began to filter through his jumbled thoughts that perhaps Gregor really had saved his daughter. 'Sorry, son,' he gasped. 'She's still our little girl, you see. Sit down and I'll put the kettle on. Hot sweet tea for shock, that's what they say isn't it?' He had to calm down. His chest was tight.

Gregor sat at the side on a dining chair by the door. He looked over at the clock. Even after all that commotion it was only five to three. 'A cup of tea would go down well thanks.' With his hands clasped tightly behind his neck like a pillow he closed his eyes. 'My taxi will have gone by now anyway.' He yawned and stretched his head back into the pressure of his hands and, rotating his head from side to side, began to massage the tension away.

Maggie cradled Catherine in her arms and spoke to her softly. 'You'll stay in bed tomorrow and I'll call Dr. Menzies. Sunday or no Sunday, I'll insist he comes in.' Catherine made no protest and snuggled further into her mother. Maggie turned her attention to Sam. 'What's the hold up, Sam,' she asked, 'it's only a cup of tea you're making, not a five course banquet.'

Sam's large frame was bent over the cooker. He turned to face them. 'I feel kind of queer,' he said, his rugged face stark white now beneath the black stubble. 'I've a terrible pain in my chest. Must be indigestion. I should never have eaten that cheese on toast. I must have a seat.' He turned away from the cooker, and before he had taken even one step, he collapsed on the floor by the sink. Gregor was over at his side in a flash. 'Lie flat, Sam, and don't move!' he commanded.

167

Meekly Sam did as he was bidden. 'Stay still and don't get up; it looks like a heart attack to me. I'll run round the corner to the phone box I saw on the way here and call an ambulance. What's the name of your doctor? I'll ring him too.'

Maggie jumped up from the chair. 'It's Dr. Menzies. Three four seven one five.'

Sam lay on his back. Sweat lay in droplets on his now ashen face. 'Hurry up, will you. The pain's getting worse.' He clutched his chest and the words rattled in his throat. His dark blue lips were speckled with white froths of saliva. Maggie rushed to his side. The choking had stopped. Sam was no longer breathing. Instantly Gregor was astride him on the floor. He put his hands together, one on top of the other, and started to thump Sam on the chest with the heel of the lower hand, counting each stroke out loud. When he reached seven, he dismounted and crouched at Sam's side. He pinched Sam's nose between his thumb and first finger and breathed hard into his mouth.

The two women watched in silence as Gregor worked on Sam. Over and over again he banged the chest and breathed for him. 'I'm sorry,' he said at last looking over at the clock. A good five minutes had passed since Sam had last breathed. 'It's no use. He's gone.'

Maggie whispered, 'He can't be. He was all right before. You must be mistaken.' With Maggie and Catherine at his head and Gregor at his feet, they lifted Sam on to the settee. Maggie sat beside her husband's body. She took his hand in hers and started kissing it. She kissed his face. She buried her face in his face. She sat up and started shaking her unresponsive husband by the shoulders with all her desperate strength. 'Sam, wake up! Wake up!' she shouted over and over and over again.

'Daddy,' screamed Catherine, 'you can't leave us!' She knelt on the floor, her head resting on his legs.

'I'll call the ambulance,' said Gregor, picking up his brown corduroy jacket and university scarf from the floor where he'd flung them.

Maggie kissed Sam's closed eyelids and then lay sobbing with her head on his chest. On his way out, Gregor glanced at Catherine who sat too stunned to move. 'Make your mother a cup of tea,' he said with newfound authority, 'and if you have any brandy or whisky add some in.' Catherine rose from the chair like a sleepwalker to do as she'd been told. Maggie glared after him.

Dr. Menzies' car screeched to a halt at the door. In seconds, he had climbed the stairs and entered the house. He shone a little torch in Sam's eyes. 'I'm afraid Sam's gone right enough. I had hoped... but...' He closed his doctor's bag and stood up. A deathly hush followed, the characters caught in a tableau as if waiting for the final curtain to come down at the end of a moving theatrical drama.

Catherine's strained voice cut eerily through the thick silence. 'You can't leave us. It's my fault. I've killed him, just as I killed little Lucy and destroyed Miss Walker. I'll never forgive myself. I'm a jinx.' She looked heavenwards and trailed her hands slowly down the front of her face, distorting her features. With clenched fingers she clung to her lower lip and dragged it down from gums and teeth so that her mouth was stretched, misshapen, and grotesque. She couldn't speak but gargled in distress.

Dr. Menzies walked over to her and took her hands in his as he crouched beside her. 'Look at me!' he commanded. 'Look at me and listen closely. You did not cause this. The unseen problem with your father's heart was like a time bomb waiting to go off. Trawlermen spend days hanging around waiting for the catch, and when it comes the inertia is followed by a frenzied working round the clock. If he hadn't had a heart attack tonight, he'd have had it sometime soon.'

'He was such a big man. Such a strong man,' sobbed Maggie, still refusing to let go of her husband's hand. 'He was a good man too. O, Sam I'm so sorry. I did love you. I did.' She left Sam's side to walk over to Catherine. 'The doctor's right, Catherine. He had a hard life at sea and he did it all for us. O my, how are we going to manage on our own?' She stroked her crying daughter's hair.

'Life goes on, Maggie,' said Dr. Menzies. He looked tired. Why did people have to suffer so much? 'You must try to be strong for each other. By the way, where's the young man who phoned me? And what on earth has happened to your face?' Tenderly he reached out to touch the dressing on Catherine's neck.

'His name's Gregor,' answered Catherine, turning her wound away from his reach. 'I was attacked. Gregor came to my rescue and took me to Casualty. But I don't expect to see him again.' The matter was closed. Dr. Menzies left it at that.

From the street below came the sound of the ambulance bell followed almost immediately by a loud knock at the door. The ambulance men rushed in carrying a canister of oxygen. 'Heart attack, is it, doctor?'

'There's nothing more anyone can do,' replied the doctor with a sigh.

Catherine and Maggie stood together at the fireplace like pillars of stone. They watched as the ambulance crew bundled Sam on to a stretcher, covered him with a red blanket and carried him out.

Maggie found her voice. 'Be careful. Don't be so rough with him,' she sobbed.

The siren-free departure of the ambulance announced to the world that the patient was dead, there being no need to hurry. They were only going to the mortuary.

'What's to become of us? How will we manage?' Maggie cried and threw herself weeping on to Sam's side of the bed. They heard Rosie's door opening downstairs. Catherine was glad. She was going to need help to look after her mother.

Chapter 36

'Who's that at the door at this time on a Monday morning?' shouted Maggie, still in bed, numb with shock and grief. She stumbled to the door in her dressing gown. 'Why can't people leave us alone?' She opened the door just wide enough to peer out. 'Yes?' she snapped at the stranger who wore a suit and looked for all the world like a salesman of some sort.

'I'm looking for Samuel Taylor,' he answered. 'I have a warrant here for his arrest. He failed to turn up at the fishing vessel Brave Harvest this morning. Can you tell me his whereabouts?' He held out the warrant as he spoke.

'Tell you his whereabouts. I'll soon tell you his whereabouts. He's in the morgue. That's where he is. And if you and your blasted piece of paper can get him to rise up and go to work I'll be delighted. I really will. Now get the hell out of here, you bureaucratic bastard, and shove your warrant . . . Do you hear me? Get out!' She lunged at the officer and was pushing him across the landing towards the stairs when Catherine emerged from her bedroom.

'Who are you? What do you want?' Catherine shouted at the Sheriff's Officer who now stood several steps down the stairs. She held tightly on to Maggie who struggled to go after him.

'I'm only doing my job. How was I to know?' he replied, his round face glowing crimson like a harvest moon. 'I'll pass on the information to the ship's agents. They'll be in touch. Sorry to have bothered you.' He crumpled the envelope in his hands and fled down the stairs two at a time, through the front lobby and away.

Catherine drew her mother back into the house. 'These people aren't worth it. Come and sit down. You know how strict the discipline is for fishermen, and that a warrant is issued for their arrest if they don't turn up for the Monday sailing. Bloody abominable Dad called it, little thinking that one day it would be his turn.'

171

'O, Catherine, what I wouldn't give to see him standing here in that great ganzy of his and those awful stinking socks.' Maggie drew so hard on a cigarette that the end flared bright red like a danger signal and its length shortened by a good half inch with only the one puff. Beside her on the arm of the chair was an ashtray piled high with cigarette butts smoked hard down to the tip. Sam's supply of duty frees was sorely dented. 'I've been thinking, Catherine,' she said earnestly, raking her latest stub through the grey ash before extinguishing it amongst the other remains, 'that man has done me a favour. I'm so riled up now that I can't lie down.' She remembered how Sam had dragged her to Lucy's funeral. She couldn't let him down at his. She had to be strong. 'We'll give your father the send off he deserves. I'm proud to have been his wife.' She lit another cigarette. 'Once this is over, I'll find work.'

'But really, Mum, you have to rest and look after yourself. You're fine as you are with your little job round at the baker's shop,' replied Catherine. She took the overflowing ashtray, which was beginning to spill its contents down the side of the chair, and emptied it into the hearth where the remnants of Saturday night's fire still lay cold and black. Maggie had lain in bed all Sunday but was now filled with a determination to survive for Sam's sake. Vigorously she started to rake over the ashes and clean out the grate. In no time at all she'd set a new fire ready for lighting later on, when even in summer a chill would come into the evening air.

Chapter 37

Maggie and Catherine sat at the kitchen table planning their future. Pieces of paper where they'd been calculating their money lay scattered in front of them. 'I'm still a young woman; I can't sit down to life yet. In this town they're always looking for fish workers. It's good money for a woman with no skills. How else can we survive and get you through university?'

'I don't have to go to university. I can easily get a job. There's the library or the bank,' replied Catherine, putting on the kettle and placing two slices of toast under the grill. 'Anyway,' she announced triumphantly, 'you can't stand the smell of fish. You keep saying so.'

'If the smell of fish means I can smell money then that's what I'll do. That's where the wages are for women like me – in the factories. We'll be fine. It might be too late for me now to get out of here. I'll never pay off a mortgage on one wage, but you're young Catherine, you can do it. You have to do it for me; and,' she paused to brush away a tear, 'more than just me; you have to do it for your father. You'll go to university and be a teacher.'

Catherine was about to say more but stopped when she heard mention of her dead father. 'All right, but we'll just take it one year at a time. I'll work in the holidays and at weekends. But no thanks to being a teacher. I want to experience the world, not live a shut away life like Miss Walker. I'll be a journalist. And when I'm a journalist I'll make all of this up to you. You'll see. We'll have a fine house and you'll want for nothing.' Catherine's face started to shine as the dream unfurled before her. Maggie's eyes glistened with happiness. 'I'll be so proud of you, Catherine,' she said, smiling up at her daughter. 'And wherever your father is now, looking down on you, he'll be proud too. He'll always be there for you, I just know it. You meant everything to him.'

'I won't let either of you down,' answered Catherine, turning her back to hide her emotion, pretending it was to check on the

173

toast in the grill. She turned the hot slices with her bare hands and muttered to herself, 'How will I ever make it up to Mum for causing Dad's death?'

Maggie was determined to be as good as her word. If Catherine were to go to university she had no choice but earn a big enough wage to keep their home afloat. Catherine would have a small grant but only enough to cover her personal expenses. The government initiative of providing less well-off students with an annual sum of money had brought opportunity to all studious youngsters, whatever their background. The drawback in Catherine's case was that the coming year's amount had been calculated on Sam's wages from the previous year and, according to the rules, could not be increased in spite of the disastrous change in their circumstances.

Maggie pursed her lips, closed her eyes and began humming a little tune to herself as she rolled her lips between her teeth. Suddenly she sat up straight and nodded. 'Nihil desperandum!' she declared and held her clenched fist high with a flourish. 'Of course we'll manage,' she said. 'We haven't struggled all these years to give up now. It's just as well we don't have a council house; we would never afford the rent, and I think I can put buying one on hold, for a while anyway.'

Catherine raised a clenched fist in agreement. She ignored the comments about a house which she thought was out of their reach. She didn't want to give her own opinion and risk dashing her mother's hopes all together. 'You're crazy,' she laughed, 'but you're right, we will manage and I can always find work in the Post Office at Christmas and hotels in the summer. My only real worry is the thought of you working in the fish.' As she spoke she started twisting the corner of the tablecloth round her nervous fingers. 'And what's going to happen to you in the future, Mum?' she asked, clearing her throat that seemed to be closing with fear. 'What if I have to move away and leave you on your own?' Catherine's anxieties poured from her, threatening to drown her

174

floundering optimism. She had her elbows on the table with her hands supporting her face which was weary from thinking. Her eyes flickered from the pieces of paper where they had calculated their finances and back to her mother again.

'That's no way to approach life,' Maggie admonished her daughter. 'Four years is a long way off. We have to do what is necessary now. Always remember that no-one knows the future and we must never allow fear to ruin our plans.' Maggie looked at Catherine directly as she spoke, passing on to her, through her eyes, her own determination, willing her to cast away all doubt.

Catherine clapped her hands together. 'Nihil desperandum!' she shouted. 'And when I've made the big time, Mum, I'll look after you. I promise.'

'Don't go thinking you're the only one with ideas,' Maggie chided playfully before reaching over and patting Catherine on the hand, 'I've signed up for a shorthand typing course to do at evening classes. I start in two weeks. So, you see, the fish is only a temporary measure.'

Chapter 38

Maggie straightened her white turban in the little mirror on the wall of the changing room where she was preparing for her first day in the fish factory. A sea of faces bobbed around her as everyone fought to see themselves in the mirror. Vanity created a sense of desperation amongst the workers as they endeavoured to retain some vestige of femininity despite their clumsy attire. Maggie's face puckered with despair as she looked down at the wellington boots, and when she tried to walk her hips and legs were constricted by the heavy rubber pinafore. 'I feel like an orange penguin,' she muttered before squaring her shoulders and reminding herself why she was there. Shoulders back and chin up, she splodded with her fellow workers through a cold stone-floored corridor that had no lighting except that which filtered in from the narrow doorways at either end.

They emerged into what looked like a grey-walled hut containing two long stretches of stainless steel tables facing into a whirring conveyor belt. Positioned along these were about a dozen women from the previous shift working on for a bit of overtime. They were glassy-eyed with the monotonous concentration of winding fish from the boxes by their side into tins that were then carried away on the belt with fishtails protruding. As if slithering on ice, Maggie's troop linked arms in pairs to enable them to hold their feet on the slippery wet flagstones. Carefully they lifted their clumsy feet over tangled hose pipes and sidestepped the precariously placed zinc buckets and slobbery mops that littered the floor on their way through to the next part of the factory.

The acrid stench of rotten fish clung to the air and hit the back of Maggie's throat. 'It's not usually this bad,' a woman called Eva reassured her. 'Fish goes off quickly in this weather and it's been lying around all night in the melted ice.'

'It'll be the mincing machine for us today then, a lovely job to launch your career in the fish,' added Sheila whom she'd already

176

spoken to at the clock-in.

'Cheer up,' interrupted Eva who seemed to have appointed herself in charge of the group, 'the first ten years are the worst.'

In yet another section of the factory, a young lad stood, feet wide apart for balance, on a high platform beside a gigantic mincing machine that churned like a cement mixer. His job was to empty the metal boxes of rotting whiting into the back of it, while at the vast front opening, an old man, who seemed to be in danger of being swallowed into its hungry jaws, had to guide the mounds of spewed out mush down a wide wooden chute. At the bottom waited two workers whose stomach turning task was to funnel the pulverised mess into metal crates. These were carried, a woman at each end, to more conveyor belts and measured into large tins which were then loaded on to a forklift and taken to the ovens for cooking.

Maggie stood mesmerised by the procedure. One or two of her companions were retching into their hands which they'd cupped over their noses and mouths in an effort to cut out the stench. 'See what goes into your fish paste sandwiches?' the young lad shouted down, recognising a new face. Sheila, who had pinched her nose tightly between thumb and forefinger, told Maggie in a Donald Duck voice not to worry, that she was sure it went for cat food and not for human consumption. Maggie shrugged. 'I don't mind what I do as long as I'm making money. I did want to be a filleter but they said I'd have to start off in the canning.'

'Filleting's a highly skilled job but great wages - for a woman,' answered Sheila. Her voice, back to normal again, was almost drowned out by the chugging of the machinery.

'Maggie, over here!' Thelma, the supervisor, shouted to her above the din. 'Change of plan, we're putting you on to canning some fresh whiting. If it's not cleared today, it'll only be fit for pet food tomorrow.' Maggie followed her. 'Sorry about the smell but the drains here are blocked,' explained Thelma as the pungent smell, even harsher than before, adhered, like a piece of plastic film that couldn't be swallowed, to the lining of Maggie's nose and throat and she started to heave. She tried taking only shallow breaths but nothing could stop the smell engulfing her with nausea.

There were two conveyor belts with five workers lined up on one side and six on the other. Maggie took her place to make them equal and Thelma gave her the rundown of what she had to do. 'You collect one of these boxes of whiting from over there by the door,' she said, pointing to a massive stack of about two hundred and fifty boxes. 'There's two stone in each.' Maggie watched a slightly built woman struggle to carry one back to her place. Although she looked older than sixty she must have been much younger. It was certainly not an easy life in the fish houses.

'The whiting have to be twisted into these cans, three pounds in each,' said Thelma, demonstrating how to manipulate the required quantity into the tin, heads first. 'Weigh your fish on the scales here at your station. Be exact or the can will be emptied back into your box and you'll never make a bonus.'

'I've never seen cans of fish like this in the shops,' commented Maggie, who had quickly calculated in her head that there were over twenty boxes for each worker making more than a hundred and eighty cans that she would have to fill.

'These are for export to America for distribution to hotels,' answered Thelma. 'They appreciate Scottish fish.' Maggie felt a twinge of sympathy for American diners. She wound yet another cold, slimy fish into the can, placed it on to the moving belt and then delved into the metal box beside her for another mound to weigh out. The grey creatures looked at her accusingly with their bulbous eyes and mocked her with their wide grinning mouths. Carefully, she weighed out the required three pounds of wet flesh and started to twist their firm resisting bodies into a can.

The smell was caused, not by the fresh fish, but by their discarded and rotting guts that floated about in the water on the floor. Particles of entrails, left behind after gutting, a mingling mass of purplish grey stomachs and bowels, had to be removed and put into the gutty bucket. The drain where these were emptied could take no more. The floor was awash with water and fragments of intestines. The women paddled rather than walked through this mire.

At least there was a wooden frame to stand on, much easier on the legs and feet than the bare stone floor. Conversation was drowned by the sound of machinery. She looked over at Sheila who struggled to can the fish with her arthritic joints. Twelve years she had been standing there at her station. Further along to Maggie's left was Stella, the machine operator. As each tin of fish passed, she jerked down a handle and the can was lidded. This was considered a better job, a clean job. Stella turned and smiled over to her. 'Here he comes,' she called, 'the Weasel!' She started to laugh as a skinny young lad in a forklift truck manoeuvred his way in to take away the stack of tins arranged on pallets by the catchers at the end of the belt. 'He does look like a weasel,' thought Maggie to herself, staring at his tight mouth, long nose and eyes that protruded, unblinking, like stitched-on glass beads.

'Stand clear!' he shouted bossily, as the high load leaned dangerously from side to side. In his arrogance he was oblivious to what everyone was thinking. Rumour had it that he slept with his mother because of overcrowding. Maggie couldn't help wondering if his mother was young, blonde and tarty or old, grey and frail. Sheila's voice rang out above the noise, 'I wonder how many cock stands he has in a night!' She ended her comment with a harsh, throaty laugh that had taken many years of smoking high tar cigarettes to cultivate. Weasel, ignoring the remarks, loaded the tins into the vast oven for cooking. 'Out of my way, you lot, or I'll run you down,' he shouted, clearly exalted by the delusion of his own authority.

The hooter blasted the signal for tea break. They needed no further encouragement and hurried as fast as their cumbersome feet would carry them to the canteen. They all stopped at the

179

entrance where there was a deep sink of disinfectant. Maggie copied the others and plunged her hands in, rubbed them together in the cold scummy liquid and then dried them on a shared soggy hand towel. 'Probably wiped on more germs than I've washed off,' she joked. The canteen was a large shed of a room with yellow Formica-topped tables and a tea urn in the corner. Maggie sat with the women and girls from her belt. At a table on the opposite side of the room sat the filleters. The Weasel and his mate Ernie, who also worked a forklift, waddled in, their vast green aprons and peaked white hats giving them the appearance of proud strutting drakes showing off their plumage to the females.

'Please, God, don't let them sit with us,' declared Nancy, a pretty faced young school leaver who spoke through a mouthful of Chelsea bun. 'These characters put me off my food.'

'They are a disgusting pair,' agreed Sheila. 'Just look at the love bites on Ernie's neck. He gets them from men, you know, men he meets in the Black Bull.'

'It's the cold sores I can't stand,' said Stella. 'He even has them on his ears.'

The others stopped eating and pushed their snacks away as the two young men took seats beside them. 'You're new, aren't you?' the Weasel said to Maggie. 'You won't stick it, you know.'

'Leave her alone,' said Sheila jumping to her defence.

'It's all right, Sheila,' Maggie interrupted, 'I can speak for myself. And what makes you so sure I won't?'

'You look stuck up. That's what,' he replied, looking away and winking at Nancy. 'The sort that's all airs and graces and no drawers.'

'You want to mind your manners, talking like that. I'm old enough to be your mother. And speaking of mothers, what would your mother say if she knew you spoke to women like that?' Her skill at rebuffing rude comments, that had been second nature to her in the bakery, returned to her automatically after a gap of twenty-one years.

'You leave my mother out of this. You don't know nothing about her,' he replied angrily, his eyes popping out beneath eyebrows that had lifted almost up to his hairline, his forehead being so low.

'You don't know who I know,' Maggie said, standing hands on hips between him and Nancy, adopting already the stance of a defiant fishwife in full flow. 'And I don't want you annoying this young girl again, or next time I see your mother, I'll put her in the picture.' She looked from him to Nancy, never wavering in her bluff.

The other women stared at him too. He didn't like it. 'Okay, I get the message,' Weasel muttered and stepped back. 'Come on, Ernie; let's find some better company to sit with.' The two louts scraped back their chairs and scuttled over to the filleters, who immediately turned their backs on the pair.

'Business good last night, Ernie?' Sheila called after them, pointing to her neck. 'Or did you bump into a vampire?'

'You don't know nothing either,' he replied, making a V sign with his fingers as he spoke. Maggie sat down and waved him away with the back of her hand as if brushing off an irritating fly. Several voices could be heard almost in unison: 'What an idiot!'

'Well, you showed them, Maggie,' Nancy said, holding Maggie's chair out for her as she sat down again. 'They've done nothing but pester me constantly since I started here.'

'And I don't agree with what that fool says,' added Sheila. 'You will stay. You've got what it takes.' She linked arms with Maggie and escorted her back to work. Maggie was successfully initiated as a fish worker.

Chapter 39

The bus home was crowded. Maggie sat inside, right up at the front on the long seat with her back to the driver facing the rest of the passengers. She was crushed between an old woman on her left and a podgy man on her right whose heavy thighs were pressing hard against her own, and making her lean into the old woman who kept digging her walking stick into Maggie's foot. Maggie could see nothing ahead of her but a sea of bodies that swung from the leather straps, clutching them tightly for dear life in case they might lurch across the bus as it swerved round corners or jolted to a halt.

'I'm turning into a fish,' Maggie muttered to herself as she picked scales off her wrists. 'These things seem to be growing out of my skin now, always there, no matter how many times I scrub myself. But can't complain. At least I'm making ends meet.' Maggie drifted off into a lovely reverie where she imagined she was relaxing in a hot scented bath.

'Well, well, if it's not Maggie Clark.' A man's surprised voice broke into her thoughts. Looking up, she saw a figure clinging tightly to his strap with one hand and to the back of a seat with the other to prevent himself from being flung on top of her.

'I don't think I know you,' she replied hastily and looked away. A few heads had turned to follow the conversation, an interesting diversion from their immediate discomfort.

'Yes, you do. You were a barmaid in the cocktail lounge of the Regent Hotel.' Maggie looked more closely. The mellow voice had a familiar ring to it. She looked up at the tall, rather dapper figure in short sheepskin coat with camel scarf tucked in at the collar. Her gaze met the liquid brown of his eyes that searched hers for the answers to lost years. His still curly hair, longer now, and flecked with grey, dripped rain over his brow and down his face like tears mourning lost time. Maggie was transported back through the years to the Regent, waving goodbye to a soldier. She put up her hand to relieve the prickling in her eyes and felt the wetness that was her own tears. 'Frank Rae,' she said, just managing to compose herself, despite the embarrassment she felt at being stared at by fellow passengers on all sides. 'I remember now. Sorry for not recognising you right away. I was lost in a daydream.'

'You wouldn't believe how often I've thought about you. How are you anyway?' His voice took on a note of concern when he saw her eyes filling up.

'I'm a widow,' Maggie said in explanation, but she knew that seeing Frank had stirred up old emotions she'd thought were buried for good. 'I'm not used to it yet, you see. My husband, Sam, died only five months ago in June.' Tears cascaded down her cheeks and spilled off her chin in large splashing drops.

The eyes of the passengers were upon him now, silent yet fiercely accusing. What had this character said to the poor woman? Frank gulped with embarrassment and reached out his hand as if to touch Maggie's cheek but the bus threw him off balance. He steadied himself by leaning hard into the back of a seat. 'Tell you what,' he stammered and, in an effort to comfort her and still the crowd, offered her a fresh white handkerchief from his pocket. Maggie took it and a tingle like electricity ran up her arm as their fingers touched. She wiped her eyes which were now beginning to sparkle with happiness. The onlookers seemed satisfied and their expressions lightened. 'This isn't the best place to talk,' he whispered. 'We must meet somewhere private and catch up on each other's news properly. I'm a widower too, by the way. Sarah died last year.' He cleared his throat and looked away.

'I'm sorry to hear that, Frank.'

'I know the perfect place. I'll be outside The Blue Danube restaurant on Friday at half past seven. Must go, Maggie, here's my stop.' Frank turned and pushed his way to the front of the bus.

Maggie watched him alight and stretched round to give him a wave. He mouthed the words 'Be there' before turning up the collar of his coat and striding off into the rain. Strangers beamed at Maggie and then flashed smiles at each other, obviously delighted by the show of tenderness. Maggie was radiant and her smile, unlike those of the audience, did not fade. She felt that some light had come into the darkness of her life at last.

Catherine was waiting for her when she arrived home and the fire was lit. Maggie hugged her. Lighting the fire after a tiring day was one of the worst aspects of working. 'Come and sit down, I've bought you something,' announced Catherine. She led her mother to the table and sat her down.

'Let me take off my coat first,' laughed Maggie without protest. 'Now that I'm sitting quietly, go on surprise me.'

Maggie had to close her eyes while Catherine went through to her bedroom and returned with something that sounded heavy as she placed it in front of her. 'All right, you can look now,' Catherine said excitedly. Maggie slowly opened her eyes. 'You're a mind reader, Catherine, where did you get it?' she screamed.

'It was in the window of a second hand shop I was passing. It really works. Try it.'

Maggie laid her fingers on the keyboard of the typewriter in front of her. 'It's beautiful. Get some paper quickly.'

Catherine fetched a writing pad and Maggie carefully wound in a sheet. Letter by letter she pressed the keys – Maggie Clark. 'See, Catherine, I've typed my name.'

Catherine looked at the paper. 'That's not your name. You're Maggie Taylor. What are you thinking of?' she asked.

Maggie looked startled too when she saw the paper. 'Would you believe it? I've typed in my maiden name. I must have been thinking back to my school days,' she stuttered in explanation. But it was not to school that she had returned, but to the Regent Hotel, talking and laughing with Frank, handsome in his uniform.

'Well I hope you work harder at evening classes than you did at school,' said Catherine sternly. 'If you pass that secretarial course, you won't have to go back to that infernal hellhole of a fish house.'

'That's all the incentive I need, believe me, to keep me working nose to the typewriter ribbon all winter,' replied Maggie.

'You're sounding cheerful. Yesterday you were ready to pack in that place. I've been scared to ask what kind of day you've had. And here you are today cracking jokes,' said Catherine, pressing down on the keys.

'Today was different though. Something exciting happened, Catherine, something totally unexpected.' Maggie went over to the mirror and peered in. Catherine was anxious to find out her mother's secret and hurried over beside her. 'Tell me, what have you been up to? Have you been promoted to supervisor already?' Maggie turned away and skipped to the sideboard and, picking up a soft brush, returned to admire her reflection as she brought a sheen to the red waves with long, sweeping strokes. Catherine followed like a faithful puppy, her impatience at bursting point. 'Mother, I insist you tell me now. The suspense is too much to bear. Come on, spill the beans.'

'All right, Catherine. I'll tell you. Today I met someone, someone you don't know yet, and he wanted to see me again.' Maggie had a dreamy, faraway look in her eyes.

'And what did you say, Mum? Who is he? Do you know him?' Catherine fired question after question at her mother.

'Give me a chance, Catherine. Of course I know him, or rather, I knew him long ago. He's asked me out and you know what, Catherine, I said Yes.' She waved the brush in the air and repeated in the shrill tones of a love-struck schoolgirl, 'I said Yes!'

'Mother!' said Catherine, clapping her hands to her face in shock. After a moment of fast thinking she exclaimed, 'Surely you're not going out on a date!'

Maggie went over to sit at the table. 'Oh dear, I'm quite

breathless. You don't think it's too soon do you?' Catherine joined her but made no reply. 'Catherine, I'm talking to you. What do you think?' But Catherine was too busy with the typewriter to listen. Maggie leaned over to see what she was doing. The words 'Maggie Taylor' and 'Sam Taylor' filled the page. Catherine looked up in embarrassment. Maggie had fallen silent. 'I didn't mean anything, Mum, honestly.'

Maggie slumped back into her chair and sighed. Her face regained the tired, drawn appearance of someone who is enduring life but not really living. 'Whatever happens, Catherine,' she said, pulling the paper from the machine and scrutinising the words closely, 'you must always remember that I loved your father. He did his best for us. But he's not here anymore and I'm still a young woman.'

'It's all right, Mum,' replied Catherine, 'I know that. I just hope you know what you're doing that's all.'

'Would you mind leaving me alone to think,' Maggie said, screwing the paper into a tight ball. Catherine set a cup of tea in front of her, and said as she left the room with a haughty toss of her head, 'I hope you're not going to be one of these women who jump into bed with every Tom, Dick and Harry.' Maggie looked after her with the look of a whipped animal. Why was every moment of joy always snatched from her?

Elation gone, hope and doubt vied with each other in Maggie's mind. Frank had married someone else all those years ago. But he had been already engaged when he met her and never made a secret of the fact. She'd been introduced to Sarah who was a good woman and in love with Frank. He'd flirted, but so did they all. It was during the war and every leave could be their last. Maggie had known they could have never tried to build happiness on the ruins of Sarah's broken life, and she respected Frank for never asking her to. But now they were both free.

Chapter 40

(Aberdeen, Summer 1966)

It was exactly a year since Sam's death. Catherine planned a cycle run in the country to be alone with her thoughts. However, Rosie got wind of her plan and sent Jimmy to ask if he might join her. Rosie's attempts at matchmaking were growing wearisome, and Catherine only agreed in order to prevent any friction on this anniversary day when she was feeling at her most sensitive. Jimmy grinned like a smug Cheshire cat as he cycled alongside her on the winding country roads. 'I'm so happy I could fly with the birds and sing to the world,' he said, taking his hands off the handlebars and flapping his arms up and down like a demented duck. 'We should do this more often. Certainly do you more good than stuck inside studying all the time.'

'It's a means to an end, and you know that perfectly well, Jimmy Simpson,' Catherine answered flippantly, hoping that their day out wouldn't finish in the endless round of arguments that they usually had. 'I love finding out about the world. It adds vibrancy and meaning to life, and, more importantly, it's liberating.'

'You'll end up like an old book yourself, gathering dust on the shelf, your pages grown dingy and dry with age, unread and never enjoyed. You may lose yourself in learning, Catherine, for now, but there will come a day when that's not enough and you'll wish you could lose yourself in love.'

'You'll never understand, will you?' she sneered and pedalled faster up the steep gradient of the road so that she could enjoy freewheeling down the other side. Having left the confines of the city, she was feeling carefree and cool in her denim shirt and shorts. Jimmy always commented that wearing denim wasn't feminine. In the breeze, her thick hair streamed behind her, secured at the front by a broad ribbon. To her great annoyance

Jimmy caught up with her. He had been singing an old Scottish folk song about a bonnie lassie and her childhood sweetheart ever since they'd left the house.

'And you can stop singing that song. You don't know just how annoying it is!' she shouted.

'You look so pretty when you're angry,' answered Jimmy oblivious in his happiness to how irritating he could be. 'I only like it because it reminds me of you. Take it as a compliment, why don't you?'

'How can I? Your raucous voice grates on me like a fingernail scraping down a chalk board,' Catherine replied, 'and put your hands back on the bike, you great buffoon. You nearly made that lorry driver swerve into a ditch!'

'You've no sense of fun. I don't think you know how to laugh.'

Catherine pedalled furiously ahead, but Jimmy kept on ringing his bell in time to the tune. After another mile or two into the countryside they both slowed down and Jimmy called after her as they drew near to a stretch of flat grass, 'Let's stop here for a picnic. There's a little path nearby that leads down to the river.'

'For once you've come up with a good idea,' she called back. Her face was flushed with exertion and a light moisture glistened her cheeks.

Jimmy looked at Catherine wistfully as she wheeled her bike towards him. 'It's not far,' he said, 'follow me.' However, instead of waiting for her so they could walk together, he headed off, emphasising that he was now the leader. Catherine felt her annoyance dissipate in the bliss of having her own space at last. The grass was dry and springy underfoot, making it easy to push her bike, and she revelled in the warm beauty of the day. The bright golden yellow of the broom was the dominating colour of the landscape, while the pinks, whites and reds of tree blossom competed enthusiastically for her attention. A community of sparrows that were hanging upside down like acrobats on the supple stems of ripe grass heads, while pecking out the seeds, suddenly fluttered as one to the high branches of a nearby birch tree, and chattered a warning at the intruders from the safety of their retreat. Some dark-chested males swooped bravely towards them and back again, protecting their womenfolk and young ones from possible danger.

Catherine took pleasure in watching their antics as she strolled along, but her reverie was rudely interrupted by Jimmy's excited shout: 'Here's the path. I knew it wasn't far.' He waited for her and she cringed at having him near. The gravel on the path crunched underfoot making it impossible for either of them to forget the other's presence. Jimmy sucked at a stalk of the moist, sweet grass as he marched onwards with the arrogant air of a seasoned explorer. Catherine tried to ignore Jimmy's male behaviour and breathed in the delicious heady smell of grass and blossom that filled the June morning.

'Just over this little stream and we're there.' Jimmy had stopped in the middle of a rough wooden bridge. He took the grass from his mouth, dropped it over the side and then rushed, almost falling over his bike, to watch it floating out from under the other side and travel, higgledy-piggledy, clearing its way past stones and clumps of reeds, downstream and away. 'Hurrah!' he shouted.

Catherine watched him impatiently before pushing her way past and down to the edge of the cool wide river. Wispy white cirrus clouds swirled delicately in a startling blue sky. The sun was generous with her heat that was relieved only by a lazy breeze that kept dropping as if it couldn't quite be bothered. The birds sang, their various chants blending together in a rapturous orchestra of sound. Catherine sat herself on one of the huge boulders that lay scattered around as if nature had deliberately placed them there for people to laze upon. Above the still little pools that were tucked amongst the reeds along the river bank, clusters of tiny flies darted and danced, enticing the birds to come and taste them, and an occasional dragonfly would stop by and hover just long enough to admire its rainbow reflection in the glassy ripples. The pebbles on the riverbed shone through the translucent water like precious stones, making the water twinkle and sparkle, tempting passersby to slake their thirst with its mountain fresh taste or have a dip in its crystal clear coolness. Jimmy picked one up and started skimming it over the smooth surface of the flow, making a series of splashes. 'Five,' he shouted competitively. 'Bet you can't better that.'

'Good for you,' said Catherine as she stretched herself languorously on the rock which had been gently warmed by the sun, 'but we're not kids anymore, trying to vie with each other at every opportunity. Why can't you grow up?'

Jimmy, whose childish behaviour was unlikely to captivate the heart of any woman, whizzed yet another stone across the slow moving river. 'Six that time!' he called out triumphantly before swaggering over to his bike that he'd flung on the ground and starting to unpack a picnic lunch from his large saddlebag. Catherine left the luxury of her sunny spot to unload her share from the panniers of her own bicycle. Placing a white tablecloth on the grass, she furnished it with sandwiches wrapped carefully in greaseproof paper, two chicken legs and a flask of tea. 'I've brought these too,' she said holding up a couple of chunky cups, 'they're plastic but they look like china.'

'You're a girl wonder,' answered Jimmy as he added some apples, more sandwiches and a couple of bags of crisps. 'A meal fit for a king,' he laughed, 'and a queen, of course.' He looked across at her affectionately. Catherine raised a wan smile. 'To us,' said Jimmy, holding up his cup of tea.

'To us,' replied Catherine laughing at last, her irritation turning to amusement. Having finished most of the food, they lay back satisfied. 'What are you going to do when you finish university?' asked Jimmy sucking thoughtfully on a flower of pink clover, his eyes closed against the glare of the sun.

'I don't really know yet,' replied Catherine, lethargically, scarcely taking the trouble to open her mouth to speak.

'Do you plan to stay at home or move away?' he asked, taking the risk that the answer might not be to his liking.

'If I make it as a journalist I'll most likely have to go away, down south somewhere,' she replied. 'I don't know yet. I don't think about it too much.'

'Your mother's here. Surely you wouldn't leave her behind.' Jimmy sat up as he said this and watched her reactions closely.

'My mother wants me to do well,' Catherine said, the power returning to her voice as she fought off the heavy drowsiness. 'She'd never hold me back for her own benefit.'

Jimmy slurped the clover through his lips one last time and tossed it away. 'I think she's hard. Too shrewd,' he said with a tell tale edge to his voice. 'Do you never question that she's trying to live through you? She's pushing you into a life of hard work and no love.'

'She's ambitious for me. There's nothing wrong in that.' Catherine glared at her interrogator and sniped back, 'What about you, no more ambition than to work for ever at the same job. You'll only have the guts to leave your mother when you've a wife to take over her role.'

'A welder's a damned good job. And it pays good money. When I finish my apprenticeship I'll make fifteen pounds a week plus bonuses,' he asserted, sitting up and looking directly over at Catherine.

'There's more to life than money,' Catherine replied and she too opened her eyes and sat up. She emptied the last of the flask into her cup and drank it down quickly.

'Such as?'

'Such as meeting interesting people, having new experiences.'

'Why can't you be normal, Catherine? Why do you have to be such a . . . Bohemian?'

'What a ridiculous comment, Jimmy Simpson! Can't you do better than that? Bohemian is such an old fashioned word, but that's why it suits you. Your whole world is old fashioned. Well, I

191

want more!' She got to her feet and started clearing up.

Jimmy got up too and stood watching her. His brow was pulled down over narrowing eyes and his lips tightened. 'You don't know what you're talking about. There's something wrong with you, Catherine. You're not like other girls.'

'Well, since I'm so strange, why did you come out with me today? What is a normal person like you doing out here with a misfit like me?' Catherine flapped the tablecloth vigorously. It thunder clapped as it caught the air. Jimmy brushed a shower of crumbs from his hair. Sparrows that had cheekily approached to snatch stray tit-bits, flurried back to the trees and followed anxiously with their keen little eyes the whereabouts of their anticipated meal. Jimmy dragged the cloth roughly out of her hands and tossed it aside. He faced her squarely and wiped his mouth with the side of his hand to make sure no sign of picnic remained on his lips. He held up his head and stood uncommonly still to attention. 'I want to marry you, Catherine. Will you marry me?' Catherine stopped picking up the debris for a minute and laughed right in his face. She started again with such increased speed there was no doubt she couldn't wait to get away from him, but Jimmy was too full of himself to take the hint. 'Well, what do you have to say?' he persisted, following her around like a lost puppy, but when he realised that she had no intention of taking him seriously, he turned nasty. 'I can still see that scar on your cheek and it's been a year now,' he mused. Catherine winced and put her hand up to touch it, but said nothing in retaliation. His remark had hit home but with more impact than he'd intended. 'I'm sorry, Catherine, I've gone about this all the wrong way.' He was desperate to salvage some remnant of enjoyment from their day out and regain Catherine's approval. 'Please say we can still at least be friends.'

'All right, we're still friends,' answered Catherine grudgingly, 'but nothing else, do you hear?' Tight lipped and silent she pushed her bike roughly back towards the road for home.

Chapter 41

(Aberdeen, August 1966)

The moon was rising red over the horizon of the sea. Maggie and Frank were snuggled together in his car that was parked high on a cliff overlooking the sea. The lights of ships berthed there for the weekend shone in the darkness of the night. Suddenly in the silence Maggie asked, 'Have you had other women since Sarah died?'

'What's brought that on?' Frank replied. 'Since Sarah died there's been no one but you. And all the time we were married I was faithful. I'm proud to say I was a good husband and I looked after Sarah as best I could, but she was never in good health. That's why we never had children. I thought I'd never come to terms with her death, believe me. I'd lived a long time in fear of losing her, but life goes on and fate has kindly led me back to you. I never forgot you and I'll never forget Sarah.'

'I don't think it's possible to forget someone you've loved. I'll never forget Sam, but we do have to make a new life. At least I have Catherine, whereas you have no one.'

'Had no one, Maggie. Now I have you.'

'That's true, Frank. We have each other now. The past nine months have flown. I don't know if I could have made it without you. You've brought me back to life.'

'Me too,' said Frank. 'Know what else I've noticed? I don't stammer when I'm with you. I developed one after the war. Trauma the specialist said. Too many comrades killed around me. And all I'd ever wanted was a quiet life.'

'I know exactly what you mean. I've seen a bit too much of life myself.'

'You know, Maggie, I wanted you from the very first day I saw you in the hotel more than twenty years ago, but how could I hurt Sarah? How could I involve you in a scandal?'

'It wasn't meant to be at that time, that's all. Anyway, I met Sam and I wouldn't be without Catherine now - even for you.'

'I never forgot you, Maggie Clark. Never forgot your pretty little face and curly hair.' He turned from gazing out across the sea and brushed her cheek with the back of his fingers. 'Time has moved on, and here we are the two of us, each on our own again. What are we going to do with the rest of our lives?'

'What do you want to do, Frank?'

'You tell me, Maggie. What do you really want?'

Maggie didn't have to think long. 'I want an end to the desperate loneliness.' The deeply felt words burst quickly from her throat like the effervescent bubbles that occasionally break the surface of a still dark pool. Her voice dropped to a whisper as she continued to reveal her private thoughts. 'I want to feel part of a family again. I am lucky to have Catherine but she has her own life to live. Sometimes such a terror grips me that it wakens me in the middle of the night, and I feel my heart thumping and my body trembling.' She paused, and her voice wavered as if she were struck with panic even at that precise moment, 'Will this fear ever go away?' She gripped Frank's arm. 'You don't think I'm crazy?'

'Of course not, Maggie, you're perfectly normal,' he replied gently. He put his hand over hers to increase her grip on him. 'You've described exactly how I feel, how I've felt for longer than I dare think. There is a solution though, a solution for both of us. Marry me, Maggie. Don't you think it was more than just coincidence that we were both on the same bus on the day that my car was in for a service? Marry me and we'll be a family. You, me and Catherine. I earn a good wage as an electrician, and when I give up my digs at Mrs. Christie's, and we join forces, we'll be able to afford a comfortable life. I'll look after you, I promise. You're the spark in my life, Maggie. Please say Yes.'

Maggie was quiet for a few moments, mulling over the options. 'I do enjoy being with you, Frank. It's our time together that makes me able to tolerate that fish house.'

194

'Is that a "Yes" I'm hearing?' asked Frank.

Maggie said nothing for what seemed to Frank an eternity, and yet it was barely a minute. She twisted Sam's ring round and round on her wedding finger. She closed her eyes to be alone with her thoughts before giving an answer. 'Yes, Frank, it is. I'm saying Yes. I want so much to be happy and all the time I'm with you that's exactly how I feel.'

'I love you, Maggie Cla . . . Taylor, and now you're going to be Maggie Rae.' Frank wound her curls tightly round his fingers. 'I'll never let you go again.'

Maggie smiled and cuddled closer. 'I like the name Maggie Rae. It has a lovely ring to it. We're going to be so happy together and make up for all those lost years.'

'I'll make you the happiest woman in the whole wide world!' shouted Frank, throwing his arms round her. 'That's a promise.'

Frank kissed her gently on the lips and drew her to him. 'I love you, Maggie, and I'm going to show you just how much.' He kissed the side of her neck and she shuddered. He slid his hand inside her blouse and moved his hands towards her breasts. Maggie moaned as he fondled them and released them from the constraints of her bra. Her nipples tingled and grew hard as he fingered them one by one. She opened her mouth wider and they tasted each other with their tongues. His hand moved downwards and slowly and patiently he gave her the loving she had never had before. Only when he was sure she was satisfied did he position himself over her and slowly bring them both to a fulfilling climax.

Maggie was weeping. 'Something inside me has melted,' she answered when he asked her what was wrong. 'I've never felt like this before. It all seems too easy. Do you think it's possible for life to run so smoothly, for us always to be this happy?'

Chapter 42

By the spring of the following year Maggie had a typing qualification under her belt and had found herself a job in the Council offices. Through it all she continued to fall deeper in love with Frank. Catherine, however, closed her mind to her mother's romance and continued to press ahead with her studies. It was unfortunate that both had been too preoccupied to notice that their dear friend and neighbour, Rosie, was having a hard time of it, but it wasn't long before the severity of her problem came to light.

'There's a prowler on the stairs,' whispered Catherine, shaking her mother awake. 'I hear him creeping about. He'll be trying all the doors till he finds one open and goes in.'

'For the love of God,' said Maggie, forcing her eyes open and dragging herself out of bed, 'it's the middle of the night.'

Catherine shushed her. 'Listen!'

'There are five other families besides us. It's just someone coming in late or going out early.' Maggie made to crawl back under the covers. 'All those books you read have inflamed your imagination. You need to give your mind a rest. We've nothing to steal and neither does anybody else in this building. If there is a prowler, he's in for a great disappointment.'

'I haven't lost touch with reality just because I study. It could be an attacker who knows there are two women alone in the house.' Catherine was adamant and pulled the collar of her quilted dressing gown tight up round her throat. She tried not to look at the prying face of the full moon leering in at them through the window as he wandered the night sky poking his nose into everybody's secrets. She put her ear to the door. 'Surely someone coming home late would just go straight to their house. Nobody's out till three in the morning. Where would they go?'

'Well, Mrs. Chisholm across the road goes to the Red Dragon gaming club till all the hours. She's well over sixty but says it's given her a new lease of life since she was widowed and couldn't sleep.' Maggie sat up in bed, nursing her knees, wide-awake now.

'Mum! I didn't ask for the life and times of every neighbour in the street. I just want you to take me seriously for once.' She had her ear against the wall next to the stairs. 'There's definitely somebody there.'

'It'll be young Jimmy coming home from one of his late dances. Maybe he's had a drink too many and can't get the key in the lock.' Maggie turned over and lay with her eyes shut. 'I've work tomorrow and the boss wants me to type up the minutes of his meeting with the Finance Committee. Three carbon copies he wants in three different colours. It'll be a nightmare if I don't have enough sleep.'

'You're only a clerkess with the Council,' Catherine tutted. 'You're not running the country. Anyway, it won't be Jimmy. He rests up on a Thursday in preparation for taking the weekend by storm.'

'Maybe the Russians are coming and they're making a start with us,' Maggie muttered as, reluctantly, she swung her legs over the side of her cosy bed. She shivered as her bare feet slapped over the linoleum. 'Wait a minute, though, I do hear a strange swishing sound and an occasional footstep. Stand back, Catherine!' and Maggie swept past her and flung open the door. 'Who's there? Give yourself up!' Maggie challenged the darkness as if she were a cowboy in a western, except instead of a gun, she brandished an umbrella that had been hanging amongst the coats in the lobby.

'It's only me,' replied a woman's soft voice.

'Rosie!' said Catherine and Maggie in unison. 'What the hell are you doing out there in the dark?' Their voices were gentle now, full of concern, always aware that extreme cleaning spelt trouble.

'I'm only in the dark because our stair light's gone and we're out of fuse wire,' came the reply as if that were explanation enough for her night time activity. Maggie switched on hers, happy now that it was safe to do so. Rosie appeared round the corner of the stairs with a mop and a tin of polish in her hand.

'But don't you know it's the middle of the night? Don't you have enough to do in the daytime?' asked Maggie, going down to her friend and leading her up to the house. 'You look awful. Your eyes are all funny. What's going on?'

'It's the tablets the doctor gave me. They make me work. There's nothing left to do in the house and Jim was moaning, so I thought I'd do the stairs.' Her usually pale face flushed red as if caught in a criminal act.

'What kind of tablets? Are you ill or something?' pursued Maggie kindly as she helped Rosie to a chair. 'Catherine, put the kettle on. There's something far wrong here.'

'I know what's wrong with Rosie,' said Catherine scornfully, peering closely at her. 'Just look at her pupils. She's out of her head on some kind of drug.'

'But Rosie never goes anywhere. I'm not joking; I really am going to take all your books away if you don't stop having these flights of fancy.' Maggie shook her head and filled the kettle herself.

'I'm afraid Catherine's right. The doctor gave me slimming pills and now I can't stop working.' Rosie took a little bottle from her apron pocket and handed it to Catherine.

'Amphetamine!' exclaimed Catherine. 'That's speed.' The kettle whistled its warning and Maggie removed it from the gas. She put tea in the pot and stirred in the boiling water with a large spoon. She was all ears now. Maybe Catherine did know what she was talking about. 'Doctors are drugs happy these days,' Catherine continued, putting a comforting arm round Rosie. 'They dish out pills willy-nilly. These are amphetamines. Not much wonder Rosie looks all in.'

'Is that right, Rosie?' asked Maggie, hastening to pour the strong tea as if it would bring an immediate cure. 'Who would

198

believe a doctor did this to you? You look bloody awful.' She clutched at her throat, distraught to think of anyone of her acquaintance being on drugs, far less her best friend.

Rosie looked up. Red-rimmed eyes protruded from black circles in a hollowed out face. No more the healthy peaches and cream complexion. She spoke like a child making excuses for silly behaviour. 'The doctor said that lots of his patients use them to help burn up calories. If they make me thin, then I'm going to keep on taking them.' Desperately, she tried to steady her trembling hands to take the cup of tea that Maggie offered, but she shook the saucer so much that the cup of scalding liquid fell off, just missing Maggie, who mopped it up, while Catherine carried another cup over and placed it angrily on the table with such a clatter it made Rosie jump and tremble even worse than before. 'You must stop taking these pills,' Catherine shouted. 'They're dangerous. They'll burn you out. For God's sake, it's not as if you were obese; you're just a bit on the plump side.'

'Well the doctor must know what he's doing. It is his job after all. I'll only take them untill I've lost two stone. Anyway, I want to be able to wear something attractive for your mum's wedding.' Rosie bent her head down to the cup and, holding it steady with two hands, slurped the hot, sugary drink.

'Don't blame me for all this,' came Maggie's quick reply. 'I've enough to contend with. Catherine, are you sure these pills are bad for you?'

'Look at Rosie for your answer. People buy them in pubs so they can get high and stay up all night dancing, studying or whatever. And as for this wedding, I've had a gutful of it! I'm off back to bed!'

'Oh, not that old chestnut, Catherine, Frank and I love each other. Surely you don't want me to be an old maid already. I'm too young.'

'You know what I'm getting at. You've seen a chance of getting a council house if Frank leaves his bedsit and lives here. He's just a means to an end. You won't be happy.' Maggie dismissed her daughter with a wave of her hand and pulled her chair over to Rosie in order to talk wedding outfits. Catherine was incensed and began waving her arms like an angry Italian waiter. The two older women became silent and seemed chastened with eyes cast downwards while Catherine ranted, but when they simultaneously looked at each other, they dissolved into nervous laughter, hands over their mouths and shoulders heaving. Catherine was furious. 'When will you two ever grow up?' she shouted. 'I've lived my whole life with the pair of you sitting in the evenings drinking stout and dreaming up one hare-brained scheme after another. I'm sick of it!'

'You've gone too far, my lady!' shouted Maggie, standing up ready for a real ding-dong with her daughter.

'Leave her be, Maggie. It's my fault,' said Rosie, tugging her friend's nightdress to make her sit down again. 'She's smarting because I said to her the other day that I thought she and our Jimmy would make a fine couple. I had no right to voice an opinion on their relationship.'

'Our relationship? There is no bloody relationship! Jimmy's nothing but a dolt and always has been!' Catherine's voice rose so high that Jim started knocking up with a broom handle from downstairs. He felt an entitlement to complain since his own wife was in the thick of it.

'Less of that infernal row can't you! Some of us have to work in the morning!' he roared.

'Quiet, Jim,' Rosie screamed back at her husband, and quickly turning to Catherine said, 'You were out with him on Sunday, weren't you?'

'I've had enough of all this. It's like living in bedlam! What do I have to do to have a private life of my own?' shrieked Catherine. 'I'm off to bed. And you, Jim, it's your own fault there's a noise. You should try keeping your wife in order. It was her that started it all!' Catherine stormed out of the living room and, on her way

200

through to her bedroom, banged loudly on the floor with the sharp end of the long umbrella her mother had left lying there. 'There, now, is that enough noise for you?'

Silence reigned in the kitchen for a full minute as the two allies clamped their lips between their teeth before the hysterical laughter burst out again. They giggled so much it brought on a coughing fit in Maggie. 'You'll have to see about that,' said Rosie drawing breath before starting to laugh again.

'I know. I'll go to the doctor and see if there's any pills he can give me,' choked Maggie and she coughed so hard she had to rush out through the door and down the stairs. 'Now I've gone and wet myself!' she called behind her.

Chapter 43

(Aberdeen, Summer 1967)

Soothed by sweet stout and even sweeter dreams of a bright future, Maggie smiled contentedly in a sound sleep. Suddenly, she sat bolt-upright drenched in sweat. Her nightie was wringing wet and clinging to her. 'For the love of God,' she exclaimed, jumping out of bed and peeling it off her. 'This is too much night after night.' She rummaged despairingly in the chest of drawers and found a clean pair of pyjamas. 'First I'm too hot and then I'm shivering. This wretched cold will never get better if I'm constantly up and down.' She hauled the soaking sheets from her bed and put on fresh. Fighting back tears of frustration and exhaustion, she crept back under the covers, where she lay coughing, drifting in and out of fitful sleep.

'I can't tolerate this much longer, Dr. Miller, it's wearing me out!' Maggie sat in the doctor's surgery, drumming her fingers impatiently on the side of her thigh. 'Surely there's something you can do.' Dr. Miller was Dr. Menzies' replacement. This tousle headed youngster, resplendent in pristine white coat, rotated himself first one way then another in the leather chair making her feel dizzy. He wore a stethoscope round his neck like an amulet. Dr. Menzies had always left his lying on the desk until needed.

The young lad asked a number of questions and, after some thoughtful deliberation, leaned forward on the desk, his hands clasped in front of him, his expression intense. 'Well, Maggie, your periods are irregular and you're having night sweats. It would seem to me that you're entering the menopause, or the "change" as it's more commonly known.' Maggie opened her mouth in protest. 'But I'm only forty-five.'

The doctor smiled, not a warm smile, merely a stretching of lips across his face. 'Some women do have an earlier menopause than others and it's quite natural at that time to have hot flushes and insomnia.' He flicked through her notes. 'You've had a lot to contend with in recent times. I see you were widowed just over two years ago. And you were studying for a new career as well as working in a factory. Now you tell me you've started a new job with responsibilities. A person can only take so much you know. Latest medical opinion has it that stress at your time of life makes the symptoms worse.'

Maggie interrupted him with an indignant tone in her voice, 'I'm not stressed. I enjoy my work, when I'm not exhausted from lack of sleep that is. Surely there's something you can give me.'

'Well, of course there are lots of new medications available these days. I'll give you something that will calm you down during the day and then you'll sleep better at night. Just let me take your pulse.' Dr. Miller walked round to Maggie and she held her wrist out to him. He pinched her wrist between his bony thumb and skinny white fingers that felt reptilian cold against her skin. 'Your pulse is rather fast,' he commented and hummed tunelessly to himself for a few moments. 'You would benefit, you know, from something to slow you down. I've helped quite a number of my patients with these already. We've found that tranqillisers can relieve the symptoms you're suffering.'

Maggie eyed the novice suspiciously. 'I don't want any drugs that will rot my brain. I've seen for myself the result of these new-fangled pills. They've already turned my neighbour into a zombie. Can't you give me a tonic or something?' Maggie pulled the sleeve of her cardigan back down over her wrist. 'I've no other problems in my life except for a bit of a cough. I don't need to calm down.'

'Look, Mrs. Taylor, why don't you take the help I'm offering?' Dr. Miller persisted, leaning back in his chair to swivel himself more energetically with his feet pressed hard on the floor for leverage. He stopped and leaned forward like a salesman determined that she wouldn't leave empty handed, and said, rubbing his hands together, 'If you don't want these then perhaps you'd be interested in some liquid iron. That should do the trick. However, you must take it with a straw,' he added as he pulled his prescription pad towards him, 'or it will blacken your teeth.'

'I'm sorry, doctor, but things are bad enough without looking like a witch in a pantomime. If that's all you have to offer, I'll carry on with aspirin and winter lozenges for this cold, thanks all the same.' Maggie rose to her feet and fastened her jacket.

'Can't beat aspirin,' said Dr. Miller approvingly yet mechanically. He considered the consultation over, and, after writing up her notes, stood up ready to call the next patient. He walked with her to the door of the surgery. 'Go easy on yourself; you're obviously under great strain. The menopause is natural, but it is a sign that you're not as young as you once were.'

A lump rose in Maggie's throat, but she swallowed it back down again. She couldn't allow this young upstart to think he was right about stress by bursting into tears.

Maggie gave way to her tears as she sat at Rosie's table. 'I'm too young to be past it,' she declared, lifting the teacup to her lips with hands as shaky as Rosie's. 'I've so much to look forward to.'

'You're not getting old. It just means that your periods will stop soon and that's a good thing. Just think, once you're married you won't have any "bad weeks" to spoil your fun. You'll be able to go at it like rabbits all the time and you won't have to worry about pregnancy either.' Rosie prattled on relentlessly like a tightly wound up record player as she went round the house tidying and polishing. 'I can't understand your turning down the tranquillisers though. They certainly help me to settle at night. He didn't tell you the name of them did he?'

'You take too many as it is,' Maggie warned her. 'Something to wake you up, something to make you sleep. It's a vicious circle. Catherine says they're addictive. That means you'll never be able to live without them.'

'Well, so what? That's not a problem. I like them. They've

helped me. Look, I've had to take in all my skirts and dresses. I wish they'd been around years ago.' Rosie ran her hand up and down her slim figure to show it off but Maggie was more concerned about how pinched and strained her face had become. Rosie misinterpreted Maggie's frown. 'Maybe the doctor's right. Why not take the pills and relax. Let it all hang out.' She put her hands under her smaller though still ample breasts and jiggled them up and down as she laughed. Maggie managed to force a smile at Rosie's antics and nodded.

'Now, Maggie, to more serious matters,' Rosie said in a conspiratorial tone. She lifted the salt and pepper pots, one in each hand, and placed them close together like the bride and groom on top of a wedding cake. 'What do you think is going on between your Catherine and our Jimmy? Do you think there's any chance they'll get together? It's always been a dream of mine, you know.'

Chapter 44

Catherine and Jimmy strolled round the Friday market. This was a pastime they shared occasionally when Jimmy was working a night shift. Catherine stopped to admire a beautifully carved wooden table. 'That's just junk,' Jimmy taunted.

'Doesn't it ever occur to you that a woman likes to be complimented? If you don't change tactics, you'll never have a girlfriend,' Catherine sniped back as she crouched beside the table. 'Anyway, I'm only looking. I'm not going to buy it. Where on earth would I put it? But if I did have the right surroundings to show it off, regardless of what you think, I'd buy it in a flash.'

'You could save it for your bottom drawer for when you get married,' he suggested pointedly.

'That won't be for a long time – if at all,' replied Catherine distractedly, caressing with loving fingertips the whorls on the legs of the beautifully styled piece of furniture. 'I wonder what tales this has to tell. I bet it's been sitting in some wealthy family's drawing room for years. I wonder where it was made, maybe in a fashionable country like Italy or even further away in the East.'

'Your head's in the clouds,' commented Jimmy. 'Why can't you look round and see this market for what it is, a pile of old tat? I wouldn't give houseroom to any of it.'

'Why come here then if it's "just junk"?' retorted Catherine.

'I like being with you. Surely that's reason enough. Why don't you come somewhere I like to go? There's a dance tonight. It's out of town but I'll take you home in a taxi,' he said, squatting down beside her. He followed her fingers with his, gently following the scrolling, before closing his hand over hers, squeezing it. It felt cold and clammy like a dead fish. She pulled away, but Jimmy held her even more tightly in his grip. 'Please come out with me,' he said, pulling her to her feet.

Two men stumbled past under the weight of an oak wardrobe. They staggered sideways and jostled the couple, causing them to overbalance into each other's arms. Jimmy steadied Catherine as she teetered on her stilettos. Impulsively, he pulled her roughly to him and kissed her full on the mouth. Catherine wrestled her way out of his clutches and rubbed her lips clean with the back of her sleeve. 'How dare you! What do you take me for? I'm not one of the good time girls from those dances you go to. Get off me!'

'Go on, kiss her again. She likes it really,' chuckled a scruffy drunk, one of the winos from the lodging house nearby. Taking a swig from a bottle, he tottered right close up to them and leered with bleary eyes into Catherine's face. Pushing a bright red tongue out through black stumps of teeth, he licked his cracked lips, and saliva mingled with special brew spilled down his unshaven chin.

Catherine's disgust overwhelmed her. She turned on her companion. 'I hate you, Jimmy, you ignorant, vacuous apology for a man. Why can't you understand that we are just friends? Nothing else!' She shoved him so hard he blundered backwards into a torn leather chesterfield. 'So keep your hands off me!' She bent to put on her shoe that had come off in the scuffle.

'You're weird you are,' shouted Jimmy, hauling himself up from the depths of the chair. He pulled his tie straight in an effort to regain his composure, concerned that passersby were stopping to gawp at them.

Catherine cared nothing for the intrigued looks of the other bargain hunters and made no effort to lower her voice. 'Not fancying you doesn't constitute weirdness in a girl. Quite the reverse. I wouldn't want you if you were the last man on earth.' Catlike, Catherine spat the words at him through bared teeth.

'Maybe it's not a man you want,' he hissed back, his eyes fixing hers in the manner of a weasel stalking its prey before the kill. He went for the jugular, hoping to fell his victim like the cruel predator that he was. 'Maybe if I were a woman you would show more interest.'

'You filthy bastard! Just because you're forever picking up women and God knows what else besides, you think it's normal to be promiscuous. You disgust me!' Catherine held his gaze as she parried insult for insult. She knew he wanted to hurt her because he couldn't have her for himself, so his words had little effect and she almost pitied him in his weakness. However, she wasn't prepared for his next thrust. Truth made it cut deeply.

'Catherine, you're still a virgin at twenty. It's not normal. You go on with your la-di-dah ideas about life and people and you know nothing. What could you know when you haven't had a relationship, when you haven't even had sex?' Jimmy's sharp words pierced her weak spot and she stepped back from him, jaw dropping, her eyes wide with disbelief and pain.

'We're no longer friends,' she gasped. 'I never want to see or hear of you again.' She turned on her heel and walked away, head bowed, past the mesmerised group of onlookers.

Jimmy called after her, 'I'm sorry, Catherine. Really I am. I didn't mean it.' Shoulders pulled forward and hands in pockets, he slouched away in the opposite direction, shamefaced in his victory. 'Have you lot nothing better to do?' he snarled at the grinning spectators who had relished the drama as if it were street theatre presented especially for them. An old woman booed and said, 'That poor girl will never forgive you.'

'Clear off, you nosy parkers,' he growled back at them. The wino chortled, 'Will you be here again next Friday? I like a laugh.' Jimmy stormed off and aimed a kick at an empty whisky bottle that sent it slithering across the cobblestones to crash into fragments against the leg of an old iron bedstead.

Chapter 45

(Aberdeen, Autumn 1967)

Maggie and Frank sat huddled together on the settee watching a play on television, but Maggie's incessant coughing made it impossible for either of them to follow it. Frank eased himself away from Maggie's side and stood up to switch off the set. 'That cough of yours is getting worse, Maggie. Is there nothing you can take for it? Can't you go back to the doctor?'

'I did go but that new Dr. Miller wanted me to try tranquillisers for my night sweats,' replied Maggie. 'I was so angry I hardly mentioned my cough and he agreed with the aspirin anyway. All I could think of was Rosie; pills to speed her up; pills to slow her down; pills to make her sleep; pills to make her happy. Surely you don't want me following her down that road.' Her eyes darkened as if a great storm would blow up if he dared to say 'Yes'. Wisely, he remained silent. 'I wish Dr. Menzies was still in the practice,' she continued. 'I'm sure he would have found a way to help me. I've never been as tired as this in my whole life and the wedding's only five weeks away. I hope you don't mind, but I must have an early night.' She stood at the mirror and brushed her hair, preparing for bed.

'But it's only eight o'clock. This isn't like you, Maggie,' sighed Frank looking closely at her face that was drained of all colour. 'I tell you, if you don't take yourself back to that doctor I'm going round to see him myself.' He went over and put a hand to her forehead. 'You're burning up.'

'Some like it hot,' Maggie joked, 'but I promise I'll go soon. If I'm no better after the honeymoon I'll insist on a check-up. Just think, Frank, a whole week at the seaside. I've never been as far as Cornwall before.'

Frank kissed the top of her head. 'We'll be like a couple of youngsters.'

'What do you mean like? We are a couple of youngsters. Our life together is only starting. Oh, Frank, I can hardly wait. Life is so good now.' Maggie's excitement gave her new found strength and she started to dance round the room in a cha, cha, cha, but she stopped abruptly, doubled over clutching her chest. Her breath came noisily and not without struggle. Frank was at her side in an instant. 'Oh, the agony,' she whimpered, leaning over the back of the settee as a searing cough tore through her. Frank helped her to a seat. She spluttered and, as Frank began to straighten himself up, he stopped, frozen in shock. 'What's wrong now?' Maggie managed to whisper.

'Your mouth is covered with . . .' started Frank.

'Blood!' they both said together as Maggie caught sight of the bright red stain soaking its way through the folds of her handkerchief.

'Good God!' shouted Frank. 'I'll fetch Rosie to sit with you while I go and phone an ambulance.'

Rosie came flying up the stairs and through Maggie's kitchen door like a gust of wind blowing up a storm. However, when she saw the weakened state of Maggie, she managed to revert to her old capable self in spite of the cocktail of chemicals that ran through her system. 'They won't let you home if you turn up at Casualty in that state,' she said, hurriedly throwing nighties and toiletries into a case. She made a comforting cup of tea and promised to pass on the news to Catherine when she came home from the debating society. Maggie's breathing became steadier but she still seemed to have difficulty getting enough air. Her eyes were wide and staring with illness, and she offered no resistance to being helped into the ambulance.

In Casualty, a nurse gently led Maggie to a cubicle and a stooping, grey haired doctor followed soon after. 'He looks old enough to be able to diagnose with one quick glance,' thought Frank, and sure enough, after only a few short minutes, the doctor emerged and went over to the desk. He spoke quietly to the receptionist and then his voice could be heard raised in annoyance, 'I don't care what time of night it is, I want a bed immediately for Mrs. Taylor in the isolation ward. There must be some nurses around somewhere who can prepare it for her.' He headed for a store cupboard and came out soon after wearing a white gown, mask and rubber gloves. His bent back became even more pronounced as he hurried to get back behind the screen where Maggie was receiving attention. The nurse in attendance was sent to the same store and returned similarly dressed.

Frank could contain himself no longer and pulled the curtain aside. 'Mr. Taylor, please be patient. Sit down and we'll talk to you presently. Don't you know that your wife is very sick?' came the doctor's voice, sharp and measured. Frank ran over to the receptionist, a young girl who was talking in a shaky voice on the phone. He listened closely to what she was saying. 'Dr. Ferguson said it had to be the isolation ward and immediately. No, I don't know what's wrong with the patient.' She paused and waited silently. In a few minutes, she spoke again. 'Thanks, I'll let him know that it's all arranged.' She looked up at Frank who was drumming his fingers impatiently on the ledge beside the glass partition. 'Your wife's in safe hands, Mr. Taylor,' she said, but without conviction. Frank allowed their mistaken assumption to go uncorrected. He knew he had more chance of information if they continued to think he was married to Maggie. The girl spoke with an authority that seemed to have been brought on by the crisis, saying, 'Please take a seat in the waiting area till the doctor calls you, I have serious matters to attend to.'

'But I need to know. I didn't come here to read magazines. Can nobody here tell me anything?' He paced up and down in front of the rows of chairs set out for waiting patients. Frank smoked his way through two cigarettes before the doctor, whose eyes above the mask had become slits from thinking so hard, finally emerged. He pulled off the rubber gloves and discarded them in the bin that was marked **For Incineration** before tossing the mask and gown into the dirty laundry bag.

'Come with me please, Mr. Taylor,' he said to Frank and led him into a side room. Frank took the seat offered him. The doctor took another chair and, ignoring his customary seat behind the desk, sat beside Frank, close and intimate. 'I'm Dr. Ferguson and I'll be handling your wife's case.' He stopped to clasp his chin between thumb and forefinger and pushed folds of loose skin up towards his mouth as if trying to prevent himself from having to say what had to be said. 'Mr. Taylor,' he continued hesitantly, 'you may have already gathered that what I have to tell you is not at all pleasant. Your wife tells me that she hasn't been to the doctor for a number of weeks despite the fact that she has felt unwell and had some worrying symptoms. To put not too fine a point on it, I strongly suspect that Mrs. Taylor has tuberculosis, although, of course, we must wait for the results of the x-rays we'll be carrying out first thing in the morning. In the meantime, we're admitting her to an isolation ward and starting antibiotic treatment immediately. Even if T.B. is not the cause of her symptoms, there is obviously a great deal of infection down there in her lungs.'

'Tuberculosis,' repeated Frank and his jaw hung limply open in disbelief.

'Tell me, why has she avoided seeking proper medical attention until now?' asked the doctor, peering closely into Frank's eyes for an answer to this conundrum.

'She did go to the doctor,' explained Frank, 'but he said the night sweats were due to the change of life and offered her some kind of tranquillisers, so she never went back.'

'Well, I am sorry about that, but I can't comment. That's another doctor's territory,' Dr. Ferguson spoke in what appeared to be his customary non-committal monotone.

'What a cock-up!' railed Frank. 'A doctor who can't tell the difference between T.B. and the change of life; what a bloody laugh! Heads will roll for this, mark my words.' Frank was punching his right fist into his left hand to emphasise that he meant business.

The doctor remained grim faced and silent.

Frank calmed himself. He didn't want to appear belligerent. 'Where could she have caught it? I thought there wasn't so much of it around these days.'

'T.B. can lie dormant for long enough and then become active during a period of stress. We'll have to test everybody who's been in close contact with her. If it's any consolation, we've more or less got it beat with the new treatments, mainly antibiotics. She's in the best place now.' The doctor continued to offer his hackneyed platitudes. What else could he do?

'You must be patient, Mr. Taylor. I'll take you through to your wife, but only a few minutes mind; she needs her rest. Oh, by the way, take these first. We can't take any chances.' The doctor handed Frank a gown, mask and rubber gloves from a trolley in the corner and took a fresh set for himself.

Maggie lay still, propped up on pillows. Her face was flushed and her eyes sunken in dark sockets. Frank looked at her, the torment of worry tingeing his pale face with a yellow hue. 'I'm tired, Frank,' was all she had to say. 'Please go home and have some sleep. Come back tomorrow. I'll be fine. We've a wedding in five weeks' time remember.' She gave a faint smile and closed her eyes.

Frank bent to kiss her but the nurse quickly stepped in. She was a dark, scowling woman with the shadow of a moustache on her upper lip. She had dead straight hair cut into a fringe that lay flat against the back and sides of her head like a Nazi helmet. She pulled her eyebrows even lower as she spoke. 'No, no! You mustn't.' Frank glared into her unsmiling eyes. 'Showing affection may mean nothing to you, but I'm going to kiss my wife. If I were going to catch anything I'd have it by now.' He bent over Maggie and defiantly pulled down the mask to kiss her on the lips. 'I love you, Maggie, and I think of you as my wife already. You get better soon, d'you hear?' Maggie smiled up at him, much more strongly

213

this time, her spirits raised by his flouting of the rules.

Maggie did in fact have T.B. and, over the next few days, tests were carried out, which showed no trace of consumption in any of Maggie's loved ones. Catherine and Jimmy had had the BCG jab at school. Frank had a natural immunity and Rosie and Jim were also in the clear.

'You're all very lucky,' explained Dr. Ferguson, 'but I can't be so positive about Maggie herself. I cannot over emphasise to you the seriousness of her condition.'

'But how did she catch it? Where did it come from?' interjected Catherine who sat white faced and anxious on the edge of her chair.

'Your mother could have caught it anywhere, a crowded bus, someone coughing on her in a shop; we can only speculate.' The doctor looked directly at her. 'I believe you have concerns that there may have been some negligence on the part of the medical profession as regards the diagnosis.' He rushed in with an explanation before she had a chance to speak. 'In both the menopause and tuberculosis there are night sweats and tiredness. Dr. Miller is young and may not have seen many cases of T.B. which is mercifully not nearly as common as it once was. He can't be blamed. Also, your mother never returned for a further consultation. If there is any blame to be apportioned, then I'm afraid it lies clearly at her own feet.' Catherine and Frank opened their mouths in protest but the doctor beat them to it. 'We have no treatment for stubbornness so may I suggest that we concentrate instead on curing the T.B. as quickly as possible.' The doctor paused and looked from Frank to Catherine and back to Catherine again. They sat silently, tight lipped this time. 'Right then,' continued the doctor, clapping his hands lightly together and taking a deep breath of relief that all fears of an official complaint were laid to rest, 'the tuberculosis is active. We must take scrupulous care that no infection is passed on. I'm afraid that, for the time being, no visits are allowed to her room. We have to eliminate any chance of its being carried beyond the confines of the isolation ward.' Frank and Catherine gasped. Doctor Ferguson continued, 'You may come to see her, of course, but you may only stand outside the window and wave to her. Medication will soon render the T.B. inactive and you may then resume normal contact. However, the illness is quite advanced and the lungs are badly damaged, especially as she's been a heavy smoker for many years.'

'She will get better, won't she?' Catherine asked with panic in her voice.

'Rest assured that we'll do our best,' was all the doctor said, and having risen from his chair, he turned his back to them and looked out of the window as if wishing to avoid any more questions.

'There is one matter of vital importance, doctor. Maggie and I are due to be married in a month. Is it possible that we can still go ahead with our plans?' Frank also made his way to the window and stood beside the doctor. For a full minute the two men stood watching a gardener raking up the cut grass outside while Catherine sat motionless, staring straight ahead and playing with the catch on her handbag.

'We'll think of something,' the doctor said eventually. 'Who's your minister?'

'Well, doctor, you see,' Frank sounded embarrassed, but continued, 'we were going to be married in the Registry Office. Maggie stopped going to church a few years ago.'

'I see,' said the doctor still thoughtful. 'There is a minister attached to the hospital you know. I'll have a word with him. Tell me, you are both church members I take it?'

'Oh yes, doctor. It's not that we don't believe or anything like that. It's just that we don't go to church. We're both members of St. Matthew's Parish Church.' Frank spoke enthusiastically, sensing that the solution he hardly dared dream of could be in the offing.

'Leave it with me, Mr. Rae. I understand fully.' The doctor turned his back again and resumed his meditative study of the busy gardener.

Catherine gave Frank the thumbs up. They offered their thanks and goodbyes and left.

'I wonder why he's being so helpful,' said Catherine as they walked along the highly polished corridor to the exit.

'It's best we don't think about that,' answered Frank.

'You know, I owe you an apology. I wasn't too keen at first on Mum marrying you . . . in fact marrying anyone.'

Frank put an arm round her shoulder. 'Don't worry, I understand. You never know; I might have been a con man out to get my hands on her fish factory wages and your grant.' He managed a spark of humour in spite of their heavy mood. Catherine joined in his laughter and linked her arm through his. Together they left the hospital, determined that recent events wouldn't grind them down.

Chapter 46

Catherine and Frank stood outside Maggie's window and blew kisses. Misery was etched on their faces as they walked away with slow, heavy steps. They had just turned out through the gates, well out of hearing, when Maggie let out a howl of anguish and turned her face to the wall. She tossed and turned in a painful sleep that was near to delirium. Out of the darkness of dreams, her mother's face appeared, smiling and youthful. She held out a welcoming hand and Maggie allowed herself to be led to a magnificent room where golds, reds and greens mingled in a wealth of textures, rich furnishings and beautiful artwork. Delicate trees and plants with a glorious profusion of fragrant flowers and plump fruit fringed the walls of the room making it difficult to know if they were indoors or outside. There was the sound of rushing water and Maggie turned to see an ornamental fountain where shafts of soft sunshine sprinkled the soft jets of water with rainbow coloured jewels. A chorus of birdsong filled the air.

A glass table was laid for a feast. Sitting at the table, were her father Joe, her sister Jane and her brother Kenny, their everyday clothes somehow visible through shining white robes draped around them like gossamer. Their shining faces smiled in welcome. Her mother went to one of two empty gold high backed chairs that were padded with red velvet and beckoned Maggie to take the other. Though seated, Joe, Jane and Kenny seemed to be able to flow like vapour and wafted towards her, seemingly near enough to touch but at the same time distant and vague. Maggie wanted to join them and tried to hurry but her feet wouldn't move. Another shadowy and yet shining figure stepped out from behind some delicate green branches that hung down like a flimsy screen. He was carrying a small child on his shoulders. Blonde hair rippled in soft waves over her shoulders. She was smiling and waved excitedly when she saw Maggie. Although their features were blurred in the iridescence of the light there was no mistaking who

217

they were – Sam and Lucy. Maggie tried to call their names but she was choking. She tried again to rush forward and grasp the ghosts of her husband and sweet baby girl in her embrace, but her mother suddenly put up a hand, indicating her stop. Maggie looked down at herself. Instead of robes, she wore only a nightie and her feet were bare. 'I have to go now,' she heard herself say. 'I'm not dressed for the occasion. I must go and prepare myself.' Her family receded into the distance and a pink mist closed round her.

Suddenly she was falling down and down and a great gust of wind rushed past her, roaring like a storm in her ears. A scorching pain that was matched only by the agony of heartbreak at leaving her loved ones, cut through her chest and back like a sword. She heard her name being called over and over, while her cheeks were stinging from someone patting her face repeatedly. Reluctantly, she opened her eyes and saw masked faces looming over her and she was aware of being pushed and pulled by none too gentle hands. Her vision cleared and she saw the dark haired nurse whose name was Sandra mopping her brow with a damp flannel. 'You gave us all a scare, Maggie, but thanks be to God you're all right now.' She spoke in a voice that was threadlike with shock. Maggie noticed bright red smears and splashes down the front of the nurse's white gown and she could taste bitter blood in her mouth and between her teeth. 'Don't try to speak,' said the nurse. Maggie saw the familiar masked figure of Dr. Ferguson advancing towards her, syringe in hand. 'We won't hurt you,' he said.

All of a sudden, a thought flashed through Maggie's mind and she tried to sit up. 'Eddie wasn't there,' she rasped. 'He can't be dead after all. He's alive somewhere and I've got to go and find him.' She tried to push the nurse away but her strength was giving out.

'It's all right, better if you don't struggle,' said the doctor, and Maggie felt a stab of pain as he plunged the needle into her arm. This was immediately followed by the cold trickle of sedative running through her muscle and she sank into the blackness, deeper and deeper into space where there was neither an up nor a down. She felt the softness of cocooning mists, cushioning her like cotton wool billows, and she hovered there, comforted like a baby in its mother's arms, and then sleep took over, restful and healing.

A week after the planned date, Maggie and Frank were married quietly in the ward. The fragile state of Maggie's health meant that they received special dispensation. Maggie wore a champagne silk negligee. However, the others were not so elegantly attired, including Catherine and Rosie the witnesses. They had to make do with matching white gowns tied at the back with frayed tapes, and on their faces, the obligatory masks. Despite the drabness of her entourage, no bride ever looked more radiant. Indeed, Maggie's frailty and the glow of happiness that enveloped her, gave her the ethereal look of an angel. The minister, Reverend Forbes, delivered a beautiful service on the theme of hope and love that brought tears to everyone's eyes, Dr. Ferguson being no exception. As they raised their glasses to the happy couple, no one in the wedding party could remember when they had ever felt such overwhelming joy.

Chapter 47

Due to the seriousness of Maggie's condition, there were no restrictions on visiting hours and Catherine called past at every possible opportunity, albeit just to wave in at the window. One day, between lectures, Catherine hurried to the hospital as she often did, carrying fruit, bottles of juice, more perfumed toiletries and several changes of nightclothes. She was heading for the duty room to deposit the stuff and get an update from the nursing sister when she was aware of a young doctor behaving in an extraordinarily strange manner. He had been leaving as she came hurrying in, but only seconds later he had re-entered the building and quickly caught up with her, but instead of overtaking, walked alongside peering at her face. 'Is there something you want?' Catherine asked sharply without taking time to look closely at him. She almost dropped her mother's goodies when he stepped in front of her and said straight into her face, 'It is you, Catherine.' Catherine stared, and a deluge of horrible memories swamped her mind. 'Gregor!' she exclaimed. Her face grew deathly pale and she had to lean against the wall for support.

'Come and sit down,' he said quickly, catching her arm and helping her to a bench further along the corridor. 'I'll fetch you a glass of water,' he said once she was safely seated. Catherine bent her head forward on to her knees to stop everything going black, while the ghost from the past disappeared off somewhere, making her wonder if she hadn't been hallucinating. However, she knew her anxious mind hadn't been playing tricks when she felt a hand being laid on her shoulders and Gregor's voice saying, 'Here, drink this; it'll do you good.' He handed her a cup of hot sweet tea from the lunch trolley in a nearby ward. 'You look all in,' he added, taking a seat beside her.

'I'm so sorry. It must have been the shock,' said Catherine, sipping the welcome drink until some colour returned to her cheeks.

'It's my fault. It seems that I turn up at the worst of times for you.' He spoke with genuine concern and in worried fashion ran his fingers back through his hair in a vain effort to hold it back. Solicitously, he took the empty cup from her and placed it on the polished floor under the seat.

'It's not all your fault I nearly fainted, Gregor, truthfully. I've had so much rushing about to do looking after Mum.' She mustered a smile for him. 'Meeting you was a shock, but it's nice to see you again, especially as I never had a chance to thank you properly.'

'I've often thought about you over the years. How are you and your mother?'

'Mum is seriously ill. It's her I've been visiting.' Catherine's lower lip trembled and she broke down in floods of tears. 'She was allowed to be married here last month. They thought she wasn't going to make it.'

'I know, everyone was talking about that wedding. When I heard the name, I checked the address with Records. I've been stalking this corridor ever since in the off chance of seeing you.'

'Quite the Sherlock Holmes,' laughed Catherine and then stopped. 'You haven't been to see her!'

'Of course not. Look at the state you're in. I wouldn't want to upset your mum in the same way.' Gregor was silent for a few moments. When he finally spoke, the words came rushing out: 'You must let me take you out some time. Get to know each other better.'

Catherine hesitated and made no sign of answering. She was far away in thoughts of her own. She knew that her mother had never forgiven Gregor. Although she had eventually accepted that he had rescued her from danger in an unsavoury part of town, she would not let go of the idea that he had been responsible for antagonising Sam so much he'd had a heart attack. Catherine hadn't felt it was worth falling out over and had stopped trying to convince her otherwise. After all, it hadn't been as if she would ever see him again.

'I should have called round to see you, but I always thought better of it. I didn't want to upset anyone.'

'You were right to stay away. Mum can be so stubborn.'

Gregor repeated his invitation. 'We've a lot to catch up on and I've a couple of free hours this afternoon. Please say you'll make it.' He spoke rapidly and looked at his watch, anxious to be off on his rounds.

Catherine's mind went into a spin of arguing this way and that but she heard herself agreeing. 'Yes, I'd enjoy that. There's a tearoom round the corner from here, the Shiny Teapot. I'll be there at half-past two. There's no need for Mum to know.'

Catherine heard him whistling as he strode away and the beginnings of a smile flickered on her lips.

The ward sister nodded. 'Yes, of course you can go in. We've done the tests and your mother's no longer infectious.' Catherine was through like a shot. Maggie patted the bed. 'Sit here. Never mind the chair. You know, I feel as if I've just been released from quarantine.'

Catherine planted a kiss on her mother's cheek. 'I've been longing to do that for months,' she sighed and squeezed her mother tightly. 'Maybe they'll let you home soon,' she whispered, frightened that if she said the words too loudly she'd waken and find that the happy news was only a dream. 'But don't raise your hopes too soon,' she warned. 'They're not too happy about your having to use an outside toilet. The doctor has written a letter for me to take to the Housing Department so I'm hoping we'll get more points.'

'I just want to be home with you and Frank,' answered Maggie. She tightened her lips and tried to blink back the tears. She couldn't pretend she hadn't missed them. 'You've no idea how much I've longed to be home. My life's at a standstill in here.'

Catherine stroked her cheek. 'Everything passes in time.' Her brow furrowed as she struggled to believe her own words. Maggie's recovery was taking a long time and although the T.B. was clearing, she still had a hacking cough and a wheeze that whistled like a singing kettle. At the end of the visit they bade each other a particularly emotional farewell with the kisses that had been denied them for so long.

Chapter 48

A bell tinkled as Catherine went through the door of the Shiny Teapot tearoom. Gathering herself together, she fought through the memories of the night of her father's death to bring herself to the present, and glanced round the linen-covered tables set with cake stands and dishes of butter and jam. Gregor was already there, seated in a quiet corner. He stood up eagerly, and in gentlemanly fashion pulled out a chair for her. It was more than two and a half years since she'd first met him at the Bosun's Locker. He hadn't changed much except that his face showed the strain of long hours and little sleep. 'You look well in spite of everything,' he commented, already sounding quite the doctor.

Catherine blushed uncomfortably under his steady gaze and turned away. Touching nervously at her hair, she inadvertently brushed it from her cheek revealing the thin red line of the scar. 'I'm sorry. I didn't mean to stare at you,' said Gregor and he too looked embarrassed. 'It's barely noticeable now,' was all he said.

'I never think about it,' she lied.

'I'm sorry,' Gregor said again.

Catherine forced a smile. 'It's you I have to thank for getting me to hospital so quickly. Otherwise it might have been a real mess.' She shrugged her shoulders and brightened up. 'Look, Gregor, let's leave that night in the past,' she said and signalled quickly to the waitress. 'I'm absolutely starving. The bacon rolls in here are fabulous and so is their coffee.'

'You have whatever you want,' he said quietly but firmly. 'Be my guest.' He ordered four bacon rolls and two mugs of coffee. 'I'm famished. I've had nothing but half a plate of hospital porridge at seven o'clock this morning!' Catherine laughed, freely this time, and they soon settled down to an interchange of news. Gregor was delighted to hear of Catherine's ambition to be a journalist. 'I knew you were different from other girls,' he said warmly. 'You're going to make something of yourself. I just know it. You have smeddum.'

'What on earth is smeddum?' asked Catherine. 'I hope it's not some kind of disease!'

'I'm surprised you don't know that word. Smeddum is a Scots word for spirit, strength, determination, and all these attributes in one. There's really no exact translation, but you certainly have it. Whatever it is you want to do, you'll do it,' he said and bit voraciously into a roll.

'Well, thank you. That's quite a compliment,' said Catherine. 'My mother certainly has smeddum and the thought of my ever having to manage without her one day frightens me.'

Gregor went on to tell Catherine how he planned to go to Canada once he was qualified. 'We have relatives over there and my parents have already joined them. My father was an engineer in the shipyards and retired last year. Nothing to keep me here now and Canada's a young country with opportunities aplenty.'

Catherine was quick to tackle him about his plans. 'You'll be part of the brain drain. That's the problem for this old country. Scotland educates a workforce for the benefit of everywhere else. People like you keep emigrating,' she argued, suddenly serious.

'It can't be helped, Catherine. That's life. And whether you want to believe it or not, it's not that easy getting a foot in the door as a G.P., unless you've a family business behind you. So let's see the politicians offer a solution,' he replied assertively.

'You're right. What's the point of a qualification if you can't use it? I don't know why I said that to you when I may leave myself.' Catherine wanted to maintain some harmony between them and added, in an effort to change the subject, 'Surely you have a girl friend. Will she go with you?'

He laughed. 'I admit I've had lots of girls, but I've always been too busy to take any of them seriously,' he answered.

'Quite the Don Juan,' said Catherine and took a quick drink of coffee to hide the blush that was spreading up over her face.

'What about yourself? I can't believe you haven't been snapped up.'

Catherine's embarrassment grew. Her face was burning now. 'I've been too busy for that sort of thing,' she said and, as clearly as if he'd been sitting right beside her, she heard Jimmy's nasty mocking voice: 'You know nothing; you're still a virgin.' Was she really such a freak?

Gregor was too polite to pursue the subject. 'I'd love to see you again,' he said and, before she could reply, he continued, leaning on the table towards her, 'I'm having a party at the Halls of Residence two weeks on Friday to celebrate the end of this stint of hospital residency. Please say you'll come. You'll be my special guest. I won't force you, but here's the address and my room number.' Gregor took a pen from the breast pocket of his sports jacket and wrote the necessary information on a napkin.

'Thanks. I'll take you up on that. I haven't been to a party for ages.' Gregor watched as she folded the napkin carefully in half and then half again before slipping it into a zipped pocket on the inside of her handbag.

'I'll count the days,' he said, helping her on with her coat. He bowed politely and planted a soft kiss on her forehead. Catherine smiled and made no protest.

Chapter 49

Frank sat brooding by the fire. He'd spent the whole day at the hospital and wasn't looking forward to yet another lonely Friday night. Catherine cleared her throat to attract his attention. 'My word, you do look good,' he said. 'Give us a twirl.' Catherine danced round the kitchen in a purple halter neck mini dress and high stilettos. Her long hair swung behind her like a bridal train.

'Heavy date? Who's the lucky man, Jimmy downstairs?'

'No, certainly not!' she shouted and stamped her foot, ruining the elegant image of the previous moment.

'One thing's for certain. I know you're not dressed like that for the debating society.' Frank couldn't resist teasing her, but there was no humourous response. Jimmy had long since ceased to be a joke.

'I'll be late, really late. So don't wait up!' Catherine shouted the words without any goodbye and slammed the door behind her.

'You're early,' said Gregor.

'I didn't want to miss anything,' Catherine laughed in reply. Gregor took her coat, threw it on the bed with a whistle of admiration and drew her to him. She was unresisting as their lips met in a long, lingering kiss. Catherine felt his heart thundering against hers and knew she would return home with the bounty she'd come hunting. Gregor drew back and cleared his throat. He was quite out of breath. 'Wow!' he said appreciatively. 'I didn't expect that. But must put you down until later and prepare for my other guests.'

'Later can't come soon enough,' smiled Catherine as she smoothed the front of her skirt slowly and seductively over the curves of her firm belly and thighs. She teetered over to the dressing table and sat on the stool, crossing her legs seductively. Taking a small silver cylinder from her bag, she removed the top and twisted the bottom of the case until a red point of lipstick emerged and grew longer. She opened her mouth and carefully applied it to her lips, which were still plump from kissing. She pressed them together tightly and then let them spring open with a pop.

Gregor stood behind her straightening his tie. His eyes had followed every move that she made and he moistened his own lips, licking them all over with the tip of his tongue. 'You're full of surprises,' he whispered huskily, 'but let's get a move on; we've a party to get going.' He gave her a quick pat on the bottom to hurry her out through the door.

The party, held in the common room, kicked off to a lively start and rolled along comfortably and predictably. Plenty loud music and alcohol with piles of the unimaginative food typical of a single male: plates of cold sausage rolls and crackers and cheese. But food wasn't Catherine's priority. Jimmy's words had stung her deeply. The word 'virgin' rang in her ears as a brutal insult. It made her feel that she had somehow failed, that perhaps she wasn't grown up.

But she had work to do, ambitions to achieve. How could she do that if she tied herself down? And yet she wasn't prepared to sleep around with any Tom, Dick or Harry. She valued her male friends too much to use them, and they in turn treated her the same way. Jimmy was a definite 'no go' area. As well as the fact that he disgusted her, he was too close to home to go fooling around with. But now there was Gregor, Gregor who could love them and leave them, no strings attached. Fate had presented him to her on a plate. She liked him, but not with the same depth of feeling she had for her longtime friends. And importantly too, he was fanciable. He was perfect for that long awaited one night stand. She would be free at last from the burden of inexperience.

Throughout the evening, Catherine danced with Gregor as well as with several other young lads, flirting and laughing, and she felt no jealousy when Gregor chatted up girls. She knew she had whetted his appetite and that he would be hers come night time.

To ensure that this night went according to plan she had to stay in control and so sipped only one glass of wine.

The party continued to go with a swing. It was nearly midnight and many of the guests had paired off and left. The number remaining had dwindled to only a handful. Gregor led Catherine to a low couch where they both sank squeezed together into its soft velvet cushions. He nuzzled the side of her neck. 'Tired?' he asked.

'Not too tired,' she whispered back suggestively, biting his ear and breathing gently into it.

A long tender kiss followed. 'Come on,' he said, taking her hand, 'time for bed.' Catherine gripped his firm hand tightly and followed him to his room.

In the early hours of the morning Catherine sauntered through the university grounds on the start of her walk home. The dawn chorus gave voice to her joy as the cheeky birds sang in the branches of trees and from rooftops. Some scampered on the empty pathways and roads to celebrate their freedom from traffic and people. She strolled on slowly through the town, absorbing the newness of the day, savouring the changes in her body. The sky filled with fresh colour and light, and she allowed a smile of smug satisfaction to spread across her face like the cat that had got the cream.

Chapter 50

Maggie's state of health fluctuated in a series of peaks and troughs which left Catherine and Frank living on a knife-edge. Even in sleep they remained alert, listening for the heavy policeman's knock on the door that would summon them to the hospital for Maggie's last moments. Some nights, Frank would scream out in terror as death visited in nightmare visions. Fortunately, Catherine understood and so did their neighbours. He was one of many who remained a life-long casualty of unimaginable wartime experiences.

Although there were days when Maggie sank weakened by the struggle for breath into states of near unconsciousness, most times she thrived and was able to walk unaided to the day room for a few hours. 'I don't know why you worry so much,' she tutted on seeing Catherine and Frank's drawn faces. 'I am getting better. And you may not believe what the hardest part of my struggle to recover has been – stopping smoking, giving up my wee pals that have seen me through so many hard times.'

Frank frowned. 'Of course you'll get better. You'll see us all out, Maggie. You're like a bulldog the way you hang on to life. As for your fags, they've only come back to haunt you and stab you in the back. That's treachery and betrayal, not friendship.'

'Please, no more advice,' she said sharply, obviously still craving the nicotine. 'Catherine, lend me your hand mirror. I haven't seen what I look like for ages.' She looked in and gasped. 'Oh, no. I don't recognise that face. My hair's hanging like mince and it's going grey.' Catherine couldn't speak and hid her tears by pretending to rummage in her handbag while replacing the mirror. Frank's stammer returned with the distress of seeing his wife upset by the reality of her weakened appearance. 'I, I'll pay a hairdresser to come in and give you the works.' Maggie seemed cheered with that idea but was quite ecstatic when he added, 'And I'll take in

230

your new catalogue so you can choose a new dress to go with it.'

Catherine bounded up the tenement stairs two at a time and burst into the living room like a storm trooper. Frank, who had been slumped in the armchair catching up on lost sleep, jerked awake with a great snort. 'What's going on?' he yelled. Straight away, when he saw Catherine standing at his side, gasping for breath and urging him to wake up, he thought the worst. 'It's Maggie! Quick, we must get to the hospital!' He reached under the chair for his shoes and hauled them on, his fingers tangling with the laces in his haste to tie them.

To his surprise, Catherine started laughing. 'There's nothing wrong, Frank,' she said, sitting down on the settee with her coat still on. Her hair was dishevelled, but her face was shining. 'Do you know where I've come from, Frank?' she said mysteriously, getting back on her feet and clapping her hands together. She jumped up and down. 'I can't stay still. I'm too wound up.'

'Catherine, I'm many things but mind reader isn't one of them.' Frank didn't want to risk feeling happy until he knew the reason. 'Sit down, take a deep breath and tell me all about it. It's not Saturday, so we haven't won the football pools. Come on, Catherine, what is it? Put me out of my misery.'

Catherine took a few deep breaths. It was obvious from the sparkle in her eyes that she was enjoying every minute of the suspense. 'Well,' she began, smiling mischievously, 'today I went in past the Housing Department to ask if they had received the medical points for Mum from Dr. Ferguson. They took out the file and, what with my being over eighteen, Mum being married and now these for ill health – we are top of the list! Do you hear that, Frank? We're getting a house. Mum will have her house at last! I want to shout and scream and sing and dance!' Catherine got up and started twirling round the room, chanting: 'Mum's got her house!' She was manic with joy.

Frank started to laugh. 'I'm speechless,' he said, grinning from

231

ear to ear. 'Just wait till your mother hears this. Did they give you any indication where the house might be?'

'I've an idea it may be one of the new two bed-roomed houses up from the hospital; you know, where the prefabs used to be?'

'That would be fantastic,' said Frank excitedly. 'The air is so fresh and clean up there and it's only ten minutes from the town centre by bus. This news should really set your mother on the road to recovery. I can't wait to see her face.' He bustled round the room not knowing whether to straighten his tie or finally tie his laces. 'There will be a little garden for her to sit out in won't there?' he asked, checking to see if the dream really had come true.

'Well, don't ask me, I'm not clairvoyant either,' Catherine answered, looking at the clock. 'I'm only guessing where the house will be, but they all have gardens,' she answered. 'But one thing I must ask you, don't tell Rosie until we have it all in writing. I don't want her working Mum up. You know what she's like. Talking of Rosie, have you seen her today? I heard her up in the night vacuuming. I don't want to start complaining, but she'll soon have us as crazy as herself. And to think this drug-taking started because she wanted to look like a Hollywood actress. The only film star she resembles now is one you'd see in a horror movie. There's precious little difference by my way of thinking between the drug pushers in the pubs downtown and the doctors with their prescription pads.'

'I'm inclined to agree with you,' replied Frank, taking a cigarette from the mantelpiece. He studied it and then put it back behind the clock. 'I can't clear my mind of the fact that it was fear of being like Rosie that prevented your mother from going back to the doctor. It won't be easy for Rosie to come off all that stuff, you know. I'm finding it hard enough to pack this in.' He nodded in the direction of the discarded cigarette as he spoke. 'I have to persevere though – for Maggie's sake. If she can do it, so can I.'

'We're becoming serious again, Frank,' said Catherine. 'Let's get ourselves along to that hospital.'

Maggie raised herself off the pillows. 'I can't believe it,' she repeated when Catherine and Frank broke the good news. With a burst of energy she continued, 'There's so much to be done, I can't stay here being ill any more. Nurse, I'm going home.' Dr. Ferguson came through instead. He was smiling. 'I know,' he said, 'but, although the tuberculosis has responded to treatment and you're no longer infectious, you'll have to continue with hospital treatment until your damaged lungs have healed some more. We're allowing you home for occasional days at a time until your new house is ready.' Maggie pouted and pulled her forehead into a frown.

The doctor managed to crack a smile on his wrinkled old face. 'You won't have long to wait. I've made sure of that.'

Maggie kept her sulky expression and looked into the distance instead of into the happy faces around her. 'It's a question of how long I can afford to wait.'

Chapter 51

(Aberdeen, February 1968)

Maggie sat triumphantly in an armchair at home in her familiar kitchen and scrutinised her domain. She was delighted that Frank had redecorated and put in a new sink. However, she looked at the empty grate behind the new triple-barred electric fire and sighed, 'I miss the coal fire. This heater you've bought just doesn't have the same life about it.'

'I hope you're not complaining, Mum. You know the smoke from a coal fire is bad for you.' Catherine tucked a blanket round Maggie and placed her feet up on a footstool.

Frank smiled. 'We've been lost without you. Nobody to boss us about.'

'Enjoy it while you can,' replied Maggie in an ominous tone, 'because I shall be cracking the whip over your heads soon enough; my mind is racing with enough ideas for the new house to keep the two of you on your toes for months to come. I can't sit around as if I've given up on life all together. I need a sense of purpose.' Maggie gave a cheeky smile as she sat back, eyes closed, while Catherine and Frank danced attendance on her, preparing a light tea of sandwiches and cakes.

'You're up to something, Mum,' said Catherine, eyeing her mother suspiciously, 'and I'm not sure if that's a good or a bad thing.'

'I do have a surprise for you as a matter of fact,' said Maggie, her eyes twinkling with devilment. 'I'll let you in on it once we've eaten. I don't want your catering skills to go to waste.'

'There's never a dull moment in this house,' said Frank, stretching over towards the teapot. 'I suppose I'll have to play mother while you two play games.'

'You already make me a wonderful wife, Frank,' jibed Maggie, enjoying the fun atmosphere of home as opposed to the austerity of the hospital ward.

'I know, I'll be the one wanting a new frock after all this, so be warned,' Frank joked back.

Once the tea dishes were cleared away, the family relaxed, Maggie on the settee, the centre of attention and Catherine and Frank on the armchairs on either side of her, impatient and curious.

Maggie took her time. 'Catherine, I want you to fetch something for me,' she said after a good two minutes.

'Anything you want, you can have,' replied Catherine. 'I can't wait to discover what you're up to.'

'You'll find out in a minute,' Maggie answered, taking a deep breath to quell the mounting excitement within her. 'Go under the bed till you find something wrapped in a towel and bring it out.'

'What? You want me to crawl under the bed and get covered in cobwebs?' protested Catherine.

'Just do it,' said Maggie, 'or you won't find out what it is.'

'I'll fetch it,' said Frank, 'whatever it is. You can't have Catherine scrambling about on the floor.'

'No, Frank, please,' Maggie insisted, 'I want Catherine to do this.' Catherine was already struggling back out from under the bed, her jeans and jumper covered in long grey strands of dust. She clutched a package wrapped in a faded blue cloth.

'Go on, Catherine, open it,' said Maggie. Catherine sat with the parcel on her knee and unwrapped it slowly, tantalisingly, as if afraid something would jump out at her. She revealed a metal moneybox. 'The key's on the top shelf of the cupboard in a little plastic egg cup,' Maggie said to Frank. 'You can fetch that if you like.' Frank went to the cupboard and returned with the key, which he handed to Catherine. 'Now, open it,' Maggie instructed, her breath coming in short shallow breaths. Catherine hesitated for a full minute and just stared at the box. When she eventually put the key in the little lock, the click filled the expectant silence. Maggie had her hands pressed against her mouth. She couldn't wait.

Carefully Catherine drew the lid back and held it open in front of her, too shocked to speak.

Frank gaped like a giddy goldfish. The box was full of bank notes and coins. 'Where has this come from?' asked Catherine. 'Have you been out robbing banks in your spare time?'

'It's my savings,' said Maggie. 'It's as simple as that. I know that you have enough to take care of us, Frank, and you are a most generous husband, but I have savings too. I've been putting past for a house ever since Sam and I first married. I never told anyone, even Rosie.' She took out the notes and handed them to Frank for counting. Under the notes lay a tobacco tin and a Post Office savings book. Maggie asked Catherine to pass them to her. 'I opened the bank account when the money started to pile up,' she said, tucking the tin into her lap before opening the book to reveal pages of neatly written columns of figures. 'Four hundred and eighty-three pounds, eleven shillings and sevenpence,' she read out with exaggerated movement of her lips, enunciating each syllable. Catherine and Frank stared open mouthed but speechless. 'Every time the cash amounted to twenty-five pounds I banked it,' she continued quickly in an almost offhand explanation.

'There's nineteen pounds here in ten shilling notes and two pounds, nine and fourpence in coins,' announced Frank, waving the sheaf of notes in the air before placing them in a neat pile on the coffee table in front of them. 'I didn't know I'd married such a wealthy woman.' However, he was too flabbergasted to laugh at his own joke.

Catherine took the bankbook from her mother's hands and scrutinised it closely. 'The entries in here go back over twenty years to before I was even born. Why didn't you tell anyone?'

'It seemed a good idea to start saving when I was expecting you,' she explained. 'I kept it secret. I even pretended to myself I didn't have it so I wouldn't be tempted to spend it. Every pound in the bank was out of bounds as far as I was concerned.' Maggie had never betrayed Sam. No-one knew the full story of how he had frittered his father's legacy. Nobody knew and they never would.

Maggie continued her explanation. 'When everyone doubted me when I spoke about buying a house, I didn't care. I knew I had more than enough for a large deposit. What I didn't have was the security of a healthy long term income to pay off a mortgage. You would need two decent wages for that so if all had gone according to plan I was going to tell everyone after the wedding . . . .'

Catherine and Frank remained silent. Their eyes were turned upwards and flickering. A lot of thinking was going on inside their heads. They looked keenly at Maggie again when she held up the tobacco tin, handling it gingerly as if it were made of glass. She removed the lid and put it on her knee. From inside she took out what looked like a folded up piece of paper, but it turned out to be an old-style British Linen Bank five pound note, yellow on one side and blank on the other. 'This is an extra special part of Sam's contribution,' she said almost reverently, glancing over at his photograph on the sideboard. 'I kept one of the fivers from his famous big win as a reminder of the day he gave up gambling for good. The rest of the money in here is from Lucy,' she said, rattling the tin gently. Her voice was shaking. 'When my little angel died I wanted her to remain a part of our future so I kept the original coins from her piggy bank in here. There's almost six pounds. I couldn't bear to put it in the bank. Now we can use it to buy something to remember her by.' She paused for breath and looked at the two pairs of amazed eyes that stared at her. 'I've always dreamed of a pretty little cherry tree that will bear blossom every year to bring her memory to life. And there should be enough for some rose bushes too, red, pink and yellow with the most fragrant of perfumes. What do you think?'

'I don't know what to think,' answered Catherine. 'I'm expecting to wake up soon.'

'Don't ask me. It's your money to spend,' said Frank still in too much of a daze to think anything.

'What I've already decided on for the house from Sam is a stereogram. We don't have room for one here, but he did buy me a record player one Christmas so I didn't have to keep on winding up the gramophone. It was wonderful; I could listen to all my favourite music without it continually slowing down to a groan. Sam always understood my need for music, especially violins.' She closed her eyes in reminiscence. 'I've already seen some of the latest ones in the shops,' she said, her voice speeding up with excitement. 'They make a beautiful piece of furniture. They've two built in speakers and a radio. The best part is that you can stack a pile of records on the long spindle part of the turn table and listen to them all in turn as they drop down. Frank, just think, we'll be able to dance without stopping.' Maggie was quite out of breath by the time she had finished.

'Sounds like magic to me,' replied Frank. 'I'd better brush up on my quickstep. But, seriously, Maggie, I have to take my hat off to you. What you've done has taken a strength of will we lesser mortals will never begin to understand.'

'Smeddum,' said Catherine. 'You've got smeddum.'

'I know what that means,' said Maggie. 'It means mettle, determination, having a back bone. I do know my mither tongue. Dad and Eddie used to love their Scots poetry. We often had Saturday soirees and they'd recite some of their favourites.'

'Well, Mum, I don't know what to say. You're just a soppy sentimentalist at heart.' Catherine was dabbing at her eyes with a hanky.

Maggie drifted into a private reverie for a couple of minutes. 'Now at last after twenty years the time is right for spending. We'll have the most beautiful house in Woodlands Lane.' She placed the lid carefully back on the tin and tears of nostalgia ran down her cheek.

Chapter 52

Maggie sat quietly pensive. It was Saturday night and her weekend home was passing too quickly. 'Just think, Catherine, in a month's time we'll be in our new home. Have you told Rosie yet?'

'No, Mum, not yet. I wanted you to have that pleasure,' she replied and hurriedly returned to the subject of new furniture. Frank's face became strangely stern at the mention of Rosie's name and then he too forced a smile and began to enthuse about studio couches and three-piece suites. 'If I had my choice, I would have red moquette.'

'Oh no, Frank,' interjected Catherine, 'that would be dreadful. Green is the colour I'd choose.'

Maggie was not to be sidetracked. 'You know, it's ages since Rosie came to visit me,' she mused, interest in her friend now taking priority over the house. 'I hope she's not still popping those pills.' There was an awkward silence so she repeated her question, this time her voice insistent as her eyes flitted from Frank's to Catherine's, probing for an answer. It was obvious she would be satisfied with nothing less than the truth. 'If there's anything wrong with Rosie, I want to know.' Hesitantly at first, Catherine unveiled the dreaded secret to her mother. Frank's face darkened as he watched anxiously for the effect the awful truth might have on his wife. 'To cut a long story short, Mum, Rosie wanted to stop and told the doctor so.' Catherine moved closer to her mother as she spoke.

'Well, surely that was a good thing, brave I'd call it,' commented Maggie, shaking her hand free of Catherine's.

'I have no doubt it was,' replied Catherine, exchanging another worried look with Frank. 'When she told the doctor she wanted off them, he studied her notes closely for the first time, and realising exactly what and how much she was taking, he cancelled the prescriptions just like that.'

'And what's wrong with that?' enquired Maggie. 'Surely that's exactly what she wanted.'

'It is, Mum, but it's not quite as easy as that. You see,' Catherine explained, 'Rosie's addicted and having bad withdrawal symptoms, especially from the tranquillisers. She can't sleep, gets panic attacks and is too frightened to leave the house. She's not been over the threshold for three weeks.'

'But surely the doctor can't abandon her like that. There must be something he can do. After all it was him that created this problem in the first place,' said a puzzled Maggie.

'Not exactly. You see, Rosie was deliberately seeing a different doctor each visit in order to mask the quantity of drugs being administered. It was a locum, an older retired doctor that saw her when she mentioned stopping. He had a word with the senior partner and there's no way now she'll be prescribed any more. Jimmy went to see the doctor himself because he was so worried. The doctor was adamant. The real problem is that because Rosie said, probably just casually, that she couldn't see a future, he'd be held responsible in the event of any overdose.'

'But surely it's the doctor's duty to treat her,' Maggie protested. Her pallid face was now flushed and she pulled at her throat anxiously. Catherine put an arm round her and Frank protested that she'd heard enough. 'No, Frank,' she persisted, 'I'm not a child; I have a right to know. Go on, Catherine, spare me none of the details.'

'Well, since you're so sure, I'll tell you; I know that if I don't, you'll go asking round the neighbours until one of them tells you,' said Catherine, relenting. 'The doctor says the withdrawals will subside, but if they don't, and Rosie gets any worse, she'll be helped, but under supervision so she doesn't take too many. You know what that means – she'll have to go into the mental hospital, and who knows what they'll do to her in there once they get their hands on her.'

'That's so true,' declared Maggie, 'she might never come out again, just like that Sunday school teacher.'

240

'Miss Walker,' Catherine replied with a shudder. 'I can't bear to think about her. It was barbaric what they did to her. They gave her a lobotomy in the end - cut bits off her brain. I wonder if she's still alive.'

'No more of all that weird stuff!' Frank interrupted angrily. 'I don't want to hear another word. It's upsetting your mother. Rosie will come all right given time.' He came and sat at the other side of Maggie and put an arm protectively around her. Maggie shrugged him off. 'Don't cosset me. I'm not an invalid or senile.'

'Okay, we'll arrange for you to see her next weekend but no more morbid talk.' He glared over at Catherine as he spoke. She visibly bit her lip and kept quiet.

'I'm not waiting till next week. I'm going to see Rosie tomorrow!' declared Maggie.

'It's great to have you back, but one thing's for sure, you haven't improved any. Still can't keep your nose out of other people's trouble,' said Frank, shaking his head.

No sooner had he spoken than there was a loud knock at the door. It opened and Jimmy came into the kitchen. 'Catherine, come quickly!' he shouted but stopped when he saw Maggie. Catherine urged him to speak. 'Sorry to interrupt your visit, Maggie, but I'm so worried,' he began breathlessly. 'You see, Mum went out earlier this afternoon to test her confidence. When she'd been out for an hour I grew worried and went looking for her. I found her in Grove Road sitting on the low wall outside Molly Gibson's, holding on to the fence for dear life. She refused to move even with my help. She's in sheer terror at being outside the familiar confines of the house.'

'Where's Jim? Why wasn't he looking after her?' Maggie asked the obvious question.

'He's out,' answered Jimmy abruptly. 'He's got an important darts away match. He'll be gone all weekend.'

'That's not much of an excuse,' muttered Maggie.

'You told me he was working away from home up north

decorating a new hotel,' said Catherine.

'He's not in. Isn't that enough?' he replied evasively and started to pace backwards and forwards, greatly agitated, berating himself for allowing his mother out by herself.

'It's too late for that now,' snapped Catherine, showing him absolutely no sympathy. 'Where is your mother now? I hope you took her home.'

'No. That's what I'm trying to tell you. She says her legs refuse to move. Molly's with her now, trying to calm her down.' Jimmy was close to tears. 'I thought that if you came we could fetch her home somehow between the two of us.'

'Of course I'll come and help your mother,' said Catherine. 'I won't be long, Mum,' she said as she strode hurriedly to the cupboard for her jacket and pulled it on as she dashed down the stairs with Jimmy hot on her heels.

Catherine and Jimmy ran to the next street where they found the panic stricken Rosie sitting on the dyke with one hand gripping her helper's hand and the other clamped tightly round a spar of the fence. Beads of sweat stood out on her haggard grey face. 'Catherine, oh Catherine,' she gasped, 'help me please.'

'I've never seen anyone so frightened,' said Molly Gibson. 'I was in the middle of my outside cleaning when Rosie came past and collapsed right in front of me. She won't budge.'

'You're going to be all right,' Catherine said to Rosie and, as she spoke, she was peeling her fingers one-by-one from the fence and entwining them with her own. Now that her hands were free, Catherine put Rosie's hands next to each other, palms upwards. 'Cup your hands over your nose and mouth and breathe out and in a few times. The increased carbon dioxide will help.' Rosie followed Catherine's instructions and was soon calm enough for Catherine and Jimmy to guide her slowly home. It wasn't until she was seated in her own chair in her own kitchen that her breathing finally steadied. 'What's wrong with me?' she cried. 'I can't spend the rest of my life in the house.'

'Where's Jim?' asked Catherine, but this question was met by a silencing glare from Jimmy who was filling the kettle for tea. Catherine said no more on the subject but she did give a long, thoughtful mmmm . . . . Suddenly there was a knock at the door and Maggie came in on Frank's arm. Rosie took one look at her friend and burst into tears. 'Stop that crying and all your other nonsense,' wheezed Maggie seemingly without sympathy. 'Come on, girl, you've got guests that need seeing to.'

Rosie smiled wanly through her tears but continued sobbing. Maggie sat beside her and held her tightly till the shuddering subsided. An awkward embarrassment kept the others silent and still in their seats.

'I have some good news that will cheer you up,' announced Maggie.

'That'll make a change,' whimpered Rosie.

'I've got a house,' announced Maggie. 'After all these years of waiting, we're moving.'

'You're what?' moaned Rosie and started to cry again. 'But it's been hell without you, absolute hell. What will I do if you leave? My life's an upside down mess.'

Jimmy sprang to his feet and went over to his mother. 'You're overwrought,' he said, ushering everyone out. 'Come on, what do you say we call it a day? Come back tomorrow when Mum's had some rest.'

'You're quite right, Jimmy,' said Maggie, 'we're all exhausted.' Jimmy couldn't seem to get rid of them fast enough.

'There's more to that household than meets the eye,' exclaimed Maggie on the way upstairs.

'I'm going down later to see Jimmy?' said Catherine. 'I'll drag it out of him over a drink. He won't say No if I ask him out and Molly said she'd sit with Rosie any time.'

Chapter 53

In the lounge of the Lochnagar, Catherine and Jimmy relaxed side by side on the plush tartan upholstery. Opposite them, up on a dais, a crooner with a trilby hat pulled down over his forehead and perched on a stool, serenaded them with jazz ballads. Catherine had deliberately steered clear of any talk relating to Jimmy's father. After the second drink, she grew bolder. 'Your mother's a bag of nerves these days, Jimmy,' she began cautiously. 'Is anything worrying her?'

'I'm not going to beat about the bush,' he said, his directness taking Catherine completely by surprise. He continued, nervously moving a beer mat around the table with the fingertip of his middle finger, 'Mum was on the verge of letting the cat out of the bag earlier.'

'What cat and what bag?' asked Catherine, burning with curiosity. She pressed her index finger on the moving beer mat and held it still. Now she had the focus of his attention, she challenged him outright. 'Be honest, your father's the problem, isn't he?'

Jimmy held his hands up in surrender. 'You're right, Catherine, as usual. I've been longing to tell you but you've been so busy.'

'Sorry, Jimmy. I shouldn't have dived in like that. You're obviously hurting.' Catherine turned her body round and leaned earnestly towards him, her eyes full of sympathy. The floodgates opened and Jimmy poured forth his secret in torrents, not even pausing for a sip of his drink. 'Dad's having an affair with a woman he met at work and he's with her now. It all blew up when you and Frank were always at the hospital. You see, Dad has spent his married life being bossed and bullied by Mum without complaint. When she began to display weakness he found he couldn't handle it. He needs a strong character to direct him through life. He's grown used to living like a puppet with rarely a thought of his own. When Mum became ill, he never saw it as an opportunity for him to reciprocate and care for her. He wanted to escape and started going out more often. He couldn't bear to be around her when it was her turn to be needy. Now he's living in the care of a widow who needed someone to take charge of after her husband died.'

Catherine shook her head, stunned. It was unlike Jimmy to be so vociferous. 'You need something stronger than beer,' she said, 'and so do I.' She waved to a passing barman and ordered two double brandies. 'I'll pay for this,' insisted Jimmy, 'and if you don't let me I won't tell you the rest.'

'How did your mother find out? Did your father confess?' Catherine asked, desperate to hear the rest of the story.

'It was my fault as usual,' continued Jimmy, taking a much needed gulp of alcohol. 'I wanted to encourage Mum to regain her confidence, so one Thursday, Thursday being Dad's darts night, I suggested we surprise him by turning up to support him. We took a cab there. Mum was great, and we were happily sitting at the side watching Dad finish his turn on the dartboard, when a woman went over and threw her arms round his neck. He kissed her back, a slow deliberate kiss.'

'Your poor mother!' declared Catherine. 'What did she do?'

'Mum grabbed me and pulled me towards the door, but not before Dad saw us and chased after. She dragged me out into the street and flagged down a taxi. Dad was left in the middle of the road waving his arms like a policeman on point duty.' Jimmy paused for breath and took another slug of his drink.

'What a bastard! I'm surprised your mother never hit him,' said Catherine angrily. 'I'd like to get my hands on him myself.'

'Mum was a woman possessed. No sooner were we in the house than she dragged the sheets off the bed, screaming that they were contaminated by his stinking two-timing body. She used them to bundle up his belongings.'

'It's a wonder she didn't burn the lot,' said Catherine, clenching and unclenching her fists.

'She made me help her drag it all down to the street and just as she had it all piled up on the kerb, Dad rolled up. Mum kicked the lot into the gutter, but it was when Dad leapt out of the cab that she finally lost her cool.' Jimmy had meanwhile ripped the beer mat to shreds which he absentmindedly swept up with his hand and deposited them in the ashtray. Without thinking, he picked up another and started tearing it to bits with his nervous fingertips.

'I hope she hit him,' said Catherine, frowning.

'Wait, let me tell the story,' answered Jimmy. 'She told him to get the hell out of her life and live with his whore. She kept kicking the bundles till they burst open. There were shirts, vests, underpants all over the street. Dad scurried around picking them out of the puddles in the potholes. His final mistake was telling her she was behaving like a madwoman. She cursed and swore, and when he came near, she kicked him high up right between the legs.'

'Good for her!' said Catherine.

'We left him curled up on the pavement crying and holding himself, while all his clothes flew around him like rubbish at the tip in the wind and the rain.'

'He deserved it. Your mother treated him like a king for twenty-five years, and look how he repaid her!' Catherine drained her glass and folded her arms. 'I'd have killed him with my bare hands.'

'Do you know the strangest thing in the whole episode?' Jimmy said.

'No, what?' replied Catherine, distractedly dreaming of the method she would choose for the murder.

'The woman he took up with, that he's living with now, is the spit and image of Mum, plump like she used to be, but with brown hair instead of blonde.' He paused and started biting the skin round his nails. 'Do you think Mum and Dad will get back together?'

Catherine shook her head. 'Never in a million years, Jimmy,

your mother may have problems but she's not insane.'

'There's something else and you're the only one I can turn to.' Jimmy called across to the barmaid for another round of drinks. 'You saw the state she was in. I can't leave her alone in the house, shaking like a leaf any time there's a knock at the door and too frightened to go out.'

'All that's to be expected, but she will return to herself gradually,' Catherine said, trying to sound convincing. 'She has to.'

'Mum would have coped with Dad's affair. It's not that; it's the pills. Her problem's physical, not mental,' said Jimmy defensively. 'You're right, my mum's as sane as anyone else, but coming off tranquillisers has proved too much.'

'I can't understand why the doctor didn't cut them down gradually,' said Catherine, suggesting a possible solution.

'I think he was scared she would take too many because she admitted to him the other week that she couldn't see a future. She didn't mean it. It was only a turn of phrase she'd got into the habit of using.'

'Do you realise that your mother's addiction is no different from that of the characters who skulk in the shadows waiting to pounce on dope peddlers for their black bombers and purple hearts? I see their kind in the pub after the debating society on Friday nights.'

A glimmer of hope flashed across Jimmy's concerned face. 'What sort of drugs do they deal? Do you think they might have any tranquillisers?' Jimmy asked excitedly.

'What on earth do you have in mind? I hope it's not what it sounds like?'

'Catherine, if they do, we can take my mother off the drugs gradually. She may have a chance of recovery after all; otherwise God knows what will happen to her. If they take her into hospital, like the doctor said, she'll be finished. I just know it. Please, Catherine, please say you'll help.' Catherine listened carefully to Jimmy's plea. What he asked was unsavoury and yet it had a ring of common sense to it. 'I've never been interested in what they sell. I'm not saying No exactly, but give me time to think it over.' She heaved a sigh. Surely Rosie wasn't the only person in her situation. Perhaps there was information to be got that would make a good story for a newspaper, and by exposure, help people out of their predicament. She gave Jimmy a nod. Rosie would get the help she needed.

Chapter 54

Two shadowy figures left the murk and mire of the foggy Saturday night streets and entered the steamy warmth of the Bonnie Prince Charlie. 'I watched the dealers in action last night,' Catherine whispered. 'You can't miss them. I think you could get almost anything you want in here. Now, play it cool. Talk to nobody. My crowd only comes here on Friday nights so we shouldn't be bothered by anyone.'

They had to struggle their way to the bar through a jam-packed crowd of young people, mostly students. The air was thick with smoke. For entertainment, two not so young men, one longhaired and bearded, one bald with a Mexican moustache, sat at a table in a corner singing folk songs along to the banjo accompaniment that the moustachioed one played quite niftily. Catherine and Jimmy managed to find a couple of seats right at the back of the lounge bar. No one would notice them there. 'Who are we looking for? Are they in yet?' asked Jimmy impatiently, scouring the crowd with narrowed eyes.

'Relax, will you,' answered Catherine who, in her efforts to appear nonchalant, had started to sing along with the folk singers. 'You don't even know who you're looking for. Pretend you're here for the music.'

'I don't know the words to these songs. It's not what I'm used to,' answered Jimmy, but after a sharp kick in the shins from Catherine, he started to nod his head in time to the music. Suddenly, Catherine stiffened. 'They're here. Keep your eyes on the singers, but discreetly allow your eyes to go towards the bar. One of them has short blond hair and is wearing a suit. The other has long greasy hair and is wearing a leather jacket,' she whispered. 'They're an ill-matched pair. Dealing drugs is probably all they have in common.'

Catherine turned to gaze at the singers with occasional glances towards the door. Jimmy looked round at the dope dealers. 'I think I see them,' he whispered, turning back towards Catherine. 'What shall we do now?'

'I'll go up for the drinks. You wait here,' she said quietly. 'Half pints only, we want to keep our wits about us.' Catherine jostled her way towards the bar and bumped herself against the blond pusher. 'Sorry,' she said quite loudly and then continued almost inaudibly, 'I'd like a word. Follow me back to where I'm sitting.' Catherine bought the drinks and returned to Jimmy. The blond guy followed and, without looking directly at her, stood beside her and Jimmy. Catherine whispered something to Jimmy who got up and went to the Gents. 'Mind if I sit here till he comes back?' the dealer asked Catherine and took the stool beside her. 'Not at all,' she answered, and as she stretched towards a table with her drink, she whispered, 'Do you have tranquillisers?'

'How many?' he asked, looking away from her. He pretended to check his watch with the time on the clock.

'Can we go somewhere to discuss it?' she asked. 'We're trying to wean someone off them gradually.'

'Is your boyfriend in on this?' he asked. 'If so, I'll go and talk to him now.' Catherine nodded and the dealer went to the Gents. Jimmy returned shortly afterwards. 'I explained the situation to him and he suggested how to cut down slowly so the withdrawals won't be so bad,' said Jimmy. 'He says a lot of his business comes from housewives who've got out of their depth with prescription pills.'

'So, when do we get them and how much will it cost?' asked Catherine.

'He's giving us sixty pills for fifteen pounds. He says it should be twenty,' replied Jimmy. 'As she cuts down, she can split them in half. We have to meet him outside the newsagent's round the corner in fifteen minutes. He has to collect them first.'

'Fine so far. Could be a bargain. You said you'd brought twenty pounds. We'll just have to trust him. We've no choice,' she answered. 'Come on, let's get out of here.'

They squeezed their way out. The greasy one with the leather jacket was deep in conversation with a white faced young couple who, by the glazed look in their eyes, looked as if they'd already had their fix.

The steady drizzle of earlier had changed to stinging rain. Catherine and Jimmy hurried through the streets. True to his word, the supplier was waiting for them in the dingy shop doorway. There was no one around and the transaction was carried out quickly and without fuss. 'Remember what I said: gradually, till she's managing on a half morning and night and then nights only and then alternate nights and then longer and longer. It won't be easy but it'll put a stop to the panic. She'll be fine, believe me.' He sounded like an everyday pharmacist dispensing cough drops and, after all, who was to know that he wasn't?

Catherine and Jimmy walked smartly back along the street with never a backward glance. Two beat policemen were heading straight for them. 'Keep walking, Jimmy. Look confident,' urged Catherine, taking his arm to stop him arousing suspicion.

The policemen were facing them now, close up. One of them, an old chap with a grey moustache nodded to them. 'Miserable old evening,' he said by way of a greeting. 'Not a night to be out.'

'Terrible weather; a night for the fireside,' agreed Jimmy giving a nervous cough.

'Best hurry along. You sound as if you've a cold already,' answered the second one.

'Yes, we're off home right now to see what's on telly,' said Catherine, trying to seem friendly, as if having nothing to hide.

'Wish I could join you,' muttered the first, wiping rain from his face as they passed closely by.

'Phew!' gasped Catherine once they were clear. 'I'm so glad that's over, though I must say it was a lot easier than I thought it would be. By the way, how did you get hold of all that money?'

'I've stayed in for the past few weekends looking after Mum. I was saving up for a holiday, but this is much more important,' he replied.

'Maybe you're not so bad after all, Jimmy Simpson,' laughed Catherine.

'You're quite surprising yourself,' answered Jimmy. Catherine turned and actually managed to raise a smile of goodwill, until he added with a smirk, 'For a virgin!'

'Why do you have to be so nasty always?' retorted Catherine, but she smiled through the rain, happy with her secret. His corny attempts at ridicule would no longer have any effect on her. 'You don't know me as well as you think, Jimmy Simpson,' she sneered. 'You don't have a clue about what I do with my life or who I see.'

But Jimmy was so impatient to make snide comments of his own that he failed to absorb the full implication of her words. 'You have the audacity to criticise me for going to the country dances and there's yourself hanging out in dives with dope peddlers. They were all students in there, you know. I think I was the only decent working man,' he said harshly.

'Get rid of that giant chip on your shoulder, Jimmy. You could study too if you wanted. Evening classes at first, and then a grant for the Institute of Technology. You have it in you to be an engineer if you wanted. My mother took exams at her age so she could better herself. You won't do it because you're just after quick money.'

'Too true. When I've finished my apprenticeship next year, I'll be well paid as a welder. I'm not sacrificing a livelihood to live on a grant. Anyway, it's not unusual to hear of students studying for years only to find there's no other work but cutting grass for the Links and Parks. That's not ambition in my book. And look at you. Do you have any idea what you want to be?' Jimmy tried his best to pour scorn on her. 'If you'd left school and worked in an office you would have a decent life and wouldn't know about places like the one we went to tonight.'

'It was yourself that asked me to take you to a place like that; you've no gratitude.' Catherine tossed her head in the air.

'You use books as a drug,' suggested Jimmy pointedly. 'They've become your whole life. You think knowledge and the success it brings will provide you with the justification for existence that you desperately need, but they won't bring you contentment.'

'You can't rile me with that old tosh, Jimmy; I've heard it all before. Change the record please,' replied Catherine rather more heatedly than she intended, annoyed with herself for rising to the bait. She took a deep breath and continued, 'To return to the point of this conversation, I do so know what I want to be, and going to these dives as you call them helps my investigation into people and their lives. You see, my ambition is to be a journalist. I want to expose the injustices that ordinary people have to endure. One day, I'll reveal the problem of prescription drugs and tonight's experience is invaluable. Your mother's story may one day help other people, so experiences such as tonight's will make me worthy of the job. And don't go thinking I won't tip off the Police, because that's the first thing on my agenda tomorrow morning.'

The pair of them had stopped walking in order to pay more attention to the conversation. They were now standing face-to-face, oblivious to the heavy rain. Catherine was excited and spoke animatedly. Jimmy's eyes, on the other hand, which had been lively and bright as he teased her, became doleful and disbelieving, like those of a faithful hound that has been brutally kicked.

'You're planning to leave here one day aren't you?' he asked, his voice shaking with agitation.

'I'll have to if I want to achieve what I know I'm capable of,' replied Catherine, her voice becoming gentler when she saw the hurt in Jimmy's eyes. 'As you know, my mother has always encouraged me. I know for sure that she would be more upset by my staying here as a nothing than if I left to follow the life that I've set my heart on.'

'Where will you go?'

'I don't know yet. That's for the future to decide. I have to pass my exams first. Catherine's step was sprightly and her voice light,

253

whereas Jimmy had become morose. 'Is there nothing I can do to make you like me?' he whined. Suddenly he looked insignificant and vulnerable as he hunched against the driving force of the rain.

Chapter 55

(Aberdeen, Spring 1968)

Outside the back door of the new house, Maggie sat on a comfortable wickerwork chair watching Frank planting the cherry tree and rose bushes. 'You know,' she called over to Catherine who was energetically raking the earth in preparation for planting new grass seed, 'I'm a lucky woman to have everything I ever wanted. My life is complete.'

'No one deserves it more than you,' Catherine replied. 'You've worked hard to achieve your ambition.'

'What are you going to do with your life, Catherine? You need a plan, otherwise life drifts on like a meandering stream that slowly dries out in the middle of nowhere.'

'I do have a piece of good news,' Catherine answered mysteriously.

'Go on, girl, tell me,' insisted Maggie. 'Don't keep me in suspenders.'

Catherine placed the rake against the wall of the house and sat on a chair beside her mother. 'You know the Easter March in London? Well, I'm going down with the local branch of the Peace Council. We're hiring a bus and a driver. That's the reason for the fund raising jumble sales and donation sheets.' Catherine spoke slowly as if leading up to something more important.

'I know all that already. I want to hear something new and exciting,' replied Maggie, sounding disappointed.

'There is more. I just got word this morning. I haven't said anything because I just can't believe it myself.'

'Well, tell me. You're too subdued for someone who's just had good news,' said Maggie.

'That's because the outcome could affect the rest of my life. You see, I won first place in an essay competition run by the "Daily Voice". I wrote about the problems faced by decent people whose lives have been affected by the random and unsupervised dispensing of prescription drugs and they've promised to print it. Mum, I'm so excited, and so nervous. The "Daily Voice" is a national newspaper. I'll be well on my way to becoming a journalist. It's just the break that I need.' Catherine became silent in anticipation of her mother's reply.

'Oh, Catherine, you're going to be famous. I knew you had it in you!' Maggie struggled to shout to Frank, but all that came out was a breathless whisper. 'Frank, our Catherine's going to be famous.'

'Mum, do be careful. You're working yourself up,' Catherine said anxiously.

'It's good for me to be happy. If there's one thing you've achieved in your life, Catherine, it's to have made me happy. You've been the highlight of my life.' They waved to Frank but he called Catherine down to the foot of the garden. He was ready to plant the cherry tree. Catherine held it steady while Frank shovelled the earth into the hole to keep it upright. 'I only wish I could live to see your success,' Maggie whispered, but Catherine was too far away to hear.

Chapter 56

(London, Easter Weekend, 1968)

'*Warmongers and playboys won't tell us what to do,*' sang the marchers. Catherine looked behind her. The march stretched back along the road as far as the eye could see. Out in front it was the same. The line averaged six people deep. 'I wonder how many thousands there are,' she commented to a fellow marcher. 'My heart races when I think of people converging from all over the world to demand peace and nuclear disarmament. It gives renewed faith in the human race and hope for the future. I love to hear the guitars, flutes and penny whistles. The music and singing create such a joyful atmosphere, and I'm part of it, part of life.'

'It's well worth the sore feet,' said her companion. 'At last, we've reached the common; we're stopping here for lunch.'

'Well done, marchers, well done,' came the voice of a woman who stood on the back of a lorry welcoming everyone on to the grass for a lunch break. Catherine wandered among the thousands of demonstrators. A Co-op van was distributing bread, slabs of cheese, bread and cups of tea. Other vans were selling teas, coffees and soft drinks. A multitude of people of all ages from toddlers to pensioners gathered on the grass, talking, debating, singing, catching up on lost sleep or tending to sore, tired feet. Reporters from around the world were asking questions and some were filming the many diverse and international banners. Catherine strolled back to her own contingent and wrote in her notebook.

The Aberdeen banner was positioned proudly against a fence. All around were banners from church groups, CND, trade unions, political parties, tenants' associations and many other organisations, all wanting peace. People approached each other's groups to chat, their town or country of origin providing an interesting opener. Catherine observed a tall middle-aged man with long, almost shoulder length auburn hair that was streaked with grey hovering around. He stroked his chin thoughtfully and looked over towards her. 'Can I help you?' Catherine called, thinking he had maybe been separated from his own group.

He walked slowly over. 'Perhaps you can,' he answered, and Catherine detected the trace of a Scottish accent. 'You see,' he continued, 'Aberdeen's my home town. I haven't been back since the war. It feels strange to see its name in large bold letters instead of merely a word fading into the dimness of time gone by.'

This had the makings of a good human-interest story for her report. 'You must tell me more. Do you still have family there? Are you ever homesick?'

'That's why I'm hesitant to go back. All my family, apart from one niece, were killed in a fire. I did try contacting her, but the neighbours told me she'd gone down south. So where would I start looking? Down south is a big place when you're starting from Aberdeen. No doubt she'll be married and have changed her surname. Of course time passes and . . .' His voice trailed into silence as he resumed his own inner thoughts. Catherine had already started writing when he spoke again. 'You must let me introduce myself. I'm Eddie Clark. I live in Basildon, Essex, and I'm a history lecturer in East London. I got myself an education after the war and settled there.'

Catherine looked at him in disbelief. 'I don't suppose by any chance that your niece is called Maggie?'

'Why, yes,' he stammered. 'How do you know that?'

Catherine's head swam and a cold rushing noise swept up past her ears. 'Are you all right? You're trembling,' Eddie said in hoarse whisper. He too had paled and his face was moist with sweat. Catherine sat on the grass and took deep gulps of fresh air. Eddie sat beside her.

'Maggie Clark is my mother. She often talks about you and says I take after you because I enjoy reading and I'm interested in politics. My name's Catherine by the way.'

Eddie scrutinised her face. 'My word, Catherine, you're

Maggie's double. You look just as I remember her, except you have brown hair and hers was fiery red.'

'Mum never left Aberdeen,' said Catherine, patting him on the arm trying to relieve his state of shock. 'You must come and visit.'

'Just try and stop me. I can't wait to see her again.'

The happy expression on Catherine's face turned to one of sadness as the vision of her now fading mother came suddenly to mind. 'Remember, Eddie, it's been well over twenty years since you last saw her and she's been seriously ill.' The call came over a loudhailer to reassemble. 'Look, why don't you march with us. It's where you belong, behind the Aberdeen banner, back to your roots.' Eddie didn't hesitate and was soon walking in line beside her. Voices from ahead had already taken up the chant: 'What do we want . . . ? Peace! When do we want it . . .? Now!'

Eddie and Catherine spoke nineteen to the dozen as they walked. 'It's only a small terraced house in Basildon, but there's plenty room for one more any time you want to stay.' In anticipation of the next question, he continued, 'The only girl I ever felt like marrying went and married someone else, my best mate as it happens. I was so caught up in local politics and union matters that I never noticed how close they'd become. Can't say I blame them. I wasn't being much of a friend to Mark and I certainly wasn't giving Marian the attention she deserved. I've never bothered much with anyone since. How about yourself? You haven't mentioned anyone. Is there a lucky young man somewhere on the scene?' Catherine hesitated before shaking her head. 'No one I'd call serious.'

'Well, don't leave it too late;' said Eddie, 'it's a lonely life on your own.'

The final day of the march dawned sunny and warm. From every corner of London and its hinterland, the marchers left their billets and assembled for the last leg. The march had wended its way towards London in a heady carnival atmosphere at a rate of seventeen miles a day. Each day the camaraderie intensified.

259

Peacefully, the march drew near to central London. Even the police were relaxed and happy as they accompanied the march in time to the sound of guitars, flutes and tambourines.

The Aberdeen marchers chanted and sang with the best of them. Catherine's head swivelled from side to side in awe at the size and beauty of London's buildings. Crowds lined the streets. Some cheered. Some heckled.

'So, you've never given up your interest in politics?' commented Catherine.

'I promised myself I'd remain an idealist no matter what. You see, there's more to life than personal survival. That's an attitude that can lead to discontent and the separation of oneself from the rest of the human race, viewing other people merely as competitors. However, when you give yourself over to a cause, you lose that sense of self, and petty insecurities are lessened as a result. Material gain becomes less important. However, the craving for power and possessions will corrupt all but the strongest. It happens in small committees as well as in governments. Therefore, the dedicated, the altruistic, never achieve power, because they never crave it; their energy goes on campaigning for what is right and just. That's why the most principled people never hold the positions that would enable them to change society for the better.'

'That's an interesting thought,' said Catherine, swapping her placard from one arm to the other. She wished she had a spare hand to take notes.

'Interesting but frightening,' Eddie continued. 'It means we're on a never ending circle of one corrupt leader after another. The voice of the people may be heard but will never carry power.'

'How come you're not disillusioned? Why haven't you given up?'

'That's simple,' said Eddie. 'I'm never disillusioned when I'm let down by people, especially politicians, because I never hold the illusion in the first place. But that doesn't mean I have to become apathetic. I never pass up an opportunity such as this to stand up

260

and be counted. I enjoy being among people who share the same views as myself. It's refreshing, relaxing even.'

Catherine handed her placard to a young woman who had just joined the march from the roadside and took out her notebook and started scribbling furiously.

The march continued through the busy streets of London until it reached Trafalgar Square. Catherine and Eddie managed to secure a stance from where they could glimpse the speakers. 'It's incredible. I'm actually seeing and hearing these famous politicians and churchmen. I'll never forget this as long as I live.'

'Nor will I. It's a first for me to be here with my grand niece. And I can't believe that this time tomorrow I'll be with Maggie.'

Chapter 57

It was a clear April morning as Catherine and Eddie arrived in Aberdeen. They watched it come to life through the windows of the bus. From a watery blue sky, the sun summoned the city into a new day. The granite buildings glistened as the sun's rays spangled the tiny mica fragments embedded in the rugged rock, making it shine. 'The Silver City,' mused Eddie, his mind heaving with nostalgia. The bright morning seemed to be enticing the early morning workers to wakefulness. Lorries trundled over the cobbles. Ships sailed in the shimmering wake of the cocky little pilot boat as it escorted them from their comfortable moorings to the uncertainties of the temperamental North Sea. Today, the sea seemed to be in one of its kinder moods, and welcomed the vessels with soft, lulling waves.

Eddie drew a deep breath. 'I would recognise that smell anywhere - the fish market. I used to go there often at half past four in the morning. My big brother Joe, your dad, used to take me. I feel my chest tighten with excitement just thinking about it: the throb of the engines as boats queued up to land the catch; the seagulls screaming like crazy; the noise and clamour of the buying and selling of fish. The whole procedure was an entertainment in itself. I remember the policemen on duty there wore coats cut off at the thigh so they wouldn't be hampered chasing thieves, and there was the occasional fracas, believe me.' His mind suffused with happy memories, Eddie's eyes never left the procession of fish lorries that headed in convoy for local fish houses, as well as for far flung destinations the length and breadth of the country.

His eyes scanned the skyline and he asked Catherine for an explanation of every new structure. 'What's happened to my sleepy little town?' Tower blocks competed with the many church spires in a race for the sky. Round the periphery of the city centre, low buildings spread from the hollow of the town towards the undulating hills of what had until recent times been farmland and countryside.

'The new buildings are nearly all houses. Everyone must have been crushed on top of each other before,' Catherine explained. 'Look over to the North West there, between the two church spires; that's the area where we live now.' Eddie pressed his face against the cold glass of the window and strained his eyes to peer at this new skyline as if expecting to see Maggie at her window looking out for him.

'I'm so nervous. The butterflies in my stomach are having a field day. Just think, in less than an hour I'll be in Maggie's house. I'm so glad the college doesn't start until next week and I was able to come with you instead of going straight home.'

'Don't talk about nerves; I think my legs are going to give way under me when I try to stand up,' answered Catherine as the bus jerked to a halt. However, they did hold up, and she was first out in the aisle collecting her bits and pieces from the luggage rack above their heads. The protesters streamed from the bus and said their farewells. Students on their Easter break could go home for a rest. Others had to go straight to work, their marching clothes in duffle bags slung over their shoulders. One young lad, Michael, had tiny patches of newspaper dotted about his face where he'd cut himself shaving with a dry razor to make himself presentable for his job in the bank. 'It's occasions like these that make the best memories,' said Eddie. 'You'll never forget these people and neither will I.' He rubbed his own bristly chin. 'I hope your mother doesn't think I always look this rough.'

Maggie watched and waited impatiently by the window, her eyes willing Catherine to appear. When she saw the taxi pull up she grew anxious. Catherine always took a bus and then walked the rest. Surely she wasn't ill. Maggie noticed there was someone else in the back of the large hackney cab, and her eyes burned their way into him, wondering who it could be. 'Frank, where on earth are you? You're never around when you're needed.' Maggie's eyes followed the tall gangly figure that followed Catherine up the path. 'My God!' she screamed, doubling over to catch her breath. She banged on the window, frustrated by her own weakness, and then, as unaccustomed strength surged through her body, she found herself hurrying out to welcome her long lost uncle. Could this really be happening? Maggie threw open the front door and waved frantically to Eddie and then propelled herself at him with never a sideways glance at Catherine whose imminent arrival had been the focus of her life only minutes before. Through tears mingled with laughter she kissed Eddie repeatedly. He didn't even have a chance to put down his bags and hug her back before she was pushing him towards the house. 'Eddie! I never gave up hope. It's a miracle. Thank you, God, thank you!' She pushed him through the door and called again for Frank. 'I give up on that man, I really do!'

Catherine followed behind. 'Hello, Mum, I'm home,' she said, amused that her mother was taking no notice of her. Frank came wandering down the stairs. 'What's all the commotion? I was just putting a plug on the new electric blanket.' He looked on in astonishment at the three figures in the hallway that were crying openly and kissing and hugging each other in turn.

'Never mind that now,' shouted Maggie, holding Eddie out in front of her like a prize she wanted to show off. 'Just look who's here!' Frank had of course heard all about Eddie but never in a million years thought he'd have the pleasure of meeting him. He put his screwdriver down on the step and joined in the jubilation.

Maggie was in seventh heaven as she relived past times with Eddie, and naturally, everyone wanted to find out what had happened to him when he went missing. He'd been taken prisoner at Anzio in Italy in the April of 1944 but managed to escape. 'I caught dysentery and collapsed at the side of a field,' he explained. 'A farmer found me and gave me into the care of a lovely old couple in the village who looked after me till the war was over.' His listeners eyes widened in disbelief and Eddie nodded to emphasise the truth of his words, adding, 'You'd be surprised how often escaped British prisoners of war were taken care of by the Italian people.' He refused point blank, however, to discuss what he'd seen in battle.

Catherine looked over at her mother and was surprised to see how healthy she looked. 'I was worried that the shock would give you a relapse,' she said, 'but it's brought new life into you instead. You look years younger.'

'Your mother always was a looker,' said Eddie, squeezing Maggie's hand affectionately. 'She was always surrounded by young soldiers home on leave. They used to call her "Honey Pot".'

'They never did! Don't listen to him,' retorted Maggie, blushing like a teenager. Maggie picked up the newspaper and swiped her uncle over the head with it. 'It's plain to see that you haven't improved with age, Eddie Clark.' The conversation turned to Mr. and Mrs. Scott who had taken Maggie in after the fire. 'I don't understand why old Sandy told you I was down south,' said Maggie. 'But we did used to call him "Odd Fellow", remember? But enough of him. Let's not think of the bad times, only the good. You know, I couldn't be happier with my life than I am right now. My life really is more than complete.'

Chapter 58

(Aberdeen, June 1968)

Maggie had been glowing with inner contentment almost spiritual fulfilment after Eddie's visit. However, the luminosity of her complexion was really only a sign of her physical frailty and the Maggie who had blossomed like a summer rose during Eddie's stay, began to fade and wilt in spite of many sunny days spent in the garden. A feeble body did not deter her, however, from the daily care she showered on the cherry tree and rosebushes. She carried the used washing-up water in a jug, so much at time, and poured it lovingly round their roots. She did the same with used tea-leaves and gently mulched them into the soil. It was her way of keeping Lucy and Sam alive in her memory. Since seeing them again in her dream, she knew for certain that they were waiting for her in Heaven. All fear had gone and been replaced by joyful anticipation.

Frank said nothing. Being a widower, he knew the pain of losing a spouse, and also that it was possible to love a new partner while remembering the first. He was happy that this loving occupation gave her the will to survive and enjoy every day. It gave her something to focus on when he was occasionally down in Perthshire helping his brother in his attempts to establish a jam making business. Frank, who had lost his own job on account of frequent absences when looking after Maggie, welcomed this opportunity to continue his trade. Catherine was busy with final exams and buried herself in study, either in her room or at the library. Neither noticed that Maggie was slowly withdrawing from them and attaching herself more intensely to her deceased family. She had frequent conversations with Sam, and no child ever heard such loving words as were spoken every day by a doting mother to little Lucy.

Sometimes Rosie came to stay when Frank was away. They

would enjoy long relaxing chats and listen to music on the stereogram. 'You do have a lovely home, Maggie,' Rosie said, running her hand along the side of Maggie's twin tub. 'I know Frank and Catherine do everything for you around the house, but I'm worried you're working too hard in that garden. You look all in.'

'I thought friends were supposed to make you feel better, not worse,' retorted Maggie. 'However, the same certainly can't be said about you. You're glowing. You look better and younger than ever, and you seem so sure of yourself. What's the doctor giving you now?'

'Nothing, as it happens, Maggie, nothing at all. I don't need it. I'm a new woman, finished with all that nonsense.'

'I wish you'd let me into your secret,' replied Maggie. Rosie looked at her fragile, fading friend and quickly turned away. Tears glistened in her eyes. 'I've a lot to tell you,' she said, blinking quickly. Maggie looked over at her. 'I miss you so much, Rosie,' she said and reached out a bony hand to touch her. 'I'm so glad you're staying over till tomorrow. Frank's down at his brother George's fruit farm in Perth this weekend. I visited there a few times with Frank before we were married. It was beautiful. The hills, the fresh air and much warmer than here. George says I have to stay with Wilma and him for as long as I want when I'm strong enough to travel. The truth is, though, I would rather spend what time I have left in my own little home.'

'At least you have the phone now to talk to Frank when he's away,' said Rosie, who'd been placing an array of cosmetics on the coffee table. The implication of Maggie's last few words didn't seem to have registered. 'I couldn't afford a phone. Anyway, you know me; I'd be on it all day long running up a bill that would land me in the debtors' prison. But Catherine must certainly be glad of it now she's going to be a journalist.'

'Did you read her article in the "Daily Voice"?' Maggie asked proudly.

'Of course,' Rosie replied, 'I wouldn't have missed it. Most professional it was. Just imagine, our little Catherine writing for a national newspaper.' She had gone over to the mantelpiece as she spoke and picked up a photograph of Maggie, Sam, Catherine and Lucy taken at a Sunday school picnic more than ten years before.

'I'm proud of my little girl,' beamed Maggie, 'and I won't stand in her way, whatever she decides to do. But let's be hearing your news, Mrs. Simpson. I want your secret,' said Maggie, lying back and closing her eyes in anticipation of one of Rosie's long stories about losing weight, the latest hairstyles or moisturising face cream.

Rosie threw herself into the soft fireside chair and, slipping off her comfy shoes, put her feet up on the pouffe. 'For a kick-off, it's not Mrs. Simpson, it's Miss Tough.' She paused, waiting for her words to take effect.

Maggie opened her eyes. 'Who on earth is Miss Tough?' she asked, struggling to raise herself to a sitting position.

'I am. So you'd better get used to it. Tough is my maiden name.' Rosie stood up and looked at herself in the mirror as if to enjoy her new identity to the full. 'Once upon a time there was a Rosie Simpson. She and her life were a mess. So she wised up. First of all she weaned herself off medication . . . ' Rosie was enjoying Maggie's suspense.

'That must have been hard; Frank and I found giving up cigarettes hard enough,' said Maggie sympathetically.

'It was hard, but I'd no choice if life was to be worth living. I'd already sent Jim packing to his floosie. I'd better things to do than cook and clean for a philanderer. She can do it now.'

'That was a terrible shock. I thought you and Jim were together for all time. So, what are you up to now?' Maggie was intrigued and urged her friend to hurry up.

'I saw a solicitor, and Jim has to give me money every week until I'm able to earn my own living. The divorce papers will be served on him in a few months. It's straightforward adultery.'

Rosie had her feet up on the coffee table now and was painting her toenails with bright pink nail varnish, the toes neatly separated with cotton wool.

'Make yourself at home,' laughed Maggie.

'You're next. Nothing better for cheering you up.'

Maggie wasn't interested in toenails. 'But divorce!' she exclaimed. 'I've never known anyone divorced before. What if he comes back? I heard he wasn't happy and was missing you.'

'Don't be old-fashioned, Maggie,' declared Rosie. 'I gave that man years of my life and he betrayed me. I could never trust him again. Never mind, I start a new job next week. It's part-time, plenty company and good money.' Rosie hesitated and put the lid back on the varnish. She moved her feet closer to the warmth of the electric fire. 'I'd started voluntary work giving sewing classes in the River Valley home for unmarried mothers every Monday evening. These poor girls have a terrible life, let me tell you. It's a draconian institution that hasn't progressed since Victorian times. Debbie, one of the girls missed my class some weeks ago and she wasn't allowed to leave the premises or have visitors for a fortnight. Now, after a few weeks of coming to my classes, she's knitted a jacket for her baby and has calmed down a lot. The matron is so impressed by how well I relate to the girls that I'm being employed as an auxiliary there four days a week to instruct the girls in baby care, cooking and needlework.'

Maggie took a sudden fit of coughing, but even that did not hide the look of bewilderment on her face. 'I can't believe how well you're coping. I really do admire you. I've never known you like this before.' Maggie was at a loss, not knowing exactly how to take this latest news.

'Just say you're pleased for me. I've seen sense at last. I've spent my life trying to be someone I'm not. So what if I carry some extra weight? That's just me. This is my life and I want what's left of it for me. I wish I'd been more like Catherine when I was her age instead of chasing boys and searching for a husband.

That girl shines for us all like a beacon.' Rosie lifted Maggie's feet and placed them on the footstool. 'Now to make you beautiful, oops, sorry, even more beautiful. What colour do you want, shocking pink or crimson cutie?'

'I'd prefer something less dramatic, but if you must, crimson cutie will do just nicely. But careful, mind, I'm ticklish.' Maggie's toes twitched, but she managed to hold steady. 'Seriously, though, I'm pleased for you. Come to think of it, I'm envious, envious of the fact that you have a life to do with as you please. Mine is nearly over.'

'Never say never. You're a fighter remember. Nihil desperandum,' said Rosie as she stroked the lurid colour on to Maggie's nails. 'I do have other things to tell you about, but I'm waiting to see how they develop before I say anything.'

'Would you mind making more tea first? I need something to wash down all the news. Is it about Jimmy? You haven't told me anything about him yet,' said Maggie. 'Has he finished his apprenticeship?'

'Young Jimmy is another story and I really don't feel in the mood for it now,' replied Rosie.

'Well, have it your own way. Whatever it is he'll grow out of it. He's young. He'll survive. Anyway, I must take this out to Lucy,' replied Maggie, heading for the back door with the teapot of cold tea leaves.

'I'm not so sure that he will,' said Rosie watching her. 'He's gone a step too far this time, I'm afraid. And as for you, you've gone and put your feet in your shoes without letting the nail varnish dry.'

Chapter 59

Later that evening Maggie lay resting in bed. Rosie and Catherine were on top of the quilt, one on either side of her. A cosy Saturday night in with the telly. 'Remember, Catherine, Rosie's staying over. She can have your bed and you can sleep with me.'

'Great!' she exclaimed. 'It will be like the old days when I was a little girl and I slept with you in the big bed on cold nights when Dad was away.'

'I hope you're not expecting a game of Fairies in the Woods,' laughed Maggie. On the television screen a juggler ran around trying to keep a dozen spinning plates balanced at once. 'Is this the best we can do on a Saturday night?' Maggie asked, flicking through the TV listings.

'I've already looked. It's either this variety show or a programme about pigeon racing on the other side,' Catherine answered. 'Never mind, the film starts in half an hour. You'll enjoy it. It's about a man who goes to Heaven and is allowed back once a year as an angel.'

'I like the sound of that. Do you think I'll come back as an angel?' asked Maggie quite seriously.

Catherine and Rosie looked at her in horror. Rosie, who had been sorting through a bag of wine gums for the black ones, corkscrewed the top of the paper bag and placed it on the bedside table. 'Right, Maggie,' she said, 'since you refuse to stop hinting at the imminence of your own demise, let's clear the air once and for all. Let's discuss it openly. I'm fed up going away from here crying all the way home on the bus.'

Catherine's mouth hung open. 'You can't talk to Mum like that. I'll have to ask you to leave if you upset her again,' she said acidly.

'Come down off your high horse, Catherine, and leave Rosie alone. She's right,' interrupted Maggie, 'it's me that's been upsetting her and it really is time to face the fact that I may not be around much longer. I'm losing weight, I'm tired all the time and

271

my body aches. Sometimes I feel as if I'm floating when I walk. It won't be long until my life here is over. It's an unfortunate fact of life that the existence of our personality is dependent on the health of our physical body, but mine has just about had it. We have to face up to that.'

Rosie and Catherine were wiping their eyes with tissues from the box they'd brought up for the movie. Maggie continued, 'Can't you understand my wish to be involved in the arrangements for my own funeral? I've arranged to say my own Goodbye. I've written it down and it will be read out at my funeral by the Reverend Forbes who gave Frank and me such a wonderful wedding. He's a gem. And it's not just the funeral I want to discuss. There's also the matter of what might happen to me afterwards. Have you never considered that I might even be looking forward to it? I'm so damned tired of this endless struggle for breath that death may come as a welcome relief. The only people who listen to my deepest thoughts now are Lucy and Sam, so much so, that sometimes I can't wait to join them.'

Catherine left the bed and pulled up a chair so that she could see her mother's face more clearly. 'I'm sorry, Mum. It never occurred to me that you might be thinking like that. I've been so selfishly caught up with my own feelings that I've neglected you. I'm a beast. From now on, you can tell me anything you want, anything at all.' Rosie stroked Maggie's hair gently. 'I'm sorry too, my love. I've been so heartless.'

'We have to face it. Every day I grow weaker and weaker. My lungs are badly scarred. It is only a matter of time. However, it's not the illness that's causing me to grow anxious and making me feel isolated and lonely, but everyone refusing to listen. Every time I try to talk about how I feel, someone changes the subject. It will be too late once I'm gone.' Maggie struggled to hold her voice steady. Catherine opened her mouth to speak but Maggie held up her hand. 'Please don't interrupt me,' she said. 'I want to see Eddie again before it's too late. What's the point of his being at my funeral if I don't see him myself one last time? And, Rosie, I want to visit you at the old street and for some of my old friends to be there too.' At length she stopped talking and sank back exhausted on the pillows satisfied that she had won a great victory.

'I'd no idea you were bottling up these thoughts. It must have been torture for you when we wouldn't listen,' replied Catherine sheepishly.

'I'm sorry too,' said Rosie, moving to sit on the edge of the bed to look at her friend. She picked up Maggie's frail hand and pressed it to her cheek.

'You see,' Maggie said, 'loving someone means being able to let them go. In the same way as I'll willingly see Catherine go away to fulfill her dreams, she must likewise allow me to move on to whatever comes next. We've had happy times together and now we must go our separate ways. You can't hide from death. It will seek out every one of us one day and we must prepare. Enjoy each of our loved ones as much as we can and take no one for granted.' Maggie's voice grew stronger instead of weaker as she spoke.

'You're right, Mum, we must take our heads out of the sand and face our own mortality as a natural part of life,' said Catherine. She too sounded braver.

'I'll organise that get together for you as soon as I can. It will be a day to remember.' Rosie, too, managed to speak without a tear.

'Thank you both so much. And you know something; I don't feel so frightened of the journey ahead any more. I can bid you all a proper goodbye before joining Lucy and Sam and Mum and Dad and Kenny and Jane.'

'Do you believe you will meet them again?' asked Rosie.

'Yes, Mum, do you really?' asked Catherine.

Maggie gave a slow smile. She spoke softly, almost in a sigh. 'I don't know for certain, nobody does, but it's just that when I speak to them in the garden, they seem so close, and sometimes in the dark of the night I see their shadowy figures flitting near my bed along with the rest of my family. When they gather round, I feel so safe and secure. The pain in my chest goes and I'm able to breathe. I see them there nearly every night, but I've still to hear them calling my name.' Rosie and Catherine glanced at each other. They knew what that would mean, but made no protest.

Instead, Catherine responded with an understanding nod of her head. 'I think I know what you're talking about,' she said. 'I like to think of Dad when I'm feeling down. I imagine he's there and I feel happier.' Maggie looked thoughtful, but remained silent. Catherine continued, her voice dropping to a murmur: 'It was the winter after Dad died. It was a freezing night and it seemed as if he came to visit me. My bedroom was icy cold and I couldn't sleep properly. I tossed and turned, and then I'm sure I saw Dad standing by my bed holding what looked like a heavy overcoat. He put it over me, in the same way he did when I was a little girl, and it wrapped itself round me like a cloak of comfort. Then he bent down and kissed me on the forehead. I felt it like a buzz of electricity. I must have fallen asleep, because the next thing I knew it was morning.'

Maggie gave a happy smile, glad that Catherine was capable of receiving such care. Her eyes closed and she allowed herself to recapture the memory of the dream she'd had in hospital that always filled her with joyful anticipation. She was sure that Heaven was waiting and that it would be wonderful.

'That's a beautiful story,' said Rosie and the three women sat quietly for a few moments, each with their own private thoughts.

'The air's cooling now,' said Rosie, shuddering as a tingle ran up her spine, and she walked over to the open window to close it, 'but it's still wonderfully bright outside. You're so close to nature here. I could watch the changing colours of the sky all night.' It was June, almost mid-summer, when the sun barely sets before rising again. Invisible hands seemed to pull the wispy clouds like candy floss across a mixture of pinks, yellows and lavender blues as the reddening sun sank slowly down on the horizon. Swifts with high piping voices swooped and soared after high-flying insects. A thousand chattering starlings had merged into one swarm that rolled in random amoeba shapes like a galaxy of stars spinning through space. Across the sky, a broad, black ribbon of crows cawed their way home to roost in the rookery in the nearby woods.

Catherine joined Rosie while Maggie lay back and allowed herself to visualise the scene. 'I enjoy hearing the birds. They hardly sleep at this time of year. Listen carefully and you'll hear my friendly blackbird singing. He's becoming quite tame. I'm sure he'll be eating out of my hand one of these days. He sits on the branches of the cherry tree and pours his heart out. I can see him in my mind's eye now, with his chest puffed out and his bright yellow beak lifted to the heavens.'

Suddenly, the loud ring of the doorbell broke their meditation. 'Who on earth can that be at this time of night?' said Catherine.

'Only one way to find out,' answered her mother. Rosie stiffened when she heard the male voice downstairs. 'That's Jimmy,' she said. 'What on earth does he want?' She rushed out the door and downstairs. Maggie shook her head. 'What a lad that is. He gives his mother no peace.' She crawled to the foot of her bed and turned up the sound on the television set. She wasn't going to let Jimmy Simpson spoil her film.

Catherine popped her head round the door. 'Don't worry yourself. It's nothing serious. You know Jimmy, can't let his mother out of his sight for five minutes. You enjoy your programme and I'll fetch you a cup of tea.'

Jimmy stood with his back to the fire in the living room, his hands hanging loosely by his sides, his head down. His face was red and he smelt strongly of drink. Rosie looked out of the downstairs window trying to recapture the pleasures of only minutes before. Suddenly, she turned and stormed towards him, exploding in his face like a canister of gas under too much pressure. 'You'll have to grow up some time, Jimmy, and handle

275

your own life. I can't fight your battles for you anymore. You're nearly twenty-three for goodness sake.' The grown man looked back at her with puppy dog eyes. His lower lip trembled and he burst into tears.

Catherine came through the door with a tray of tea. She took one disgusted look at the pathetic wimp and joined in. 'For Pete's sake, man, stop blubbering and tell us what's wrong.' She put the tray on the coffee table beside him.

'My girlfriend is expecting,' he announced.

'I knew that already. Tell me something new,' quipped his unsympathetic mother who was tearing into a ham sandwich in much the same way as a tigress would devour her kill. 'Patsy herself told me she was going to do something about it. There's a new law you know, and her mother's threatening to throw her out if she carries on with the pregnancy.'

Catherine perched herself on a chair opposite Rosie and put a hand over her mouth to stifle her amusement. Here was a story worth hearing. Jimmy stood between them, his face buried in a hanky.

'Come and sit down, Jimmy. I've made you a strong cup of coffee,' said Catherine, her voice cracking with stifled laughter as she pretended to be sympathetic. She guided him to the settee and pushed him down on it before picking up his strong coffee from the tray and placing it in his hands. 'Drink this and tell us all about it.' Catherine was determined to worm this intriguing story out of him. Rosie carried on eating.

'Patsy told me she would talk to the doctor. I even offered to go with her,' he whined.

'You mean, have an abortion. Go on say it. Face the consequences of your actions. If she's so young, why did you take advantage of her?' Catherine couldn't resist shoving some punishment his way.

'Catherine, please, Jimmy's not that bad. He's only made a mistake like many before him,' interrupted his mother, calmer now she'd eaten. 'Jimmy,' she said softly to her son, 'tell me what's gone wrong?'

'Patsy wants to keep the baby now. To get an abortion, you've to see a psychiatrist as well as the G.P. and her parents rebelled at that. The upshot is that they've all changed their minds, even her father. They want the baby now. I don't know what's got into them.' His voice tailed off in bewilderment.

'Maybe they've realised they don't want to kill a baby,' said Catherine.

Rosie glared at her. 'It's not like that anymore. They do it properly in a hospital.'

'It comes to the same thing,' Catherine dared to answer back, 'whether in a hospital or a back street.'

'That's not true, Catherine. In a hospital it's legal, it's safe,' Rosie argued.

'Anyway, Jimmy,' Catherine asked him pointedly, 'what's wrong with having a baby? Did the psychiatrist not want to see you as well?'

Jimmy ignored Catherine's snide comment and carried on with his complaint. 'I don't want to marry Patsy, and her father said he'll beat me to a pulp if I don't. He's a six foot two docker with muscles like Tarzan. What am I going to do?'

Rosie ordered him to drink his coffee and he did so at last in one gulp.

'Patsy's young but she's all right, although I did think you could do better,' Rosie said looking out of the corner of her eye at Catherine. 'But you could do a helluva lot worse. Patsy will be good for you, settle you down.' She took Jimmy's cup from him and offered him a sandwich. He peered between the slices of bread and moaned, 'There's mustard in these,' and returned the sandwich to the plate.

Rosie yawned. 'Marriage and a baby could be the making of you,' she continued, eating the discarded sandwich. 'You'll be a family. Your apprenticeship's finished and you make good money.

Take Patsy to live with us and when the baby's a few months old they'll give you a council house. There's no problem as I see it.'

'It might sound fine to you, but to me it's a disaster. I don't want to marry Patsy. I want to marry Catherine. Patsy and the baby can go to Hell.' His words met with a stunned, embarrassed silence.

A deep flush, starting at her neck, spread upwards to colour Catherine's face a deep red that was partly embarrassment, partly anger. Tight lipped, she gathered the dishes back on to the tray and crashed her way through to the kitchen.

Rosie grabbed Jimmy by the shoulder of his jacket and hauled him to his feet. 'You get out of here with that language right now, my lad. You're marrying Patsy and that's an end of it.' Jimmy stiffened. He wrenched his mother's hand roughly from his shoulder, spun her round and threw her sprawling backwards on to the settee. Head down and shoulders bent forward like an all-in wrestler, he crashed through the kitchen door towards Catherine. He rushed her where she stood shocked and rigid with her back to the sink. He pulled her face towards him by the neck of her blouse and, spilling out of his spoiled, blubbering mouth came a torrent of hideous threats. 'Catherine, I'll have you one day, no matter how many times I marry, or however far you go from here. Mark my words; one day you'll be glad to be mine!' Evil had replaced stupidity now that life had pinned him with his back to the wall with no way out.

Rosie had followed him through. 'Don't you think I've suffered enough?' she screamed. 'I wash my hands of you.' She tried to force herself between him and Catherine, digging her elbow hard into his stomach. He flinched, and still holding Catherine firmly at the throat with his right hand, he brought his left back and punched Rosie with full force on her ear. She staggered sideways against the wall and leaned against it, still dazed. 'Catherine, I'm sorry. It's the drink. He doesn't mean it,' said the mother, protecting her nasty son to the end.

'Of course I mean it,' snarled Jimmy, staring hard into Catherine's eyes as if laying a curse on her. 'You'll be glad of me one day. What are you anyway, Miss Catherine high and mighty Taylor, a cross between your mother and your Uncle Eddie? Where's the you in you? You've never been a normal little girl. Your mother's moulded you. You're a clone. You've no spunk. You're not even alive. You only exist. I pity you.'

Jimmy pushed her roughly out of the way and vomited into the sink. He rushed cold water over his head, sobering and cleansing, but there was no way he could run his filthy words and actions down the drain and away. Catherine staggered over to Rosie who folded her into her arms. With lips curled back in disgust, she hissed at her son through bared teeth, 'I'll bloody swing for you, Jimmy Simpson. A rat from the drains is better than you.'

'I'm sorry, really sorry,' he wept, wiping his mouth on a tea towel. The demon had left him and he was a pathetic little boy again.

But Jimmy's threats still hung heavy in the air like a curse. 'You've no part in my future!' shouted Catherine. She spat out the words as if ridding herself of poison. She looked up at Rosie. 'Just get him out of here, out of my sight!'

'I'll come and see your mother during the week. I'd better walk Jimmy home. The fresh air will do us both good.' Rosie spoke with resignation. She couldn't abandon him as she had Jim. Jim was only her husband and another woman's son. She marched Jimmy out of the house and along the road, chastising him vehemently with harsh words and an occasional slap.

Catherine removed the blouse, screwed it up like a dirty rag and flung it in the bin. As she climbed the stairs, Jimmy's words followed her. She turned quickly as if sensing some devilish entity behind her. 'Who's there?' she whispered hoarsely. There was no answer, but in her mind she heard Jimmy's sneering laugh and saw his mocking eyes leering ever closer. 'Go away! Get out!' She forced the words from the back of her throat that was dry with dread. Catherine threw open the door to her room. It was dark, and she switched on the light quickly. Her eyes scanned the room. 'He can't be in here, you fool,' she snapped at herself. 'He's gone and won't be back.'

'Hurry up, Catherine! You're missing a good programme here,' called Maggie over the cacophony of a jazz band that was playing at a New Year party in her film. 'And where's that tea you promised me?'

'Sorry to be so long, Mum,' she called. 'We'd a bit of trouble with Jimmy. Too much drink.' She reached into her wardrobe for a fresh blouse. As she did it up, she looked at herself in the mirror, searching her own eyes for clues. 'Who am I?' she whispered. Her mind grew numb with fear and her stomach gave a lurch. However, another call from her mother made her abandon these eerie thoughts. She gave herself a shake and joined Maggie to watch the movie. 'I'm damned if I'll let that moron spoil the rest of our evening.'

Maggie felt the tension coming off Catherine but made no comment. 'I'm so glad you let me talk earlier. You must always remember, Catherine, that even when I'm gone, you'll never be alone. If times are hard, you only have to reach out and I'll be there for you, I promise.'

'I believe you, Mum,' she whispered, pulling the blankets up over her sleepy mother's shoulders, but all the while she was thinking inwardly to herself, 'How am going to manage on my own without you? How can I stand up to anyone without you at my back?'

Chapter 60

(Aberdeen, July 1968)

It was graduation day and Catherine walked proudly and steadily up to the podium. It had taken three years of hard work and now her reward was only seconds from her grasp. The applause rang in her ears, but there were only four people in the auditorium that mattered, Maggie, Frank, Eddie and Rosie. Maggie had struggled into the building supported by Eddie and Frank on either side. Now they watched, hearts bursting, as their little Catherine collected her degree and returned to her seat, a fully-fledged graduate with a dazzling future ahead of her. The four of them clapped till their hands stung.

'Put that away! This is my treat!' insisted Eddie in the restaurant afterwards, pushing Frank's wallet aside. 'You treated me like a VIP on my last visit. It's my turn now.' They sat at a round table and were able to talk comfortably to each other as they reminisced about Catherine's childhood.

'You will look after her, won't you, away down there?' whispered Maggie to Eddie.

''Course I will,' he replied warmly. He turned to Catherine. 'You'll be fine. You can commute from Essex to London for as long as you want until you find a place of your own.' He took Maggie's hand. 'Don't worry, Maggie, it's a direct line home from London to Aberdeen by train so you'll still see her often.' They all knew that Maggie wouldn't hear of Catherine staying put and losing a year's contract with the "Daily Voice".

'It would kill me faster if she stayed here,' said Maggie. 'Catherine's future is my main preoccupation now. She'll be with me all the time in my thoughts. I'll just have to close my eyes and I'll see her.'

Frank raised his glass. 'We wish you all the best in the Smoke,

Catherine.'

'It's your turn next for glory, Rosie, in a few weeks as mother of the groom,' smiled Catherine. She felt embarrassed and wanted to shift the attention on to someone else. Mischievously, she added, 'How is the husband to be bearing up?' She felt her mother's kick under the table.

Rosie ignored Catherine's sarcasm. Since early childhood Catherine and Jimmy had sniped at one another. Why should they stop now? 'Jimmy's fine. He even said the other day that he was breaking with the family tradition of James for the oldest son and giving the baby a name of its own. And he won't hear of it being a girl.'

'What's he going to do if it is, send it back?' laughed Catherine.

'I thought you'd just graduated,' said Maggie, kicking her harder this time. 'I hope you're not going downhill and stupid already.' Catherine thrilled to the reprimand, delighted her mother still had a sharp sense of humour.

'Jimmy will make a good father,' insisted Rosie. 'You should see him fussing over Patsy. He won't let the wind blow on her. He even washes the dishes when she's round for tea.'

'Of course Jimmy will be a good husband. I think Catherine's missed out there,' said Maggie in agreement. She nudged Catherine in the side as she said it, knowing it would infuriate her. It was Catherine's turn to give Maggie a kick. Maggie smiled with pleasure. She was enjoying this little game. Catherine and Rosie exchanged a quick look. Maggie knew nothing of his attack on Catherine. 'Did you know that Eddie's staying for the wedding?' Rosie announced. 'He's going to be my partner.' This little snippet made them all sit up and take notice.

'Yes,' said Eddie, clearing his throat. 'Rosie's taking me old-time dancing at the Plaza later tonight so that I can have a taste of old times.'

'As long as it's only a taste,' laughed Frank. It was his turn now to have his shins kicked hard by both Maggie and Catherine.

Rosie blushed like a young girl. Eddie stroked her leg with his foot. 'Eddie and I have been writing to each other,' she said, putting her arm through his. 'That was the other bit of news I was telling you about.'

'I once had a pen friend,' said Frank, 'a boy from Dundee that we met on a caravan holiday in Ayr.'

'Hush, Frank,' said Maggie, frowning at him and shaking her head. 'I think Eddie's more than a pen friend.'

'We certainly are. Rosie's joining me in Basildon next month after Jimmy's wedding. He and Patsy are taking over the tenancy of the flat. And, furthermore, to top it all, I know a cloth merchant in the East End who wants to commission Rosie to do embroidery for his customers.' Eddie grinned from ear to ear and kissed her full on the lips in front of everybody.

'I'm so pleased for you, Rosie,' said Maggie and she clapped her hands gleefully.

'This is the best day of my life!' exclaimed Catherine and she too clapped her hands together like a delighted child. She stood up and waved over towards the door. 'O, here's my friend now; he had to go to work, but I'd like you all to meet him.' And, in line with many of the other tables across the restaurant where graduates were introducing fellow students to family, there was a happy exchange of handshakes and hugs. 'I don't know why you kept Gregor a secret from me for so long,' Maggie whispered to Catherine. 'I've been so happy for you since you took him home last week. Did you think I would eat him or something?' Gregor overheard and he and Catherine exchanged looks. Maggie shook her head as if still puzzling over her daughter's behaviour. 'You must have known how grateful I always was that he took care of you. But what neither of you knows is that I saw Gregor a couple of times in the hospital when I was being wheeled to x-ray or the day room. When I saw what a fine young doctor he'd become, I had a good long think to myself. If your father hadn't already had heart problems he would have taken a family row in his stride.

283

There was nothing to forgive poor Gregor for. My only regret is that I didn't see sense sooner. But all's well that ends well.'

Maggie stood to her feet, face shining like the sun in a distant island paradise. 'Here's to the future! To Catherine and Gregor, Rosie and Eddie, Jimmy and Patsy and, of course, Frank and me.' She had managed to speak loudly, raising her glass high, cocking-a-snook at Fate, defiant to the end.

Everyone stood and raised their glasses. 'The future!' they all shouted in unison.

A few mornings later, when Frank brought Maggie breakfast in bed, he found that she was in the deep slumber of death. She had slipped peacefully away in the quiet sleep of velvet night. No more pain or suffering. Her face had acquired the soft, smooth texture of a young girl's. Her hair had regained its lost lustre. Lines etched on her face by constant pain and the struggle for breath were gone. Maggie was at peace and smiled contentedly. A line of crows, resplendent in dark mourning attire, strutted in funereal procession across the lawn, while on the topmost branch of the cherry tree her favourite blackbird sang his heart out. The sun greeted the news from a rained out sky and the roses burst their pink and yellow petals wide open to the world.

Chapter 61

Sorting through Maggie's possessions, Catherine and Frank worked in silence. Frank stopped and drew a deep breath. 'I'm leaving too,' he announced, giving up on the heart-rending task. He sat cross-legged on the floor in front of a pile of papers and documents. Catherine had been upstairs among the clothes and had likewise found she could only take so much pain and had taken a break. 'Why would you leave? This is your home,' she said.

'I'm going to Perth to work with my brother, driving and maintenance. The scenery's beautiful and the people friendly. I'll be too busy to brood,' he replied robotically. It was obviously a speech he'd been rehearsing over and over in his mind.

'What about the house, Mum's dream?' asked Catherine.

'That's it precisely. The house was your mother's dream, just as she was mine. But she's gone now; the house means nothing without her,' he answered.

'But you can't abandon her like that.'

'Maggie achieved her ambitions. We have ours. We're not deserting her; we're just moving on the same as she has. The house has played its part. We can't let it become a mausoleum. Think about it. The cherry tree and bushes will find a happy home in my brother's garden. You can see them any time you want. Eddie's taking cuttings back to Essex to flourish there and Rosie will be there to look after them. As for your dad's stereogram, it's yours any time you want to fetch it. I'll take good care of it in the meantime. It'll be playing music for many years to come. Catherine, please think this through. We're not forsaking your mother. Wherever any of us goes, she'll be there too. She'll never be forgotten.'

'Have it your own way,' snapped Catherine. She'd been making tea but didn't bring a cup for Frank. 'There'll be no one left.'

'Surely you don't grudge Rosie and Eddie their happiness. Rosie will thrive in Basildon. You'll see them all the time.' He went and made a cup of tea for himself.

Still Catherine sulked. 'But there won't be anyone here!' she said.

'So, life must go on hold for everyone else but Catherine Taylor?'

'All right then. Have it your own way,' she said between sobs. 'We'll all move, and everything that's gone before need never have happened.'

Frank tried his best to calm her. 'We'll have our memories and our love for each other, no matter how far away we travel or for how long. Surely you don't want me to tie myself to a three-piece suite and a coffee table for the rest of my natural. Let's face it, pieces of furniture haven't a lot to say for themselves.'

'Okay, Frank, just leave it.'

But Frank couldn't resist the temptation. He thought a little joke would lighten the atmosphere. 'You can always visit Jimmy and Patsy, and the baby when it comes.' He expected a fiery exchange but got more than he bargained for.

'Never ever mention that beast again! I'll accustom myself to everyone taking off given time but never Jimmy. You don't know him like I do. He's evil.' She fled from the room, slamming doors behind her. Frank heard her crying. 'Poor lass. I must stop pulling her leg like that.'

A couple of hours later, a little face peeped round the door of the living room. 'Come here, you daft thing,' said Frank holding out his arms to Catherine. She smiled a watery smile and walked slowly over to him.

'I'm sorry,' said Catherine and hugged him close. You're right, Frank. We can't stop time. I can't believe my own selfishness. Of course we all have our lives to live. One thing you must realise about me, though, and that is that Jimmy Simpson fills me with disgust.'

'I know that. I'm sorry, Catherine,' said Frank. He sat down on the edge of the settee and looked at her. 'I've to start treating you as a grown up now instead of teasing you all the time. I know something happened between you and him. Your mother told me there was some kind of trouble the weekend I was away.' Catherine sat facing him on the chair and told him all about Jimmy's violent outburst. Frank listened closely and you could tell from the clenching of his fists and the tightening of his jaw that he was finding it hard to control his temper. 'Stay away from that so and so,' he said, pacing backwards and forwards and seething with rage. 'He deserves a right good going over. Not much wonder you can't even stand the sound of his name.'

Later that evening, after taking a warm bath and changing into her dressing gown, Catherine snoozed in front of an old black and white movie on the television. Frank had decided on the spur of the moment to drive to Perthshire for a few days to clear his mind. Glad of time to herself, Catherine relaxed and allowed the pictures of her happy future to mingle with the characters in the Hollywood romance she was watching. Suddenly, a persistent ring at the doorbell jolted her back to reality. With a heavy sigh she uncurled her feet and shoved them into the slippers that she'd let fall on to the floor. 'It's been nothing but visitors since Mum died,' she said to herself, not in any hurry to answer.

The bell continued to ring long and loud. She stopped in her tracks. Through the frosted glass she recognised the tall figure that was stooped forwards, peering into the hallway, hand leaning on the jamb, finger on the bell. This was no welcome guest. It was Jimmy.

'What do you want here?' she shouted. Instinct made her push up the bolt.

'I only want to talk, to see you before you go. I thought you might want some company.'

'I don't want company. I'm better on my own.'

'I get married next week. I want to put things right between us.

You mean too much to me.'

'Things are fine as they are.' Catherine's voice shook. She put a hand to her throat.

Jimmy tried the door handle. 'Come on, Catherine, for old times' sake. Just let me in. I won't stay long.' As if realising that his nearness was intimidating her, he stepped back from the door, much as a snake draws back before it strikes. Catherine pulled her towelling robe tight round her till her knuckles shone white. She remained motionless and silent, hoping he would tire of waiting and go away. 'Please, Catherine. This is my last chance to make amends. I promise I won't argue with you. I just want to wish you luck.'

Her shoulders relaxed. Maybe he had learned his lesson.

He lifted the flap of the letterbox and called in, 'I know I've done some terrible things, but I am your friend after all.'

'Please, Jimmy, I've heard it all before.'

His voice grew quiet, almost gentle. 'Please, Catherine, we've known each other all our lives and we've been through such a lot together.'

She took a deep breath. Obviously he wasn't going to leave. Best get it over with, and he didn't seem drunk or upset. 'Okay, but only half an hour,' she said feeling worn out and desperate for rest. She was so sure that this would be the last of him, that she had allowed herself to be taken in, and drop by drop she had swallowed his words that flowed as sweet as any soothing linctus. She reached up to release the bolt before slowly unlocking the door. Jimmy was already turning the handle and pushed it open. His arms reached for her and he tried to pull her to him. 'O, Catherine, I've missed you so much.'

Catherine pulled away, and keeping a firm grasp on the neck of her dressing gown, hurried into the living room. She remained standing and made no move to switch off the television, hoping that would make it clear that he wasn't entirely welcome. Jimmy followed, marching in as if he owned the place. 'Take it easy,

Catherine, it's only me.' He glanced at the screen. A man and a woman gazed into each other's eyes before embracing. Music played. 'The End' came up on the screen. 'That should have been us,' he said matter of factly. 'We could've had a happy ending.' He took a step closer and looked down on her, fixing her with his stare. Catherine looked up at him. His breath was warm and moist against her face. She caught a whiff of alcohol. He was drunk after all. Catherine screwed up her face and choked back the nausea.

'Don't give us all that tosh, Jimmy. You're marrying Patsy. I feel nothing for you. In fact, if anything, you revolt me.'

'Come on, Catherine. You know you want to.' Jimmy puckered up his fat lips and made a kissing noise. His face was suspended just above her line of vision, distorted. It began to blur. Catherine tried to blink it into focus but had to close her eyes. In doing so she lost her guard. He was in control.

'Come on, Catherine, just once. I'll make you enjoy it.' Suddenly, his lips were on hers, pressing down hard so she could hardly breathe. When his arms tightened round her she squirmed, but he was too strong. He pushed his knee hard up between her legs, forcing them apart. He pulled roughly at the belt of her robe. His tongue was in her mouth making her gag and unable to scream. His hands were everywhere. Catherine struggled to free an arm and twisted the skin of his face, digging her nails in. She tried to reach further upwards for his eyes but Jimmy caught her hand and bent it backwards. He spun her whole body round and pushed her to her knees. Deftly he whipped off her dressing gown and flung it aside. Taking hold of the hair at the nape of her neck, he shoved her flat on to the floor, grazing her forehead on the carpet. Mustering all her strength, Catherine tried to call out. Jimmy grabbed a cushion and held it to her mouth.

Catherine lay face down spread-eagled beneath his weight. He was still for a few seconds, breathing heavily. His grip on her wrist tightened like a vice and then he dragged her arm up behind her back. Catherine clawed at the carpet with her free hand but there was nothing to catch hold of. She heard him unzip himself and shuddered as he lifted her nightie and she felt his rough hand on her. She began to pray. Surely this couldn't be happening. She was on the point of blacking out when loud noises made it seem as if the world was crashing upon her. The floor under her shook and a man's voice resounded about her. Jimmy's body was hauled off her and there was an almighty crash and then silence. Gentle hands helped her to her feet and comforting arms enfolded her. She knew without looking that it was Gregor. She dared to open her eyes. Jimmy lay unconscious beside the still open door. Blood streamed from his nose and his face already showed signs of bruising. 'I changed shifts and got away early,' said Gregor by way of explanation. 'There was some exciting news from Canada and I couldn't wait to tell you.'

Jimmy moaned and struggled to his feet. Catherine held tight to Gregor. He gently released himself from her grip and approached the snivelling brute. Taking him by the scruff of the neck, he shoved him to the door and threw him out where he lay defeated on the path. 'Clear off, you worm. And don't show your nose round here again. You won't get off so lightly next time.'

'Okay. I get the message,' he lisped through bleeding lips, but he couldn't resist a final taunt now that he realised there had always been more to Catherine and Gregor's friendship than he'd thought. 'What a waste of a bloody evening!' he shouted loud enough for Catherine to hear. 'You won't be seeing me again, you filthy slag. At least Patsy was a virgin when I first had her.'

As the door slammed behind him, Catherine slumped onto the sofa staring sightlessly ahead. Gregor brought her a stiff brandy and put it to her lips. She managed a few sips. She couldn't even look at Gregor and her voice was little more than a sigh as she thanked him and signalled for him to leave. She had to be alone. Gregor, sensitive to her needs, knocked back the drink he'd poured for himself and left, but not before holding her tightly to him and assuring her that he'd be round first thing in the morning.

Blindly she dragged herself upstairs to the bathroom. She rushed the hot water full force into the tub and poured disinfectant into the steaming water until it turned white. She immersed herself in the scalding water. 'Why do I always bring such horrible things on myself,' she wondered, 'as if I'm being punished? What have I done?' Her conscience provided her with the answer as the faces of Lucy, Sam and Miss Walker seemed to float in the steam in front of her eyes. She mulled over the circumstances of each tragedy and it finally dawned on her that each tragic event had happened independently of her influence, and that the punishment that she seemed to subconsciously attract must stop. She couldn't be held accountable for her father's heart attack; he'd been having chest pains for weeks. The scarlet fever that killed Lucy couldn't logically be spread by a jealous sister's wishful thinking. As for Miss Walker, she had been heading for a breakdown ever since the day her fiancé was bayoneted in the Great War and the gruesome treatment of mental patients in the asylum was well beyond her control.

As Catherine scrubbed her body red raw, it seemed as if she were cleansing herself of all the badness and guilt of the past. She pulled on a pair of jeans and a jumper, gathered up the nightie and dressing gown she'd been wearing and carried them out to the dustbin where she dowsed them in paraffin and set them alight. Once that was done, she hoovered and polished the living room before having a second antiseptic bath. It was morning before she was ready to fall into bed and lose herself in sleep.

Chapter 62

(Aberdeen, November 1968)

Catherine hesitated on the doorstep of the doctor's surgery chewing her lips as if trying to cause such intense pain she wouldn't feel the shock of the news the doctor had just given her. A young man jostled her, intent only on deciphering what was written on his prescription. Catherine remained frozen to the spot. It was as if roadblocks had been set up to hold her back from the happy future that she'd promised herself. Another patient pushed past complaining that she was causing an obstruction. Catherine allowed herself to be shoved out of the doorway and continued with uncertain steps down the path and along the street, staring straight ahead but seeing nothing.

'Mum!' she called aloud. 'I need you now.' A young woman walking towards her sidestepped with her child and hurried on. Catherine stopped walking and blew her nose. 'I'm so sorry for letting you down,' she whispered, imagining her mother's presence. 'I know this isn't what you wanted for me.' She walked on like a zombie towards the Shiny Teapot a few streets away, but, as she walked she allowed her thinking to become clearer. This might not have been how her mother had wanted things to turn out, but with each step her concept of what life was about seemed to be changing. Her purpose wasn't to please her mother but to live as she herself wanted to. She felt a soft breeze brush past her cheek just like a kiss and she realised that what her mother really wanted for her was happiness. And that's exactly what she could have with this new turn of events. She paused in the doorway of the toyshop next door to the tearoom, took out a compact and lipstick and covered her tear stained face with fresh make up. 'At last, I feel free,' she said inwardly, 'as if a great weight has been lifted from my shoulders.' With one final check that the seams of her stockings were straight, she entered the Shiny Teapot. Must be looking her best for what was coming next.

The bell tinkled to announce her arrival. A tall young man at the table in the corner rose quickly to his feet and welcomed her with a warm embrace. 'This was a truly romantic idea of yours to come here one last time,' he said pulling out a chair for her. Catherine sat down and nervously twisted the diamond ring on the third finger of her left hand.

'There's something you have to know,' whispered Catherine. She turned away.

'Look at me, Catherine. What's wrong?'

'I'm pregnant. I've just come from the doctor's.' She watched for Gregor's reaction.

He stared at her, motionless and mouth open at first, and then his eyes lit up and he grinned from ear to ear. 'But that's wonderful news. Why have you been crying? Our plans will just need altering a bit, that's all. We'll get married right away.'

'What, you mean you really don't mind? I thought you were looking forward to going to Canada while I did a year in London with the "Daily Voice" before joining you.'

'I'd never leave you alone now. I'll support you every step of the way. I can look after the baby until your stint is over.' Gregor leaned across the table to take her hands tightly in his, fixing her eyes with his own, ardently presenting a solution. When your year's up we'll go to Canada then. My work can wait.'

'You're a man in a million, Gregor,' said Catherine, 'but you don't understand. I've been lying awake for nights sorting things out in my mind. It doesn't matter if we live here or London or Canada. And it's of no consequence when we do the things we've planned. The only thing that matters to me is now, and that we're together. And please listen; I don't want anyone looking after this baby but me. I don't want work and ambition to spoil our family. As long as you love me and want the baby, then I'm happy. Anyway, there's no telling what the future will bring.'

'And maybe just as well,' said Gregor wisely, 'but whatever

happens there is only one way to face life: Nihil desperandum, never give up,'

'Why did you say that? It's what Mum used to say.'

'I don't know. I must have heard it somewhere before, probably at school. It just popped into my head.'

'Never lose hope,' Catherine said in agreement.

'We'll make a great team, you and I;' Gregor said firmly, 'and the little one too.' They both looked down at Catherine's tummy with fondness.

Gregor put his arm around her protectively. 'What would you like to eat?' he asked. 'We'll have to make sure you're properly looked after.' He waved to the waitress who stood puffing on a cigarette at the kitchen door, following with her eyes the smoke rings that drifted upwards before disintegrating into vapour.

Catherine shushed him before he could place an order and pointed to the transistor radio on the shelf. 'Listen,' she said, 'it's Mum's favourite piece of violin music.' They listened to the soulful melody as it stirred their hearts with its poignant beauty. Catherine glanced upwards. 'Thanks, Mum,' she said quietly, 'I knew you were there.'

She turned to Gregor and reached over to take his hand. 'Now it's time for our dreams,' she said and they kissed.

The End.

Other Titles From Cauliay Publishing

Kilts, Confetti & Conspiracy *By* Bill Shackleton
Child Of The Storm *By* Douglas Davidson
Buildings In A House Of Fire *By* Graham Tiler
Tatterdemalion *By* Ray Succre
From The Holocaust To The Highlands *By* Walter Kress
To Save My Father's Soul *By* Michael William Molden
Love, Cry and Wonder Why *By* Bernard Briggs
A Seal Snorts Out The Moon *By* Colin Stewart Jones
The Haunted North *By* Graeme Milne
Revolutionaries *By* Jack Blade
Michael *By* Sandra Rowell
Poets Centre Stage (*Vol One*) *By* Various poets
The Fire House *By* Michael William Molden
The Upside Down Social World *By* Jennifer Morrison
The Strawberry Garden *By* Michael William Molden
Poets Centre Stage (*Vol Two*) *By* Various Poets
Havers & Blethers *By* The Red Book Writers
Amphisbaena *By* Ray Succre
The Ark *By* Andrew Powell
The Diaries of Belfour, Ellah, Rainals & Co *By* Gerald Davison

Books Coming Soon

Underway, Looking Aft *By* Amy Shouse
Silence of the Night *By* Sandra Rowell
The Bubble *By* Andrew Powell
The Trouble with Pheep Ahrrf By Coffeestayne
Spoils of the Eagle By Alan James Barker

Lightning Source UK Ltd.
Milton Keynes UK
26 August 2010

159013UK00001B/28/P